MYSTICMOON

A LUNAR ODYSSEY

Rao Achutuni, PhD

Copyright

Mystic Moon: A Lunar Odyssey

ISBN: 979-8-99159790-6

Copyright © 2024 by Rao Achutuni

All rights reserved. No part of this book may be reproduced, distributed, or transmitted in anyform or by any means, including photocopying, recording, or other electronic or mechanical methods, without written permission from the author, except as permitted by U.S. copyright law.

Disclaimer: This book reflects the author's personal views. References to religious texts serve purely illustrative and anecdotal purposes and do not aim to promote any specific religious beliefs. The conclusions based on Hasselblad and other imagery are the author's interpretations and may not encompass all possible conditions on the lunar surface. The opinions expressed herein are independent of any governmental or academic position.

To my beloved family

MYSTIC MOON : A LUNAR ODYSSEY

Purpose and Scope of this Book

Our Moon is an exciting and mystical natural satellite of the Earth. Ancient cultures worshiped both the Sun and the Moon; the full Moon was important to some cultures and the crescent Moon to others. Ancient civilizations built elaborate stone observatories to monitor the precise movements of the Sun, the Moon, the Earth, and other heavenly bodies. Some ancient Hindu and Buddhist temple architecture incorporated the precise seasonal movements of the Sun in the positioning of their deities to ensure that the Sun's rays would fall at the feet during the solstices.

The discovery of the telescope during the early 17th century in Europe ushered in a whole new world of optical astronomy, and soon, people began to observe the Solar system with all its planets and moons with great interest. The Moon, our closest heavenly object, is the first and easiest target. Over the years, people observed the Moon regularly and soon began to observe strange transient phenomena such as blinking lights, multiple bright spots in or near craters, brightening up of crater floors, lightning on the face of the Moon, and white smoke, to mention a few. An exhaustive chronology of transient events observed on the Moon by renown astronomers and scientists has been documented by NASA (1968). Some of these observed events piqued my interest in the Moon.

The advent of NASA's early Lunar Orbiters (1-5) during the Apollo era marked a significant milestone in lunar exploration, reigniting humanity's curiosity about the Moon. The far side of the Moon was exciting, a perpetual mystery hidden from Earth's view. The Lunar Orbiters (LOs), with their groundbreaking views of the Moon, including the enigmatic far side, opened a new chapter in our understanding of the Moon. The vast LO database and the Hasselblad imagery archives, made accessible by NASA, have since been a treasure trove for scientists and enthusiasts alike.

Several Apollo-era Hasselblad imagery magazines are in the public domain and available online through the Flickr platform. Their appropriate sources have been credited accordingly. Each Apollo mission documented these images by their corresponding number in each film magazine.

This book explores several mystical features lurking in these extensive Apollo Hasselblad archives, available on Flickr, from the independent perspective of a remote-sensing scientist with a passion for space exploration. The book is based on analyzing numerous Hasselblad images taken during Apollo 8 through the Apollo 17 missions.

Many of the pictures were taken from the orbiting command module (CM) around a height of about 100 kilometers (~62 miles), and others by the crew on the lunar surface.

This book presents and discusses various intriguing and enigmatic artifacts visible in lunar imagery. Many casual online observers will be left in awe by these images, prompting them to express their admiration through online comments such as "Like" or "Fave" for their favorite scenes.

Users should be aware of potential data processing and quality control issues in NASA's archives to avoid misinterpreting blemishes and those due to contaminants associated with thrusters firing during orbital corrections and spacecraft ascent or descent. Debris can inadvertently accumulate on the lens of the Hasselblad camera carried by the crew. Only images without systemic blemishes were included in the analysis.

I have avoided presenting scenes with astronauts in them or with NASA logos per se. I have also avoided mentioning astronauts' names within the text to respect any privacy concerns.

Considerable time was spent researching ancient religious texts from Hinduism, Buddhism, Christianity, Judaism, Zoroastrianism, Islam, and others in my quest for answers. I had to comprehend various concepts presented in Vedic cosmology, including the cyclical evolutionary cycles of the *Yugas* to explain certain situations.

This book is not a novel by any stretch of the imagination; there are no characters or storyline per se. It is designed to educate and inform readers about the complexities of lunar missions and space exploration.

The casual reader may find many of the scenes presented jaw-dropping or exciting and may wish to view the archives online, which contain new information and insight into the various chapters.

A brief introduction to some basics of *Orbital Science* and *Propulsion* in support of lunar and deep space exploration is also provided. Space is indeed the proverbial final frontier. I hope my book entices the youth to consider exciting opportunities in space exploration and related technological development. I passionately believe that space exploration and rapidly advancing Artificial Intelligence will provide many exciting opportunities for the next generation.

I do not claim to have all the answers, but I tried to address various puzzling situations with current scientific explanations and anecdotal evidence from religious texts.

The Moon, in all its splendor, is very mystic and full of surprises, possibly dating back to millions of years ago and some more recent. The reader is expected to be able to appreciate some of the interesting ones presented in the various chapters.

The findings and conclusions presented in this book are entirely my own and do not reflect those of any government or academic entities in the U. S. or anywhere else.

Mystic Moon is genuinely a Lunar *Odyssey* encompassing the role of spacecraft from ancient times to modern human exploration of space. It is a journey illustrated with anecdotal evidence from religious texts to the extensive Apollo-era Hasselblad archives, elucidated with my thoughts and conclusions. Enjoy!

Table of Contents

PURPOSE AND SCOPE OF THIS BOOK	V
CHAPTER 1: HISTORY IN THE MAKING	1
CHAPTER 2: THE SETTING FOR THE BOOK	11
CHAPTER 3: IN SEARCH OF CLUES FROM THE ANCIENT PAST	14
CHAPTER 4: THE GREAT BIBLICAL FLOOD	31
CHAPTER 5: SOARING INTO THE SKY	41
CHAPTER 6: SECRETS OF THE MOON	52
CHAPTER 7: MORE LUNAR SPACECRAFT	61
CHAPTER 8: LUNAR DRONES	76
CHAPTER 9: MASTERS OF LIGHT	89
CHAPTER 10: ANCIENT GLASS ARTIFACTS	103
CHAPTER 11: CREEPY STUFF GREETING LUNAR VISITORS	108
CHAPTER 12: WHAT'S IN A FACE?	114
CHAPTER 13: SACRED RELIGIOUS SYMBOLS	122
CHAPTER 14: KNOCKING ON MYSTERIOUS DOORS	133
CHAPTER 15: SUSTAINABLE LUNAR EXPLORATION	144
CHAPTER 16: A REVIEW OF NASA'S PLANS FOR LUNAR EXPLORATION	147
CHAPTER 17: THE NEW SPACE RACE TO THE MOON	153
CHAPTER 18: EPILOGUE	158

REFERENCES 161

APPENDIX-1A: LUNAR NEAR SIDE 166

APPENDIX-1B: LUNAR FAR SIDE 167

APPENDIX-1C: LUNAR SOUTH-POLE AITKEN (SPA) BASIN 168

APPENDIX-2: BASICS OF SATELLITE ORBITS 169

APPENDIX-3: PROPULSION 181

APPENDIX-4: ACCESSING THE APOLLO IMAGE ARCHIVE ON FLICKR 184

Chapter 1: History in the Making

My infatuation with the Moon started in my early childhood during the magnificent U. S. Apollo Program (1963 – 1972). Growing up in the early sixties in Calcutta, now renamed Kolkata in its native Bengali, life was simple, with the proverbial social media limited to books, newspapers, and the almighty radio. I always made it a point to read newspaper headlines from *The Statesman* before going to school, an act which my mother inevitably reminded me was a colossal waste of time and ought to be deferred to retirement. Sadly, modern media communications with their 24-hour news channels had inadvertently reduced all but the major newspapers to mere purveyors of obituary columns, advertisements, and shopper's coupons. Media headlines of today are cringe-worthy with details of murders, rapes, brutality, gun violence, and endless wars, reducing civilizations to a new soil type that can be rightfully termed rubble.

The *Voice of America* (VOA) was one of the major sources of information to the outside world, especially in the sixties when there were no 24-hour news channels providing live coverage at the drop of a hat. People without TV sets had to view recorded Metro Goldwyn Mayer (MGM) *Newsreels* of major newsworthy events shown before the screening of every motion picture on the silver screen. As a young lad of 9, I humbly tuned in to the VOA on my parents' radio set at an ungodly hour to hear the live broadcast from Mission Control in Houston. I mentally traced every step of Apollo 8, and then, sometime later, even the moon landed on Apollo 11 with great enthusiasm.

Legacy of Wernher von Braun

Towards the end of World War II, the United States, and the Soviet Union (USSR) embarked on their respective secret missions to offer asylum to hundreds of German scientists, including nuclear physicists, engineers, and others, before the impending collapse of the Third Reich. Several top German rocket scientists, physicists, mathematicians, and other noted space-age personages emigrated to the United States or the Soviet Union (USSR).

The Marshall Space Flight Center (MSFC) was established on July 1, 1960, in Huntsville, Alabama. President Dwight Eisenhower dedicated it to General George C. Marshall, the founder of the Marshall Plan for European Recovery after World War II. Huntsville was nicknamed *Rocket City* in the 1950s due to its contributions to aerospace and rocketry.

Post-WWII, the Cold War with the Soviet Union was heating up amidst the nuclear arms race and military buildup across Eastern Europe. Both the United States and the USSR were busy harnessing the scientific benefits from their recently acquired scientific talent to immediately work on ambitious space exploration and nuclear weapons programs.

On April 12, 1961, the Soviets launched Yuri Gagarin, the first human to orbit Earth. On June 16th, 1963, the USSR broke the gender barrier by launching the first female cosmonaut, Valentina Tereshkova, into orbit. The United States had much to catch up on to gain the lead over the USSR in the space arena.

In his early years, Werner von Braun (2009) was experimenting with rockets in Germany. Post WWII, he emigrated to the United States and relocated to Huntsville, Alabama, where he successfully developed the famed Saturn V rocket technology that would serve as the workhorse for the American space program. This provided NASA with launch capabilities to deliver heavy payloads into Earth orbit for its numerous rapidly developing space programs. The Saturn V series of launch vehicles delivered all Apollo missions into Earth orbit. The trans lunar injection and the subsequent orbital insertion and then to the Moon and back were attributed to rocket engine companies such as Rocketdyne.

Wernher von Braun was not content with just going to the Moon. His heart was set on conquering Mars, and he was confident he could deliver. However, budget limitations, the protracted Vietnam War, and other political hurdles set limits to his ambitions. Unfortunately, von Braun passed away in the summer of 1977 after a prolonged battle with cancer.

The Apollo Program: A Historical Perspective

A brief review of the Apollo program is provided to facilitate the understanding of the various lunar missions, including the terminology, configuration, and physical process of getting there and returning safely to Earth. Many of the basic principles shall also apply to future missions such as the ARTEMIS[1] Program.

The Hardware

Figure 1.1 illustrates the Saturn V Launch Vehicle configuration used in the Apollo Program, which consists of three rocket stages.

The *First Stage* consists of a set of five (F-1) engines (at the tail end of the rocket) delivering a maximum combined thrust of 7.6M lbs. for liftoff (Biggs, 2009). The F-1 uses a bipropellant fuel combination of liquid oxygen (LOX) and Refined Petroleum (RP-1) such as kerosene.

---

[1] NASA ARTEMIS: https://www.nasa.gov/feature/artemis/

Chapter 1: History in the Making

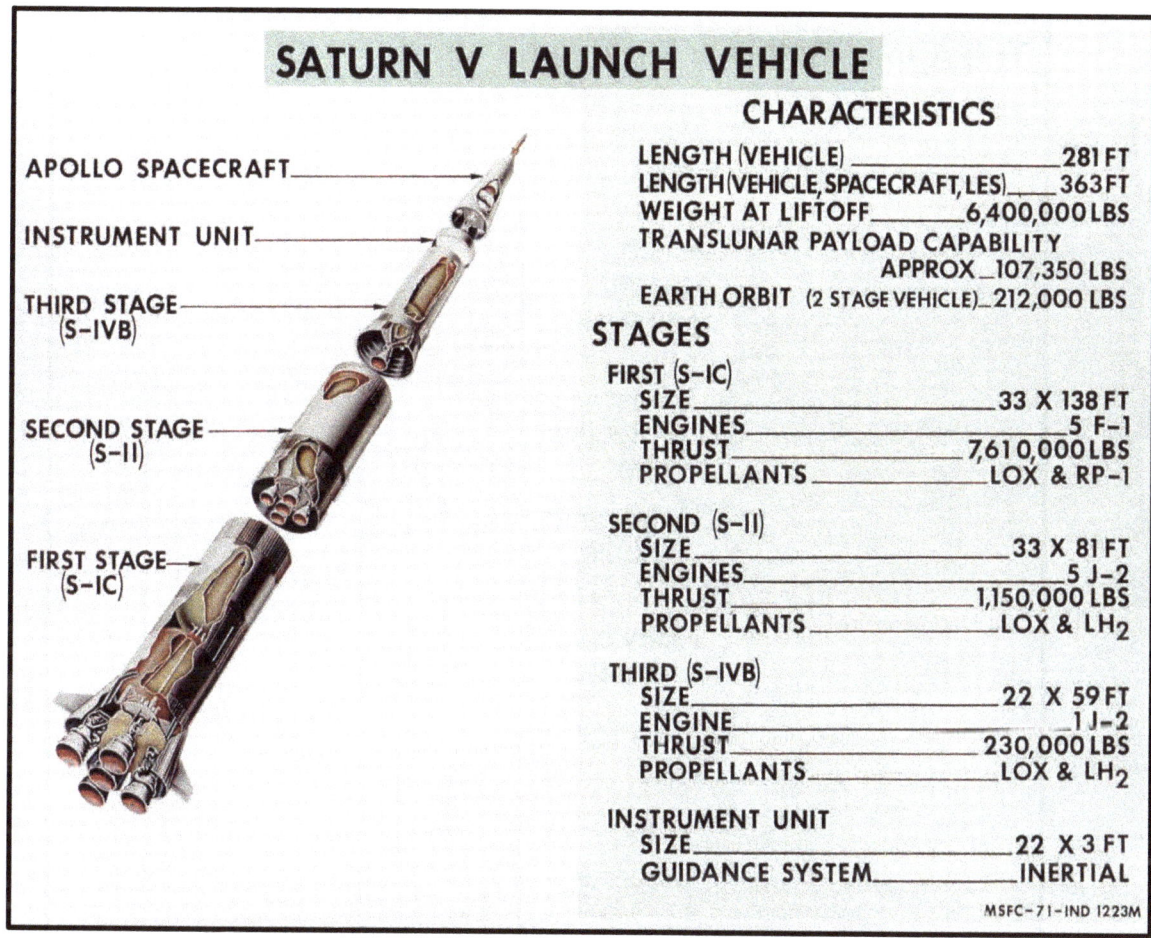

Figure 1.1 Saturn V Launch Vehicle Configuration (Credit: "NASA Image Collection" /Alamy Stock Photo)

The *Second Stage* had five J-2 engines powered by a combination of liquid oxygen (LOX) and liquid hydrogen (LH$_2$), delivering a combined thrust of 1,150,000 lbs. These stages are primarily used during liftoff and for placing the spacecraft into Earth orbit, known as a *Parked Orbit*. Following stage burn-out, both stages are sequentially ejected (Coffman, 2009).

The final *Third Stage* consists of a single restartable J-2 engine capable of delivering a thrust of 230,000 lbs. This engine is responsible for any orbital corrections and maneuvers and for placing the Apollo spacecraft into Trans Lunar Injection (TLI) towards the Moon by providing the required escape velocity to leave Earth's orbit and enter a lunar orbital trajectory.

Details of the spacecraft's configuration riding above the *Third Stage* (Fig. 1.2) show: (1) The nose section, which is always dedicated to the emergency *Launch Escape System* (LES) which can jettison the crew seated in the LM to safety in case of a launch mishap; (2) the Command Module (CM); (3) the Service Module powered by the Service Propulsion System (SPS); (4) the Lunar Module (LM) with both its *Ascent* and *Descent* propulsion stages for landing and subsequent lift-off maneuvers; and (5) the *Adapter* or Spacecraft LM Adapter (SLA) for protecting the LM assembly during launch.

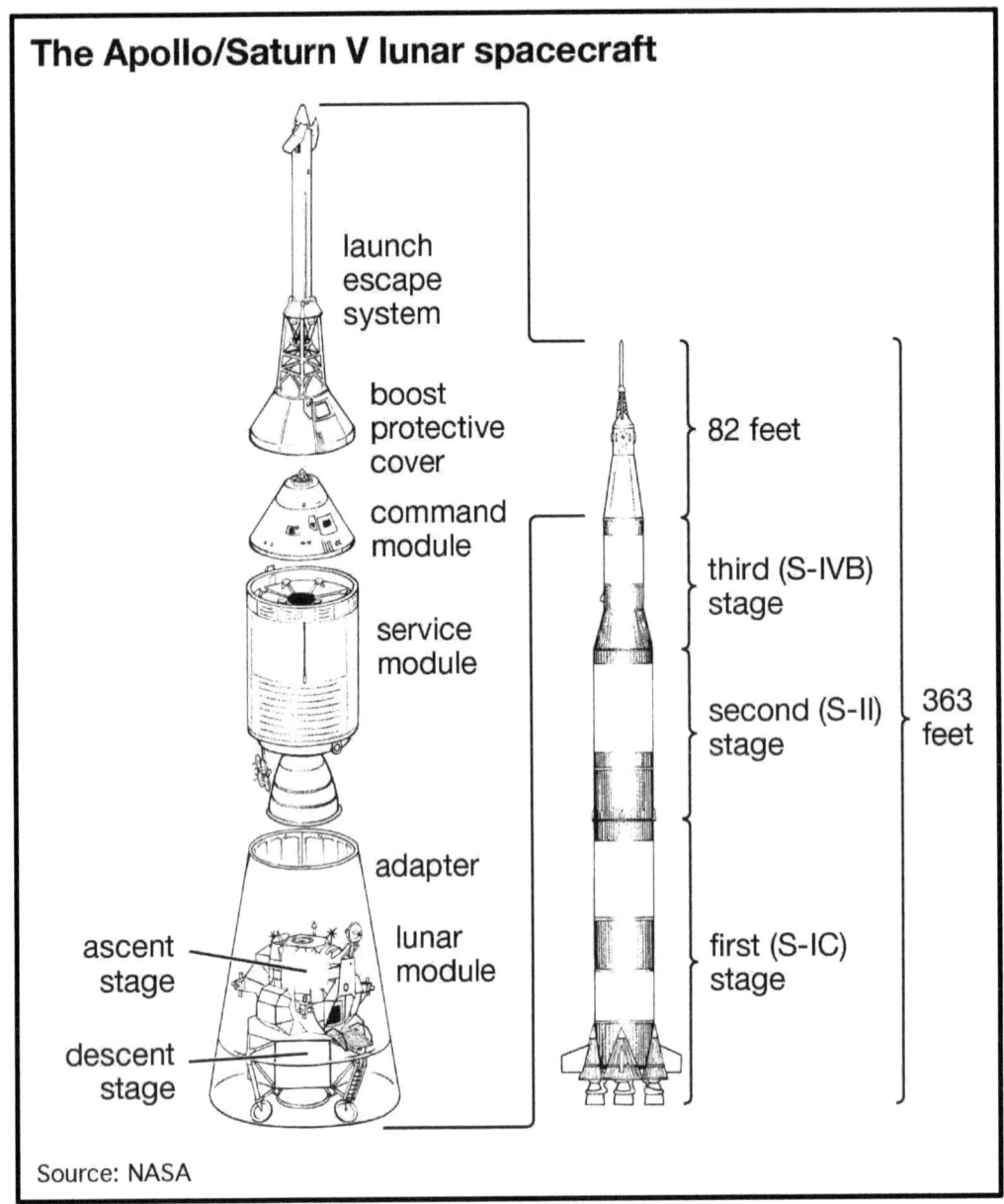

**Figure 1.2 Apollo 11 Spacecraft Configuration Showing LES, CM, SPS, SLA & LM components
(Credit: "Universal Images Group North America LLC"/ Alamy Stock Photo)**

The Descent Stage of the Lunar Excursion Module (LEM), subsequently known as the Lunar Module (LM) was developed by Rocketdyne (Elverum, 2009). It used Nitrogen Tetroxide (N_2O_4) as oxidizer and hydrazine as fuel. The throttleable J-2 engine had a unique built-in feature that could automatically revert to its full thrust position in case of a power failure during descent. This safety feature would enable the crew to abort landing and return safely to dock with the CM.

The Apollo program is said to be equipped with redundant engines at every stage to guarantee success. The only exception to this redundancy requirement was the unique Apollo Lunar Module Ascent Engine (LMAE); it had to work under any circumstances for the crew to return home safely. The pressure-fed engine was equipped with a simple on/off switch to deliver a thrust of 3,500 pounds of force, had a Specific

Chapter 1: History in the Making

Impulse of 310, and incorporated hypergolic propellants (Harmon, 2009). It used Aerozine 50 for fuel and N2O4 as oxidizer.

The entire Apollo lunar mission - now Moon-bound (Fig. 1.3) depended upon the flawless performance of a single gimballable SPS engine capable of delivering a thrust of 20,000 pounds. Its surefire reliability is attributed to using Aerozine 50 (as fuel) and dinitrogen tetroxide (N_2O_4) as oxidizer. Both are stored in separate tanks and spontaneously ignited upon demand. A throat-gimballed rocket engine is said to provide more precise spacecraft control (Boyce, 2009).

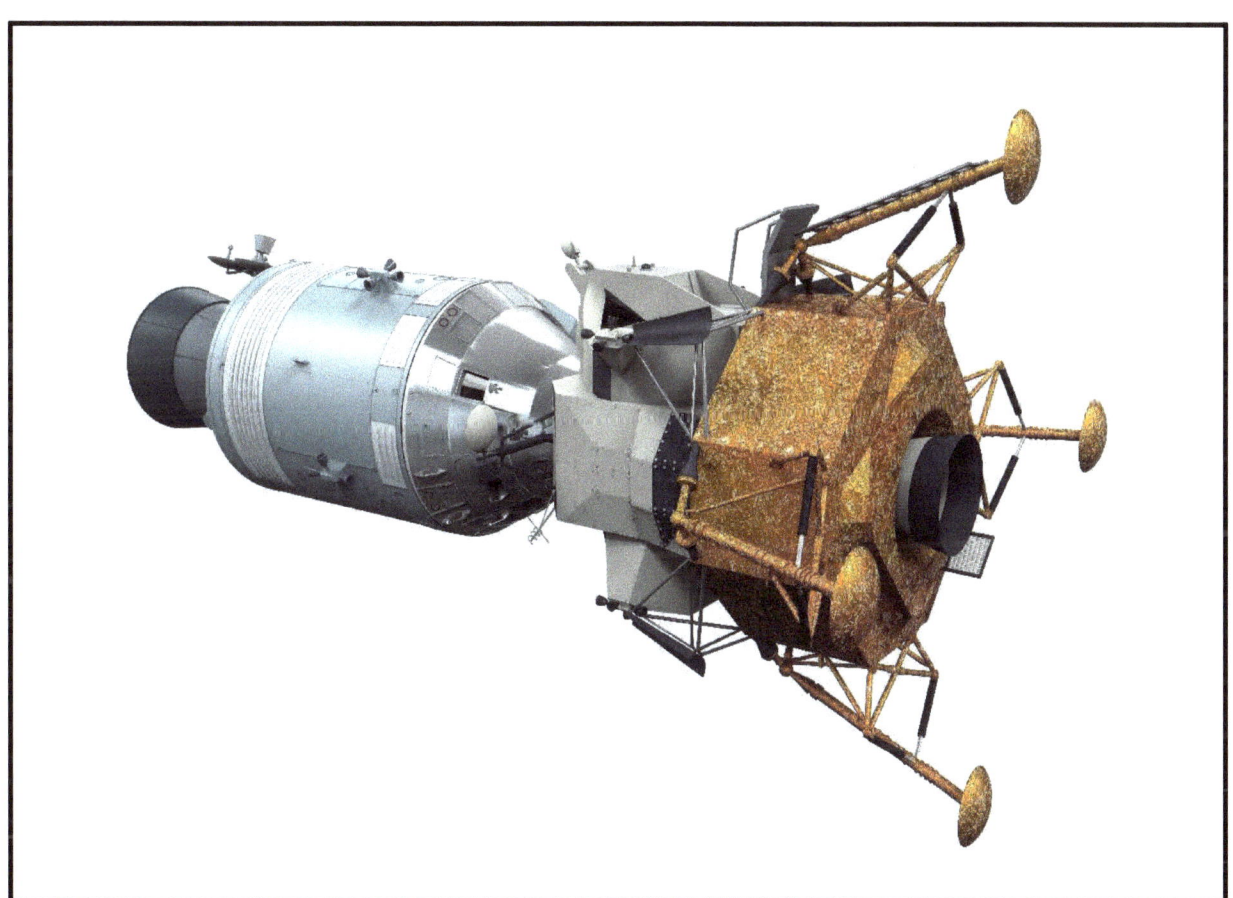

Figure 1.3 Docked configuration of the Apollo Service Module, Command Module, and Lunar Lander. (Credit: "Nerthuz" - stock.adobe.com)

A Generic Apollo Flight Path to the Moon and Back

Let us take a quick step-by-step look at how the Apollo missions traveled to the Moon and returned safely to Earth. Establishing a generic flight path for all the missions to the Moon and back simplifies project control and streamlines the engineering aspects of the program. Individual missions can deviate from the plan due to changes in the scope of the mission itself or due to the development of unforeseen events along the way.

After liftoff at Kennedy Space Center (symbol "1" in the figure), the spacecraft is placed into an Earth Parking orbit utilizing both Stages 1 and 2 of the Saturn V rocket (Fig.1.4).

Protective shields called *fairings* are used to enclose all payloads to withstand the launch process and must be ejected with the help of explosive "Pyro-bolts" that can be activated by Mission Control.

The final Saturn Stage 3 rocket engine places the spacecraft into a Trans-Lunar Trajectory (2) enroute to the Moon, and the adapter panels over the LM are then ejected.

Recall that the Apollo LM sits on top of both the Ascent and Descent Stages, and all of them are enclosed within the Spacecraft Lunar Module Adapter (SLA). Also, the CM and the Service Module containing the all-important SPS motor are stacked above the SLA using an adapter ring. After launch, these components must be reassembled in flight for landing on the Moon and safely returning the crew to Earth.

The Command and Service Modules jointly separate from the Saturn Third Stage and flip over by 180° to dock with the Lunar Module (3) for the trip to the Moon and back. By the end of this maneuver, the LM is docked to the Ascent Stage.

The trajectory of the spacecraft will initially take it towards the far side of the Moon, Once the spacecraft is over the far side of the Moon, the Service Module engine slows the spacecraft to insert it into the desired lunar orbit (4). There is no radio communication until the spacecraft emerges once again from behind.

Next, the Lunar Module, which carries the two astronauts, separates, and descends to the Moon's surface with the help of the Descent Stage, which faces the Moon. Meanwhile, the Service Module and the Command Module, carrying the third astronaut, remain in lunar orbit (5).

Once the lunar mission is completed, the Ascent Stage lifts the Lunar Module from the surface of the Moon, leaving the Descent Stage behind (6). After achieving lunar orbit, the Ascent Stage docks the attached Lunar Module to the Command Module (7). The Ascent Stage is then jettisoned towards the Moon after both crew members join the third member in the Command Module. The SPS Service Module Engine takes over and places the spacecraft into a Trans Earth Trajectory. The Service Module is jettisoned as the Command Module approaches Earth with its bottom facing down to slow the spacecraft and prepare for a parachute landing in the ocean (9). Finally, the Command Module splashes down in a predetermined location to be picked up by the awaiting recovery team (10).

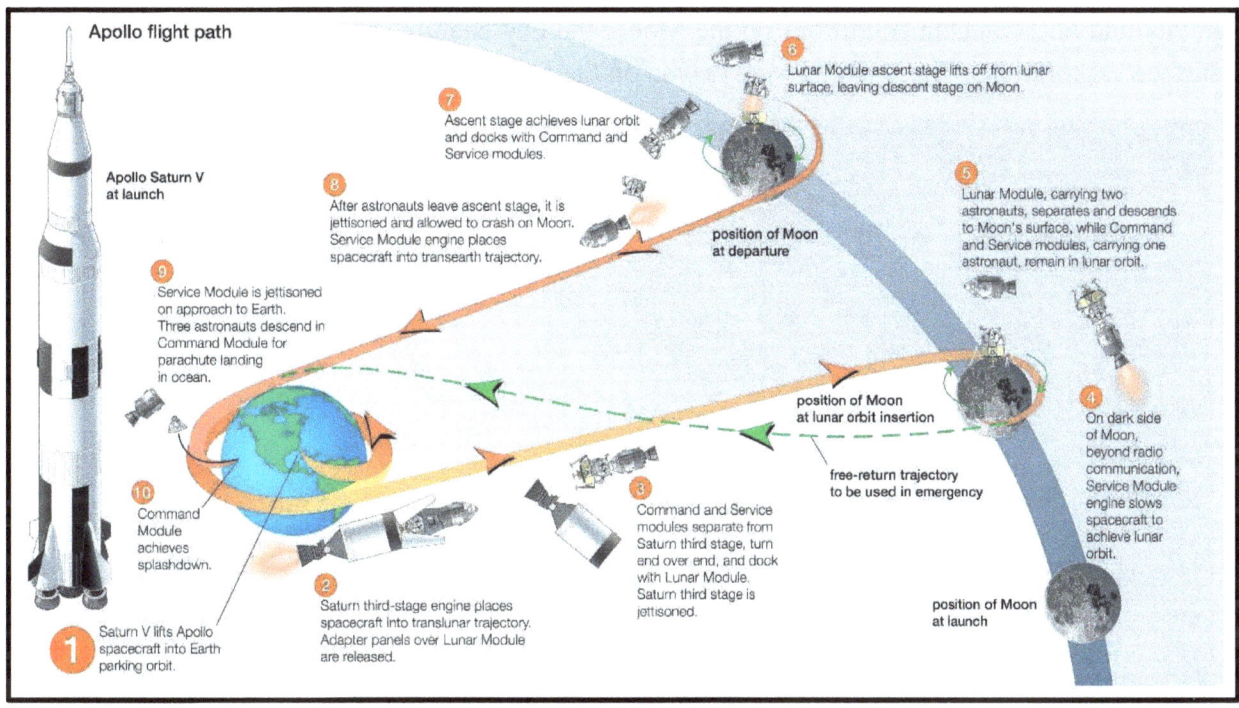

Figure 1.4 Generalized Apollo Flight Path to Moon and Back Showing Details of the Various Orbital Maneuvers (Credit: "Universal Images Group North America LLC" / Alamy Stock Photo)

An overview of the Apollo missions is summarized in Table 1.1. Apollo missions 7, 9 and 10 were primarily for testing and evaluating various features and components before the lunar missions. Apollo 8 was the first crewed mission with three members orbiting the Moon. This was humans' first flight around the hitherto hidden far side. Apollo 11 was the first mission to land a crew of 2 on the Moon. Apollo 13 had to cut short its mission due to an unfortunate onboard incident. The table also summarizes the crew's time spent on the Moon and the number of lunar orbits made by the CM.

TABLE 1.1 OVERVIEW OF APOLLO MISSIONS

MISSION	MISSION TYPE	COMMAND MODULE	LUNAR MODULE	LAUNCH	RETURN	TIME ON SURFACE	LUNAR ORBITS
Apollo 7	Earth Orbit	CSM	NA	11-Oct-68	22-Oct-68	NA	NA
Apollo 8	Lunar Orbit	CSM-103	LTA-B	21-Dec-68	27-Dec-68	NA	10
Apollo 9	Earth Orbit	Gumdrop	Spider	03-Mar-69	13-Mar-69	NA	NA
Apollo 10	Earth Orbit	Charlie Brown	Snoopy	18-May-69	26-May-69	NA	NA
Apollo 11	Lunar Landing	Columbia	Eagle	16-Jul-69	24-Jul-69	21:36:00	30
Apollo 12	Lunar Landing	Yankee Clipper	Intrepid	14-Nov-69	24-Nov-69	31:00:00	45
Apollo 13	Lunar Fly-By	Odyssey	Aquarius	11-Apr-70	17-Apr-70	NA	Fly-By
Apollo 14	Lunar Landing	Kitty Hawk	Antares	31-Jan-71	09-Feb-71	33:30:00	34
Apollo 15	Lunar Landing	Endeavour	Falcon	26-Jul-71	07-Aug-71	67:00:00	74
Apollo 16	Lunar Landing	Casper	Orion	16-Apr-72	27-Apr-72	71:02:13	64
Apollo 17	Lunar Landing	America	Challenger	07-Dec-72	19-Dec-72	75:02:00	75

In addition, some of the missions carried an electric *Lunar Roving Vehicle* (LRV), which was an electric vehicle developed exclusively for the Apollo program (Fig. 1.5). It was designed to operate under low-gravity and near-vacuum conditions on the Moon, thereby enabling the crew to extend the range of their surface explorations. These LRVs were driven on the Moon during the Apollo 15-17 missions.

Figure 1.5 The Apollo 17 Lunar Rover (Credit: "Artsiom P" -stock.adobe.com)

All Apollo spacecraft are typically assembled inside a hangar and transported to the launch pad. Figure 1.6 shows the entire Apollo 11 Saturn V rocket assembly being transported to the launch pad.

Chapter 1: History in the Making

Figure 1.6 The Apollo 11 Saturn V Rocket Assembly makes its Way to the Launch Pad (Credit: "Imaginechina Limited" / Alamy Stock Photo)

Historical Lunar Data Archives

Exploring the Moon or any other planetary object requires studying the body's physical environment and surface characteristics over an extended period to understand seasonal and daily changes. Understanding atmospheric characteristics, such as the nature and density of gases a spacecraft must endure during entry and landing maneuvers, is critical in mission planning, design, and execution.

Mapping surface characteristics such as the terrain (mountains and valleys), volcanoes, impact craters, ice and water, methane, etc., will help in mission planning and design. The importance of historical lunar data archives in this process cannot be overstated, as they provide a wealth of information for mission planning and design and contribute to the overall success of space missions.

Many Hasselblad images are available in the public domain through the popular internet URL platform Flickr.com. The interested reader may visualize these images as described in *Accessing the Apollo Image Archives* provided in the Appendix towards the end of the book.

* * * * * *

Chapter 2: The Setting for the Book

Our beautiful planet Earth is truly a gem in our galaxy. Tens, if not hundreds, of light years away, there appears to be nothing comparable to our planet. If real estate on our planet were ever to be traded on a universal platform, none of us could afford even a square inch of it. That is how valuable our planet is for being so unique. However, we abuse it in many ways instead of preserving its beauty and passing it on to the following generations.

Over millions of years, our planet has experienced numerous natural disasters, including earthquakes, volcanic eruptions, droughts, massive floodings, epidemics, and cataclysmic events such as asteroid strikes. However, it has managed to bounce back over time. Rapid industrialization, global warming, and constant conflicts are taking a toll on humanity and the planet.

Our nearest neighbor, the Moon, has been a silent witness to the numerous happenings on our planet. During its 4.5 billion-year history, it has experienced volcanic eruptions, quakes, and showers of large and small meteorites. Early on in its history, it suffered one of the most significant asteroid strikes in the entire Solar system over what is known as the South Pole-Aitken (SPA) basin, a prevalent region in modern-day lunar exploration.

The *synchronous rotation* of the Moon around the Earth, also known as tidal locking, causes it to always show its same side. We can never see about 40 percent of the Moon, known as the far side, as opposed to the always visible *near side*. Many moons in our Solar system are tidally locked with their host planetary bodies. If a moon gets closer than the *Roche radius* of the planet, it will begin to disintegrate. We will not have to worry about this happening to our Moon as it drifts away by about 3.8 centimeters (1.5 inches) annually.

A *lunar day* is about 29.53 Earth days, resulting in long days and nights (14.77 Earth days each). This window poses some challenges to lunar exploration, especially in the polar regions.

Why Bring up Religion?

Religious texts offer a peek into the distant past if we are interested in learning about what transpired in the ancient past. When one studies more than one religion, some commonalities emerge among them. This convergence of evidence assures us of their authenticity. Some ancient religions, such as Hinduism, are significantly older than the modern ones and can, therefore, take one back farther in time.

The interesting common factor is that God appears to travel by spacecraft and address His subjects sometimes from the air, like when talking to Noah about the Ark. Hindu Gods also frequently utilized spacecraft or Vimana. The Persian Prophet Zoroaster is also believed to have traveled in His own Vimana.

In his runaway bestseller *Chariots of the Gods* (Däniken, 1999), Erich von Däniken theorized that ancient aliens visited Earth in spacecraft numerous times and transferred knowledge to humans for their betterment. We may even have inherited some of their physical traits by design. He presents numerous examples that suggest ancient aliens or alien Gods may be responsible for many of the world's megalithic structures, pyramids, and other unexplainable artifacts attributed to many cultures.

Almost all religions allude to giants tormenting humankind; such convergence of evidence conveys credibility to their claims. We will examine some of them in greater depth.

The repetitive *Mahayuga cycles* described in the ancient Puranas allude to humanity's evolutionary cycles integrating into the larger life cycle of the Universe itself. According to the Puranas, each Mahayuga cycle, which is 4.3 million years in duration, can be further subdivided into four yuga cycles: *Satya yuga, Treta yuga, Dvapara* yuga, and *Kali-yuga*. Each of the four yugas has preset limits on human lifespans, stature, intelligence, and social traits.

By Divine design, all these human traits decrease according to a prescribed ratio with each successive Yuga, and then the cycle repeats itself indefinitely. Paradoxically, this concept contradicts modern-day evolutionary theories that define our present civilization as the most advanced.

Each Mahayuga cycle is assigned a number, and we live in the Kali-yuga associated with the 28th Mahayuga cycle. The next chapter describes the Mahayuga cycles during which the epics of Ramayana and Mahabharata are said to have occurred.

The origins of giants described in religious texts in Christianity, Judaism, and Hinduism may be traceable to characteristics observed in some of the earlier yugas.

We will explore how the intellectual superiority of inhabitants during a Satya yuga may have enabled our ancient ancestors to achieve marvels in engineering, construction, and more.

The characteristics of evolutionary cycles are intriguing and even paradoxical. Human lifespans and physical, intellectual, and social characteristics are unique to each cycle. We are all extremely comfortable discussing extinct giant dinosaurs, large birds, and massive reptiles but immediately shy away from discussing giant human populations. Historically, most religions have acknowledged the presence of giants.

Individuals in the epic Ramayana are said to be very tall and endowed with long life spans. The famed *Hanuman* could transform himself into a towering 36-foot giant. Several temples worldwide have erected giant statues dedicated to *Hanuman*, as described in this epic.

Noah and his descendants were tall and lived around a thousand years. These characteristics can be observed during the peak of any Dvapara yuga. The Maha Yuga cycle during which *The Great Flood* took place may be traceable to a similar flood described in the *Matsya Purana*.

According to the Puranas, the Gods or Alien Gods are believed to have traveled around the world millions of years ago in Vimanas; this may be why we find religious symbols such as Mandalas and Sri Chakras scattered over many parts of the world. The Gods may have also traveled to the Moon and other parts of our Solar system.

We will examine the relevance of some artifacts and anomalies appearing in the Apollo Hasselblad Imagery available in Flickr's public domain archive. The reader must be cognizant that these lunar images were taken nearly sixty years ago, and the situation on the ground could have changed considerably by now.

This book also discusses the recently renewed space race to the Moon's South Pole-Aitken Basin by a growing list of countries in quest of its limited natural resources.

The Moon is a fascinating and mysterious place for anyone interested in exploring and colonizing it. Investigating and deciphering its fascinating mysteries may take much time and effort. In the interim, competition for lunar exploration is once again heating up.

* * * * *

Chapter 3: In Search of Clues From the Ancient Past

Ancient religious works such as *the Ramayana, the Mahabharata, the Book of Genesis, the Book of Numbers,* and several others offer a rare glimpse into society when God or His messengers interacted with humans in various situations worldwide, such as *the creation of Man*, historic epic battles, mass destructions, *the Great Flood*, the triumph of good over evil, and so forth. These works have survived for thousands of years because ancient societies nurtured these great writings for the benefit of future generations.

Major religions evolved successively over time in history across the globe, ranging from Hinduism (ancient), Zoroastrianism (600 BCE), Buddhism (500 BCE), the birth of Jesus Christ and Christianity (1st Century CE), Islam (7th Century CE), and Sikhism (16th Century CE). Several religious instances illustrate that God or Alien Gods appeared on Earth to defend humanity from evil forces or "speed up or jump-start" the human evolutionary process by modifying the genetic stock or steering humankind onto righteous paths. However, humankind often chose to revert to the status quo soon after the Gods or their messengers departed Earth.

An unbiased exploration of diverse religions can help us understand God's handling of disagreement and non-acceptance. Civilizations have gone through a pattern of creation and re-creation throughout history. Humanity's age is significantly older than modern science is willing to acknowledge.

A common denominator in several religious texts is numerous references to their Gods using spacecraft during visits to Earth or sojourns. It is very plausible that the Moon may have been used as a base to launch terrestrial missions.

ANCIENT ASTRONOMY

Ancient civilizations worldwide spent considerable time, effort, and resources in mastering astronomy. Ancient Babylonians, Egyptians, Mayans, Incas, Greeks, Hindus, and Moghuls studied astronomy and constructed elaborate observatories. Ancient Egyptians from the *Pharaonic* period maintained a vast database of astronomical tables, diagrams, and texts. Stonehenge in England and the Carnac stones in France are examples of early European attempts at studying astronomy. They all monitored the progression of the seasons by observing the vernal and autumnal equinoxes for both astrological and religious purposes.

In 129 BC, the Greek astronomer *Hipparchus* noticed a systematic shift in the stars from earlier Babylonian measurements. Hipparchus correctly attributed this shift to the periodic wobble of the earth's axis in what is now known as the *precession of the equinoxes*. In ancient astronomy, the intersection of the ecliptic by the Sun during the vernal (spring) equinox was observed in the constellation of Pisces. However, it is currently transitioning into the constellation Aquarius. The Earth's precession is about 25,772 years and is attributed to the combined gravitational pull of the sun and the Moon on the Earth's equatorial bulge (Britannica, 2023[2]).

---

[2] Britannica, The Editors of Encyclopedia. "precession of the equinoxes". Encyclopedia Britannica, 29 Mar. 2023, https://www.brittanica.com/science/precession-of-the-equinoxes. Accessed March 2024.

Ancient Hindus introduced the concept of *Navagrahas* (nine planetary Gods) into their religious rituals. These consist of (1) Surya (Sun), (2) Chandra (Moon), (3) Mangala (Mars), (4) Budha (Mercury), (5) Brihaspati (Jupiter), (6) Shukra (Venus), (7) Sani (Saturn), (8) Rahu (Neptune), and (9) Ketu ("DhumaKetu", or comet in Sanskrit). According to the Vedas, both Rahu and Ketu, described as demons, are said to have found their place in the *Navagraha* count through deception. The *Navagrahas* occupy a prominent position in Hindu-temple architectural layouts and are worshiped by devotees to dispel any perceived adverse planetary influences from an astrological perspective.

THE PURANAS AND VEDAS

Sanatana Dharma was the original name of what we now know as modern Hinduism. It believes in a universal God who can manifest in different forms, such as the Trinity of Chatur-Mukha (four-headed) Brahma (the Creator), Vishnu (the Preserver), and Shiva (the Destroyer). This God is responsible for various aspects of cyclical creation, preservation, annihilation, and eventual recreation of our universe. According to this belief, our universe was created and destroyed six times before this seventh cycle.

A series of eighteen sacred ancient scriptures called *Puranas* (Veda Vyasa) describe the cycles of creationism, preservation, annihilation, and recreation as narrated by God to a chosen group of seven *Sages* known as *Saptarishis*.

In Vedic cosmology, the seven brightest stars in the Great Bear (Ursa Major) constellation, also known as Saptarishi Mandalas, are named after these sages. The Pole Star (*Dhruva*), as well as the location of the abodes of the Hindu Gods dwelling beyond the Ursa Major constellation, is discussed in the Puranas. The eighteen Puranas are supplemented by another eighteen secondary or *Upa Puranas*. The great epics such as *the Ramayana* (Valmiki and Griffith) and *the Mahabharata* (Veda Vyasa, Veda Vyasa and Swami Paramananda (2020)) were included later in a collection collectively known as the *Sacred Hindu texts*.

The eighteen *Puranas* consists of: (1) Brahma Purana, (2) Vishnu Purana, (3) Shiva Purana, (4) Bhagavat Purana, (5) Bhavishya (Future) Purana, (6) Narada Purana, (7) Markandeya Purana, (8) Agni Purana, (9) Brahma Vaivarta Purana, (10) Linga Purana, (11) Padma Purana, (12), Varaha Purana, (13) Skanda Purana, (14) Vamana Purana, (15) Kurma Purana, (16) Matsya Purana, (17) Garuda Purana, and (18) Vayu Purana (Veda Vyasa, Kindle Books). The *Vishnu Purana, Brahma Purana, and Shiva Purana* are the most widely read.

The Vedas, Sanskrit for *knowledge*, refers to a collection of four scriptures known as (1) *Rig Veda*, (2) *Sama Veda*, (3) *Yajur Veda*, and (4) *Atharva Veda*. These four Vedas are attributed to *Brahma*, the four-faced Creator of the Universe. According to *Vishnu Purana*, Brahma recited the four Vedas for the benefit of humankind after the end of each *Kalpa* (see below); Lord Brahma recited the *Rig Veda*, Gayathri mantra, and Yagyas from His east-facing head. The *Sama Veda* was recited from His west-facing head. The *Yajur Veda* was recited from His south-facing head. And the *Athar Veda* was recited from His north-facing head. An authoritative translation of the Puranas is available online courtesy of the *Kanchi Kamakoti Peetham* (Kamakoti.org).

Western scholars translated the Vedas and other ancient sacred texts by the early nineteenth century. A nineteenth-century German-born Sanskrit scholar and Philologist named Max Muller is said to have translated the *Upanishads* into German. He later moved to Oxford, England, where he is credited with overseeing the translation of several other sacred scriptures, including the Rig Veda, under the aegis of the British East India Company. Later, while in Oxford, he published *the Sacred Books of the East*.

In 1870, Ralph Thomas Hotchkin Griffith translated the *Valmiki Ramayana* into English (Valmiki and Griffith). He later translated all four Vedas into English as well. The translated works by RTH Griffith[3] are now available online in their entirety. Vedic philosophy influenced several early 20th-century scientists and mathematicians. Nobel Laureates in quantum physics, such as Niels Bohr (Denmark) and Erwin Schrodinger (Austria), are both said to have studied the Vedas.

German scientists such as Robert Oppenheimer and Albert Einstein learned Sanskrit to gather information first-hand rather than through third-party translations. Oppenheimer was able to find references to the deployment of small-scale atomic weapons during the *Mahabharata* battle. Albert Einstein was able to quantify some of the qualitative concepts of the Creation of the Universe following the explosion of Lord Vishnu's *cosmic egg* analogous to the modern *Big Bang theory*, the role of energy and matter in creation, concepts of time travel, multiverses, etcetera.

Both *the Vishnu Purana* and *Shiva Purana* allude to episodes in which God uses concepts of DNA (e.g., strands of hair), in-vitro fertilization, and even non-invasive fertilization techniques to manifest various avatars in their chosen ones. Religious texts convey some of these modern scientific concepts in the form of anecdotes for the benefit of humanity. Anecdotes are always easier for anyone to remember and relate to, so all religious texts incorporate them effectively and successfully.

In both *the Ramayana* and *the Mahabharata*, the battles, the deployment of Star Wars weapons and their usage, and the nature of damage to life and property are all vividly described. The most feared weapon in battle was always the *Brahmastra*; it was also the weapon of choice when all else failed. It is the hand-launched equivalent of a modern nuclear weapon in its destructive ability. However, the delivery mechanisms were simple arrowheads that were 'programmed' with appropriate mantras (codes) acquired by warriors from Gods due to their divine ancestry, such as Krishna, or royal lineage such as Rama and Lakshmana, or based on religious devotion and penance. Even tyrants such as Ravana, the evil king of Lanka who abducted Rama's wife, Sita, are said to have acquired some of these dangerous weapons through the intense religious devotion of Lord Shiva, who inadvertently granted him wishes that would transform him into a formidable enemy in the battlefield.

Nuclear physicists such as Robert Oppenheimer (Bird and Sherwin, 2016), the father of the atomic bomb, studied the *Bhagavad Gita* in search of references to advanced weapons used in battle. The vivid accounts of the fallout from the blasts, the ensuing civilian toll, soldiers jumping into the water, battle horses and elephants screaming and burning to their deaths, birds with feathers turning white, and contamination of food are all fallouts of atomic weapon warfare. Evidence of vitrification of glass in the form of beads scattered in the soil is the classic tell-tale evidence of atomic warfare. Commenting on his success in detonating the first atomic explosion, Robert Oppenheimer quotes from the Bhagavad Gita:

---

[3] https://hinduwebsite.com/

"I become Death, the destroyer of worlds" (Hijiya, 2000[4]). Later, when asked by a student if he was the first person ever to detonate an atomic weapon, Oppenheimer replied, "Well, yes, in modern times," implying that similar weapons had already been used earlier in the battle of the *Mahabharata*. There are reports of some locations in India, such as the one near Jodhpur, Rajasthan, where a thick layer of radioactive ash was found during excavations over a three-mile area. Excavations at other sites in northern India also revealed the vitrification of ancient pottery, bricks, and dwelling walls due to the extensive heat accompanying an atomic blast.

THE YUGA CYCLES AND BRAHMA'S CLOCK

Ancient texts are our only sources of information regarding our distant past, dating back perhaps to the Big Bang or even earlier. Vedic texts such as the *Vishnu Purana* (Wilson, 1884), the *Brahma Purana,* or the *Matsya Purana* provide us with an insight into the life cycle of the universe in terms of S*rishti* or creation; *Sthithi* or continuation, and subsequent dissolution or annihilation (*Pralaya*) through the concept of *Yuga*s which are inherently cyclical spanning over trillions of years. In Hindu cosmology, Brahma is associated with creation or Srishti; Vishnu is associated with *Sthithi* or continuation, and Shiva is associated with *Pralaya* or dissolution.

Humankind may have been subjected to periodic *mini Pralayas* in natural calamities such as famine, droughts, floods, plagues, epidemics, pandemics, and viral infections. Global outbreaks of pandemics such as MERS, SARS-CoV2, and, most recently, COVID-19 have resulted in massive infestations and deaths, coupled with economic upheavals reminiscent of the *Great Depression*. In modern times, airline passenger traffic from infected areas has facilitated the rapid spread of pandemics such as Ebola, SARS, Covid-19, and others. These *mini Pralayas* are nature's way of regulating human populations worldwide. Mortality rates may have been exceedingly high during ancient times, but they did not benefit from modern-day healthcare, sanitation, or the availability of vaccines to curtail their spread. However, humankind hobbled along and prevailed.

The Puranas describe the universe's age in terms of Brahma's life cycle without using complex equations and the need for supercomputers. One starts with simple numbers in the millions describing Earth's cycles that soon transcend into billions and eventually into trillions of years, describing the universe's life cycle. This simple computational journey describes the mathematical means to cycle through the universe's past and about 130 trillion years into the future.

Imagine a situation where people are to be identified by a number, such as their passport number, social security number, or email, instead of their name. On a personal level, it is always easier to communicate by name rather than by numbers. A similar logic is used in the Puranas to describe the flow of time. They may identify large chunks of time by name to facilitate matters. For example, consider our current *Manu*, which is known as *Vaivaswata*. He is not someone sitting behind a Divine desk regulating time and human evolution; a name is always easier to relate to than a number running into millions, billions, or, at times, into the trillions!

---

[4] Hijiya, J.A. (2000): The Gita of J. Robert Oppenheimer.
https://ia802907.us.archive.org/8/items/gitaandoppenheimer/Gita%20and%20Oppenheimer_text.pdf

I doubt whether anyone of human origin could have ever conjured such an elaborate process without fully comprehending how the universe functions. This method can be used to create an equation describing the age of our universe. The ancient Vedas used simple daily examples to explain complex and challenging concepts, many of which remain unknown. Some of these concepts will challenge our conventional wisdom, especially regarding human evolution, ancient civilizations, and ancient history.

BRAHMA'S CLOCK AND THE CYCLICAL YUGAS

The Earth's movement over time is measured in Yugas, which are part of a larger cycle of the Universe, which I would like to coin as Brahma's clock. These definitions can be found in several of the Puranas. Let me try to present these concepts succinctly.

Brahma's lifespan is divided into one hundred Divya or Divine years, after which the entire Universe is dissolved and starts fresh with a *Big Bang*. Some definitions are in order:

- Full Day (Daylight period + Night)
- Month (30 days)
- Year (360 days)
- Brahma's Lifespan is one hundred Divine years

The Earth's recurring evolutionary cycles are known as Mahayuga Cycles, subdivided into four parts called *Yugas*.

Several Puranas, such as the Vishnu Purana (Wilson, 1884) and the Brahma Purana, describe the four Yugas and their temporal characteristics in terms of Divine years and Deva Vatsaras in Sanskrit and their equivalent human years (1 Divine Year = 360 solar years), as shown in Table 3.1.

The basic block of time in Yugas is measured in terms of a *Charana* consisting of 1,200 Divine years (432,000 solar years). Comprehension will be easier if you stick with solar (human) years

The four Yugas in Hindu Cosmology are as follows (Table 3.1, Fig. 3.1):

(1) **Satya or Krita Yuga** (4 *Charanas*: 4,800 Divine years or **1,728,000** solar years)

(2) **Treta Yuga** (3 *Charanas*: 3,600 Divine years or **1,296,000** solar years)

(3) **Dvapara Yuga** (2 *Charanas*: 2,400 Divine years or **864,000** solar years)

(4) **Kali Yuga** (1 *Charana*: 1,200 Divine years or **432,000** solar years)

- Sum of all four Yugas is an important measure known as a **Maha or Chatur** (four) Yuga
- Evolutionary cycles are referred to by the appropriate *Mahayuga*; for example, we are currently in the 28th Mahayuga cycle

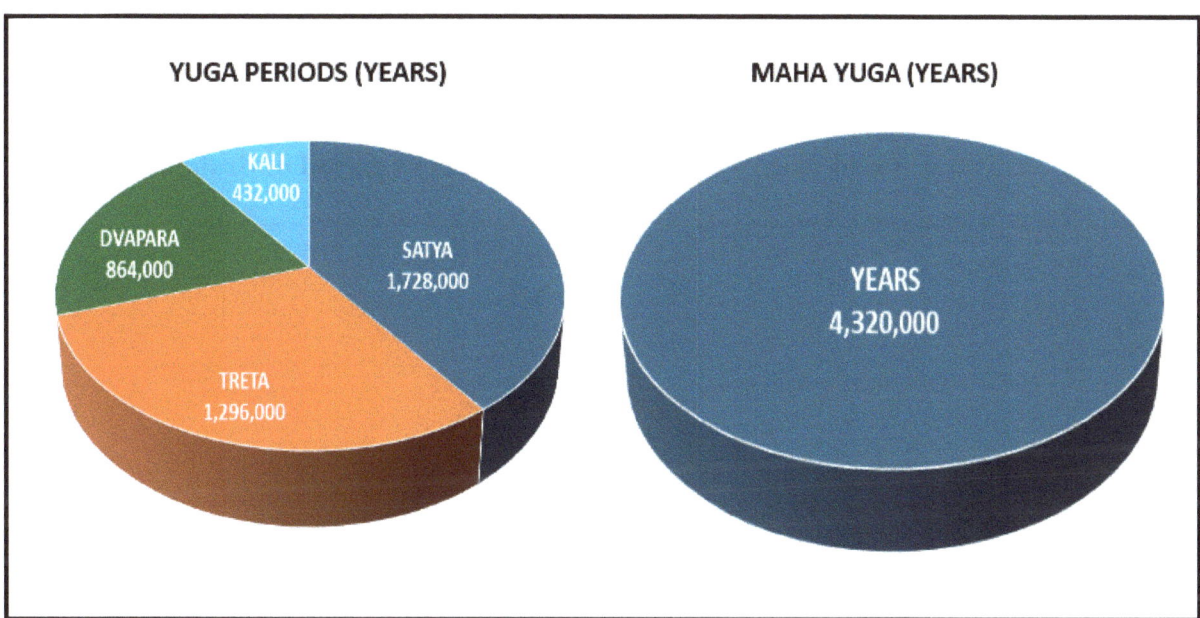

Figure 3.1 A Mahayuga cycle consists of (1) Satya, (2) Treta, (3) Dvapara, and (4) Kali Yugas

By Divine design, the duration, physical and mental attributes, and moral values of humans in each successive Yuga are reduced using the **Divine Ratio 4:3:2:1**. Note that the duration of the four Yugas decreases in the ratio of 4:3:2:1 *Charanas*.

- **Divine Ratio: 4:3:2:1** by which the duration of Yuga periods and human characteristics (through a DNA switch) are diminished within each *Mahayuga*; and once again, all four Yuga cycles are repeated in perpetuity

Each Yuga period may be visualized in the form of the familiar statistical bell curve with leading and trailing edges (Fig.3.2). A ten percent overlap of the leading cuspal period to the left is known as ***Sandhya*** (dawn) of the Yuga; human populations with a mix of characteristics from preceding as well as the next successive Yuga may appear. Over time, this leads us into the central ***Core*** period of each Yuga when its characteristic features are firmly established. Similarly, a ten percent overlap or cuspal period is appended towards the tail-end of each Yuga, known as ***Sandhyansa*** *(Sunset)*. A mix of human characteristics from the current and the next successive Yuga may appear. Some important terms and duration-wise definitions.

- Duration of each **Yuga = (*Sandhya* + *Core* + *Sandhyansa*)** (Fig.3.2)

- **Mahayuga** Cycle = Sum of all four Yugas = 4,320,000 **(4.32M)** solar years

- *Manvantara* = 71 Mahayuga cycles = 306,720,000 **(306.72M)** solar years

- **Full Day = (Daylight +Night)** in Life of Brahma **(8.64T)** solar years

- **Adi Sandhi = 1.728M solar years.** It precedes the ***start of*** the ***first*** **Manvantara** only

- **Sandhi Kala = 1.728M solar years = Earth Flooded** at the **end of each Manvantara**

- *Kalpa* = **(Adi Sandhi + 14 Manvantaras + Sandhi Kala)** = **4.32B** solar years

- ➢ *Kalpa* = **Daylight or Night** in Life of Brahma (4.32B solar years) = **1000 Mahayugas**
- ➢ **Full Day (Daylight + Night) = 2 Kalpas = 8.64** billion solar years
- ➢ **Life in the universe is said to exist only during the Daylight period of Brahma.**

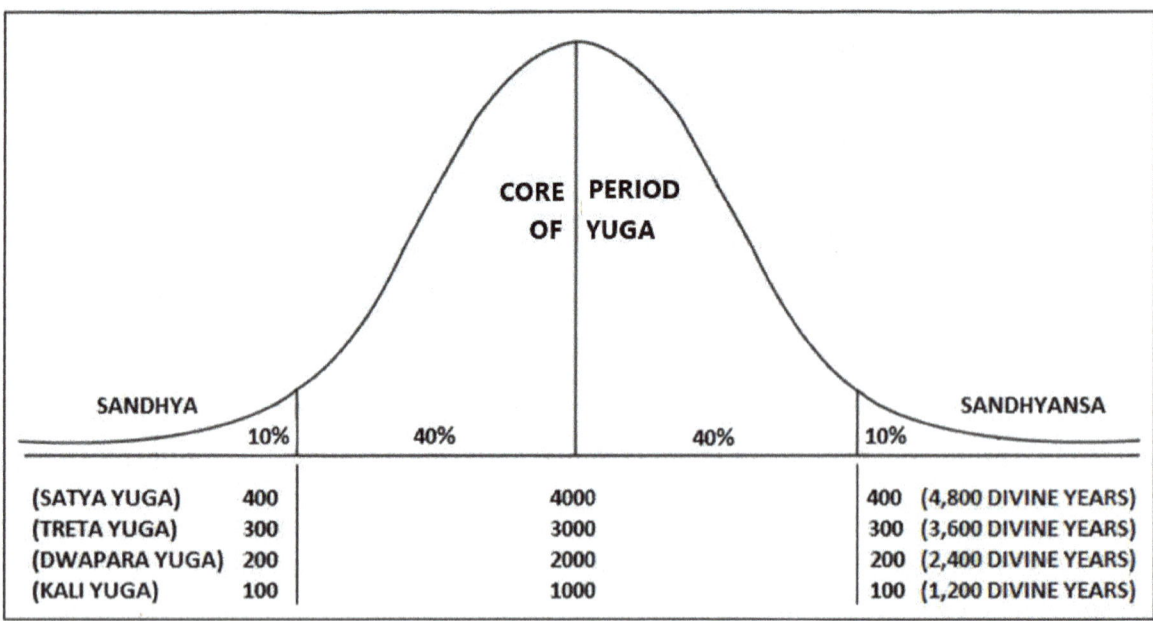

Figure 3.2 Delineation of Sandhya (10%), Core (70%), and Sandhyansa (10%) periods in each Yuga

MANVANTARAS AND KALPAS

TABLE 3.1 The Yuga Cycles and Brahma's Clock

YUGAS	PERIOD (Divine Years)			DURATION OF EACH YUGA	
	Sandhya	Core	Sandhyansa	Divine Years	Solar Years
Satya/Krita Yuga	400	4,000	400	4,800	1,728,000
Treta Yuga	300	3,000	300	3,600	1,296,000
Dvapara Yuga	200	2,000	200	2,400	864,000
Kali Yuga	100	1,000	100	1,200	432,000
Mahā Yuga/*Chatur* Yuga = Sum of all 4 Yugas				12,000	4,320,000
Manvantara = 71 Mahā Yuga Cycles				852,000	306,720,000
Adi Sandhi (Precedes 1st of 14 Manvantaras)				4,800	1,728,000
Sandhi Kāla (End of each Manvantara)				4,800	1,728,000
Kalpa = [Adi Sandhi+14 (Manvantaras + Sandhi Kāla)]				12,000,000	4,320,000,000
Full Day (Day + Night) of Brahma = **2 *Kalpas***				24,000,000	8,640,000,000
Month in life of Brahma = 30 Brahma Days				720,000,000	259,200,000,000
Year in life of Brahma = 12 Months in Brahma Year				8,640,000,000	3,110,400,000,000
Life of Brahma/Universe = 100 Years = *Mahā Kalpa*				864,000,000,000	311,040,000,000,000
Brahma completed 50 Years known as *First Parardha*				432,000,000,000	155,520,000,000,000

Each Manvantara encompasses 71 Mahayuga cycles (306.72 million solar years) and is ruled by a pre-assigned Manu for that period (Matsya Purana). We are now in the *seventh* Manvantara cycle, therefore our ruling Manu is *Vaivasvata* (Table 3.3). The names of all 14 Manvantaras, including the seven future ones that are to follow the current *Vaiswata* Manu over the next 2.16 billion years, have already been assigned by some entity prior to the commencement of this Kalpa, and these are listed sequentially in Table 3.3. The names of the 14 Manus groups keep changing with every new *Kalpa*.

Incidentally, we just crossed the halfway point in the life of Brahma vis-a-vis the age of our Universe (155.52T years).

A *Kalpa* refers to a daylight or nocturnal period in Brahma's life and comprises one thousand Mahayugas (ref. Table 3.1). Consequently, a full day in Brahma's life includes two Kalpas (Day + Night). According to Hindu cosmology, creation starts with each daylight *Kalpa*, and the universe dissolves during each night *Kalpa*.

We are now near the beginning of Kali Yuga of the 28th Mahayuga cycle; this implies that the current *Vaiswata Manvantara* commenced about 120 million years ago. A total of 504,000 Manus appear during the lifetime of Brahma.

Life on Earth is said to exist only during the daylight *Kalpa*, followed by a night Kalpa of equal duration. The nocturnal period that follows the end of each daylight period is known as Pralaya Kalpa.

At night, the Sun and Earth enter a suspended transition period, and our planet becomes completely uninhabited. The next morning, Brahma wakes up and recreates all of life again with the start of the next daylight Kalpa.

The *Matsya Purana* provides the names of all 30 Kalpas, beginning with the current daylight Kalpa in which we are living, *Sveta* or *Sveta Varaha Kalpa*; this will be followed by *Nilalohita Kalpa* (Table 3.2), and others.

Table 3.2 Sequence of the 30 Kalpas Based on *Matsya Purana*

NO.	KALPA	NO.	KALPA
1	*Sveta* Varaha (Current)	16	Nanarasimha
2	Nilalohita	17	Samana
3	Vamadeva	18	Agneya
4	Rathanantra	19	Soma
5	Raurava	20	Manava
6	Deva	21	Tatpuman
7	Vrhat	22	Vaikuntha
8	Kandarpa	23	Laksmi
9	Sadya	24	Savitri
10	Isana	25	Aghora
11	Tamah	26	Varaha
12	Sarasvata	27	Vairaja
13	Udana	28	Gauri
14	Garuda	29	Mahesvara
15	Kaurma	30	Pitr

According to the *Puranas,* each Kalpa begins with a leading period of 1.728 million solar years, known as *Adi Sandhi*. This is followed in sequence by 14 *Manvantaras*; a *Sandhi Kāla* follows each Manvantara, during which time the entire Earth is completely flooded before the commencement of the next *Manvantara* cycle. Each *Sandhi Kāla* lasts 1.728 million years, during which all life on Earth ceases to exist.

The *Sandhi Kāla* is characterized by massive flooding of the Earth for an extended period of about 1.728 million years. This could probably be due to relentless rainfall engulfing the entire planet during this long period.

Adi Sandhi and the *Sandhi Kāla* are inherently cyclical and have long periods of massive and sustained flooding on Earth. This period can be characterized as an existential threat to many species on Earth, especially those living on land. Marine life may have a better chance of survival, provided sunlight is not a limiting factor.

According to Hindu cosmology, life begins once again with the onset of the next Manvantara after Lord Brahma initiates His creation process. The Puranas describe each cycle of our universe based on Brahma's lifespan for easy understanding.

Table 3.3 The 14 Manvantaras and Manus in the Current *Sveta Varaha* Kalpa

NO.	NAME OF MANU	NO.	NAME OF MANU
1	Svayambhuva	8	Savarni
2	Svarochisha	9	Daksha Savarni
3	Uttama	10	Brahma Savarni
4	Tamasa / Tapasa	11	Dharma Savarni
5	Raivata	12	Rudra Savarni
6	Chakshusha	13	Raucya / Deva Savarni
7	Vaivaswata (Current)	14	Indra Savarni

During Brahma's lifetime, known as a Maha Kalpa (311.04T years), 504,000 Manus are present.

The entire universe is said to be destroyed at the end of each *Maha Kalpa*, after Brahma's life, and this event is known as a *Maha Pralaya*. The universe is re-created with the birth of the next Brahma, and the cycle repeats itself.

BRAHMA'S CLOCK AND THE EQUATION OF TIME

Brahma's Clock is a synonym for the *Age of the Universe*, as described earlier with the help of the Yuga cycles. The mathematical formula for the *Age of the Universe* is as follows:

TIME = [2 X KALPA] X 30 X 12 X 100 years   (Eq. 3. 1)

➢ = [2 X Adi Sandhi + 14 (Manvantaras + Sandhi Kala)] X 30 X 12 X 100

   = [2 X 1,728,000 + 14 (306,720,000 + 1,728,000)] X 30 X 12 x 100

   = 311,040,000,000,000 years = 311.04T years

Therefore, the total duration of the *Age of the Universe* is 311.04T years. We are currently at the halfway point in the life of our Universe.

LONG-TERM CYCLES OF GLOBAL FLOODING

From the description of the Manvantaras, it is clear that massive global floods recur predictably and cyclically. These flooding events deposit significantly more volumes of water than continuous rainfall events alone can contribute.

➢ The Earth is wholly flooded for 1.728 million years during the *Sandhi Kala* that follows the end of every Manvantara (306.72 million years)

- There are 14 Manvantaras in each Kalpa, and therefore, the Earth is wholly flooded fourteen times in each Kalpa

- Flooding during the *Adi Sandhi* (1.728M years) precedes the very first Manvantara

- The total cumulative period the Earth is flooded in each Kalpa (4.32B years) amounts to 25.92M years or 7.1 percent of the time.

The above periods of massive flooding are probably part of the Earth's hydrological cycle on geological time scales. The Manvantara-based flooding is cyclical and very predictable. The unique aspect of this flooding is that it is said to engulf the entire Earth in water.

There may be several potential sources for this massive influx of water:

- Heavy rainfall over several millennia

- Cyclical melting of polar Ice, global warming, etcetera.

- Delivered by ice-laden asteroids originating from the *Oort cloud* as the Sun traverses through its *galactic year*.

- Massive upwelling of water from deep below the Earth's surface. This subterranean water may have been deposited during earlier global flooding events.

The fact that massive flooding is said to occur at the end of every Manvantara (306.72M years) implies that the process may be self-contained within the Earth-atmosphere system. The massive quantities of water deposited at the end of the previous Manvantara must have eventually trickled deep into the Earth's inner layers. There may be some reverse mechanism by which this water finds its way back towards the surface. More research is warranted to explain some of these hypothetical scenarios.

CHARACTERISTICS OF THE FOUR YUGAS

In each cycle of Mahayuga, human civilization exhibits various characteristics such as height, longevity, intelligence, and values. Interestingly, these traits are genetically programmed to decrease with each successive Yuga by the ratio 4:3:2:1, and the reason for this phenomenon is not clear. This contradicts the theory of evolution, which suggests that humanity should evolve steadily over time without external stimuli. However, there are religious texts that describe instances where God or alien Gods intervened in the evolutionary process by providing periodic external stimuli to jump-start evolution. Examples can be found in the Book of Genesis and the Bible.

Satya Yuga or Krita Yuga (The Golden Age)

According to the *Purana*s, the *Satya* or *Krita Yuga* is the epitome of human evolution, followed by *Treta*, *Dvapara,* and *Kali* Yugas in any Mahayuga cycle.

Satya (Truth) or *Krita Yuga* is also known as the *Golden Age* of humanity and has a total duration of 1.728M years, the longest run amongst all four Yugas. The Golden Age is characterized by societies in which human values such as virtue and honesty are valued as paramount, with no place for sin. The Gods reserved it exclusively for their chosen ones.

The evolutionary ratio of 4:3:2:1 assures that Individuals in the *Satya or Krita* Yuga are endowed with supreme levels of intelligence while also enjoying the longest lifespans amongst anyone in all four Yugas. They could have been four times smarter than us in the Kali Yuga. It is possible that they accomplished significant advances in the sciences and technology, enabling them to develop advanced societies.

With its extended duration, access to large populations with long lifespans, and superior intelligence, the Satya Yuga could have made significant advances, especially in areas such as the development of science and technology. Likely our ancestors from this Yuga could have explored our solar system and nearby constellations. Such capabilities would have provided them with the means to escape from Earth before impending cataclysms such as asteroid strikes, massive floods, and other existential threats.

Visualize the technological advancements humankind had made in the post-industrial revolution era. We put Man on the Moon and are getting geared up for human exploration of our Solar system. Imagine the technological advances we could have achieved if we had access to a large pool of intellectuals and geniuses such as Einstein, von Braun, Ramanujan, and others when endowed with exceptionally long lifespans.

The Puranas tell us that the average lifespan of humans during the *Satya* Yuga was over 100,000 years, with death deferred to one's own discretion. Human beings of this Yuga are believed to be extremely tall in stature, reaching staggering heights of up to 21 *cubits*[5] or 9.6 meters (~31.5 feet) at the peak of this Yuga.

According to mainstream archeologists, modern Man evolved to be the smartest of all earlier human species. However, paradoxically, the *Puranas* state that human intelligence diminishes from a peak during each *Satya Yuga* and attains a minimum by the arrival of *Kali Yuga*. The gods or alien gods could have genetically programmed such a declining sequence into the human DNA.

In ancient Hindu mythology, there are four Yugas or eras—Satya Yuga, Treta Yuga, Dvapara Yuga, and Kali Yuga. According to the myth, the Gods or Alien Gods reserved the Satya Yuga exclusively for their chosen Divine stock and blessed them with superior intelligence and exceptionally long lifespans. They also built enough genetic safeguards to ensure that future generations in the three subsequent Yugas would be inferior to them in all aspects, including longevity, stature, intelligence, and social behavior.

Treta Yuga (The Silver Age)

The *Treta Yuga*, or the Silver Age, stretches over 1.296 million years. The leading and trailing cusps stretch for 108,000 years each. The cuspal periods between two successive Yugas can be categorized as those during which one can observe a mix of characteristics or traits from both Yugas.

The *Puranas* tell us about human virtue declining during the *Treta Yuga* to about seventy-five percent of the preceding *Satya Yuga* levels due to the moral decline of its populace. Human beings are also said

---

[5] Cubit (Def.): A *cubit* is an ancient forearm measure averaging to about 18 inches or 44 centimeters or eighteen inches in length.

to have a diminished stature with maximum heights of up to 14 cubits or 6. 4 meters (21 feet) and enjoyed average lifespans of about ten thousand years at the central peak of this Yuga.

According to the Matsya Purana, Lord Rama was born sometime towards the end of 24th Treta Yuga (~6,750 years + 18.149M = 18.156M years ago). Swami Prakasanand Saraswati (2007) suggests 18.144M years ago, that is 5,000 years into the 25th Dvapara Yuga. Some historians and theologians believe that the Rama empire existed during the current 28th Mahayuga cycle, based on the positions of planets in Rama's astrological birth chart corresponding to the zodiac on December 4th, contradicting the puranas.

One must be aware that identical combinations of stars and planets appearing in an astrological chart can recur cyclically over time due to the phenomenon known as the *precession of the equinoxes*. This rotational shift or wobble of the Earth's axis has a cyclical period of about 25,572 years, over which time the twelve astrological constellations appear to rotate around the Earth in the shadow of the rising sun during the vernal equinox (University of Michigan[6]).

Dvapara Yuga (The Bronze Age)

The Dvapara Yuga, also known as the Bronze Age, is said to last for approximately 864,000 years. During this era, human virtues are believed to have decreased even further compared to the previous Treta Yuga. It is said that about fifty percent of human behavior was virtuous, while the other fifty percent was sinful. The average lifespan of humans during the central peak of the Dvapara Yuga is said to be around a thousand years. Additionally, the average height of people living during this period is believed to have decreased to approximately seven cubits (10.5 feet or 3.2 meters).

The *Kurukshetra* battle in the epic *Mahabharata* happened around 3,102 BCE, towards the end of the most recent 28th *Dvapara Yuga*, about 5,000 years ago. This is approximately 18.156 million years after the birth of Rama during the 24th *Treta Yuga*. According to the *Bhavishya Purana*, a great flood is said to have occurred towards the end of the recent *Dvapara Yuga* following the Mahabharata battle. A sizable portion of Krishna's hometown of *Dwaraka* is said to have been submerged. Recent archeological searches appear to have identified parts of the submerged ancient city of *Dwarka*.

The *Dvapara Yuga* also witnessed the *Last Glacial Period* (LGP) or the Last Ice Age, which lasted from about 115,000 BCE to 11,700 BCE (Wikipedia). This also marked the end of the Pleistocene epoch, which began about 2.6 million years ago towards the tail-end of the 28th Satya Yuga. Global sea levels rose in response to warmer temperatures, melting sea ice, and retreating glaciers. The steadily rising sea's waters engulfed a substantial portion of Dwarka.

Kali Yuga (The Iron Age)

According to Hinduism, each Kali Yuga lasts for 432,000 years. Our current Kali Yuga is associated with the 28th Mahayuga and began on February 18, 3102 BCE, or about 5,126 years ago.

By the onset of the Kali Yuga, the average lifespan drops to about one hundred years, with humans attaining an average physical height of about 3.5 cubits or 1.6 meters (5.25 feet). Human traits such as

---

[6] University of Michigan: https://dept. astro.lsa.umich.edu/resources/ugactivities/Labs/precession/)

intelligence, physical stature, and longevity all declined from their peak during the *Satya Yuga* to a low in the *Kali Yuga* according to the prescribed evolutionary ratio of 4:3:2:1.

Social values, honesty, and morality during *Kali Yuga* are predicted to be the lowest amongst all four Yugas, with only about twenty-five percent of the population being virtuous and seventy-five percent living in sin. Any current television newscast or newspaper headline can vouch for this dismal decline in human values and morality worldwide.

It is a matter of concern that the current state of society seems to align with the prophecy of the Kali Yuga. There is a decline in moral and religious values, and incidents of corruption, wars, and terrorism are becoming increasingly common, affecting societies worldwide. The growing number of refugees fleeing from one country to another is consistent with the predictions made in the Markandeya Purana. It is said that God will rescue humanity in the form of the Kalki Avatar, which will be the final incarnation during the Kali Yuga. The Puranas have been remarkably accurate in predicting the arrival and purpose of each Avatar thus far.

RECENT ADVANCES IN CYCLICAL COSMOLOGY

We have seen how Hindu Cosmology describes the current age of our universe in terms of Brahma's age. Brahma has completed the first *Parardha* (the first 50 years of his life) and has only recently entered the second Parardha (phase). In short, we are currently halfway in the universe's life.

The 2020 Nobel Prize in Physics was awarded jointly to the British Mathematician and Physicist Sir Roger Penrose and his colleagues Reinhard Genzel and Andrea Ghez from Oxford. Sir Roger Stone received half of the Nobel Prize for his work on the formation of black holes and the other half jointly with his colleagues for discovering a supermassive compact object at the center of our galaxy (The Nobel Prize in Physics 2020).

The eminent British mathematical physicist Sir Penrose (2006 and 2012) introduced the concept of *Conformal Cyclic Cosmology (CCC)*, by which the universe undergoes cycles of cosmic extinction and rebirth. The remote future of one phase of the universe leads into the Big Bang of the next phase, and so on (Cartlidge: Physics World 2020). Penrose terms the period between successive and cyclical *Big Bangs* as an *Aeon* (Wikipedia). The Independently developed Penrose's *CCC* concept is a vindication of the life cycle of our universe, as stated in the Puranas. He further reaffirmed that our universe is indeed in its seventh cycle. Sir Penrose was awarded the Nobel Prize in 2020 for his finding that the formation of black holes is a robust prediction of Einstein's general theory of relativity (The Nobel Prize in Physics 2020).

Modern-day astronomical estimates of the universe's age differ significantly from the 311.04 trillion-year estimate of the *Puranas*. NASA's estimate, based on its WMAP satellite, is about 13.79 billion years. The European Space Agency's (ESA's) estimate of 13.82 billion years is based on its *Planck* spacecraft measurements of cosmic background-thermal radiation associated with the most recent Big Bang. This, in turn, provides an estimate of the rate of expansion of our universe known as the *Hubble constant*. Astronomers can determine the universe's age by working backward from this constant. Therefore, the scientifically accepted age of the universe is around 13.8 billion years.

Another technique adapted by Italian scientists to estimate the age of our universe involves the measurement of the half-life of radioactive isotopes present in elements. A group of scientists at the *INFN*

Gran Sasso National Laboratory in Italy directly observed two-neutrino double electron capture in ^{124}Xe with the help of the XENON1T dark-matter detector, the half-life of which is a trillion times the currently accepted age of our universe (XENON, 2019). Consequently, the full-life period of the isotopes is more than two trillion years.

Depending on which methodology is chosen, there appears to be considerable variance in estimating the age of our universe.

MULTIVERSES, PARALLEL UNIVERSES AND MORE

Lately, everyone has learned terms like Multiverses, parallel Universes, exoplanets, and others. The Multiverse theory argues that several other universes may exist parallel to one another in addition to our own. These universes with distinct characteristics are known as *parallel universes*.

Advances in space-borne telescopes, such as NASA's Hubble, Spitzer, Webb, and others, provide spectacular images of our universe. Scientists are beginning to discover other Earth-like planets known as Exoplanets. We will soon find a clone of the Earth somewhere within our galaxy or beyond. However, what if a similar Solar system with its planets and exoplanets already exists in another parallel universe?

The world-renowned astrophysicist Stephen Hawking suggested that *black holes* and *wormholes* could serve as conduits for reaching out to other parallel universes. Some Sci-Fi movies have already explored themes involving travel through black holes for intergalactic travel.

THE MATSYA PURANA AND RESURGENCE OF LIFE ON EARTH

A long time ago, there was a king named Vaivaswata Manu. After abdicating his throne to his son, Manu retired to the foothills of Mount Malaya and performed penance in the name of Lord Brahma for thousands of years. Pleased with his penance, Lord Brahma appears and grants Manu a boon of his choice. Manu was curious to know the onset time for the next *Pralaya* that would end all forms of life on Earth. As for his boon, Manu requests Lord Brahma that he be the one who saves the world following one of the Pralayas. Lord Brahma grants him his wish and disappears.

The *Matsya Purana* is attributed to Lord Vishnu and dates to a time in Earth's early history when an epic flood completely engulfed all land masses following massive rains. Lord Vishnu takes on the form of a Matsya (fish) to save the world. The *Matsya Avatara* is one of the Dasa (ten) Avatars of Vishnu. Interestingly, seven types of destructive Cush (rain) clouds are identified by unfamiliar names, such as Samvarta, Bhimananda, Drona, Chanda, Valahaka, Vidyutapataka, and Kona, capable of unleashing floods of epic proportions. In modern weather forecasting, heavy flooding is frequently associated with *supercells* and *atmospheric rivers* of moisture.

It narrates how one day, while Vaivaswata Manu, the seventh and current Manu, was performing his prayers in a nearby pond with both arms cupped with water, he noticed a small fish swimming around. He immediately placed it in his sacred water vessel known as a *Kamandalam*. Soon, the small fish outgrew the Kamandalam, so he transferred it to a large container, but the fish outgrew it, too. The bewildered Manu then dropped it into a well, then to a nearby pond, and finally into the holy river Ganga. However, the fish soon outgrew even the mighty Ganga River. Baffled by the sequence of events, Manu manages to transfer the fish into the ocean, but to his dismay, it soon begins occupying a significant portion. Manu soon realizes that Lord Vishnu Himself may be behind all these illusions. So, he then asks the fish to reveal its identity. Lord Vishnu appears and reminds Manu of the boon once granted to him by Lord Brahma.

Lord Vishnu informs him that the Earth will soon be flooded with water and instructs *Vaivaswata Manu* (the seventh and current Manu) to gather all living beings into a boat to be constructed according to His specifications. Manu obliges and loads a large ship with living beings and ties it to Lord Vishnu, who appears as a gigantic fish to save the world. Soon after the flood waters receded, *Vaivaswata Manu* populated the world with the living beings he had nurtured in a boat. This pins the flood to the *Sandhi Kala* preceding the 7th Manvantara of the current *Sveta Varaha Kalpa*.

What is utterly amazing is that the above massive flooding incident, in which God instructs Vaivaswata Manu to construct a boat per His specifications and save living beings, is strikingly like Noah's Ark, elucidated in *The Book of Genesis*. Incidences of extremely massive flooding are common when one considers geological timescales. As discussed earlier, the Yuga cycles tell us that the Earth is completely engulfed in water at the end of every Manvantara during the Sandhi Kala period.

MASS AND MINI EXTINCTIONS ON EARTH

According to Hindu cosmology, at the end of every Manvantara period, which lasted for 306.72 million years, a transitional period called Sandhi Kala followed, lasting for 1.728 million solar years. During this time, the entire Earth is believed to be submerged under water and devoid of any life form. With the arrival of the next Manvantara, life resurges and continues until the following Sandhi Kala. This cycle repeats itself for the duration of the universe's lifespan.

In addition to such cyclical extinctions after each *Manvantara*, other mass or mini extinctions on Earth can also be triggered by several extraneous factors. The Sun and billions of other stars revolve around the center of our Milky Way Galaxy. The Sun takes about 225 million years to traverse around the center of the Milky Way galaxy. This orbital period of the Sun is known as the *Galactic Year*. During its long journey, it traverses several spiral bands within the galaxy containing millions of stars. Scientists believe these stars cause random or cyclical perturbations that are transferred to the *Oort cloud* (Filipovic et al., 2013) and then eventually to the Kuiper belt, triggering an increase in the frequency of asteroid strikes on Earth.

The Oort cloud is a massive reservoir of billions of icy particles, asteroids, and comets with long orbital periods. Its sphere of influence stretches beyond the Kuiper belt and outer limits of the Solar system to distances over 50,000 AU. It can be quickly excited by external gravitational forces and perturbations transferred by other stars and nebulae in the spiral bands of our Milky Way galaxy. The Kuiper belt is situated beyond planet Neptune and contains many short-term comets, asteroids, and large icy particles. Any extraneous perturbations can set off some of the larger asteroids or comets into motion toward the Earth and other planets within our Solar system. Some of these asteroids can cause massive damage to Earth, resulting in mini or mass extinctions.

The *Permian-Triassic Extinction*, also known as the *Great Permian Extinction,* occurred about 252 million years ago and is believed to be one of Earth's worst-known mass extinctions. It impacted over 95 percent of all marine and 70 percent of terrestrial species (Hickey, 2018).

A more recent mass extinction known as the *Cretaceous-Paleogene* extinction occurred about sixty-six million years ago and is believed to have been triggered by a massive asteroid impact. Numerous species, including the dinosaurs, are believed to have perished during this cataclysmic event.

According to another cyclical extinction hypothesis, variations in the Sun's cosmic-ray (CR) flux have a 64-million-year period as it traverses across the Milky Way. The CR flux is believed to increase significantly due to motion across the Virgo Cluster (Medvedev & Melott, 2007). Significant increases in the CR flux can adversely impact, if not wipe out entirely, all biological life on Earth as the Sun traverses its *galactic year*. Unfortunately, cosmic rays can penetrate everything along the way, making it impossible for anyone to escape their wrath.

More recently, Rice (2020) brought my attention to a scientific study by Rampino et al. (2020) in which the authors investigated the nature and temporal frequency of several extinction episodes of non-marine tetrapods over the past three hundred million years. They observed a peak in periodicity of about thirty million years between passes of the solar system as the Sun traverses through its *Galactic Year*.

Many of the mass extinctions on Earth appear to be associated with the Sun's movement along its *Galactic Year*. Apparently, perturbations associated with the Sun's galactic travel are subsequently transferred to the Kuiper belt, which harbors numerous large asteroids; in turn, these are set into motion toward the planets in the solar system.

* * * * *

Chapter 4: The Great Biblical Flood

The American Standard Version (ASV) of *Genesis 7*[7] Describes *The Great Flood and the Story of Noah's Ark*.

God finds that Noah and his immediate descendants were the only ones leading righteous lives as He prescribed. He finds the rest of humanity to be corrupt and filled with violence. So, God decided to dissolve the rest of humanity and all the animals, reptiles, insects, and plants He had created.

During the *Great Flood* about 4,350-4,500 years ago, Jehova instructed Noah to build the Ark from the sky above. God is traditionally depicted as interacting with humanity from the sky above.

He then commands Noah to build an ark out of cypress wood and seal it inside out with pitch (a natural polymer). The ark itself is said to be three hundred cubits (450 feet) in length, fifty cubits (75 feet) across, and thirty cubits (45 feet) in height. It has two upper decks and a lower one (Fig. 4.1).

He then commands Noah to pick seven pairs of each species (beasts, cattle, birds, and creepers) from His stock and two pairs from Noah's along with his family members for the long voyage to tide over the upcoming flood said to arrive in seven days.

And then it rains continuously for forty days and forty nights, destroying everything living. Flood waters rose to a height of fifteen cubits (about 22.5 feet) and did not recede for one hundred and fifty days. Everyone in the Ark survives the flood. Noah is said to be six hundred years of age at the time of the Great Flood.

Genesis (Chapter 7) is simple to follow, and yet powerful in its message, and is presented here in its entirety:

"[7.1] And Jehovah said unto Noah, Come thou and all thy house into the ark; for thee have I seen righteous before me in this generation.

[7.2] Of every clean beast thou shalt take to thee seven and seven, the male and his female; and of the beasts that are not clean two, the male and his female:

[7.3] of the birds also of the heavens, seven and seven, male and female, to keep seed alive upon the face of all the earth.

[7.4] For yet seven days, and I will cause it to rain upon the earth forty days and forty nights; and every living thing that I have made will I [a]destroy from off the face of the ground.

[7.5] And Noah did according unto all that Jehovah commanded him.

[7.6] And Noah was six hundred years old when the flood of waters was upon the earth.

[7.7] And Noah went in, and his sons, and his wife, and his sons' wives with him, into the ark, because of the waters of the flood.

---

[7] American Standard Version (ASV) Genesis 7.1-7.24, 8.4-8.5, 8.13-8.19 and 9.28-9.29.

7.8 Of clean beasts, and of beasts that are not clean, and of birds, and of everything that creepeth upon the ground,

7.9 there went in two and two unto Noah into the ark, male and female, as God commanded Noah.

7.10 And it came to pass after the seven days, that the waters of the flood were upon the earth.

7.11 In the six hundredth year of Noah's life, in the second month, on the seventeenth day of the month, on the same day, all the fountains of the great deep were broken up, and the windows of heaven were opened.

7.12 And the rain was upon the earth forty days and forty nights.

7.13 In the selfsame day entered Noah, and Shem, and Ham, and Japheth, the sons of Noah, and Noah's wife, and the three wives of his sons with them, into the ark;

7.14 they, and every beast after its kind, and all the cattle after their kind, and every creeping thing that creepeth upon the earth after its kind, and every bird after its kind, every bird of every [b]sort.

7.15 And they went in unto Noah into the ark, two and two of all flesh wherein is the breath of life.

7.16 And they that went in, went in male and female of all flesh, as God commanded him: and Jehovah shut him in.

7.17 And the flood was forty days upon the earth; and the waters increased, and bare up the ark, and it was lifted up above the earth.

7.18 And the waters prevailed, and increased greatly upon the earth; and the ark went upon the face of the waters.

7.19 And the waters prevailed exceedingly upon the earth; and all the high mountains that were under the whole heaven were covered.

7.20 Fifteen cubits upward did the waters prevail; and the mountains were covered.

7.21 And all flesh died that moved upon the earth, both birds, and cattle, and beasts, and every creeping thing that creepeth upon the earth, and every man:

7.22 all in whose nostrils was the breath of the spirit of life, of all that was on the dry land, died.

7.23 [d]And every living thing was [e]destroyed that was upon the face of the ground, both man, and cattle, and creeping things, and birds of the heavens; and they were destroyed from the earth: and Noah only was left, and they that were with him in the ark.

7.24 And the waters prevailed upon the earth a hundred and fifty days."

8.4 And the ark rested in the seventh month, on the seventeenth day of the month, upon the mountains of Ararat.

8.5 And the waters decreased continually until the tenth month: in the tenth month, on the first day of the month, were the tops of the mountains seen.

[8.13] And it came to pass in the six hundred and first year, in the first month, the first day of the month, the waters were dried up from off the earth: and Noah removed the covering of the ark, and looked, and, behold, the face of the ground was dried.

[8.14] And in the second month, on the seven and twentieth day of the month, was the earth dry.

[8.15] And God spake unto Noah, saying,

[8.16] Go forth from the ark, thou, and thy wife, and thy sons, and thy sons' wives with thee.

[8.19] every beast, every creeping thing, and every bird, whatsoever moveth upon the earth, after their families, went forth out of the ark

[9.28] And Noah lived after the flood three hundred and fifty years

[9.29] And all the days of Noah were nine hundred and fifty years: and he died.

Humanity is set in its ways and tends to take things for granted until it is too late. Maybe it is time to amend our ways and not give God another opportunity to push the 'Reset' button again on us.

REVISITING FOUNTAINS OF THE GREAT DEEP (GENESIS 7.11)

It is interesting to note that Genesis 7.11 alludes to two sources of water contributing to the massive flood. One from the windows of heaven (sky) opening above, and the other from water gushing out of fountains (springs or wells) of the great deep:

"In the six hundredth year of Noah's life, in the second month, on the seventeenth day of the month, on the same day were *all the fountains of the great deep broken up*, and the windows of heaven were opened."

Rolf Bouma provides an interesting scientific commentary on Genesis 7.11[8] in which he states that the concept of the flood being the result of both excessive rain and waters gushing from below the Earth is consistent with the Old Testament's three-tiered universe: a dome containing the heavenly waters, a flat Earth with surface waters, and water under the Earth's surface.

In addition to the classical Earth's water cycle involving the atmosphere, oceans, and surface waters, Schmandt et al. (2014) have shown that it can also extend deep into the Earth's interior mantle transition zone some 410-660 km below the surface that acts as a large reservoir of water. It is believed that this transition zone may hold up to three times the water held by all of the Earth's oceans put together.

The implications are that the Earth's interior mantle acts as a sponge to absorb large quantities of surface water, possibly following periods of massive surface flooding as predicted during the Manvantara cycles (ref. Chpt. 3). Conversely, there may be some as yet unknown mechanism by which this massive reservoir of trapped water from below the mantle may gush to the surface, and contribute to massive flooding in addition to the heavy normal rainfall amounts from the sky.

---

[8] Rolf Bouma: A Scientific Commentary on Genesis 7.11: https://biologos.org/articles/a-scientific-commentary-on-genesis-711

GENEALOGY OF ADAM & EVE AND THEIR DESCENDANTS

A characteristic feature of the Yuga cycle is that people had long life spans during the Dvapara Yuga. This can also be observed in the documented life spans of biblical characters.

The genealogy of Adam and Eve's descendants from Seth to Noah, along with their lifespans, is shown in Table 4.1. Interestingly, *Genesis* (5:1 to 5:32) provides the father's age at the birth of the principal child and the father's full lifespan. Noah was six hundred years old at the time of the Great Flood (Genesis: 7:6) and lived for nine hundred and fifty years (Genesis: 9:29). People had long lifespans of almost a thousand years. These lifespans are strikingly like those during a *Dvapara Yuga*. My curiosity took me deeper into the *Puranas* to ascertain whether there were any references to Adam and Eve, Noah, and the Great Flood. After considerable research into several Puranas, I was amply rewarded. The *Bhavishya Purana* (Purana of the Future) refers to Adam and Eve as *Adama* and *Havyavati* (Table 4.1).

Table 4.1 Lifespans of Biblical Characters Cited in *Genesis* (ASV) and in *Bhavishya Purana*

BIBLICAL NAME	LIFESPAN IN YEARS (BIBLICAL)	PURANIC NAME	LIFESPAN IN YEARS (VEDIC)
ADAM /EVE	930	ADAMA/HAVYAVATI	930
Seth	912	Sveta-Nama	912
Enosh	905	Anuta	815
Keenan	910	Kianasa	840
Mahalalel	895	Malahalla	895
Jared	962	Virada	160
Enoch	365	Hamuka	365
Methuselah	969	Matocchila	970
Lamech	777	Lomaka	777
Noah	950	Nyuha	950
		Sima	
Shem		Hama, Kusa, Misra, Kuja, Kanaam	
Ham			
Japeth		Yakuta	
		Kusa: Havila, Sarva, Toragama, Savatika, Nimaruhal, Mahavala	

Table 4.1 includes the corresponding Vedic names and lifespans for comparison. There is considerable agreement between both religious sources, with some minor exceptions. Based on the lifespan and physical attributes of individuals from Adam and Eve to Noah and his sons, it is reasonable to assume that they may have lived during a *Dvapara Yuga*.

Chapter 4: The Great Biblical Flood

Soon after the Great Flood, people began to multiply and had daughters, and the sons of God fancied and married them. The Lord is terribly upset with this unexpected turn of events and downgrades the human lifespan from one thousand years to one hundred and twenty years. Note a similar drop in life expectancy from the *Dvapara* to the *Kali* Yuga. The average height of humans also dropped from a peak of about eight feet during each *Dvapara Yuga* to about six feet by every Kali Yuga.

Figure 4. 1 Artist's rendering of Noah's Ark (Credit: "A_A88" - stock.adobe.com)

At the end of 40 days, Noah opens the window and sends out a raven, but it flies back and forth and returns. He then sends a dove to see if the waters have subsided, but it, too, returns. He sends it again after a week, and it returns in the evening with a freshly plucked olive leaf. He waits another seven days and sends it out again, but it does not return this time.

It is remarkable that the *God Number 7* keeps recurring in everything associated with *God's* creation.

The appearance of an Ark-like feature observed in modern high-resolution satellite imagery over Mt. Ararat in Türkiye is commonly referred to as the *Ararat Anomaly*.

GREAT FLOOD IN THE EPIC OF GILGAMESH

The *Epic of Gilgamesh* is an anthology of poems about King Gilgamesh of Urk from about 2,100 BCE. The information is deciphered from a series of clay tablets gathered over an extended period. Some gaps in the lines still exist, slowly getting filled with each new find. Figure 4.2 shows an example of a 3,500-year-old Gilgamesh clay tablet.

The Legend of Gilgamesh as Narrated by Uta-Napishtim

Sir Ernest Alfred Wallis Budge (1857-1934) was an eminent British Egyptologist, philologist, and Orientalist who worked for the British Museum as curator of Egyptian and Assyrian antiquities. He authored numerous studies, one of which focuses on *"The Babylonian Story of the Deluge and the Epic of Gilgamesh"* (Budge, 1920). A brief narrative of his version is presented below.

Gilgamesh was besieged by fear of mortality following the death of his beloved friend and companion, Enkidu. He knew that his ancestor, Uta-Napishtim, had attained immortality, so he set out to find his secret to immortality. Guided by a dream, he set out to where Uta-Napishtim once lived. The immortal came down and narrated the story of the deluge to Gilgamesh.

The city of Shuruppak, situated on the banks of the Euphrates River, is an ancient city, and the gods living within it convince the great gods to stir up a *windstorm* and bring it down. Anu, the father God, Enlil the Warrior Lord, En-urta the messenger, Prince Ennugi, Nin-igi-azag, and Ea were all in council, during which Enlil presented his plan to unleash a powerful cyclonic rainstorm. Following the council meeting, Ea rushes over to his friend Uta-Napishtim and warns him of the impending rainstorm. He then commands him to build a boat and set sail.

On the fifth day, he plans to build a boat according to Ea's specifications. From the description, it appears to be cubic in shape, with each side measuring 120 cubits (180 feet). The walls were sealed with pitch (natural polymer) and bitumen to prevent leaks. Once the boat is finished, Uta-Napishtim loads it up with all his belongings, jewelry, grain, cattle, family, kin, and the ship craftsmen who helped build it.

Finally, the cyclone landed ashore with such violent fury that even the gods were terrified. Water from the deluge reached the mountains. It rained for six days and nights, and on the seventh day, both the cyclone and the rainstorm dissipated.

On the seventh day, he lets out a dove, and it comes back, the same with a swallow and, lastly, a raven; she never comes back. The ship finally comes to rest on a mountain known as Nisir. Eventually, God Ea bestows Uta-Napishtim and his wife immortality by joining them into the ranks of the gods.

Chapter 4: The Great Biblical Flood

Figure 4.2 A 650 BCE Assyrian Flood tablet of the Epic of Gilgamesh
(Credit: "Imaginechina"/Alamy Stock Photo)

The Matsya Purana describes a similar flooding event during the recent Dvapara Yuga. This Yuga period was characterized by people of about eight feet in stature and life expectations of around one thousand years.

GIANTS OR NEPHILIM

Several religious texts, including the Ramayana, Mahabharata, The Book of Genesis, the Bible, The Book of Numbers, and Torah, mention the existence of giants or Nephilim. They are often believed to have tormented and terrorized their smaller cousins.

In the *Ramayana*, for example, young Rama's first order of business was to destroy thousands of giants that were tormenting local people and causing a ruckus during religious Yagyas performed by the sages.

Moses is also known to have had difficulty convincing his followers to settle in the new lands frequented by Nephilim.

Mystic Moon: A Lunar Odyssey

Ancient skeletons of giants continue to appear worldwide during building excavations or accidental archeological findings. Many of these are discredited or debunked. A Stonehenge-like structure known as *Rujm El-Hiri* (The Wheel of Giants) was discovered by Israeli archeologists in the Golan Heights after the 1967 war (Fig. 4.3). The massive stone structure with five concentric circles is believed to be an astronomical observational site located in the vicinity of the Biblical site where the gigantic OG, the king of Bashan, was slain along with his sons by Moses during the battle of Edrei. His giant bed is described to be made of iron, measuring more than nine cubits (13.5ft) in length and four cubits (6ft) in width (Deuteronomy 3:1-13)[9].

**Figure 4.3 Aerial view of Rujm El-Hiri in Golan Heights
(Credit: "Duby Tal/Albatros"/Alamy Stock Photo)**

---

[9] American Standard Version of the Bible, 1901: Deuteronomy 3:1-13 https//www.biblegateway.com

Chapter 4: The Great Biblical Flood

As mentioned earlier, human beings typically attained heights of eight to ten feet during various stages of *Dvapara Yuga*. The *Book of Genesis* also mentions similar heights attained by Noah and his descendants.

Human beings from the *Satya Yuga* period are believed to have attained gigantic heights of about thirty-two feet. Their heights dropped during the successive Treta Yuga. It is possible that skilled giants from the distant past may have engineered some of the megalithic stone structures on Earth. Alternatively, human civilizations from the past are credited with transporting huge megalithic stones from distant quarries by boat or some other ingenious way.

The *terraces of Ollantaytambo* in Cusco, Peru (Fig. 4.4) are believed to be farm terraces dating back to the Inca period (1400-1533 CE). One cannot help but wonder about the real necessity for such massive stone terraces to meet the farming requirements of the Inca people. The construction of such colossal structures requires considerable engineering skills to shape, move, and place huge boulders, sometimes weighing over 70-100 tons and with great precision. Magnificent examples can be found in Sacsayhuaman, the Inca stronghold of Cusco. Is it possible that these megalithic structures were already in place when they arrived, enabling them to adapt to terraced farming quickly?

Figure 4.4 Stone Terraces in Inca Ruins of Ollantaytambo, Sacred Valley, in the Peruvian Andes (Credit: " Андрей Поторочин "-stock.adobe.com)

No other civilization of that period comes close to matching their advanced technological skills. Is it possible that they may have encountered these massive stone structures and adapted them to meet their needs, or did they actually build them?

Recently, paleontologists unearthed fossils of the world's largest prehistoric parrot (*Heracles Inexpectatus*) in St. Bathans in New Zealand's southern Otago region (Worthy et al., 2019). The sizeable flightless parrot measuring a meter (3. 2ft) in height and weighing about seven kilograms (15.43 pounds) is believed to belong to the early *Miocene* period (23 to 16 million years ago). St. Bathans is well known for its rich trove of bird fossils from the same period.

The legendary Jatayu mentioned in the Ramayana was also a giant bird (Worthy et al., 2019) belonging to the Treta Yuga of about 18.156 Million years ago, coinciding with the *Miocene* period. Jatayu tries to stop Ravana from kidnapping Sita, but he is seriously injured, yet somehow manages to inform Rama about the kidnapping.

The presence of giants described in religious books across several religions is also supported by the human traits associated with both Satya and Treta yugas. This suggests that giants roamed freely in many parts of the Earth in the distant past. It is highly probable that they may have been involved in the construction of megalithic stone structures observed in many parts of the world.

* * * * * *

Chapter 5: Soaring Into the Sky

The eternal human desire to soar into the sky like birds remained unfulfilled until the invention of the Wright Brothers' biplane. Nowadays, most people can afford the experience of flying worldwide or even locally in the comfort of pressurized aircraft cruising at about 35,000 ft, where the outside temperature can drop to a chilling -54°C (-65°F).

The journey of hot air balloons began in 1783 when Joseph and Stephen Montgolfier invented the first one in France. Fast-forward to 1961, and we see the birth of the modern-day hot air balloon, complete with a nylon fabric cover and a controlled propane burner, thanks to the innovation of Ed Yost at Raven Industries.

In 1960, U.S. Air Force Captain Joe Kittinger achieved a significant milestone in high-altitude human flight. He became the first person to reach a height of about nineteen miles above the Earth's surface in a massive helium-filled balloon. This feat was part of NASA's Excelsior Project, a crucial initiative designed to evaluate the airworthiness of parachutes for future astronauts during re-entry (Dave Kindy, 2023).

An impressive milestone was achieved in 1987 when Sir Richard Branson and Per Lindstrand became the first to cross the Atlantic in a hot air balloon, traveling about 3,075 miles in their *Virgin Atlantic Flyer*.

Later, in 2012, Felix Baumgartner became the first person to dive from a helium balloon at a stratospheric height of about twenty-four miles and landed safely on Earth as part of the *Red Bull Stratos Project*[10].

More recently, private entrepreneurs such as *Blue Origin's* Jeff Bezos[11] (blueorigin.com) and *Virgin Galactic's* Sir Richard Branson[12] (virgingalactic.com) are credited with commercializing space tourism for civilians. Elon Musk's SpaceX successfully launched and returned four private astronauts after spending three days in orbit as part of the *Inspiration4* mission. Eventually, such technology will become more affordable to everyone.

Nowadays, anyone with internet access to social media websites may be familiar with many blogs and short clips on sightings of *Unidentified Flying objects* (UFOs), preferably known as *Unidentified Anomalous Phenomena* (UAPs). Modern-day cell phones with megapixel capabilities enable one to record events in split seconds. Consequently, sightings of UFOs or UAPs have significantly increased worldwide. The increased sightings may be attributed to improved monitoring techniques as well as the efforts of popular social media platforms to inform people. These UAPs may have also visited Earth in ancient times. However, back then, the ancient world was much less populated and lacked the means to document these events. UAPs, both large and small, could land anywhere without much fanfare. However, rapid

---

[10] Red Bull Stratos Project; Felix Baumgartner's Space Jump: https://www.redbull.com/us-en/stratos-space-jump-key-facts-numbers
[11] https://www.blueorigin.com/
[12] https://www.virgingalactic.com/

industrialization and population growth worldwide may have prevented these UAPs from landing freely on Earth.

VIMANAS AND TEMPLE ARCHITECTURE

Many religious texts mention the presence of spaceships seen by someone or used by the Gods to descend to Earth for their missions. In Hinduism, it is believed that several avatars of Gods traveled to Earth using Vimanas or spacecraft from the distant Saptarishi Mandala (Great Bear) constellation. The spires of many temples in India mimic the shape of the Vimana supposedly used by the temple deity.

Figure 5.1 The 13-storied Vimana Shaped Spire of Brihadisvara Temple with its 80-ton stone Gopuram (Dome) in Thanjavur, TN, India. (Credit: "dbtravel"/Alamy Stock Photo)

The Brihadishwara temple in Thanjavur, Tamil Nadu, India (Fig. 5.1), dedicated to Lord Shiva, was built during the Chola dynasty by Emperor Rajaraja Chola I in the early 11th century A.D. It has a 13-storied Vimana-shaped spire on top of which sits a single-piece 80-ton Gopuram (dome). The other unique engineering marvel is that the temple never casts its own shadow on the ground; the shadow falls on itself through the tiered conical spire. Legend has it that the 80-ton dome is required to absorb the energy generated by the 12-foot Shiva Lingam in the main altar.

The Samarangana Sutradhara, a Sanskrit treatise of Vāstu-Shastra, is a treasure trove of ancient knowledge. It covers a wide range of topics, such as temple architecture, iconography, creation theory, etc. However, what truly stands out is its detailed description of mechanical contrivances and yantras in

Chapter 5: Soaring Into the Sky

chapter 31 (Roy, 1984). The construction of bird-shaped cars and robots that serve as guards, presented in verses 95-107, highlights the intricate understanding of engineering principles in ancient times, leaving us in awe of their knowledge.

Some temples also have golden domes indicative of the type of Vimana the deity uses when visiting Earth. One of the famous temples adorned by such a golden Vimana dome (Fig. 5.2) belongs to Sri Venkateswara Temple in Tirumala, Andhra Pradesh, India.

Figure 5.2 The Majestic Golden Vimana-shaped dome of *Sri Venkateswara* Temple, Tirumala, AP, India (Credit: "Exotica.im 4" / Alamy Stock Photo)

According to the Matsya Purana (Basu, 1916), the seventh manifestation of Vishnu was in the form of Sri Rama during the 24th Treta Yuga, with the specific purpose of killing Ravana. It is astonishing that the Puranas identify all ten Avatars of Vishnu by the corresponding Mahayuga cycle and the individual Yuga within that cycle. They also identify the purpose for which each Avatar shall be born long before the event occurs. Each Mahayuga cycle, as mentioned earlier (Table 3.1), lasts for about 4.32 million years. Therefore, the timing of the Rama Avatar is about 18.156 million years ago (assuming about 6,750 years before the end of the 24th Treta Yuga).

In ancient Hindu astrology, the time of an individual's birth is recorded in terms of the birth star, positions of five planets (Mercury, Venus, Mars, Jupiter, Saturn), the Sun, and the Moon, and another non-planet pair known as Rahu and Ketu. Fortunately, Sage Valmiki correctly mentions the astrological details of Sri Rama's birth star (Punarvasu) and planets at the time of His birth but not the Mahayuga in which the birth took place.

So, some early twentieth-century religious pundits and Sanskrit scholars may have assumed that Valmiki could have been referring to the most recent zodiacal position of the birth-star Punarvasu and planets associated with Sri Rama's astrological chart, all of which may have last appeared about 7,000 years ago.

In addition to the Earth spinning on its own axis over twenty-four hours, the axis wobbles around a circular path like a spinning top but in the opposite direction. This is referred to as the Earth's *cyclic-axial-precession* (axial wobble) and is known to have a period of about 25,771.5 years (NASA, 2020[13]).

Some people have introduced shorter cycles based on the Earth's cyclic-axial precession. These shorter cycles have the same names and ratios as the larger cycles, and they introduce the concept of up-and-down cycles as they repeat.

In other words, the positions of the stars and planets in Rama's astrological chart repeat every 25,771.5 years during the 18.144-million-year period. Therefore, Sri Rama's birth chart configuration would have appeared hundreds of times during this extended period. By accepting its recurrence about 7,000 years ago in the 28th Dvapara yuga, we may be questioning the Puranas by almost 18.156 million years.

The currently accepted date for the Ramayana is about 7,000 years ago, in the 28th Dvapara yuga and not the 24th Treta yuga as mentioned in the Puranas. This may have gone unnoticed because the timing of the epic Mahabharata (~5,000 years ago) aligns with the revised date of the Ramayana (~7,000 years ago). Mainstream historians may have welcomed this switch, as it would not challenge conventional human evolutionary concepts. Swami Prakasanand Saraswati (2007) questions their real motives.

In ancient times, it was believed that certain kings and rulers possessed ancient Vimanas, which were said to have been gifted to them by the Gods. There were fierce battles fought to gain control of these Vimanas from weaker monarchs. Legend has it that the evil king Ravana defeated his half-brother, the ruler of Lanka (Sri Lanka) Kubera, in battle and usurped the famed mantra-activated (voice-activated) Pushpaka Vimana. Kubera, known as the Lord of Wealth, is the banker to the Gods and the guardian of the cardinal direction of 'North.' After his defeat, Kubera fled to seclusion in the Himalayas. Legend has it that the fair-complexioned Kubera was Lord Brahma's grandson.

PUSHPAKA VIMANA OF RAMAYANA

---

[13] NASA 2020: Why Milankovitch (Orbital) Cycles Can't Explain Earth's Current Warming.
https://science.nasa.gov/earth/climate-change/why-milankovitch-orbital-cycles-cant-explain-earths-current-warming/

Chapter 5: Soaring Into the Sky

After defeating Ravana, Rama and his entourage reportedly returned to Ayodhya in the same Pushpaka Vimana. Their journey back is well documented in the Ramayana. The Vimana was later returned to its owner, Kubera, after dropping Lord Rama and his entourage in Ayodhya. An abstract image of the Pushpaka Vimana is illustrated in Figure 5.3. The original Vimana is described as being elaborately decorated with numerous gems and ornaments.

Figure 5.3 An Abstract image of a Mantric Vimana (Credit: "Adriano"- stock.adobe.com)

The amazing Pushpak was said to be a 'plus-1' seater as it could always accommodate an extra passenger by changing its size. Another interesting design aspect was that it could accommodate large and tall giants native to Lanka during the time of Ravana. Such technologically advanced and sophisticated Vimanas were exceedingly rare, as only a few privileged individuals had access to them in ancient times.

The potential implication is that large, sophisticated spacecraft of alien origin were not only present on Earth about 18.156 million years ago, but some were gifted to staunch devotees, kings, and other powerful individuals. Some of these Vimanas may have inadvertently ended up in wrong hands, causing considerable agony. Both large and small Vimanas continued to exchange hands throughout ancient times.

THE LEGEND OF KING SALWA IN THE MAHABHARATA

As the Kurukshetra battle in the Mahabharata drew close, an unexpected turn of events unfolded. King Salwa, the lord of Saubha, attacked the city of Dwaraka, the capital of Lord Krishna's kingdom, while Krishna was away. This audacious move was made possible by Salwa's possession of a colossal Vimana, a flying chariot named Saubha. The Vimana, a symbol of Salwa's power, was acquired through his intense penance to Lord Shiva.

Interestingly, the gigantic Saubha Vimana is often called the *car of costly metals* because of the expensive composition of metals that went into constructing its shell. Legend has it that residents of Dwarka sometimes saw it afloat in the ocean as well. Salwa's men are believed to have showered torrents of rocks from the sky during a fierce battle with Vasudeva of Dwarka; he finally manages to dig himself out and successfully conquer the Danavas using Indra's thunderbolt.

Upon His return to Dwarka, Krishna is met with a scene of devastation. Determined to avenge the attack, He engages Salwa in a fierce battle in the sky. With His mighty Sudarshana Chakra, a fast-spinning sharp wheel capable of causing significant damage, Krishna brings down the Saubha Vimana. He then commands the Chakra to seek out and destroy Salwa, marking the end of one of the last battles of the Mahabharata war.

The Mahabharata refers to a Vimana involved in a fierce battle from the sky, firing powerful weapons at Krishna's army.

The technological achievements of our ancient ancestors were not limited to Vimanas. They may also have possessed an array of highly destructive weapons used in warfare. It is widely believed that some of the weapons used during the great Mahabharata battle were miniaturized versions of nuclear weapons capable of causing extensive damage.

The Brahmastra is one such weapon used in the battles of Ramayana and the Mahabharata, capable of causing extensive damage. The ultimate weapon of mass destruction is the Brahmashirsha Astra, which is believed to be four times deadlier than the Brahmastra.

THE VAIMANIKA SHASTRA OF BHARADWAJA

Maharishi *Bharadwaja*, one of the seven great sages (*Saptarishis*) assigned to the current *Vaivaswata Manu,* is believed to have handed down the original version of the *Vymaanika- Shaastra* (science of aeronautics in Sanskrit) for the benefit of humankind (Josyer, 1973, Childress, 2004). However, another sage, Bharadwaja, happens to be a contemporary of Sri Rama in the 24th *Yuga* cycle. Yet, another *Bharadwaja* happens to be the father of *Dronacharya*, the guru of both Pandava and Kaurava cousins from the Kuru Kingdom in the epic *Mahabharata*, which took place about five thousand years ago towards the end of the recent Dvapara Yuga (28th *Mahayuga* cycle).

How, then, could Bharadwaja have lived for over nineteen million years? I raised this issue with our family priest and Vedic scholar, Sri Seshadri of Frederick, Maryland. He was quick to point out that *a Bharadwaja* always appears in each *Mahayuga* cycle (i.e., every 4.32M years), as elucidated in the Puranas. So, he said that it is difficult to pinpoint precisely which Bharadwaja from the past five Mahayuga cycles (24th to 28th) may have been responsible for authoring the original *Vaimaanika-Shastra*.

A *Bharadwaja* from the 28th Mahayuga cycle (current), and not the *one* from Sri Rama's era, may have undertaken the daunting task of revealing the workings of ancient Vimanas in his original *Vaimanika Shaastra* version believed to be in Sanskrit.

Chapter 5: Soaring Into the Sky

The *Vaimaanika Shaastra* was translated into English by Josyer (1973) based on a 1923 version by a pandit *Subbaraya Shastry*, who claimed that a saint had personally narrated the entire contents to him. The original Sanskrit version of Bharadwaja is unavailable.

Descriptions of the space environment, the incorporation of mirrors in the design of spacecraft instrumentation, and the other capabilities of the Vimanas appear convincing. Figure 5.4 shows an example of a Rukma (Gold) Vimana (After Josyer, 1973).

Figure 5.4 The *Tantric* Rukma (Golden) Vimana with thrusters (After Josyer, 1973)

Thrusters are typically arranged in opposing pairs and fired simultaneously to stabilize a spinning spacecraft. Figure 5.5 shows the Apollo Reaction Control System (RCS) Quad-Thrusters. Each thruster is mounted at a 90-degree angle to provide precise spin and navigational control of the spacecraft. These thrusters were fueled by gaseous helium to ensure reliable performance when needed, eliminating the problems associated with engine failure during landing maneuvers.

In crewed missions, the captain of the Lunar Module (LM) assumes control of the landing process, guiding the craft to a level surface. The success of lunar descent in unmanned missions, on the other hand, hinges on the precise firing of all thrusters and the successful performance of the landing instruments. The presence of any rocks or crevices can significantly impede the spacecraft's ability to land upright. Notably, we cannot currently recover from any deviations from right-side-up landings.

Interestingly, the aerodynamic shape of the LM riding up front is somewhat similar in shape to the Rukma Vimana. The earlier Mercury and Gemini capsules also have a similar shape, suggesting the possibility that the Rukma Vimana may have been capable of low Earth orbit when equipped with proper propulsion technology.

The upward lift of a Vimana is a function of the amount of thrust delivered by its engines; insufficient thrust may limit its utility to only low-level flights. On the other hand, the much larger *mantric* type Vimanas described in the epics Ramayana and Mahabharata may be incorporating some form of advanced propulsion systems.

Figure 5.5 Apollo Reaction Control System (RCS) Quad Thrusters placed on the Service Module (Credit: "Riko Best"- stock.adobe.com)

Interesting reading aside, Bharadwaja's treatise on hardware, which includes spacecraft metallurgy and Vimana's propulsion systems, has some shortcomings. Many of the metals mentioned in Sanskrit are currently unknown to humankind, and more research may be needed to identify them.

Scientists at the Indian Institute of Science in Bengaluru, India, questioned the ability of the Vimanas described by Josyer to deliver sufficient thrust for lifting such large and heavy objects off the ground (Mukunda et al., 2021). The description of the propulsion systems may have been limited by the technical understanding of the authors of the Vaimanika Shastra, who may have been trying to explain advanced technology using their scientific knowledge.

PROPHET EZEKIEL'S VISION

In my quest to find references to spacecraft in other religions, I came across Prophet Ezekiel's vision of God landing in what appears to be a spacecraft. He describes the landing process quite vividly, even though it may have been his first experience.

In the *Bible's American Standard Version (ASV)* (Ezekiel **10** 1:1-28), the Prophet Ezekiel elegantly describes His vision of a spacecraft landing from the north.

On the banks of the river Chebar, in the land of the Chaldeans, the Prophet Ezekiel witnessed a phenomenon unlike any other. A powerful storm, heralded by intense winds, approached from the north. This storm, however, was soon engulfed by a cloud of fire, revealing a metallic object, a spacecraft, which defied all known descriptions.

From this enigmatic object emerged four humanoid figures, all males. Each figure was a marvel in itself, with four faces, four wings, and hands. Their feet, described as shiny brass-like hooves, added to their mystique. The four faces were equally intriguing human faces in front, a lion's face on the right, an ox's face on the left, and an eagle's face at the back, a sight that surely left the prophet and his readers in wonder.

The upper pair of wings were joined while the lower ones covered their bodies. All of them emanated a fiery glow accompanied by lightning flashes. They moved very quickly on wheels-within-wheels, some form of a gyroscopic mechanism (Fig. 5.6). The rims of the wheels had the appearance of eyes engraved on them. The wings fluttered as they moved, and the wheels also moved up and down. There was also a platform placed over the heads of the four creatures on which a sapphire throne appeared. Ezekiel saw a man seated on the throne. A fire engulfed the metal frame, and a bright aura or halo surrounded the seated Man. Such was Ezekiel's description of Lord Jehovah.

Finally, when the Prophet Ezekiel sees the face of the Lord, he falls face down prostrate. The Lord asks Prophet Ezekiel to rise and explains His mission for Ezekiel.

Prophet Ezekiel's account of his vision of how Lord Joshua landed on Earth is a truly fascinating account of something he had never seen nor experienced before. During those times, people were unaware of human flight to be able to describe such events.

Nowadays, most people are familiar with fiery and thunderous spacecraft launches, capsule re-entry, and landings over water or on land. The re-entry process is also quite fiery due to the intense frictional heat, as one might have observed during earlier space shuttle landings.

Imagine a different scenario where the capsule could land and take off into space from anywhere without the need for elaborate launch systems. Such a capability would fundamentally change our understanding of space travel, echoing the transformative nature of Prophet Ezekiel's vision.

Figure 5.6 Gyroscopic principles are often used to maintain directional orientation and angular Velocity (Credit: "Olekcii"/Alamy Stock Photo)

VIMANA OF ZARATHUSTRA

The Persian prophet Zarathustra (628-551 BC) founded the Zoroastrian religion. It is believed that he moved to Persia, modern-day Iran, and finally settled in northeastern Afghanistan during the later stages of his life. Some believe that he was in possession of an ancient Rukma Vimana, which he used to travel and preach.

WHAT IF …

The concept of ancient Vimanas, or flying machines and rocket ships, is found in many ancient religious texts worldwide. I have focused on the Puranas, which can take us back thousands, if not millions, of years into the past. However, the technological descriptions of these Vimanas in the Puranas remain shrouded in mystery, whether by chance or design. It is possible that many of these ancient aircraft were equipped with advanced propulsion technologies, enabling them to take off and land from any location.

The large and complex Vimanas mentioned in the epics Ramayana and Mahabharata were all gifted to numerous devotees by Lord Shiva himself. It is overwhelming that Lord Shiva could have produced a very sophisticated spacecraft millions of years ago. The Pushpaka Vimana is the first documented case of an advanced spacecraft hailing from the Ramayana 18.144 million years ago. The most recent one was shot down during the final stages of the Kurukshetra war about 5,000 years ago. The spacecraft debris from this documented event may be located under 100-200 feet of the Arabian Sea near sunken Dwarka.

If this is true, it could have far-reaching implications for humankind. It is possible that many of the gods, alien gods, and their emissaries from different religions may have traveled to Earth in ancient spacecraft. Over thousands, if not millions of years, they could have traveled across the globe, the Moon, and possibly even other planets and their moons.

It is myopic to assume that our generation is the only one to explore the solar system and beyond. We have seen how evolutionary cycles may be inherently cyclical in nature, suggesting the possibility of ancient space explorers exploring space. It may be true that the proverbial wheel gets reinvented repeatedly within each successive cycle.

Planetary laws of motion, gravity, mathematics, and others may have been independently discovered several times. In perspective, Oppenheimer's proverbial adage "…in modern times" may apply to many of our scientific and engineering accomplishments.

It is difficult to comprehend how the engineering marvels mentioned in ancient religious texts are associated with the Gods or Alien Gods. Without factories, blueprints, or manuals, nature can produce beautiful flowers, birds, and animals. On the other hand, humankind requires thousands of pages of documents, adequate financing, and a team of scientists, engineers, technicians, and contractors to produce a modern spacecraft. Perhaps another unknown process, unknown to us in our limited dimensionality, leads to the creation of such things.

* * * * *

Chapter 6: Secrets of the Moon

In Chapter 3, we delved into the intriguing concept of the Yuga cycles and their possible correlation with the existence of super-intelligent races during the Krita (Satya) Yuga period. Could it be that during the 1.728-million-year span of the most recent Krita Yuga, humanity advanced technologically enough to venture beyond Earth and establish a presence on the Moon or elsewhere within our Solar system?

NASA's deep-space telescopes recently unveiled the closest Earth-like exoplanets, located at staggering distances of at least 10 to 20 light years away. Unlike highway automobile gas stations and their food courts, spaceports may be several light years apart, necessitating travelers to carry supplies and fuel for the arduous journey. One might have to traverse at overwhelming velocities, approaching the speed of light or greater, and exploit wormholes and black holes to warp travel distances and time. Scientists are now pondering the notion of traveling faster than the speed of light.

Our Solar system can be a very inviting and lucrative destination for any unsuspecting alien space traffic. The Earth, with its air, water, and food reserves, is like an oasis in the vastness of space. Our Moon, located at a short distance of only 384,400 kilometers (238,900 miles) from Earth, is an ideal destination for potential visitors from outer space. For millions of years, the far side of the Moon may have shielded visitors from outer space. The exploration of our Moon by the United States, Russia, Japan, India, and China has added numerous high-resolution orbiters to scan and map the lunar terrain, including its far side. Our Moon is no longer a haven for travelers from outer space desiring to remain incognito.

As mentioned in Chapter 3, it is conceivable that our alien Gods and their emissaries could have used the Moon as both a space station for deep-space travel and a springboard for launching their Earthly liaisons. Numerous religious instances depict God conversing with Man from the sky above, as depicted in religious books, paintings, and murals.

As we explore the solar system and beyond, we may also encounter signs of ancient alien or ancestral activity, past or present.

LUNAR SPACECRAFT

It will be more appropriate to call spacecraft on the Moon l*unar spacecraft* instead of extraterrestrial spacecraft as we do on Earth. The presence of a lunar spacecraft can be observed in select scenes in the *Flickr Project Apollo* image archive. These scenes were examined in detail to identify the nature of each incidence. Some of the Hasselblad images on *Flickr* taken during various Apollo missions reveal these observed on the Moon. This is not a comprehensive list of all types of lunar spacecraft but rather a preliminary effort at identifying some of them.

CYLINDRICAL SPACECRAFT

Unlike a conventional Sci-Fi novel, this book involved considerable real-time research to independently validate some of the features and artifacts observed in the imagery. Some scenes reveal features that resemble linear or cylindrical-shaped spacecraft.

Chapter 6: Secrets of the Moon

NASA/JSC's Project Apollo Archives, a treasure trove available on *Flickr*, is a collection of 70mm Hasselblad camera photographs. These images were captured during the various Apollo missions, offering a unique glimpse into our space exploration history. The collection includes both black and white and color photographs. All of these images are now archived in *Flickr*.

Let us look at the first example, a captivating scene from the Apollo 17 mission. Several large linear or cylindrical spacecraft are captured, seemingly flying in formation over the lunar sky (Fig. 6.1). These are not your typical time-lapse photographs showing streaks of starlight. These spacecraft are bright and shiny and exhibit an intriguingly uneven texture. They appear to be flying in parallel formation, with the larger ones may be closer than others in the distance. A large and brightly glowing spacecraft, perhaps a mothership, is visible towards the southeast corner of the scene. Its aura of brightness somehow illuminates the emptiness of the dark sky, creating a mesmerizing contrast.

An inspection of a few sequential scenes in the archive shows that the fleet grew visibly smaller and eventually disappeared into space. Stars and planets are far away and will not fade during such a short observation period. Initial observations of these mundane-looking spacecraft may prove to be quite misleading. Their technology level may be beyond comprehension, as they can bend like pretzels, take off and land from anywhere, and travel at insane velocities through space.

A closeup of the cylindrical spacecraft (Fig. 6.1-A) indicates a wavy kink towards the left third of the craft. Also, notice that the bright craft towards the southeast is significantly larger than the rest and has a distinct aura.

Figure 6.1 Several cylindrical spacecraft observed in flight
(Image Credit: NASA/JSC/Project Apollo Archive/Flickr)

Mystic Moon: A Lunar Odyssey

Another interesting observation about lunar spacecraft is that there are no visible signs of windows or portholes. However, they have no difficulty navigating through space while in formation.

The requirement for windows and artificial lights in spacecraft is driven primarily by crewed missions. Human vision is limited to the visible portion of the solar spectrum, which requires light for nocturnal vision. An advanced civilization capable of building huge spacecraft is highly likely to have resolved this issue. Also, windows and portholes may have problems when traveling through space at extremely high velocities.

Figure 6.1-A Magnified image of the cylindrical spacecraft in flight

The Apollo 17 crew captured the next tantalizing image of a linear spacecraft landing on the lunar surface (Fig. 6.2). The landing process appears to generate a plume of dust emanating from the surface to a considerable distance behind the spacecraft. Interestingly, the propellant plume also appears to be ejected towards the front of the spacecraft, suggesting it may be firing thrusters to slow it down for landing. Surprisingly, this propulsion technology is akin to our own, with the notable exception that this craft is

Chapter 6: Secrets of the Moon

capable of firing thrusters from both ends simultaneously while landing freely on the lunar surface. Also, notice the wide plume of lunar dust kicked up during the landing.

One would have expected this craft to be equipped with more advanced propulsion systems such as nuclear or magnetic levitation associated with UAP technology. This suggests the possible presence of a diverse mix of both old and modern technologies associated with spacecraft observed on the Moon.

Figure 6.2 A cylindrical spacecraft kicks up a plume of dust as it prepares to land on the lunar surface. (Image Credit: NASA/JSC/Project Apollo Archive/Flickr)

A modern-day space enthusiast used to Hollywood's portrayal of sleek, sexy spacecraft and *motherships* in Sci-Fi movies might be a bit disappointed by the plain appearance of the workhorses observed on the Moon.

TRAPEZOIDAL & RECTANGULAR SPACECRAFT

The lunar sky is occasionally graced by massive trapezoidal (eraser-shaped) and rectangular spacecraft photographed at night during the Apollo 14 mission (Fig. 6.3a-d). What is impressive is their technology, which allows them to maintain a stationary position in the lunar sky. These windowless behemoths may be designed to withstand the perils of deep-space travel at velocities approaching that of light.

It is interesting to note that the shape of a spacecraft depends upon the viewing angle. One observer may perceive it as cylindrical, while another a few miles away may see it as rectangular or trapezoidal. Both may be correct in their interpretation of the spacecraft from their respective positions.

Mystic Moon: A Lunar Odyssey

The first three spacecraft (Fig. 6.3a-c) appear to be trapezoidal with some subtle variations in shape. The fourth one (Fig. 6.3d) is distinctly rectangular in shape. However, all of them appear to have a shiny metallic luster and seem to be about the same length. There appear to be no visible signs of portholes, lights, or protruding propulsion systems that are commonly associated with them. One can only speculate on the nature of their advanced propulsion systems that may possibly be incorporating electrostatic particle accelerators.

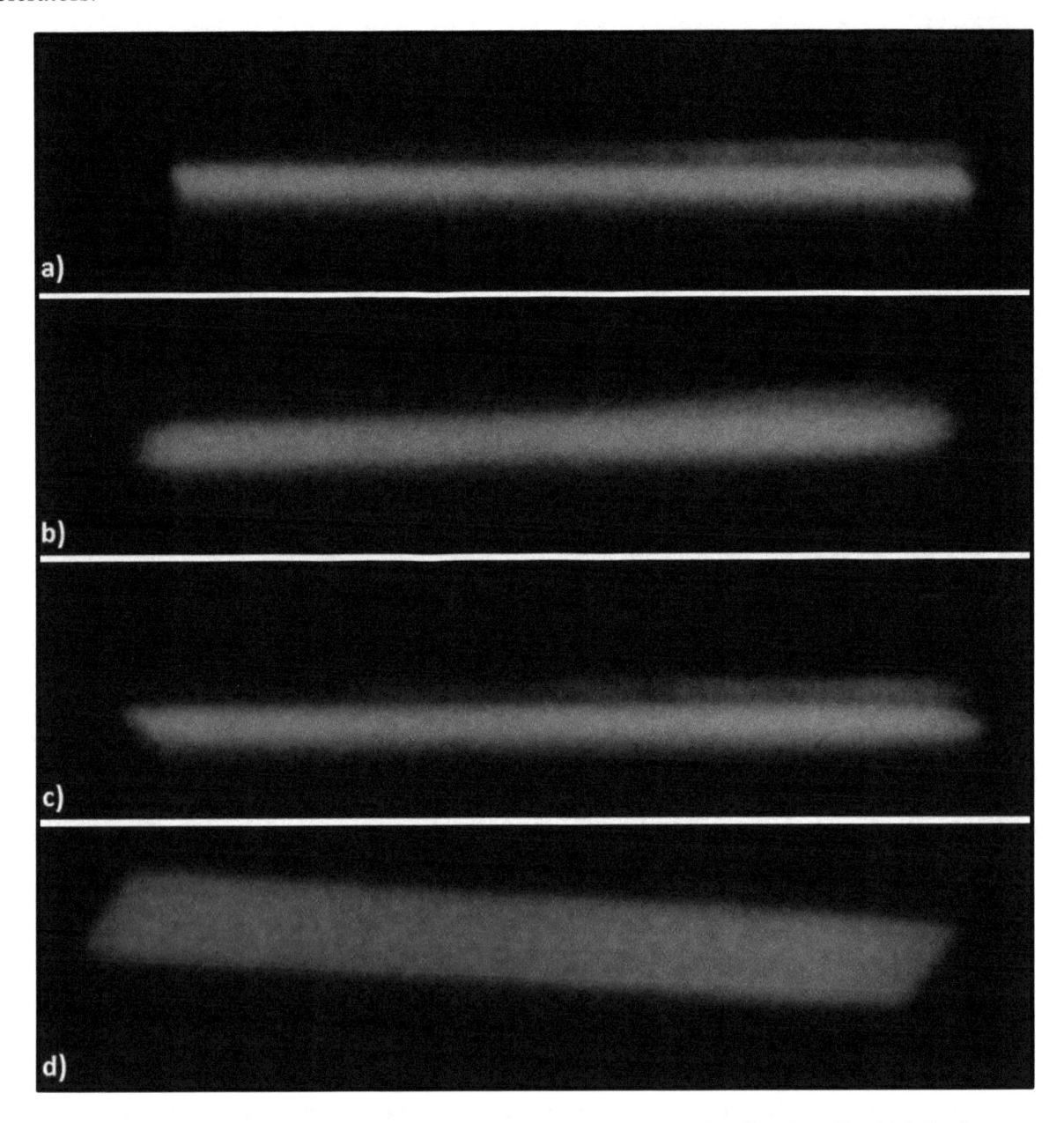

Figure 6.3a-d Four types of large spacecraft observed during Apollo 14 Mission (Raw Images Credit: NASA/JSC/Arizona State University)

Electromagnetic fields are known to accelerate charged particles to near-light velocities in our universe. Scientists have successfully accelerated photons under laboratory conditions in the Large

Hadron Collider (Mersmann, 2019). It is possible that these behemoths utilize similar principles in the design of their spacecraft with advanced propulsion technology.

One of the major limitations to human travel at near-light velocities is a phenomenon known as *pancaking* due to the sudden impulse of excessive g-forces on the body. The alien entities may have developed compensating technologies to circumvent this problem. Modern spacecrafts are equipped with momentum wheels to compensate for internal cabin torques generated by repetitive motion of exercising astronauts. On a larger scale, the spacecraft's *Attitude and Orbit Control System* provides three-axis stabilization utilizing a combination of onboard trackers, sensors, and propulsion systems.

SPHERICAL SPACECRAFT

In addition to the numerous cylindrical, trapezoidal, and rectangular spacecraft on the Moon, one may occasionally encounter smaller spherical or saucer-shaped spacecraft. Based on their size, these spherical spacecraft may belong to an alien group of short stature. Incidentally, these small saucer-shaped spacecraft may have been sighted on Earth.

Ever notice how a flying aircraft casts its shadow on the surface of the Earth? Anyone who has flown on a sunny day seated near a window may have also observed shadows of cumuliform clouds cast on the ground below. These shadows tend to be smaller when viewed perpendicularly and appear elongated when viewed at an angle. A shadow is a clear indication that some physical object is present between the Sun and the surface. Similarly, a low-flying object, such as a spacecraft flying over the lunar surface, will cast a shadow during the day.

Figure 6.4 embeds a spherical spacecraft, which can be seen by zooming and panning the full image. A low-flying spherical object can be identified to the north of Mare Spumanis in Figure 6.4A. This image is a subset of the larger one captured during the Apollo 11 Mission. The shiny spacecraft is zipping across the lunar surface, casting a distinct shadow below.

These lunar spacecraft may have been inhabiting the Moon for an exceptionally long period of time, perhaps for millions of years. The Apollo missions ended in the early seventies, and this was followed by a fifty-five-year lull in human exploration of the Moon.

Mankind's recent renewed interest in lunar exploration has brought on a new reality that alien entities may no longer remain undetected on the secluded far side. Future lunar missions are likely to make it even more difficult for them to remain isolated from Earthlings. It remains to be seen how this renewed interest in lunar exploration by several new players may likely change the dynamics. Is it likely to forge new alliances or spur bitter confrontations?

In the distant past, the Earth was sparsely populated, and most alien visitors could easily find secluded spots to safely land and park. Unfortunately, the Earth has been mostly built up and offers limited possibilities that can serve as discrete landing areas for extremely large spacecraft without drawing too much public attention. For this reason, alien visitors may prefer to return to their bases on the Moon.

Recently, there have been reported sightings of unknown disk-shaped spacecraft disappearing into lakes on Earth. This technique may be an adaptation to remain incognito. The less traveled oceans of the southern hemisphere can also present numerous opportunities to dive in undetected in search of seafood.

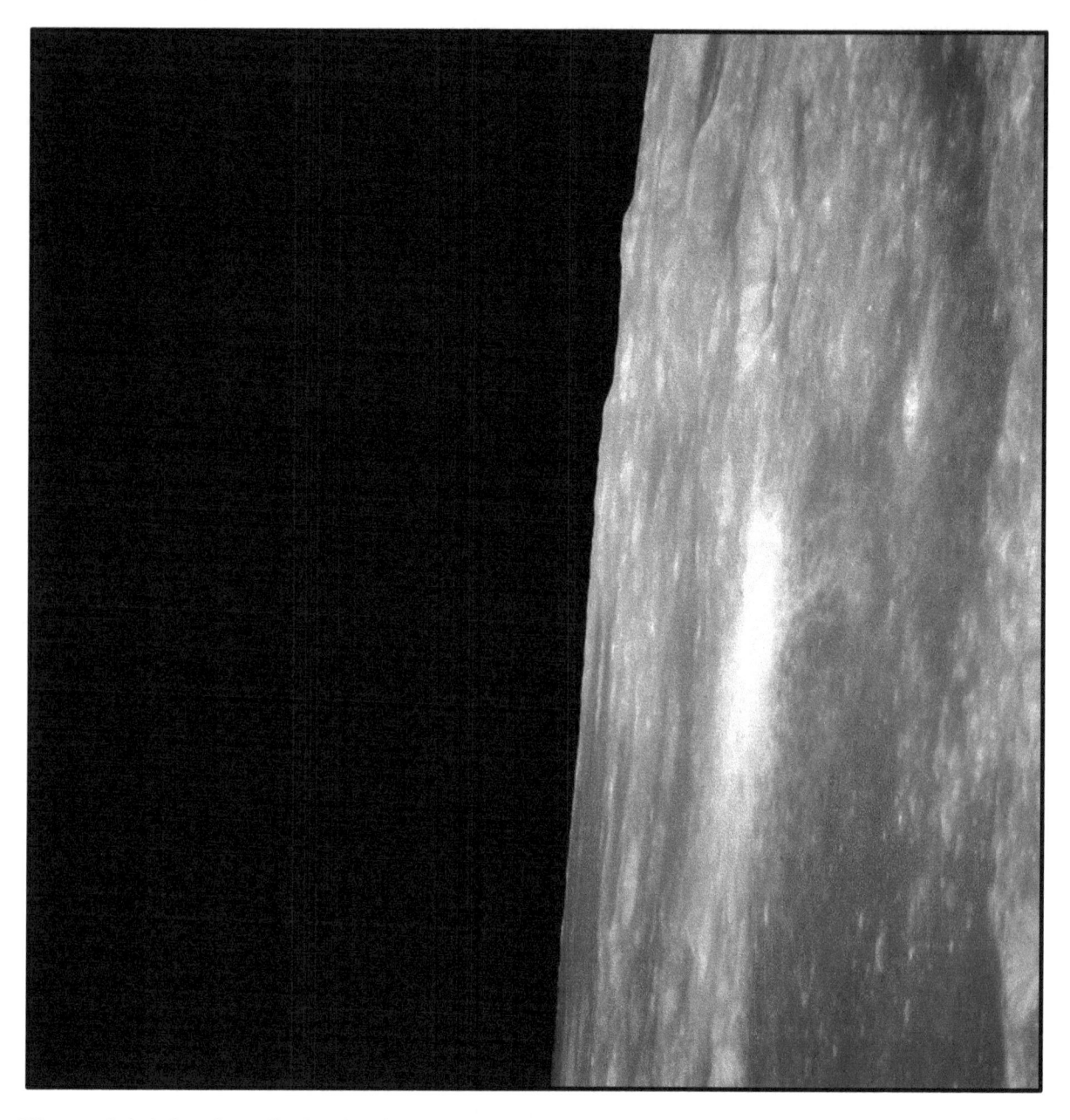

Figure 6.4 A hard-to-find spherical spacecraft flying over the lunar surface eludes the eye
(Image Credit: NASA/JSC/Project Apollo Archive/Flickr)

Chapter 6: Secrets of the Moon

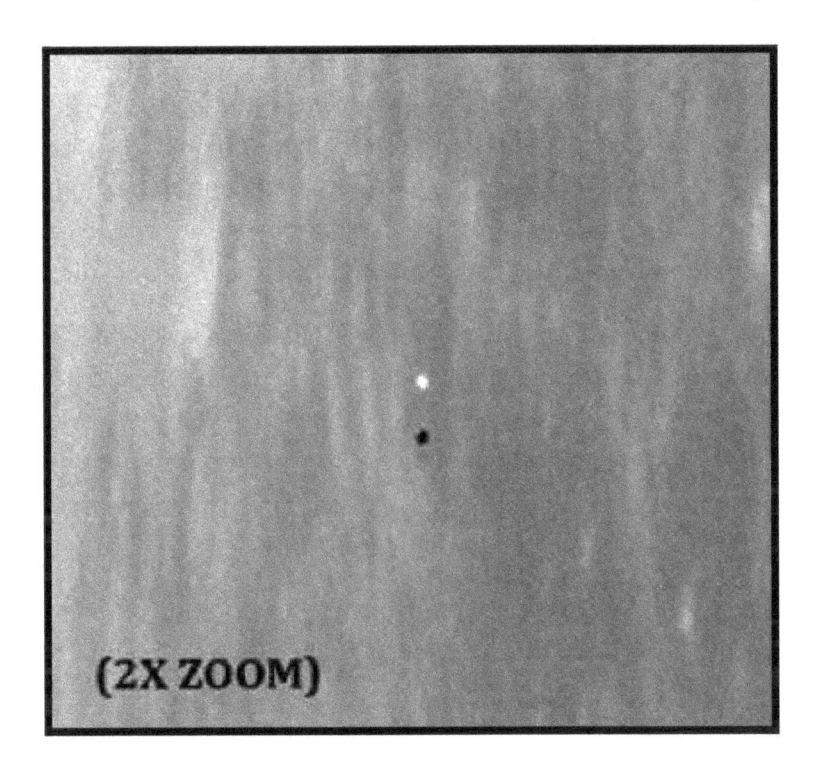

(2X ZOOM)

Figure 6.4-A The 2X Zoom reveals the spherical spacecraft

Mankind's ability to travel to the Moon has brought about a new reality: lunar entities may no longer remain undetected, even if they inhabit the secluded far side. Future lunar missions to the South Polar regions will likely make it even more difficult for alien entities to enjoy their privacy.

Suddenly, space is becoming crowded as we begin to explore our solar system. Unbeknownst to us, the competition for natural resources within our Solar System is critical for developing advanced spacecraft and sustaining life that may have already begun long ago. We are still in the early developmental stages of rocket technology, converting from bulky solid and/or liquid propellants to dynamic nuclear propulsion systems that can provide us with the much-needed ability to quickly change both speed and direction of travel as and when needed without the fear of running out of fuel.

We must graduate from bulky expendable sources of rocket fuel to alternative propulsion systems utilizing nuclear technology incorporating anti-gravity technology. This may take considerable time, funding, research and development efforts to advance to the next phase in human space exploration.

One can logically speculate on Earth's role as a life-sustaining reservoir for the survival of lunar inhabitants. The presence of any large spacecraft on the Moon poses another dilemma for the continued exploration of our Solar system. Are we likely to encounter alien traffic or traces of their enduring presence on other planetary destinations such as Mars, Europa, and others? It is highly probable that we will encounter their presence either directly or indirectly very shortly.

On Earth, archeologists can analyze prehistoric dinosaur fossils dating back to 250M years towards the end of the *Permian* period. Modern satellite technology is aiding them in unearthing ancient trade routes, hidden riverbeds, and ancient city blocks buried deep under mounds of tropical vegetation. This is made possible because ancient civilizations have left traces of their sojourn on Earth.

Similarly, the Moon may also be harboring vestiges of alien visitors dating back to millions of years. The diverse group of unknown lunar visitors could include those hailing from distant civilizations several light years away. The diversity of spacecraft and differences in propulsion systems present the possibility of diverse groups of aliens. One can also include visitors from neighboring Earth in their ancient *Vimanas* into the mix of lunar visitors. The extremely cold polar regions of the Moon, combined with its thin anaerobic exosphere, could help preserve any ancient alien DNA material for future lunar explorers.

Scientific experiments conducted during the Apollo 17 mission revealed that the lunar exosphere consists primarily of equal amounts of neon, helium, and hydrogen with some trace amounts of methane, carbon dioxide, and ammonia water. Consequently, any lunar debris attributable to alien activity may remain undisturbed over time. Space debris attributable to human exploration of the Moon is more recent and can be traced back to its country of origin. Remnants of any space debris preceding human exploration can be attributed solely to the activity of alien entities.

The universe has existed for billions of years, the Yuga cycles describe human evolution as inherently cyclical. Intelligent civilizations from the distant past may have acquired advanced technology and left planet Earth to settle elsewhere in our Solar system or beyond before any impending existential threat.

The pressure for human generations to colonize space is burgeoning from two fronts: competition from new countries in the space race and competition for life-sustaining resources on the Moon, Mars, and other destinations. It may already be time for us to follow in our 'ancient ancestors' footsteps and quickly colonize the Moon and other parts of our Solar system.

The Moon, our nearest neighbor, is an ideal destination for preparing humans for the future colonization of other planets and their moons. It is a cost-effective and time-saving option for learning the trials and tribulations of colonization of non-terrestrial objects. The lessons learned in lunar exploration can be implemented with some adaptations to other locations such as Mars and other destinations.

* * * * * *

Chapter 7: More Lunar Spacecraft

In 2022, the U.S. Defense Department refined the use of the term *Unknown Flying Objects* (UFOs) with new terminology known as *Unidentified Anomalous Phenomena* (UAP) as a preferred way to describe any objects that could pose a threat to national security.

In 2023, a congressional subcommittee heard testimony from former military officers about their experiences with UAP. A few videos were presented to support their claims. Their main concern was that these UAPs equipped with advanced technological capabilities were posing a problem for both military and civilian pilots and their safety. They also alluded to how these UAPs, without any visual signs of propulsion, could stay indefinitely in a stationary position and dart away at high speeds.

The probable presence of lunar spacecraft of unknown origin could possibly fall under the general UAP category. Still, these do not appear to have been sighted over Earth in the past fifty-five years. However, we will now consider them lunar spacecraft of unknown origin.

The presence of lunar spacecraft and drones of different shapes and sizes renders a high probability of the presence of unknown entities on the Moon. One can also look for other tell-tale signs of their existence, such as habitats, dwellings, creations, and any other metric that may vindicate their presence. However, the spatial resolution of the available Apollo imagery may limit one's ability to identify such objects with confidence clearly.

SPACECRAFT OBSERVED IN-FLIGHT OVER THE MOON

Earlier, we saw several examples of cylindrical, trapezoidal, or rectangular spacecraft over the Moon. All of them can take-off and land from any type of terrain, or remain suspended in space. A few variants of the cylindrical type of spacecraft may also have been sighted in flight across the lunar sky.

Some Apollo missions presented opportunities for astronauts to observe interesting alien spacecraft while in orbit or during docking maneuvers. These encounters may have been playful overtures for the entertainment of the terrestrial visitors and nothing to be construed as confrontational. Suffice it to say that these distant interactions seemed very cordial and did not threaten the safety of their mission.

An important element in all such episodes is the incredible and outstanding courage demonstrated by the crew during all these seamless interactions. Being an astronaut demands considerable courage, sacrifice, determination, and the ability to remain calm and reason when the situation demands. The Apollo crew demonstrated all of these attributes during their missions.

In another interesting encounter, a huge cylindrical spacecraft can be seen behind a light drone (Fig. 7.1). The cylindrical spacecraft cleared the drone and moved away. After the departure of the cylindrical UAP, the drone spun around fast and transformed itself into a four-pod drone (Fig. 7.2) before returning to its original state. It could be an optical illusion, but it was caught on camera.

Mystic Moon: A Lunar Odyssey

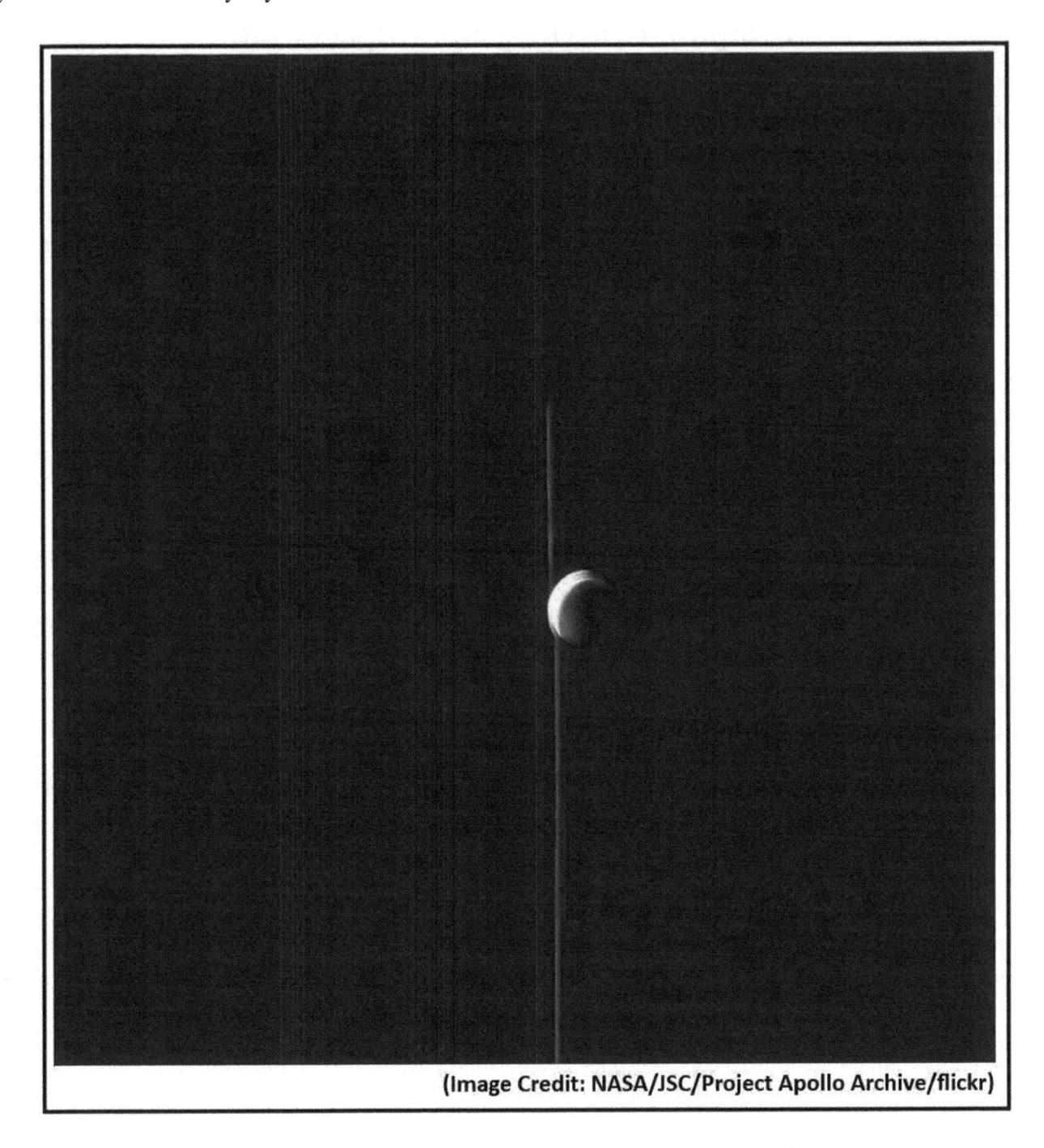

(Image Credit: NASA/JSC/Project Apollo Archive/flickr)

Figure 7.1 A huge cylindrical UAP appears behind a spherical light drone

Chapter 7: More Lunar Spacecraft

(Image Credit: NASA/JSC/Project Apollo Archive/flickr)

Figure 7.2 The light drone quickly transformed itself into a multi-pod drone

The gigantic cylindrical spacecraft is indeed an engineering marvel. It does not appear to exhibit any visible propulsion system but can move quickly.

The Wright Brothers, pioneers of aviation, could never have fathomed the modern marvels of air travel, like the wide-bodied Boeing 777 series. Similarly, we struggle to grasp the sheer scale and power of the gigantic spacecraft that patrols the Moon.

It is highly likely that such a huge spacecraft may be designed for traveling at extremely high velocities and, therefore, may be equipped with an outer protective shield.

Mystic Moon: A Lunar Odyssey

Such a huge spacecraft could easily transport numerous occupants at a time. History is replete with examples of ancient civilizations suddenly believed to have vanished without a trace- or did they?

Some of these spacecraft can transform their shape in flight in addition to their incredible size and speed. Super-advanced engineering skills are required to accomplish such marvelous acrobatic feats in space without hurling the spacecraft into a tailspin.

A fleet of lunar spacecraft capable of completely transforming their shape during flight may have been spotted during the Apollo 17 mission (Fig. 7.3). The logical assumption is that the scene represents a time-lapse picture of the night sky with characteristic streaks associated with the movement of planets and stars within the camera's field of view.

However, a more careful examination shows the spacecraft before its linear transformation (Fig. 7.3) in the shape of an inverted 'V' with a long cylindrical body attached to it at right angles. Another larger spacecraft, probably a Mothership, emanating a characteristic bright glow or aura, is easily identifiable. The spectacular linear transformation is almost complete in Figure 7.4. as the fleet moves away. Stars and planets in the sky are not capable of such quick motion.

(Image Credit: NASA/JSC/Project Apollo Archive/flickr)

Figure 7.3 A fleet of shape-transforming lunar spacecraft in flight

Chapter 7: More Lunar Spacecraft

(Image Credit: NASA/JSC/Project Apollo Archive/flickr)

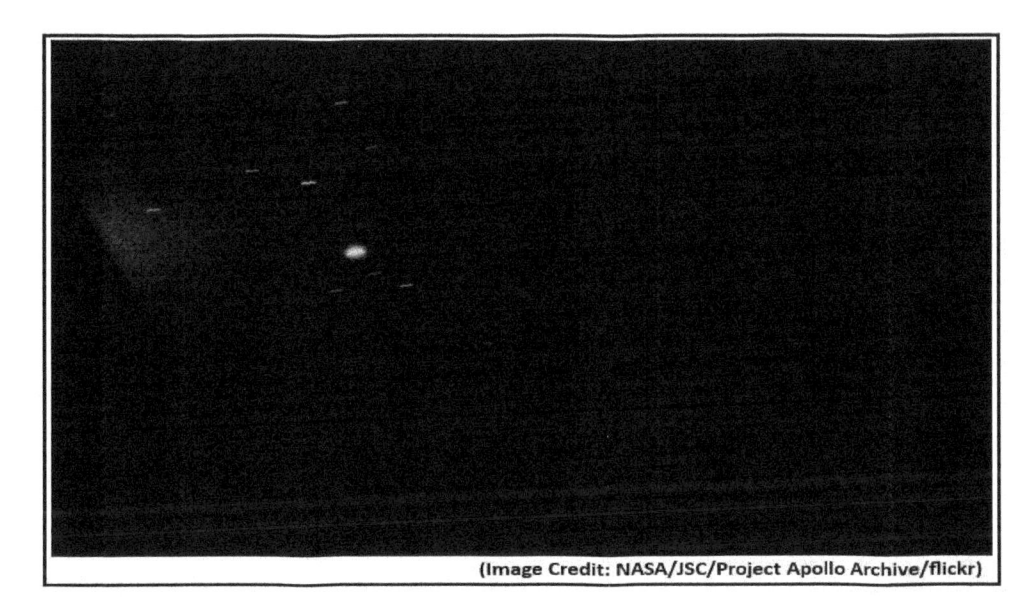

Figure 7.4 The fleet of spacecraft straightens shape as it moves away

The rapid linear transformation of these spacecraft from their original shape is truly an engineering marvel. The spacecraft may be equipped with flexible joints capable of fully unfolding into a contiguous linear shape. The reader may be familiar with children's toys capable of magically transforming themselves from one shape to another.

The lunar night sky offers an interesting display of spacecraft and drones of different shapes and sizes. The next example shows an interesting giant bluish 'Screw' shaped spacecraft emanating a blue glow in the distant horizon (Fig. 7.5) on the Moon. A 2-X zoom of this feature is shown in Figure 7.5-A, revealing more details of its shape. The spacecraft has a broad base that tapers off towards the nose and appears to have a helical twist. These UAPs keep appearing at different locations in the lunar sky.

Figure 7.5 A bluish helical screw-shaped spacecraft appears over the distant northeastern horizon (Image Credit: NASA/JSC/Project Apollo Archive/Flickr)

Mystic Moon: A Lunar Odyssey

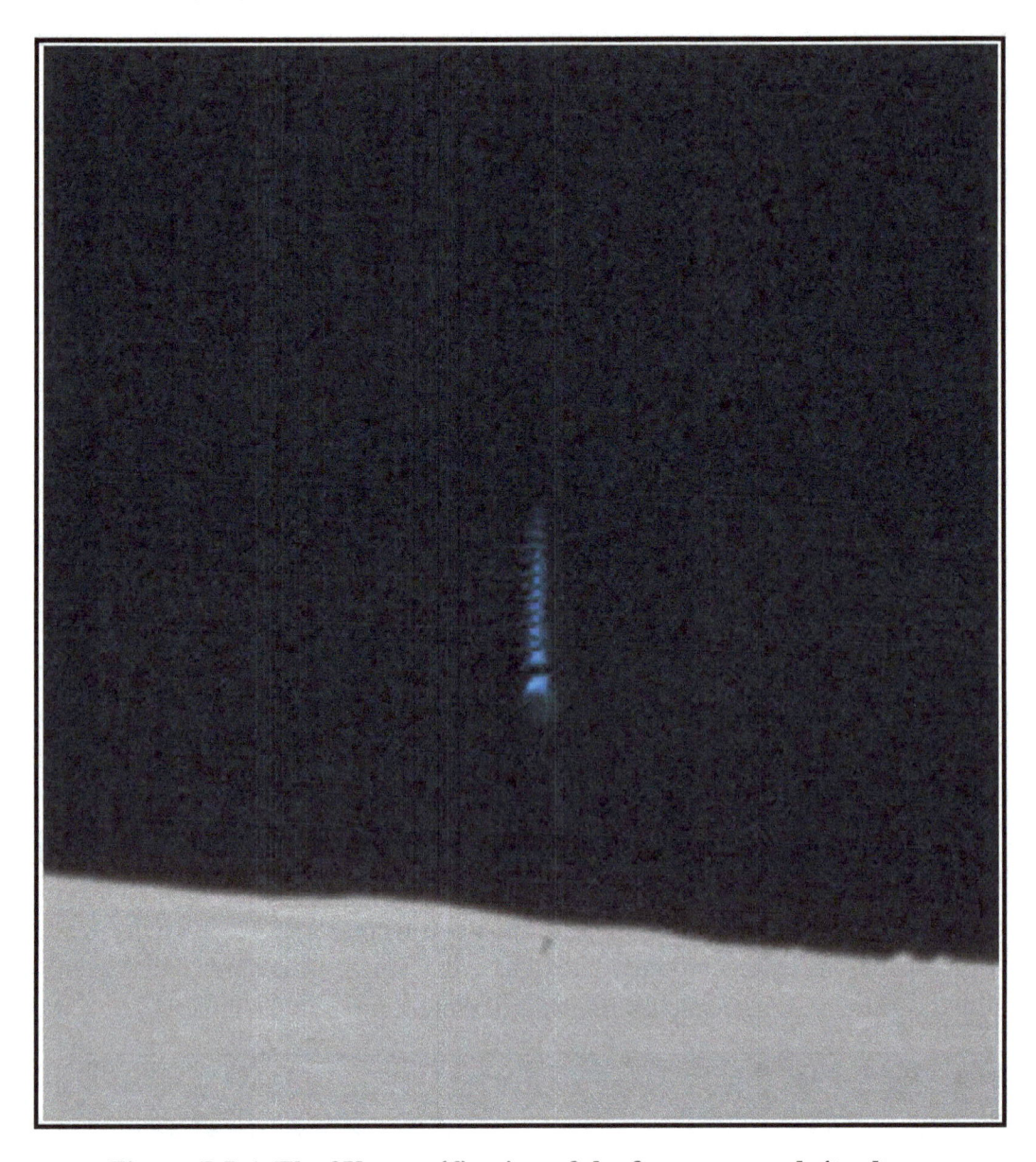

Figure 7.5-A The 2X magnification of the feature reveals its shape

Another differently shaped bright bluish spacecraft prepares to land over the lunar horizon (Fig. 7.6). This particular spacecraft has been observed in several scenes involving various Apollo missions. It has a characteristic bluish aura surrounding it (Fig. 7.6-A), as visible in the magnified image. A Xenon thruster probably generates its characteristic bluish flame.

One interesting aspect of these lunar spacecraft is their apparent ability to navigate across the Moon's surface, much like we do with helicopters and airplanes on Earth. They seemed to have mastered taking off and landing from any point, eliminating the need for complex launch pads and supporting infrastructure.

Chapter 7: More Lunar Spacecraft

(Image Credit: NASA/JSC/Project Apollo Archive/flickr)

Figure 7.6 A bright bluish spacecraft appears near the Apollo 14 Landing area of *Fra Mauro Formation*

Figure 7.6-A The 2X zoom provides a better view of the spacecraft

Spacecraft of various sizes and shapes frequently appear in the lunar sky, many of which have been captured on film by the Apollo astronauts.

Chapter 7: More Lunar Spacecraft

Some other spacecraft appear to have recognizable geometric shapes that are more familiar to us. In Figure 7.7, this spacecraft is shaped like an arrowhead and displays no visible propulsion system associated with it. A 2X zoom of this feature (Fig 7.7A) reveals a bright Delta-shaped spacecraft with three components: a leading edge and two wings on either side. All three of them appear to be almost identical.

These spacecraft will not require a conventional rudder or aileron to maneuver itself in deep space. The three wings may be flexible and change shape when the craft encounters any dense medium along the way. It is quite probable that the three segments may be able to change their configuration in flight.

(Image Credit: NASA/JSC/Project Apollo Archive/flickr)

Figure 7.7 A Delta-shaped spacecraft sighted in the northern lunar sky

Mystic Moon: A Lunar Odyssey

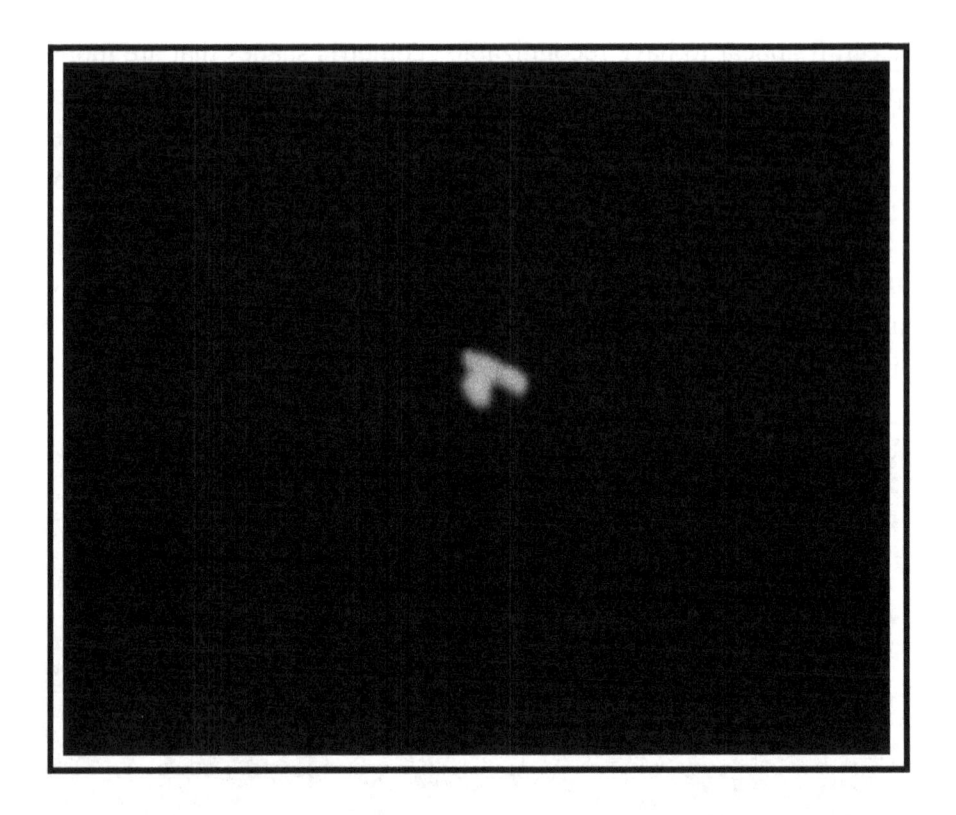

Figure 7.7-A The 2X Zoom reveals structural characteristics of the Delta-shaped spacecraft

A diverse variety of spacecraft appearing on the Moon suggests the irrefutable presence of a technology-savvy, well-established civilization with unlimited technological and financial resources.

A variety of spacecraft are apparently being used to perform everyday tasks on the Moon, much like we use airplanes, helicopters, trains, ships, cars, trucks, and heavy equipment on Earth.

An interesting rectangular wing-shaped spacecraft also appeared in the lunar sky. The following image (Fig. 7.8) reveals a sizeable rectangular wing-shaped spacecraft equipped with pods located on either end of the wing. Image magnification reveals a slightly bulging pair of pod-like features on either end of the wing (Fig.7.8-A). The shiny spacecraft is brightly illuminated by the incident sun's rays against the dark backdrop of the lunar sky.

This magnificent piece of space engineering was photographed from the lunar surface around fifty-two years ago during the Apollo 17 mission. The unique propulsion system of this spacecraft appears to leave no residual propulsion plume.

On Earth, modern-day delta-wing-shaped aircraft have no fuselage like both spacecraft (Figs. 7.7 & 7.8) presented above. Fuel for the engines, along with the crew and cargo, is stored in the wing itself.

Chapter 7: More Lunar Spacecraft

(Image Credit: NASA/JSC/Project Apollo Archive/flickr)

Figure 7.8 A large wing-shaped spacecraft with pods defines its unmistakable presence

Mystic Moon: A Lunar Odyssey

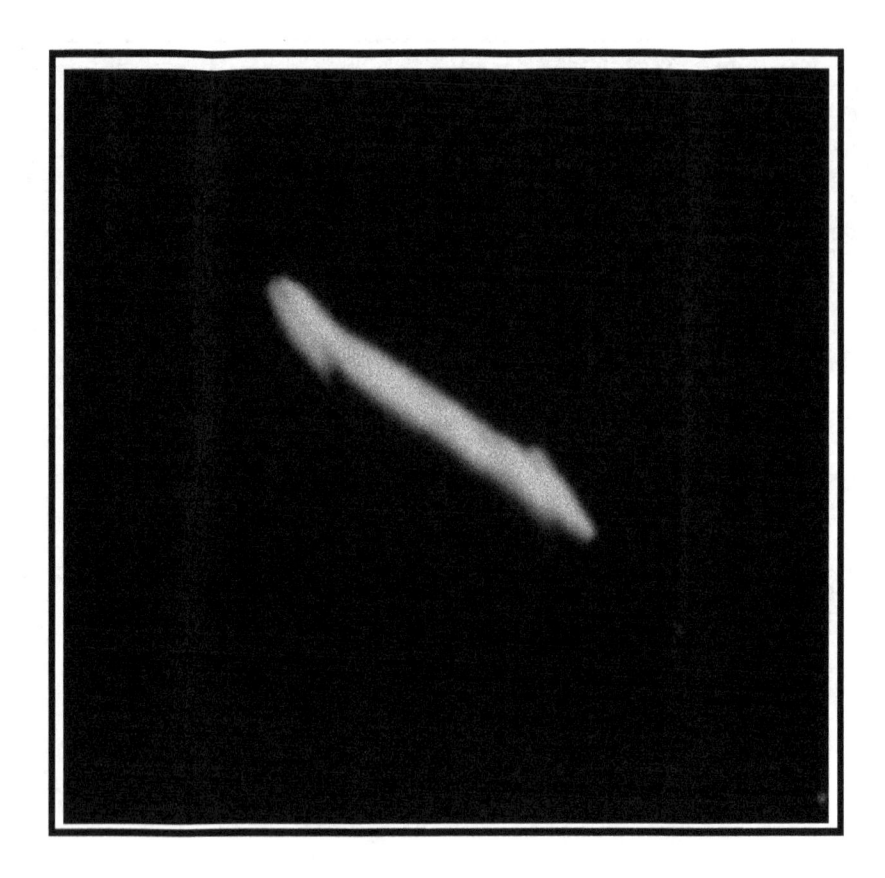

Figure 7.8-A A 2X Zoom of the wing-shaped spacecraft

SOME CLOSE ENCOUNTERS

There can be occasions when one encounters alien entities on the Moon. The best response may be to ignore their presence and continue with the business at hand. This appears to be the response taken by the Apollo astronauts during their close encounters with alien entities while on lunar excursions. An analysis of the image archives reveals a few instances in which the Apollo missions may have experienced close encounters with lunar spacecraft, including the light-bearing drones.

The lunar spacecraft appear to have kept a close watch on the surface activities. Their unique ability to take off and land from anywhere or stay suspended in space is quite intriguing from an engineering perspective, but it can be a hindrance when one is trying to do some serious work 294,000 miles away from home.

In the next scene, a huge rectangular spacecraft awaits the arrival of a Blue spacecraft near the Apollo 14 landing area of *Fra Mauro Formation* (Fig. 7.9a-b). This rectangular spacecraft stays suspended in the sky as the Blue spacecraft approaches. Both the raw (unenhanced) image (a) and the enhanced clearer image (b) are shown side by side for comparison. The plume of the Blue spacecraft is also shown magnified (Fig. 7.9b) in the inset towards the right corner. Interestingly, the enhanced image reveals a rectangular spacecraft identical to the one presented earlier in Figure 6.3d. This particular picture taken by the Apollo 14 astronauts clearly substantiates the presence of alien spacecraft in the lunar sky.

Chapter 7: More Lunar Spacecraft

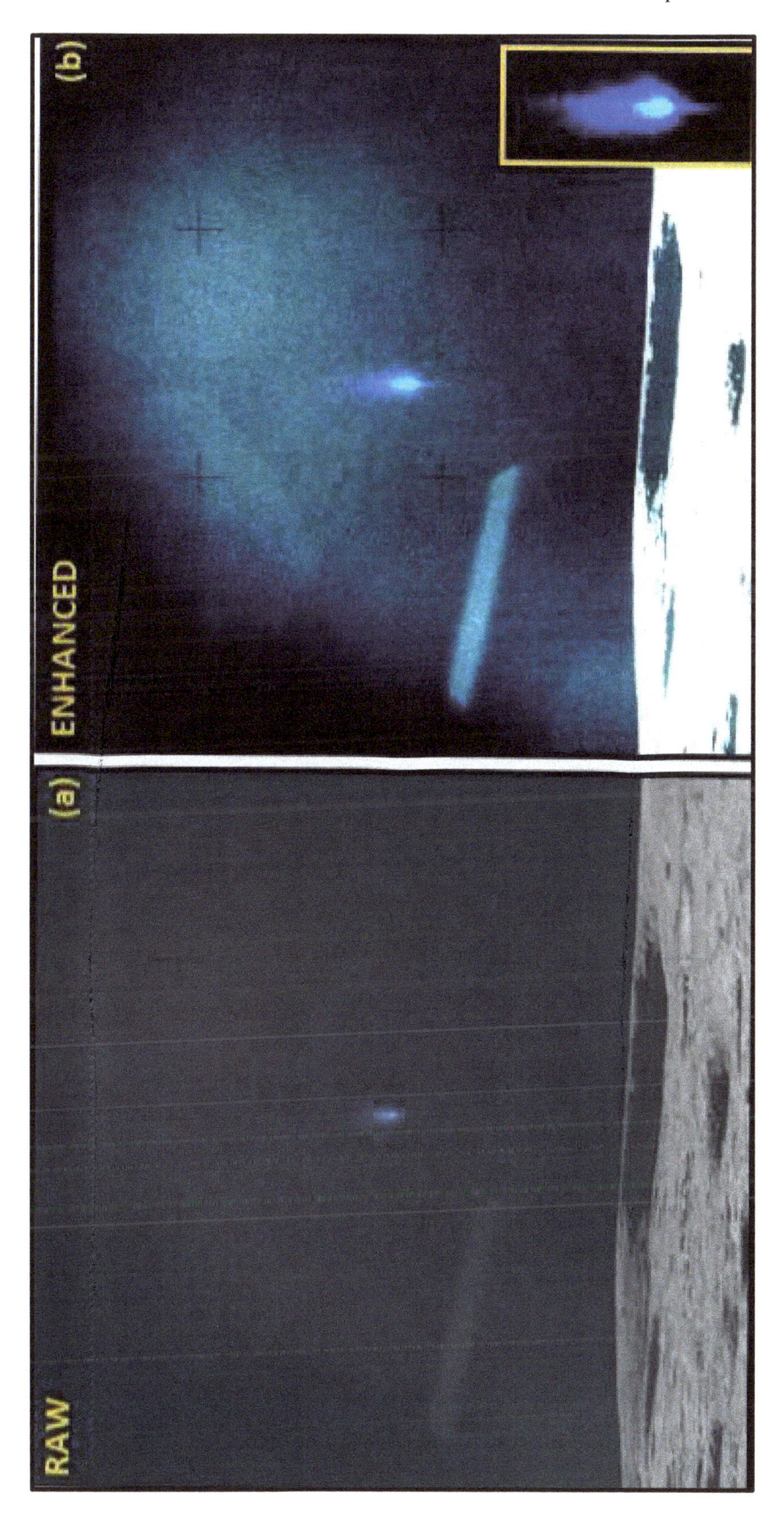

Fig. 7.9a-b Raw (a) and enhanced images showing Rectangular & Blue spacecraft near Apollo 14 landing site of *Fra Mauro Formation* (Image Credit: NASA/JSC/Project Apollo Archive/flickr)

Mystic Moon: A Lunar Odyssey

Interestingly, the propulsion system for the blue craft appears very conventional compared to that of the huge rectangular craft which may be incorporating advanced anti-gravitational technology. This picture clearly illustrates the use of a mix of advanced spacecraft alongside older and conventional ones. Both spacecraft exhibit significantly diverse types of propulsion technology.

It appears that the lunar entities are using spacecraft like we deploy aircraft or helicopters on Earth. This means that they have perfected space technology to the extent that they can deploy these spacecraft anywhere and anytime.

(Image Credit: NASA/JSC/Project Apollo Archive/flickr)

Figure 7.10 CM *Kitty Hawk* with blue spacecraft in background as viewed from LM *Antares*

In another close encounter, the Apollo 14 LM *Antares* captured a blue spacecraft in the background of the CM-*Kitty Hawk* at a safe distance towards its northwest (Fig. 7.10). Incidentally, this blue spacecraft appears identical to the one observed earlier over the *Fra Mauro Formation* (Fig. 7.6). It is highly probable that these spacecraft may have been following all of the Apollo missions.

Several examples of lunar spacecraft presented in this chapter illustrate the engineering prowess of the technologically advanced entities encountered on the Moon over fifty years ago.

The imagery presented in this chapter hints at the probable presence of unknown entities on the Moon during the Apollo missions. These entities may or may not be present on the Moon now after over fifty years. What is unclear is their true origin. Are they descendants of our ancient ancestors or are they part of a different group of aliens from somewhere else?

If their presence is true, then it is certainly comforting to feel that all encounters were very friendly in some way. These distant interactions were friendly, harmless, and thankfully uneventful. So, it is safe to assume that they did not wish to put the crew in harm's way at any time during their mission.

These lunar entities must have settled on the Moon long before the arrival of the Apollo missions and their crew. They are probably fully aware of life on Earth and familiar with its flora and fauna, as well as the availability of life-sustaining resources such as food, water, and air. The level of sophistication of their spacecraft implies that they may be able to visit Earth without us being fully aware of their presence.

* * * * * *

Chapter 8: Lunar Drones

The Moon, a celestial body that has captivated humanity for centuries, is not just a passive observer in our exploration of space. It is also home to various spacecraft or UAPs, including several smaller ones that can be categorized as drones or service vehicles. These unmanned drones, easily identifiable by a trained eye, are deployed to perform routine tasks, adding a dynamic element to our lunar observations.

Here on Earth, the U. S. Military initially developed drones to reduce the dependence on piloted fighter planes in both conventional warfare and in our war against terrorism. However, nowadays, drones have become a familiar feature ranging from children's toys to futuristic package delivery systems for courier companies. One can take this technology to the next level by utilizing drones with robotic crews, reducing risk and lowering costs associated with crewed planetary exploration. Currently, robotic rovers are doing an excellent job for NASA in the exploration of Mars. In the future, human-like robots may assist astronauts in performing some of their tasks and functions.

It Is hard to imagine that robotic drones may have been deployed on the Moon over sixty years ago by some unknown advanced alien civilization. Typically, drones are autonomous or 'unmanned' but controlled by some responsible entity. They can be programmed to perform repetitive tasks and are smaller in size than regular spacecraft. Some of these lunar drones can also be seen in high Earth orbit. Could they fetch water, air, and seafood supplies without our notice?

It is difficult to conceptualize spacecraft and drones equipped with advanced propulsion systems that enable them to land and take off from anywhere without the need for massive supporting infrastructure. However, by developing advanced propulsion systems, we may soon attain that level of sophistication.

A large red bat-wing-shaped object was sighted flying in a high Earth orbit (Fig. 8.1). The enlarged inset reveals greater details; notice the inwardly curled edges of wings as it maneuvers the Earth's upper atmosphere. Its unique wing shape allows it to enter the Earth's atmosphere in a gliding motion reminiscent of the Space Shuttle. However, this does not appear to be hardware debris from any spent stages of the Apollo 9 mission.

Figure 8.1A shows the interesting flying Batwing feature zoomed in. It is uniquely shaped and appears to be able to change its shape, like curling towards the edges of its wing. This could be a UAP flying at orbital heights over the Earth.

Chapter 8: Lunar Drones

(Image Credit: NASA/JSC/Project Apollo Archive/flickr)

Figure 8.1 A batwing shaped object seen above Earth's upper atmosphere by the Apollo 9 CSM

Mystic Moon: A Lunar Odyssey

Figure 8.1-A. A 2X Zoom of the feature

Another exciting example captured during the Apollo-10 mission reveals four drone-like features (Fig. 8.2) seen flying at varying heights and distances against the backdrop of the Earth. Unlike their larger counterparts, many of these drones may be utilizing conventional propulsion, which can levitate or float easily, change travel direction, and accelerate rapidly. One can often notice a blue plume emanating from the drones whenever their thrusters are fired. Another drone with a long red plume can be seen moving away from Earth (Fig. 8.2-A).

The presence of these large drones high above the Earth's atmosphere raises the logical question, "Are they being used for harvesting life-sustaining supplies of water, air, and possibly food?" Unbeknownst to us, the Earth may have been sustaining lunar entities for a long time. Needless to say, the Earth can sustain the needs of the lunar entities over the long haul.

If this assumption is indeed plausible, then it is ironic that future terrestrial visitors plan to harvest life-sustaining water and air supplies on the Moon. Instead, we should plan to haul these life-sustaining supplies from Earth by building larger spacecraft.

Chapter 8: Lunar Drones

(Image Credit: NASA/JSC/Project Apollo Archive/flickr)

Figure 8.2 A series of 4 Drones (1 red & 3 blue) captured flying high above the Earth by Apollo 10

The moon is said to have a rare (thin) atmosphere known as the *exosphere* that consists of rare gases such as sodium and potassium that contribute to its halo-like glow. Extremely trace amounts of other gases such as helium, argon, neon, ammonia, methane, and carbon dioxide are also present (NASA, 1975[14]).

---

[14] NASA1975: Apollo 17 Lunar Atmospheric Composition Experiment. Final Report. The University of Texas, Dallas

Mystic Moon: A Lunar Odyssey

Figure 8.2-A Magnified sub-image showing locations of the four drones flying near Earth

Unlike on Earth, the lunar exosphere does not scatter any Solar radiation, and the sky is dark. Consequently, the lunar environment appears dark even during the lunar day. The lunar entities solved this problem by introducing drones capable of illuminating the lunar surface.

Some drones appear to be remotely controlled or programmed to perform specific tasks. One such drone can be seen sampling the side of a large boulder near the Apollo 17 landing area in the *Taurus-Littrow Valley* (Fig. 8.3). Notice the supersonic *Concorde-shaped* wiry nose section with deep brown thrusters in its tail section. The advantage of this type of fascinating nanotechnology is that it can be deployed anywhere over a large area. Our exposure to such completely alien technology can indeed be rewarding.

Chapter 8: Lunar Drones

Figure 8.3 A robotic drone nesting on a large boulder photographed during the Apollo 17 mission

The small robotic drone appearing in Figure 8.3 can be seen clearly when magnified and enhanced (Fig. 8.3-A). It has a wiry supersonic Concorde type of a nose with quad-thruster-like tail section. The alert crew member deserves credit for noticing the drone in the narrow opening.

Mystic Moon: A Lunar Odyssey

Figure 8.3-A The drone after magnification and enhancement

The Apollo 11 mission encountered several spacecraft, drones, and interesting optical phenomena. In one such encounter, two parallel sets of four drone-like features appeared (Fig. 8.4) over its landing area in *Mare Tranquillitatis*. This unexpected spectacle must have surprised the first batch of astronauts to the Moon. No one could have anticipated being able to witness such an optical display in a celestial body with a very thin exosphere. One wonders about what goes through the minds of astronauts witnessing such phenomena during the very first lunar landing mission.

Chapter 8: Lunar Drones

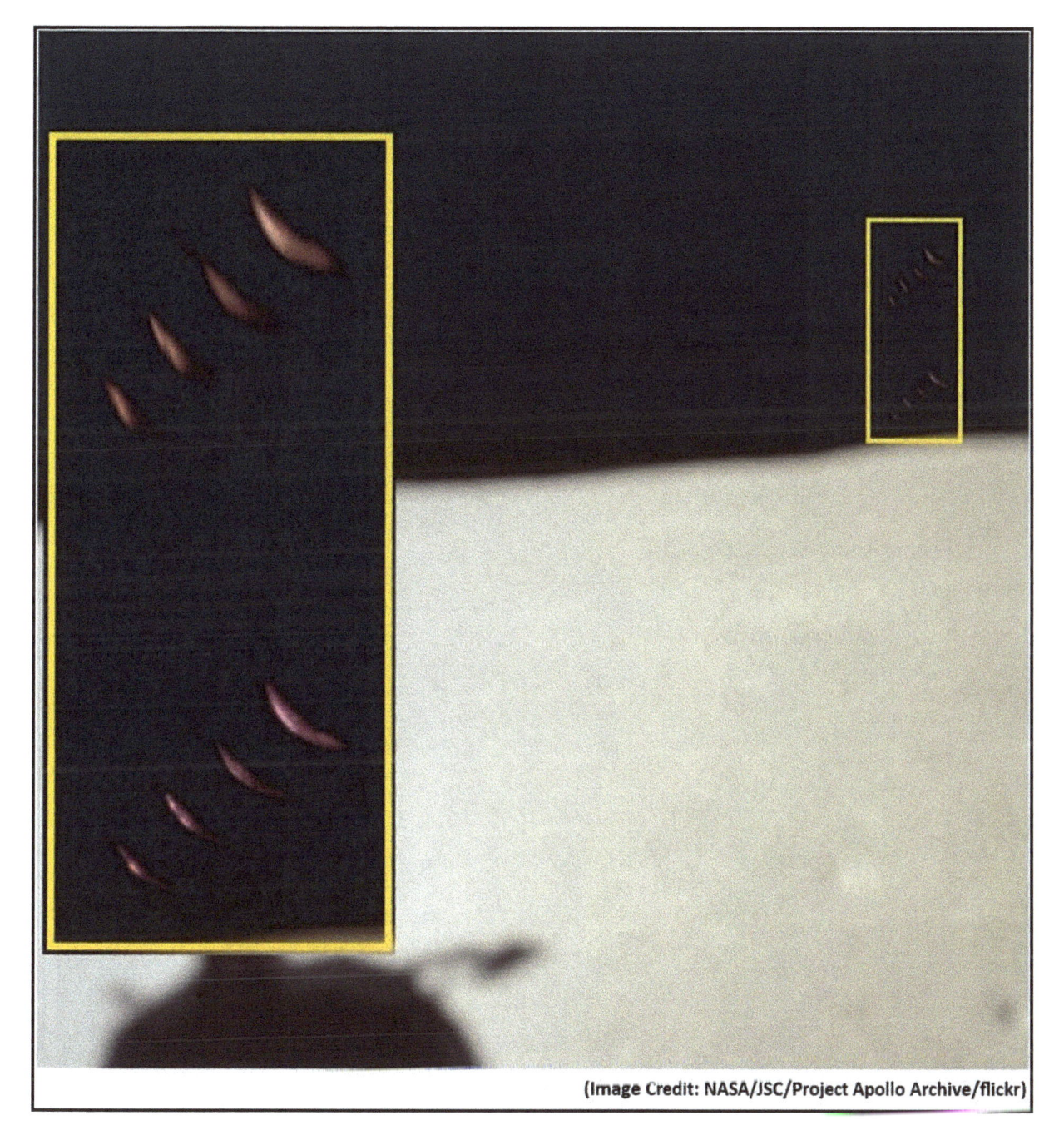

(Image Credit: NASA/JSC/Project Apollo Archive/flickr)

Figure 8.4 A rare optical phenomenon in parallel formation over the APOLLO 11 landing area

One of the most common uses of lunar drones appears to be the illumination of large dark surface areas during the long nights, which last about 14.75 Earth days. A large truffle or dome-shaped source of light (Fig. 8.5) hovering over the lunar surface was captured during the Apollo 15 mission. A 2X magnification (Fig. 8.5-A) reveals a large dome-like source of light.

Mystic Moon: A Lunar Odyssey

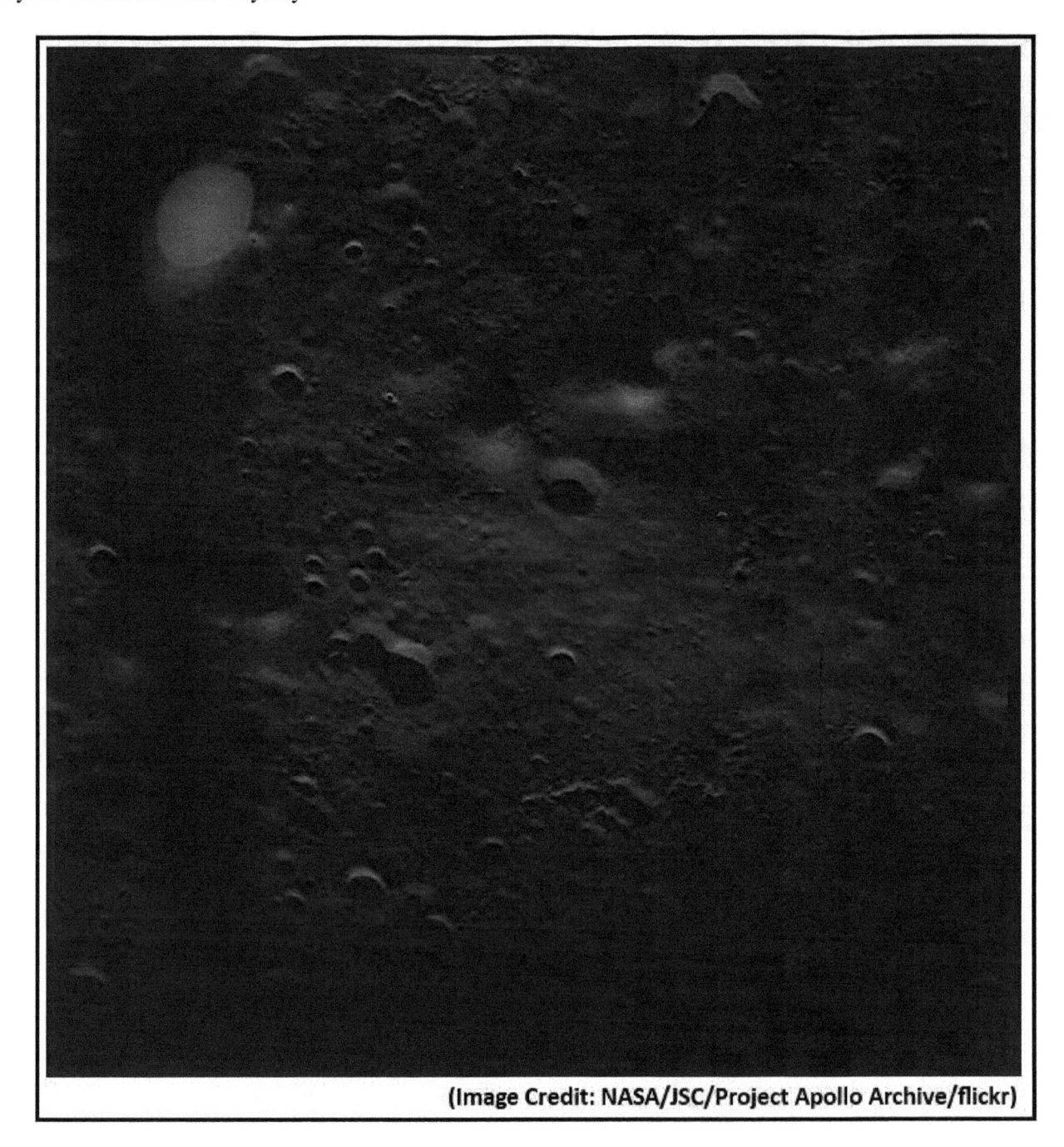

(Image Credit: NASA/JSC/Project Apollo Archive/flickr)

Figure. 8.5 A dome-shaped light drone close to the lunar surface

Chapter 8: Lunar Drones

Figure 8.5-A A 2X magnification of the light drone

Unlike the Earth's atmosphere, the lunar exosphere lacks the capacity to scatter an incident beam of light. For this reason, any artificial source of light should be able to illuminate a wide area.

Here on Earth, our concept of drones is limited to remotely controlled unmanned military craft used in warfare. Nowadays, smaller versions with cameras are used in photography, agriculture, land surveys, roof inspections, package deliveries, and other applications. There are also amazing, remotely controlled toy versions.

The concept of drones appearing on the Moon is a little different. Someone may still control them but are service vehicles performing repetitive tasks such as going around and illuminating areas while in low-level orbits? One naturally wonders who is deploying them, and why. The concurrent sighting of advanced spacecraft near them suggests that the responsible parties may be tracking crew activities. Future lunar explorations may be able to provide us with a better understanding of the technology behind these engineering marvels.

SOME INTERESTING PHENOMENA

As humanity explores the Solar system and beyond, we will undoubtedly encounter many artifacts in imagery sent back to Earth by scientific probes and orbiting satellites that will challenge our imagination, rattle our own scientific foundations, and possibly challenge our religious beliefs.

On Earth, all modes of human transportation are always equipped with glass windshields and or port holes for ease of visibility. Self-driving cars of the future may be equipped with 360^0-FOV cameras that may minimize or even eliminate the need for windows and windshields. Most spacecraft observed on the Moon have no visible signs of windows, hatches, or antennas that one commonly associates with UFOs or UAPs. Further, their linear structural format may be optimized for high-speed travel through deep space.

Similarly, imagine the communications network needed to track hundreds of spacecraft of various shapes and sizes deployed on and around the Moon. Moreover, these spacecraft can all land and take off from anywhere on the Moon and even remain suspended in space. How are these epitomes of technology communicating with each other in harmony?

LUNAR PLUMES

Nikola Tesla, the great Serbian American inventor who provided us with alternating current, visualized the possibility of wireless power transmission; unfortunately, he faced numerous technical challenges, social restraints, and financial difficulties that derailed his dream. Had he been successful, we would all have enjoyed wireless charging alongside Wi-Fi. Imagine not huddling around cell phone charging stations at airports and other public places.

In this regard, a couple of stunning images captured by Apollo 11 and then later by Apollo 15 while flying over the far side of the Moon deserve attention. The first image (Fig. 8.6) of Apollo 11 shows a tall, bright plume near the *Lamont* crater on the western edge of *Mare Tranquillitatis*. The flame could be the result of gases venting out from below the lunar surface. The flame also appears to be somehow sheared off to the left.

The lunar surface appears to host more than one such plume. A more complex-shaped plume was captured during the Apollo 15 mission while orbiting over the Humboldt region of the Moon (Fig. 8.7). The large 'door handle'-shaped bright plume appears to extend vertically for several miles above the lunar surface before veering off in the form of a door handle. Any noticeable blurriness could be due to the venting of hot gases from below the surface. The *Humboldt Region* extends into the far side of the Moon.

We do not yet know with certainty how plumes behave on the Moon. These plumes may be due to the venting of ionized gases from below the ground.

Chapter 8: Lunar Drones

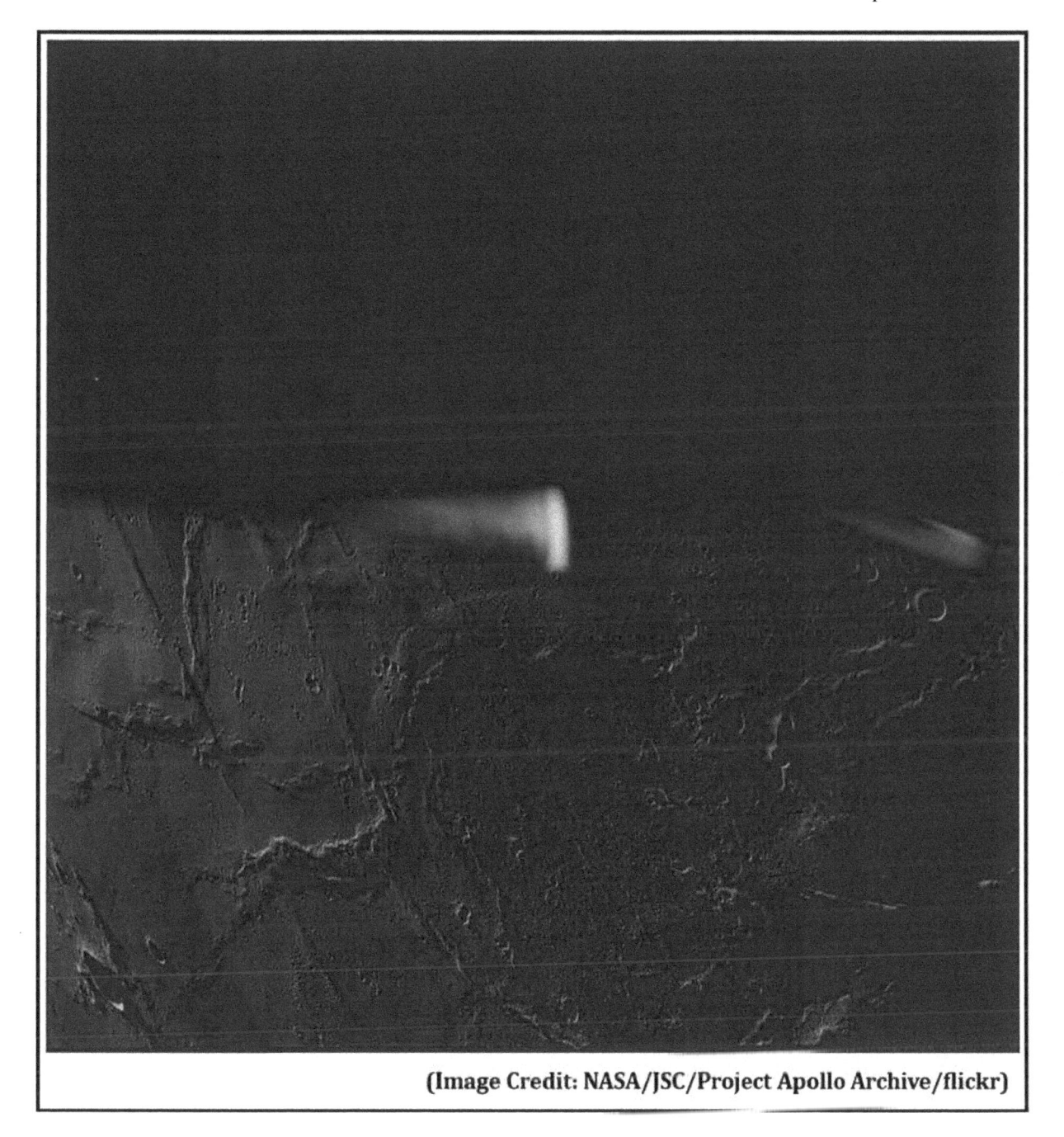

(Image Credit: NASA/JSC/Project Apollo Archive/flickr)

Figure 8.6 A bright vertical plume appears to shear off to the left near the *Lamont* crater

Mystic Moon: A Lunar Odyssey

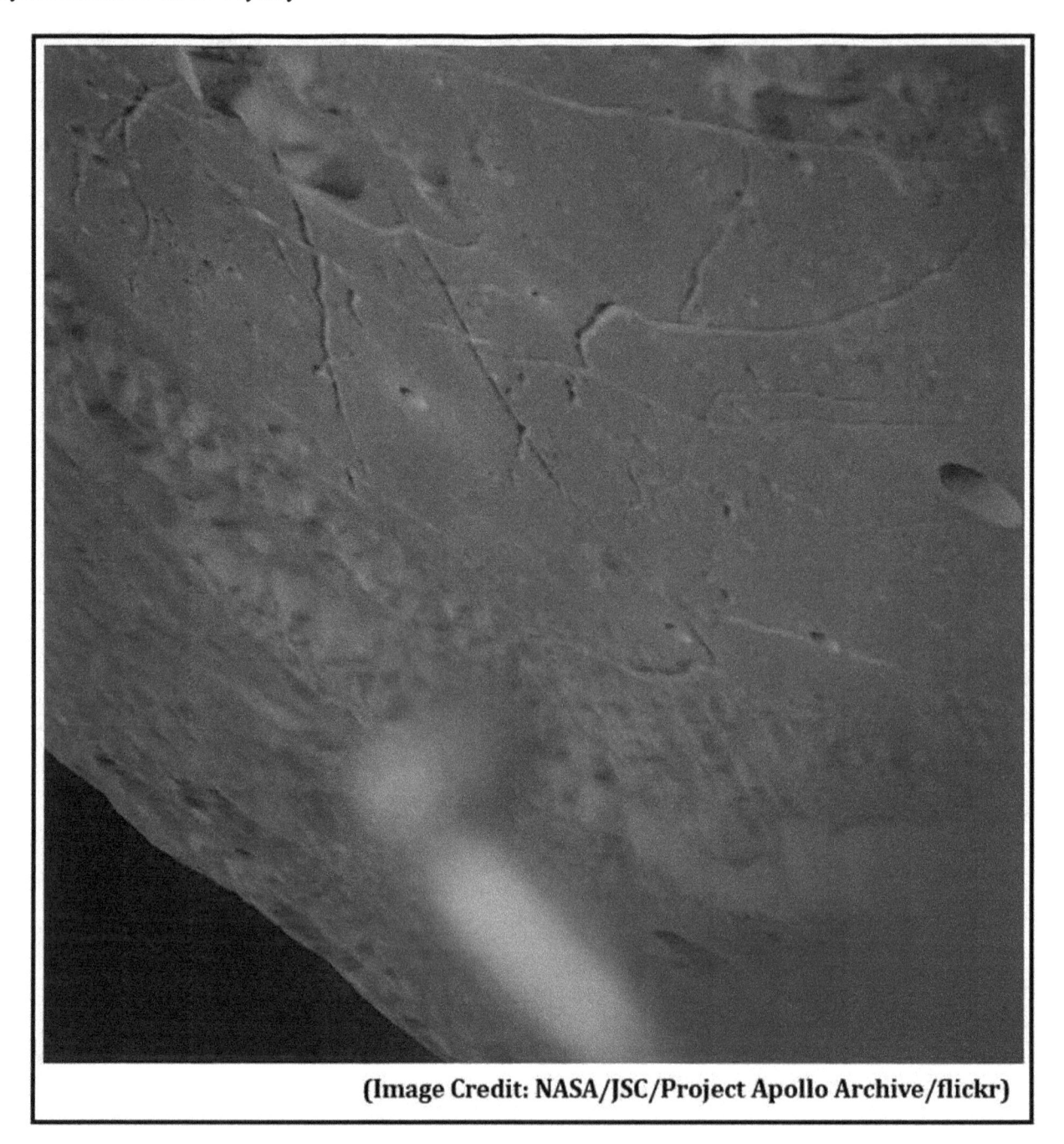

(Image Credit: NASA/JSC/Project Apollo Archive/flickr)

Figure 8.7 Apollo 15 image of a 'door handle' shaped plume captured in orbit over the Humboldt region on the far side of the Moon

Several examples of drones identified during the Apollo missions were presented. Many of them were designed to possibly perform specific tasks. Some of these drones appear to be capable of functioning independently without much guidance. These advanced drones were certainly developed by some well-established lunar entity of unknown origin.

* * * * * *

Chapter 9: Masters of Light

Our eyes can visualize light in the electromagnetic spectrum's visible (400-700 nanometers) range. Atmospheric processes such as reflection, diffraction, transmission, and scattering determine how much light is visible on any given day on Earth. Clear days are bright and sunny, while cloudy days are dull due to diffuse radiation penetrating clouds layers.

On Earth, light is scattered whenever it impinges on particles of dust or other material close to the wavelength of light. On a clear sunny day, the sky's blue is attributed to light scattering in shorter wavelengths. On the other hand, the evening sky appears in several shades of yellow and red due to the scattering of the longer wavelengths of sunlight.

Deep space is devoid of any atmosphere, so there is no possibility of scattering without some gaseous, liquid, or solid medium. Sunlight impinging on any surface along its path can make it appear bright. For example, the side of a spacecraft facing the sun will appear bright and become extremely hot, while the shaded side of the spacecraft and the surrounding space environment will appear dark and extremely cold; it is estimated to be at 30K (-243.15°C, -405.67°F). Stars and other heavenly bodies will appear bright to the naked eye in the darkness of space.

Sunrise and Sunset on the Moon

We are all familiar with local times of sunrise and sunset on Earth. However, sunrise and sunset on the Moon occur over an extended period. This section briefly overviews some basic concepts associated with sunrise and sunset on the Moon.

The Earth rotates around its axis once every twenty-four hours (23 hours, 56 minutes, and 4.09 seconds) and revolves around the Sun in an elliptical orbit over a year (365.25 days). Mars rotates around its axis in just over 24 hours, 37 minutes, and 22 seconds.

On the other hand, the Moon rotates around its own axis in 27.32 days relative to the stars, and this is known as a *sidereal month*. However, the Moon takes 29.53 Earth days (708.73 hours:29 days, 12 hours, and 44 minutes) to return to the same exact position relative to the Earth, and this time interval is known as a *synodic month*. This difference of 2.2 days between the synodic month and the sidereal month of the Moon arises because the Earth moves during the 27.3 days the Moon takes to rotate around its axis. Consequently, the Moon takes an additional 2.2 days to compensate for this difference and align itself precisely at the same position relative to the Sun (Ahrens, C).

This implies that if one were to observe the Sun on the lunar horizon during sunrise, it would take about 29.53 days to return to the same exact position in the sky, whereas, on Earth, the Sun returns to the same position approximately once every twenty-four hours. On the Moon, the Sun rises at 0.51° per hour (Fig. 9.1).

> ➤ *Lunar Day:* The time between two Noons or sunsets on the Moon is 708.73 hours (29.53 Earth days).
>
> ➤ *Daylight:* Daylight on the Moon lasts continuously for 14.765 Earth days (~14 lunar sidereal)

Mystic Moon: A Lunar Odyssey

> *Night:* A night on the Moon lasts continuously for about 14.765 Earth days (~14 lunar sidereal)

An informative animation of a lunar day is available from NASA's Scientific Visualization Studio at the Goddard Space Flight Center (NASA/GSFC, 2017)[15].

Lunar days are extremely hot, peaking around 270°F (132.2°C), and lunar nights tend to be extremely cold, dipping to around minus 280°F (-173.3°C).

Figure 9.1 A *synodic* month on the Moon lasts for 29.53 Earth days. Both night and day last for 14.75 Earth days each, and the Sun rises at the rate of 0.51° per hour over the lunar horizon

The position of the Sun in the sky is defined by a set of three angular measures known as (i) the *elevation angle* (h), (ii) the *zenith angle* (z), and (iii) the *azimuth angle* (A) (Fig. 9.2). The angle made by the Sun with the local horizon is defined as the *elevation angle* (h), and it indicates how high the Sun is above the horizon. The *elevation angle* ranges from 0° (just before sunrise) to 180° (at sunset). Shadows tend to be cast longest when the Sun is at low or high elevation angles and shortest at midday or noon. Note that the Sun is directly at *nadir* (overhead at 90°) on the Moon only after about 7.4 Earth-days from the onset of local sunrise. The elevation angle can also be used to refer to the angle made by any flying object within the lunar surface.

Similarly, the angle made by the Sun with the local vertical is known as the zenith angle (Z). It also complements the elevation angle (i.e., Z = 90°– h). The Sun is said to be at the zenith (h = 90° and z = 0°) at noon on Earth.

On Earth, the *azimuth angle* (A) tells us in which compass direction the Sun is located at that moment and is always measured clockwise from the north.

Tourists wake up before dawn and have their cameras ready to glimpse spectacular sunrises on the beach in Key West, Florida, in the United States. On a sunny day, the Sun rises slowly on the horizon in the shape of a bright arc and becomes a full disc in about five minutes. The Sun rises at a rate of about 15°

---
[15] https://svs.gsfc.nasa.gov/12739: NASA/GSFC (2017).

per hour in the terrestrial sky. The Earth's angular rotation around its own axis is responsible for this apparent movement of the Sun from east to west. Tourists gather again in the evening to watch spectacular sunsets in the west.

Unlike on Earth, the thin lunar *exosphere* eliminates the scattering of light resulting in a dark sky. The limited scattering of light in the upper levels of the lunar exosphere by non-homogenous dust particles results in what is known as the *Lunar Horizon Glow* (LHG) (Richard et al., 2011). The bombardment of the lunar surface by meteorites may generate localized showers of dust, sand, and rocks that can temporarily modify the environment for incident radiation as a direct consequence of the negligible exosphere, sunrise and sunset on the Moon occur abruptly.

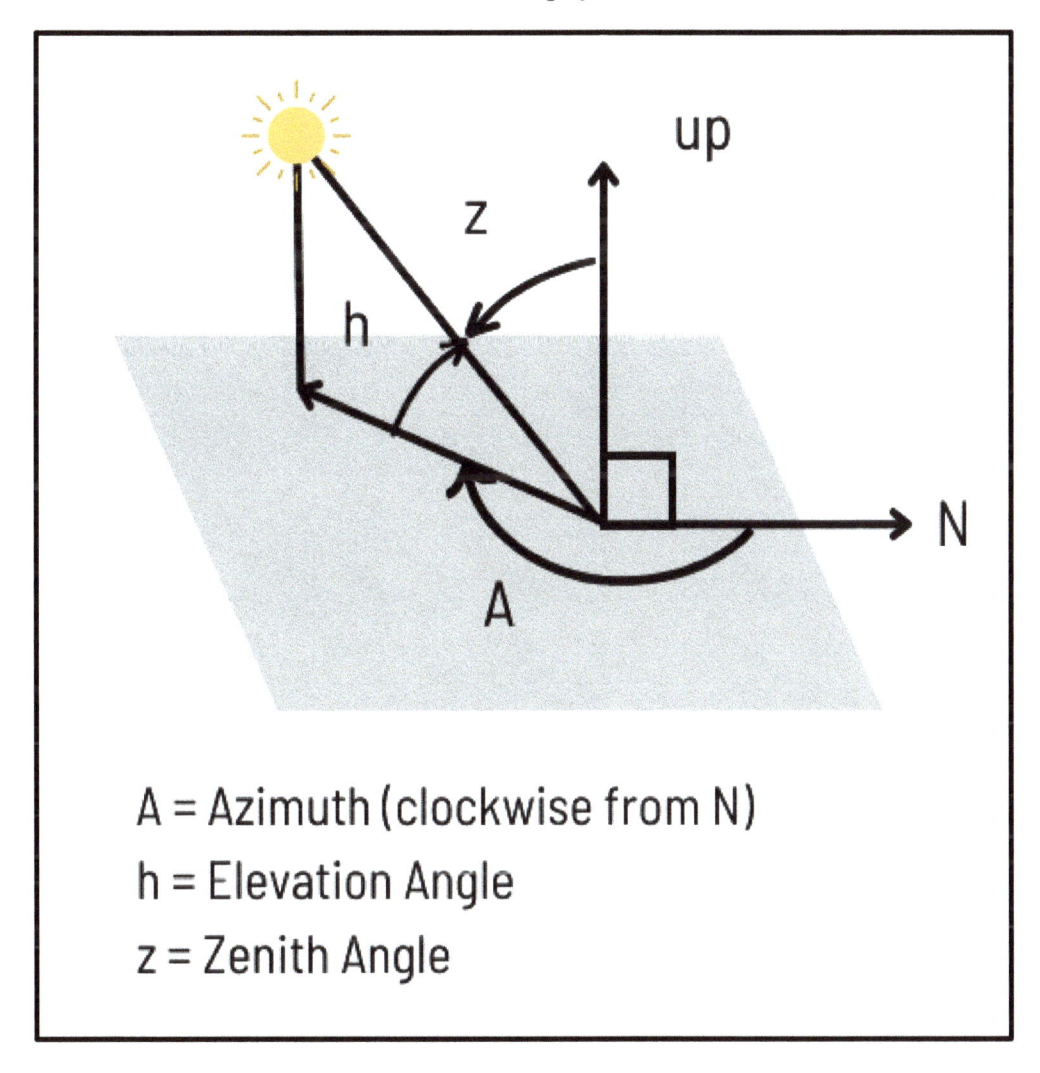

Figure 9.2 Angular positions of the Sun relative to any point on the surface

Similarly, nightfall lasts for another 14.75 Earth days. The long duration effectively shuts down all lunar exploration-related equipment powered by solar arrays. New alternate sources of power are being developed to overcome this problem.

The brightness of the lunar surface creates the optical illusion of a pitch-dark sky when one looks up at it suddenly. The high reflectivity of snow on a bright, sunny winter day can cause temporary blindness if one is not wearing protective sunglasses; the eyes will take some time to readjust themselves. Even modern cell phone cameras have difficulty focusing under low light conditions when subjects are viewed against a dark backdrop.

An imaginary moving line known as the *terminator* (Fig. 9.3) marks the demarcation between the illuminated and unlit sides of the Moon. It has a transition zone in which the Sun's oblique rays can illuminate slopes and other higher surface terrain casting long shadows. Careful planning on the part of NASA scientists and engineers ensured that all the Apollo lunar landing missions were conducted during the long daylight periods on the Moon.

(Image Credit: NASA/JSC/Project Apollo Archive/flickr)

Figure 9.3 The *terminator* demarcates sunlit and shadow segments of the Moon as it revolves

One Sun Too Many

The orbital geometry of Earth-Moon (libration) is such that about 41 percent of the Moon is never visible from Earth. The far side or dark side of the Moon is the hemisphere always facing away from Earth. Not that it is dark out there, but just not visible from Earth. Probably unknown entities or distant visitors to the Moon may have capitalized on this orbital niche to settle there to remain incognito.

Consequently, anyone inhabiting the far side of the Moon may have enjoyed an uninterrupted way of life until the advent of modern-day space travel. Recently, missions such as Russia's Luna, NASA's Apollo Missions, India's *Chandrayan,* and China's *Change'* have all challenged this tranquility. Even the hitherto hidden far side of the Moon no longer provides a safe refuge for anyone.

The lunar sky always appears dark in the background (Fig. 9.4) in pictures due to a lack of scattering by the extremely rare exosphere. The average albedo of the lunar surface is only 0.12 (12%) compared to that of the Earth 0.37 (37%) and Mars 0.11 (11%). The surface albedo may vary based on the Sun's elevation angle. Readers may have noticed that pictures from Mars appear much brighter than on the Moon due to the larger scattering associated with its denser atmosphere.

Figure 9.4 The dark sky and dimly lit surface are a direct result of the extremely rare lunar exosphere (Image Credit: NASA/JSC/Project Apollo Archive/Flickr)

This tranquility was suddenly broken by the unexpected arrival of a bright light source from the right (Fig. 9.5) near the Apollo 12 landing site in *Oceanus Procellarum*, a rift valley (Jeffrey, 2014). Suddenly, the lunar environment immediately lit up in a flash. The artificial bright beam of light emanating from possibly a drone of unknown alien origin can be seen piercing through the surrounding darkness of the lunar sky. It was as if someone had turned on a giant flashlight to brighten things up for the crew.

Two characteristic light beam components, disk-like and funnel-shaped, can be seen along its central axis. The Sun's rays cannot illuminate any part of the lunar sky; only sunlight incident on the surface can illuminate it. Our eyes can visualize light in the visible part of the Solar spectrum; therefore, the source of light from the alien craft must generally be operating in the visible spectral range. Unlike the Sun, rays from this source can brightly illuminate the lunar surface in the immediate vicinity. Such a light source must have been developed exclusively to brighten darkness during long lunar nights.

It is highly likely that someone on the Moon may have been intently watching the Apollo 12 astronauts conducting activities under the dim natural sunlit conditions and decided to surprise them. Whether this can be construed as a gesture of goodwill or just being disruptive is debatable. The astronauts themselves may be aware of the circumstances but are forbidden to discuss such incidents on camera. Nonetheless, these repetitive visitations by unknown alien drones beaming lights over the astronauts continued to plague all of the Apollo Program's lunar surface EVAs and scientific experiments.

Hints of unknown alien spacecraft around the Moon may have been noticed as early as the Apollo 8 mission that orbited it as a precursor to lunar landings. The Apollo 9 mission conducted the separation and subsequent rendezvous of the Lunar Module (LM) with the Command Module (CSM) while in low-Earth orbit. The Apollo 10 mission successfully executed all aspects of an actual moon landing, but it was also in low-Earth orbit as a precursor to the actual moon landing by Apollo 11. Extraterrestrial spacecraft may have been sighted over the distant horizon high above the Earth, as evidenced by several pictures taken by the crew.

The frequent presence of lunar drones and the spectacle of lights showered upon the crew trying to conduct experiments may have been both eerie and annoying. It is difficult to ascertain whether these unsolicited gestures of lighting up the lunar sky were meant as a friendly gesture or a form of harassment by the hovering drones above. Several incidents of this type have been encountered during lunar surface explorations, beginning with Apollo 12 and persisting through the final Apollo 17 mission.

Typically, each light drone moves very rapidly from either northeast-to-northwest or northwest-to-northeast direction illuminating a large swath of the lunar surface. A pair of funnel-shaped features always accompany the leading edge of the beam; these may be used in controlling both its intensity and the areal extent of coverage. In response, the dimly lit lunar surface suddenly brightens up and attains light saturation as the drone passes through and quickly returns to its previous state.

The Apollo 12 crew spent a total of 31.6 hours on the lunar surface. The Sun's elevation angle could have only risen over the horizon by about 16° from its initial position when the LM landed. During this mission, the crew conducted two separate EVAs totaling 7 hours, 45 minutes, 18 seconds. In an unexpected close encounter, a huge linear spacecraft (Fig. 9.5) cast a watchful eye on another alien source of bright light illuminating the Apollo 12 ALSEP area from around the two o'clock position in the sky.

Chapter 9: Masters of Light

The cylindrical spacecraft may actually be trapezoidal in shape. This is not part of the light source or any camera-related optical illusion or reflectance. The large octagonal-shaped disk towards the right is due to reflection on the camera lens itself.

(Image Credit: NASA/JSC/Apollo Image Archive/flickr)

Figure 9.5 A huge linear UAP watches over the area as the drone moves away

Unlike On Earth, the lunar exosphere offers negligible resistance to the Sun's rays falling on the surface. There is no mechanism for incident solar radiation to be scattered and brighten the sky or the environment. The low surface albedo implies that the lunar surface absorbs all the heat, resulting in extremely high temperatures approaching 260°F (127°C) near the lunar equator during the long daylight hours. Temperatures during its long lunar nights can dip to a frigid minus 280°F (-173°C), with even cooler

Mystic Moon: A Lunar Odyssey

temperatures in regions permanently shielded from sunlight (NASA: Moon Facts)[16].

Paradoxically, the Sun appears significantly brighter on the Moon than on Earth due to the rare exosphere. Without a sunlight filter, one can never contemplate taking a picture of the bright Sun on Earth. Two things would happen: the camera would be ruined, and more importantly, the photographer would lose eyesight in one or both eyes.

For these reasons, it is unlikely anyone would point a Hasselblad camera directly at the Sun. Moreover, in the Sixties, carrying a camera weighing two pounds on a lunar mission would have cost about a million dollars. Here on Earth, one can take spectacular pictures of the Sun during sunrise or sunset over the ocean. However, on the Moon, both sunrise and sunset take place rather abruptly like turning a light switch on or off. The surrounding skies always remain dark during both lunar day and night.

Given this background, let us examine an incident in which a suspected light source traversed *Oceanus Procellarum*, where the Apollo-12 crew was conducting experiments. An earlier scene shows normal-light conditions on the surface during their mission (Fig. 9.4). A series of images demonstrates the sequence of events that took place (Fig. 9.6a-f). In the first scene (Fig. 9.6a), a powerful light source appears towards the northwest. It then moves towards the northeast of the scene (Figs. 9.6 (c-e)) and finally moves away (Fig. 9.6f), leaving behind the levitating rectangular spacecraft. This is a transient artificial light source moving along an arc from northwest to northeast in this sequence of image frames.

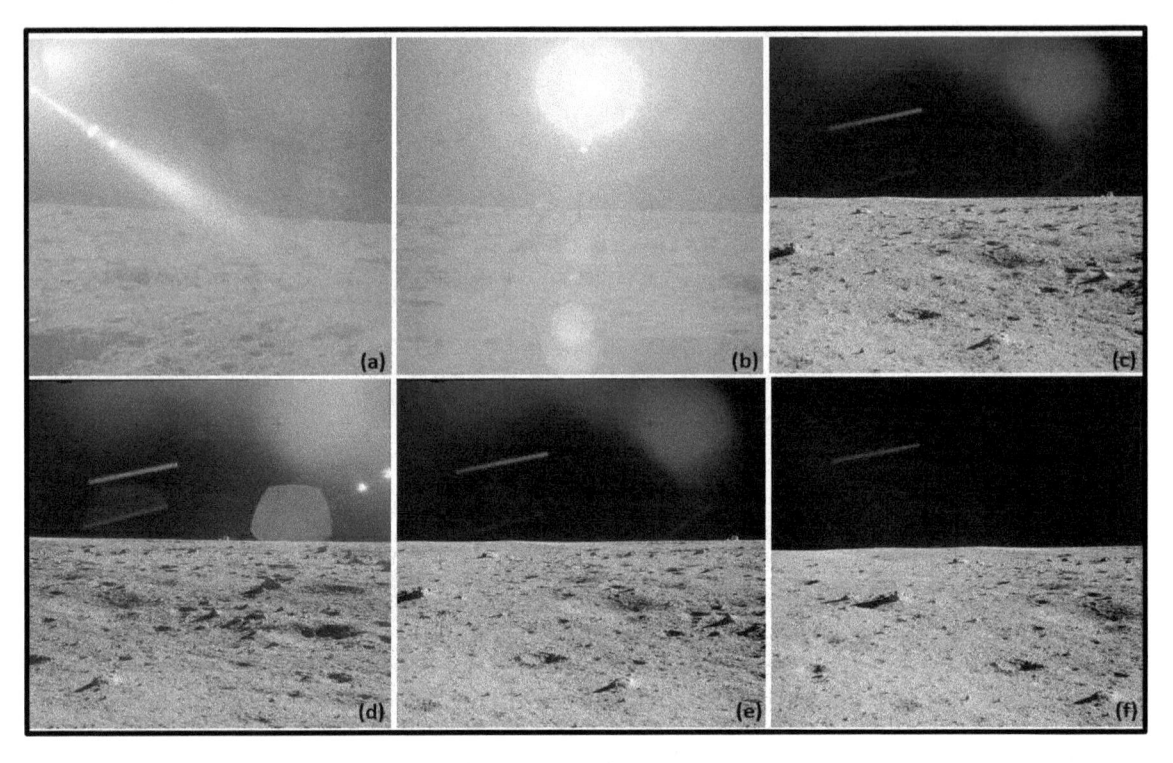

Figure 9.6 (a-f). A light drone moving northwest-northeast illuminates the Apollo-12 work area in *Oceanus Procellarum* under the watch of large linear spacecraft
(Image Credits: NASA/JSC/Project Apollo Archive/Flickr)

---

[16]NASA Moon Facts: https://science.nasa.gov/moon/facts/

Chapter 9: Masters of Light

The Apollo 14 mission, which landed in the Fra Mauro region of the Moon, also experienced its share of visitations by the light drone (Fig. 9.7a-f). It shows a relatively serene scene with a light beam just about to emerge from the northeast (Fig. 9.7a). The next two frames show that the entire area was quickly saturated with light (Fig. 9.7b-c). The drone then proceeded to head in a northwesterly direction (Fig. 9.7d) and kept moving away westward (Fig. 9.7e) before finally disappearing (Fig. 9.7f).

It appears that the light source is the drone and may not be the sun since it rushed rapidly from the northeast to the northwest; the scene quickly returned to normal with the drone's disappearance (Fig. 9.7d-f). If it were the sun, all six scenes would exhibit similar brightness.

Figure 9.7 (a-f) A light drone flies northeast-northwest over Fra Mauro's Apollo 14 landing area (Images Credit: NASA/JSC/Project Apollo Archive/Flickr)

The Apollo 15 mission landed on the Imbrium Basin's eastern edge in the Palus Putredinis region. It was the first of the 'J' missions, equipped with considerably expanded capabilities for conducting science experiments. It conducted three 7-hour Extravehicular Activities (EVAs) such as walking around, sampling rocks, and conducting scientific experiments; it was also the first mission to deploy the four-wheeled Lunar Roving Vehicle (LRV) on the surface of the Moon (NASA-15)[17]. This mission also experienced some disruptions in the form of unsolicited displays of bright lights by drones.

In this remarkable example, a lunar light drone casts a narrow but powerful beam of light toward the

---

[17] NASA-15: https://www.nasa.gov/mission_pages/apollo/missions/apollo15.html

Mystic Moon: A Lunar Odyssey

surface (Fig. 9.8a) and illuminates the Rover's communication antenna (Fig. 9.8b). In Figure 9.8a, the light beam appears to cast a bulbous ring, suggesting the possibility that the source may be a large artificial bulb.

Figure 9.8 (a-b) A lunar light drone casts a powerful narrow beam onto the surface (a), and bounces off the LRV's communication antenna (b)
(Image Credits: NASA/JSC/Project Apollo Archive/Flickr)

The Apollo 16 mission's LM *Orion* landed on the Descartes Highlands at coordinates 8.97°S, 15.51°E and spent a total surface time of 71 hours, 2 minutes, and 13 seconds on the surface. During this time, the astronauts conducted three EVAs totaling 20 hours (NASA-16)[18]. The Apollo 16 astronauts also reported encountering several fly-by incidents.

One such incident is documented in Figure 9.9 (a-d). In the images, a light source can be seen around the 1 o'clock position (Fig. 9.9a) and then moving, emitting a powerful beam of light (Fig. 9.9b). The source then moved to the 11 O'clock position (Fig. 9.9c) before finally moving away towards the northwest corner (Fig. 9.9d). Unlike on Earth, the Sun rises at a rate of 0.51° per hour on the Moon. This suggests that the moving light source is not the Sun but likely a drone. Absolutely, the light source moving from right to left is a drone. The brightness of the Sun remains constant, but its shadows can be cast by hills and in craters depending upon the viewing angle. The light drones also appear able to change the intensity of light they emit and may be able to adjust the speed of light emitted.

---

[18] NASA-16: https://www.nasa.gov/mission_pages/apollo/missions/apollo16.html

Chapter 9: Masters of Light

Figure 9.9 (a-d) A fast-moving light source casts a powerful beam over the Apollo-16 landing area. Enhanced images (b) and (c) reveal a narrow beam moving from northeast to northwest. (Images Credit: NASA/JSC/Project Apollo Archive/Flickr)

The Apollo 17 crew spent three days in the Taurus-Littrow Valley in Mare Serenitatis. During this time, the astronauts conducted three lunar-surface Extravehicular Activities (EVAs) for about 22 hours and 4 minutes. The Lunar Roving Vehicle (LRV) was driven over 35.9 kilometers, making it the longest EVA among all the Apollo missions (NASA-17). Throughout their mission, the Sun's elevation angle would have shifted by approximately 38.25 degrees across the lunar sky (Fig. 9.10).

Mystic Moon: A Lunar Odyssey

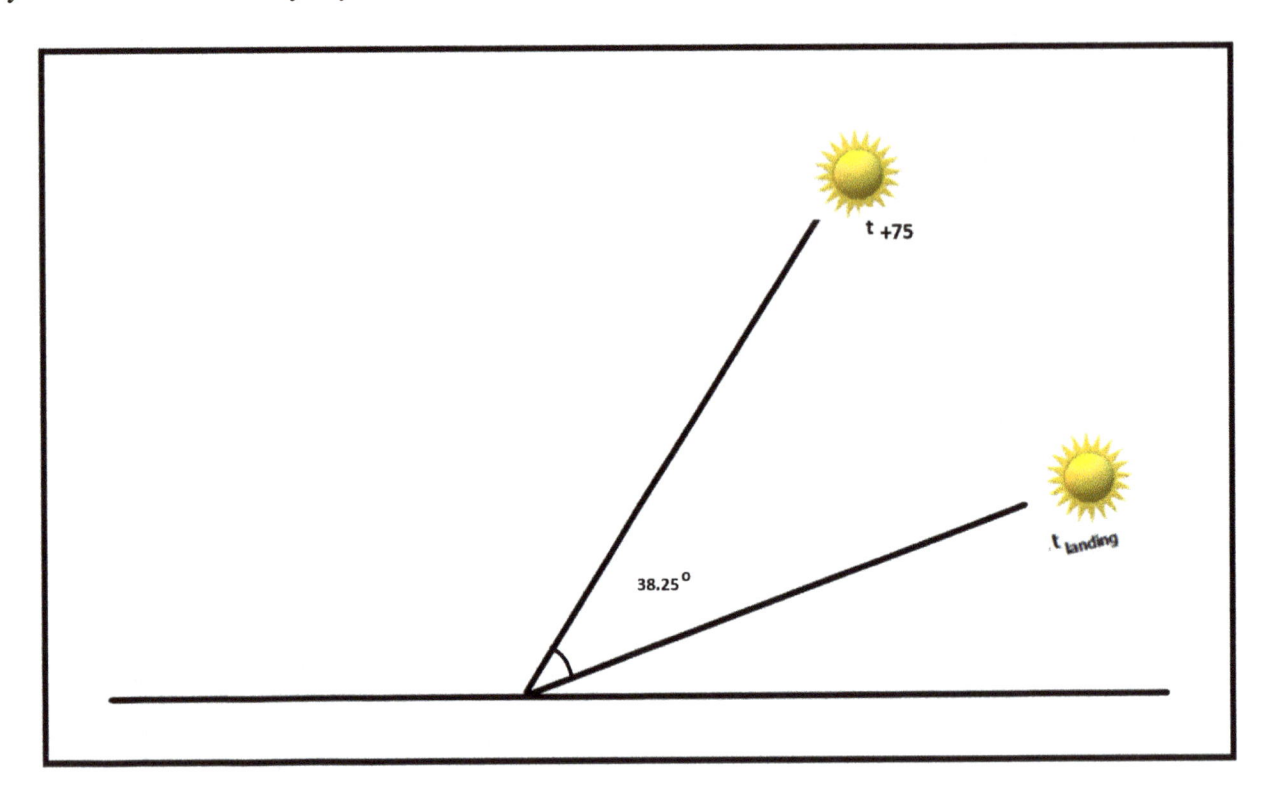

Figure 9.10 Elevation angle of the Sun at Apollo 17's landing (t $_{landing}$) would have shifted by about 38.25° at the conclusion of its mission some 75 hours (t $_{+75}$) later

The Apollo 17 mission may have experienced multiple encounters with light drones. At times, these encounters caused the Apollo 17 crew's EVAs to come to a standstill by saturating the entire environment with blinding light, leading to overexposed camera shots. It is evident that the intensity of solar radiation cannot suddenly change and reach saturation levels.

Four different types of film were used during their mission, depending upon the application. High-speed black-and-white (HBW), Plus XX, and ASA80-125 film were used in the 70mm magazines G, H, I, J, K, M, N, and R. It is quite possible that the unknown entities responsible for these lights may have higher light tolerance levels than human beings.

It is important to consider the optical properties of light beams cast by lunar alien sources from a scientific standpoint. An intriguing image shows a beam of light hitting the Apollo 17 S-band antenna (Fig. 9.11) and appears to follow the Law of Reflection in optics. According to this law, "the incident reflected, and normal rays to the surface should all be in the same plane, and the angle of reflection should equal the angle of incidence." It is fascinating to capture an incident beam of light on film, resembling an illustrative diagram in a physics textbook on optics. In other words, the entire path of the incident beam of light was captured on film as if it were in slow motion. This raises the astonishing possibility that the alien entities are manipulating the speed of light emitted by the drones. This is truly an incredible scene captured during the Apollo 17 mission and can be classified as one of the best images in all of NASA's lunar archives.

Chapter 9: Masters of Light

**Figure 9.11 A miraculous image of a beam of light bouncing off Apollo 17's S-band antenna
(Image Credit: NASA/JSC/Project Apollo Archive/Flickr)**

Sometimes, in image analysis, it is beneficial to examine multiple scenes to gain a clear understanding of the situation. Reviewing a sequence of images often reveals information that might otherwise be overlooked. These lights on the drone seem capable of moving from either west to east or east to west quickly.

The sequence of the following six images (Fig. 9.12a-f) vividly depicts a light UAP swiftly traversing the Taurus-Littrow Valley during Apollo 17's mission before vanishing. Initially, the scene was tranquil, with the Sun softly illuminating the valley as anticipated (Fig. 9.12a); note the small hill in the upper part. Suddenly, the drone materializes in the northeastern sky, projecting a potent light beam (Fig. 9.12b). It

Mystic Moon: A Lunar Odyssey

then proceeds to move towards the north (Fig. 9.12c-d), and subsequently to the northwest, where it emits a powerful beam of light (Fig. 9.12e) before gradually fading away (Fig. 9.12f). The gently undulating hill in the background acts as a topographical ground control point, clearly delineating the drone's trajectory from northeast to northwest.

9.12 (a-f) A light drone moves across *Taurus-Littrow Valley*, shining a powerful beam of light. It quickly moved over the small hill in the background, revealing that it may not be the Sun. (Images Credit: NASA/JSC/Project Apollo Archive/Flickr).

These low-flying light drones may have been developed to illuminate the lunar surface during long nights or even under dimly lit conditions during daylight. They may fly low to light up the terrain as and when needed.

If confirmed, the presence of alien light drones would require future crews to be more vigilant during lunar surface explorations. Fortunately, the interactions during the Apollo missions seemed harmless and friendly. However, those interactions were limited to the Apollo program around fifty-five years ago. Now, the frequency of lunar missions has significantly increased as multiple countries are heading to the SPA basin. Private contractors are also evaluating their launch capabilities to support the Artemis Program. It remains to be seen how the increased lunar traffic, driven by several countries pursuing lunar missions, will ultimately unfold.

* * * * * *

Chapter 10: Ancient Glass Artifacts

Our moon, a celestial body that has captivated humanity for centuries, is not without its mysteries. Its history, veiled in historical archives, presents a tapestry of enigmatic and perplexing scenarios, inviting us to delve deeper.

I spent much time researching the Apollo archives for clues about anything unusual, and this effort paid off in several instances. Since this was uncharted territory, I had to trust my intuition and scientific judgment in the investigative process. The weekend astronomer in us might feel challenged to make sense of the Apollo archives available on Flickr. Many people can identify strange and perplexing features but cannot make sense of them. Visitors to these sites may be awestruck and post a comment or even "Fave" their favorite scene.

Among the numerous images, we have witnessed a recurring theme of bright lights, gigantic "*U*" and "∩" shaped insignias or arches in the sky above and on the land below. The question of who or what is responsible for these patterns remains a mystery, inviting us to speculate.

The Yuga Cycles suggest the possibility of a highly intelligent ancestral human civilization that may have existed millions of years ago. This raises the probability that some artifacts observed in the Apollo imagery could be millions of years old. Additionally, there is evidence of a more recent presence of lunar spacecraft, or Unidentified Aerial Phenomena (UAPs) observed on and around the Moon.

It is possible that intelligent beings have left their mark on the Moon throughout its long history. This means we could encounter a mix of civilizations responsible for what we find on the Moon, including ancient artifacts from millions of years ago and more recent contributions. These ancient civilizations on the Moon likely depended on Earth for their survival.

Some researchers have suggested the presence of possible lunar inhabitants, as they have observed structures and settlement patterns in satellite imagery of the far side of the Moon. G. Leonard (1976), Barra (2012), and others have contributed to this research. This book, however, focuses exclusively on analyzing images from the Apollo Hasselblad archives, which are accessible on Flickr.

Scientists are considering establishing human colonies on the Moon within large lava tubes that crisscross the lunar landscape. These hollow lava tubes could protect against meteorite bombardment and insulate inhabitants from temperature fluctuations. Additionally, human habitats could be built within hemispherical glass domes, where people can live, grow food, and conduct scientific experiments. However, all necessary raw materials and supplies must be transported from Earth.

OMG! Glass!

The Apollo 16 LM Orion seems to have landed very close to a large vertical glass wall in the Descartes Highlands. Just behind the wall is a tall, glass tower shaped like a chess "rook". The tower looks old and worn, indicating that it could be of very ancient origin.

A luminous light source emanates behind the tower, revealing horizontal rope-like reinforcement striations. These features, used to fortify the wall and the tower, bear the marks of time and meteorite bombardment. With its weathered facade, the tower stands as a testament to the forces of nature it has endured over the years, further enriching this visual observation.

While the image of interest is in Flickr, I have chosen not to include it entirely to respect the privacy of the astronaut near the LM. I invite the curious reader to explore this captivating image in the Apollo 16 Flickr archive, fostering a deeper engagement with my findings.

In a previous image, there are some details of the Apollo 16 LM standing near a glass wall with the silhouette of the Rook-shaped tower (Fig. 10.1). The crew member in the distance is not identifiable. An unknown light source brightly illuminates a large vertical sheet of glass. The uniform scattering of light behind the wall suggests that the wall could be part of a larger glass enclosure filled with a gaseous substance such as air. Under normal conditions, the lunar sky would appear pitch dark.

The Rook-shaped glass tower (Fig. 10.2), a subset of the original image with the astronaut, is magnified to reveal spiraling striations that reinforce its structural integrity. These striations also extend across the vertical wall, indicating similarities in their construction. The amber color may be associated with the scattering of light within the medium.

The tower appears dilapidated, signifying its ancient origins, possibly several million years old. The Moon may have served as a spaceport in the very distant past. Future missions to the Moon may be able to revisit this site to learn more about the nature of its setup.

The physical dimensions of the glass wall and tower are unknown, but they both appear to be significantly taller than the LM parked in front. The lunar regolith may be the source of the glass used in their construction.

Has anyone considered using glass as a construction material in an environment where meteorite impacts are a reality? Have they developed a form of tempered glass that can withstand meteorite impacts on the lunar surface? Someone from the distant past produced a solution that would transform the construction of structures on the Moon.

Chapter 10: Ancient Glass Artifacts

Figure 10.1 The Apollo 16 LM landed near a glass wall silhouetted by a *Rook*-shaped glass tower. Notice horizontal reinforcement striations running across the wall and tower.

Mystic Moon: A Lunar Odyssey

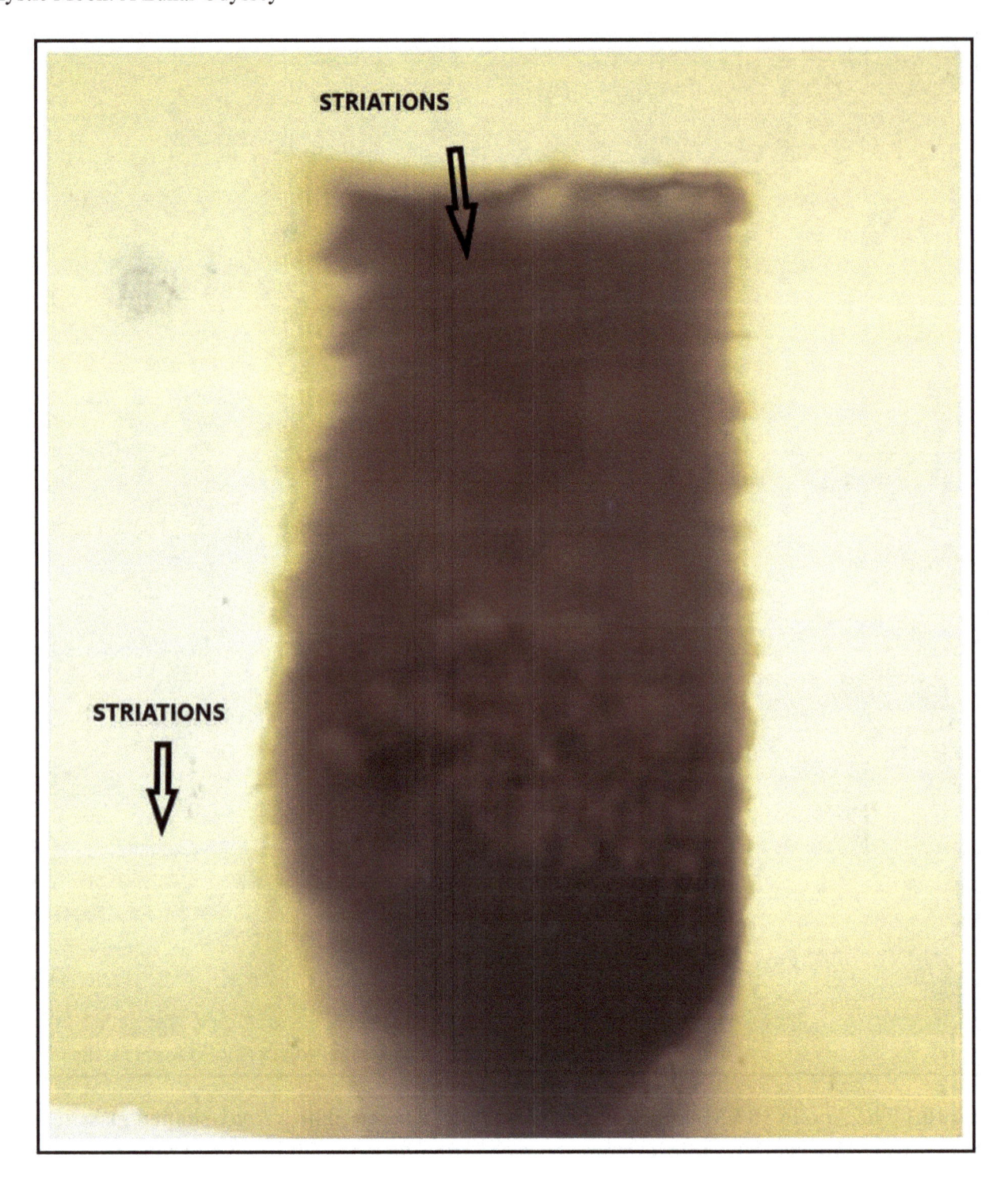

**Figure 10.2 Magnification of the tower reveals spiraling bands across the translucent glass sheet and the *Rook-shaped* tower behind the wall.
(Image Credit: NASA/JSC/Project Apollo Archive/Flickr)**

Typically, civilizations use locally available materials to construct homes and other structures. Throughout history, materials such as mud, clay, cow dung, bricks, bamboo, straw, and others have been utilized for building homes.

Chapter 10: Ancient Glass Artifacts

Glass beads from previous volcanic eruptions are abundant in the lunar regolith, as confirmed by the analysis of samples brought back by the Apollo and recent Chinese Change' missions.

Imagine the engineering skills required to construct a glass tower and wall on the Moon. The entire perimeter may have originally been enclosed by a glass ceiling and filled with air to support life.

The glass could have been mined and manufactured on the Moon. If that is the case, remnants of the manufacturing facility might still be waiting to be discovered by a future lunar mission. Another possibility is that these materials might have been transported to the Moon in large spacecraft from their original location.

The purpose behind constructing such tall walls on the Moon is still unknown. If more such walls exist on the lunar surface, then they may have to be systematically mapped for the safety of future missions. The presence of glass walls and other structures on the Moon would imply that future lunar missions must consider them.

The discovery of ancient ruins on the Moon, possibly created by unknown beings who may have colonized it a long time ago, is truly remarkable. It raises questions about how advanced their technology may have been compared to ours and whether we would be able to understand their existence.

Glass beads deposited in lunar soils by earlier volcanic eruptions may provide the raw material for manufacturing glass sheets and other building materials. The abundant supply of natural resources for making glass may have favored it as the construction material of choice for early settlers on the Moon. Over time, they may have perfected the glass manufacturing technology to withstand the impact of meteor showers.

Future lunar missions are planning to build habitats for long-term exploration of our Moon. The lunar caves and empty lava tubes may provide shelter from the cold and meteor showers. In addition, they will also have to find sources of water and air to achieve sustainability over the long term. The Moon is full of amazing things that continue to baffle the imagination.

* * * * * *

Chapter 11: Creepy Stuff Greeting Lunar Visitors

Mankind's early probes sent to the Moon were primarily flyby or impactor missions. The first spacecraft from Earth to perform a flyby of the Moon was the Soviet Union's Luna 1 in 1959, which flew within about 6,000 kilometers. This was shortly followed by Luna 2, the first impactor probe. However, the Luna series experienced several failures that slowed the Soviet lunar program.

The earliest attempt by the United States at sending probes to the Moon was spearheaded by the Ranger series of spacecraft (1962-65). On February 2nd, 1964, Ranger 6 crash-landed on the lunar surface without transmitting any imagery during its descent. Full success for the United States would be delivered a little later by the impactor probes Ranger 7 (1964) and Ranger 8 (1965), opening the door for NASA's lunar exploration. NASA later followed this up with the successful launch of the Surveyor series (1966-67), which was designated as soft landers on the Moon in preparation for the Apollo missions. Crewed missions to the Moon commenced with the Apollo 8 mission. The United States had established itself as the pioneer in human exploration of the Moon.

Visitors from Earth may not be new to the Moon. References to ancient spacecraft and Vimanas can be found in Vedic texts dating back to the Ramayana and the Mahabharata. These oldest surviving texts give us a peek into ancient history dating back several million years.

The Sumerian and Zoroastrian cultures also hint at spacecraft's existence, possibly used by their religious hierarchy for travel. However, it is important to note that these are speculative claims and lack tangible evidence. Moreover, they underscore that spacecraft and space travel are not new to ancient civilizations.

Imagine that the lunar entities, from the safety of the Moon, may have observed several mass or mini extinctions on Earth. Our planet would have undergone numerous cycles of ice ages followed by inter-glacial and warmer periods, ideal for the development of life. These cycles may have evolved and eventually perished without experiencing cataclysmic events.

Ancient civilizations, like our own, may have experienced a long period of favorable climatic conditions on Earth, potentially enabling them to advance in space technology and visit the Moon and beyond. It is also possible that lunar entities may have originated from early Earth.

The lunar entities seemed weary of visitors from Earth and other places, so they acted. They excel at creating large-scale visual special effects that frighten casual visitors.

ANGELS, MONSTERS, AND DEMONS

The fear of demons and monsters has been a universal phenomenon throughout history. Good and evil, angels and demons, are concepts in all major religions worldwide. These beings are often depicted in paintings, works of art, and the architecture of temples and churches. Caricatures of angels, monsters, demons, and dragons can be found guarding altars, arches, and gateways to places of worship in various religions. Additionally, commercial trucks and buses in south and southeast Asia are often adorned with elaborate caricatures of demons and dragons to ward off evil and bring good luck.

Famous artists such as Hieronymus Bosch, Hans Memling, Francisco Goya, Francis Bacon, and Lucas Cranach the Elder were all well-known for their depictions of demons and werewolves. In medieval Europe, many Catholic Churches incorporated intricate animal, dragon, and demon-shaped gargoyles in the design of waterspouts to divert rainwater runoff, similar to modern-day gutters. Hindu temple architectures incorporate demonic figurines with bulging telescopic eyes or angel-like figures with wings guarding entrances to altars. Buddhist temples and monasteries also incorporate wall paintings of colorful dragons, lions, and other creatures.

Nowadays, people are willing to pay deftly for amusement parks and movie studios to scare them out of their wits. Halloween costumes have become so creepy that little children are scared to wear them. Nowadays, Halloween decorations have surpassed those during Christmas; small to giant skeletons adorn people's front yards and even rooftops.

Popular novelists have authored hair-raising stories dwelling upon the macabre. The movie industry also capitalized on the audiences' appetite for fear and horror by producing numerous scary movies. Halloween has become a multi-billion-dollar industry catering to various products such as scary masks, candy for trick-or-treating, and costumes for kids and partying adults. Theme parks typically include scary rides or exhibits to appease patrons of all ages. Thanks to modern-day media, most folks can rationalize fear, especially visual fear. We often associate real fear with war, crime, terrorism, gun violence, and so forth.

In a bid to deter unsuspecting space travelers from encroaching on their skies, lunar aliens constructed a series of technologically advanced and brightly illuminated monstrosities, complete with claws and dragon-like faces. This elaborate spectacle was designed to instill fear in the hearts of intruders long before the advent of the Apollo missions. While modern humans may be immune to such fear tactics, they would have undoubtedly had their desired effect on casual visitors and curiosity seekers from ancient times. The very existence of these intricate measures is a testament to the enduring influence of fear across different historical periods.

The users of the image archives must be aware of some known imperfections in some of the Apollo 15 and 17 archives that may be attributed to blemishes and imperfections during film processing, time of filming (lunar nights), and so forth. A summary description of these types of errors is provided by ASU[19]. Following ASU policies on using NASA data archives, the images presented in this chapter were downloaded from the collection in their "Raw" format. The raw images were rotated, cropped, and processed with Photoshop© software.

A 24/7 HALLOWEEN EXTRAVAGANZA

People always associate the Moon with romantic evenings, weddings, honeymoons, and tides. The phases of the Moon are also associated with the timing of religious events in many religions. Folklore has it that the full Moon is believed to influence eccentric or lunatic behavior in some individuals. In English folklore and European legends, some individuals were believed to be able to transform themselves into werewolves. Medieval European history is strife with witch trials and wolf trials.

---

[19] ASU: https://apollo.sese.asu.edu/ABOUT_SANS/index.html

Mystic Moon: A Lunar Odyssey

Many eons ago, the lunar entities devised a unique strategy to deter unwarranted infringement of their skies. They welcomed visitors with a series of eerie laser light shows, visible from orbiting satellites or approaching spacecraft. This peculiar approach, though seemingly bizarre to the uninitiated, holds a fascinating surprise upon closer inspection.

Upon closer examination of one of the images, a large circular *"colosseum"*- like arena is visible, displaying a spectacular array of lightning patterns. Each panel starts with a large circular arena several miles in diameter with intricate patterns of lightning streamers, balls of light, claws, and other impressive formations. Each circular panel typically consists of three components: (1) a large circular ring of light enclosing the arena, (2) a perfectly spherical disc of light usually in the eastern part of the panel, and (3) a long horizontal light bar at the bottom of the panel stretching for several miles.

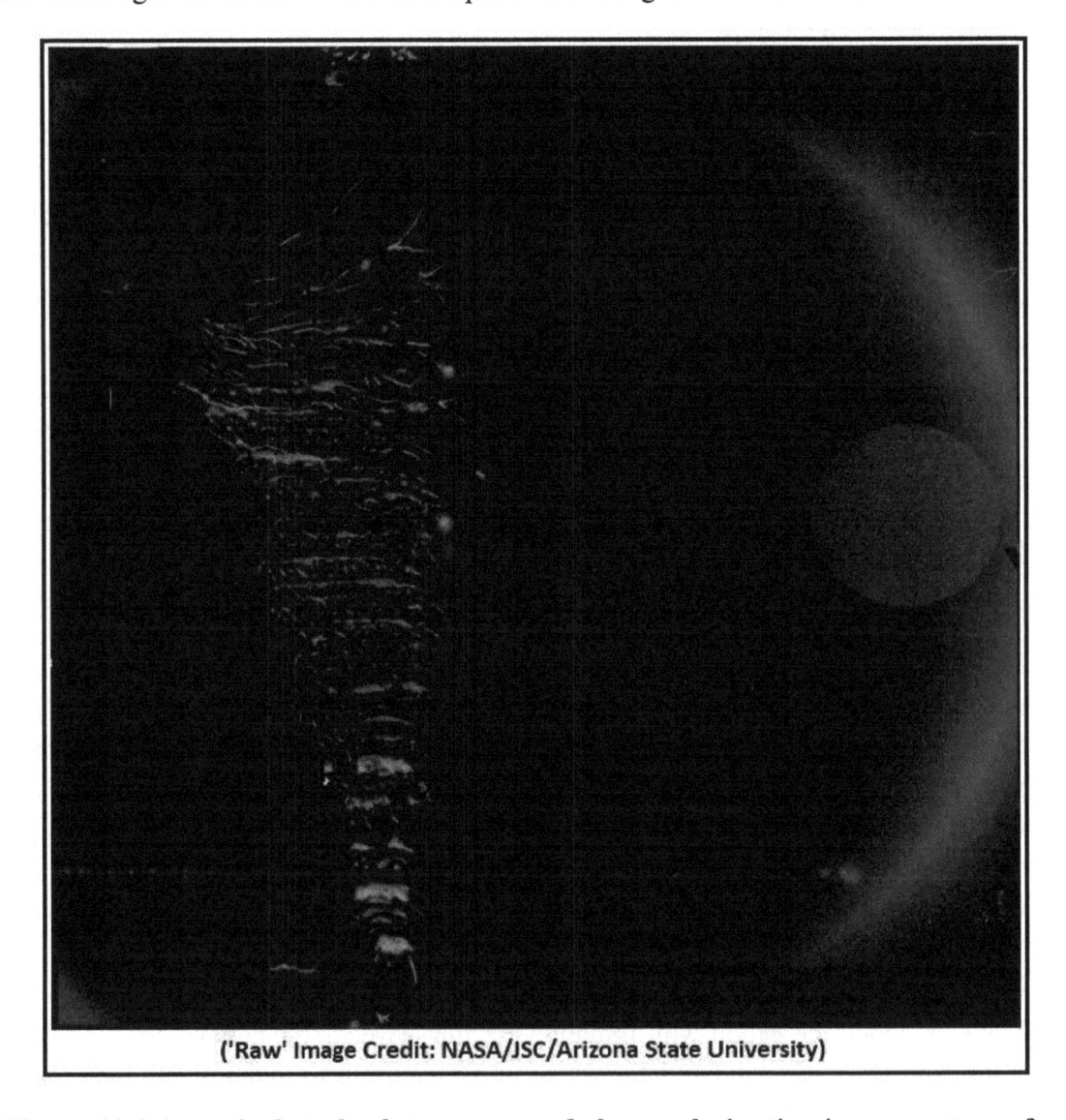

('Raw' Image Credit: NASA/JSC/Arizona State University)

Figure 11.1 A vertical stack of streamers and claws culminating in a monstrous face

In Figure 11.1, we can see the arena with a towering array of horizontal lightning streamers and claws, culminating in a monstrous face toward the floor of the circular arena.

Chapter 11: Creepy Stuff Greeting Lunar Visitors

The uncanny resemblance to depictions of dragons and monsters on Earth is quite startling, especially when one considers its facial characteristics such as eyebrows, telescopic eyeballs, uneven whiskers, claws, and a large wide mouth grasping an otter-like creature (Fig. 11.2).

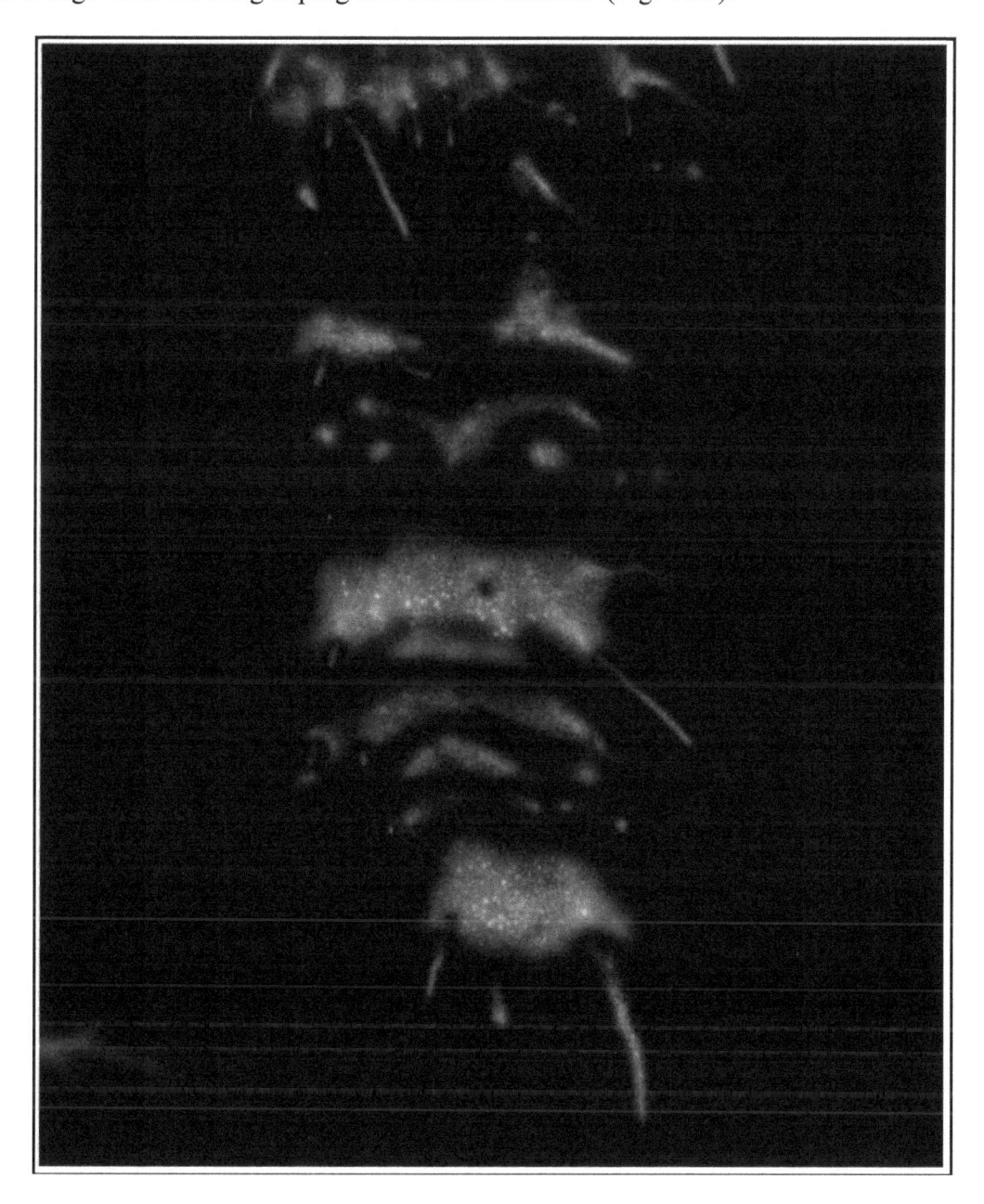

Figure 11.2 A magnification of the monster's face reveals its salient features

The lifelike otter or badger in its mouth will surely grab the attention of any terrestrial visitors orbiting above the field of view of this arena. Analysis of the raw images suggested that some of the lightning streamers may possibly be emanating from below the floor of the circular arena itself. These projection capabilities will enable lunar entities to quickly change the show's contents.

Unveiling these mysterious images from beneath the lunar surface is a fascinating way to create captivating new scenes that can perplex even the most experienced observers in orbit. It is almost like witnessing a series of modern-day digital billboards, each displaying a different commercial in rapid succession.

Interestingly, this elaborate light show appeared on the near side of the Moon, the side facing Earth. However, such a light show may not be visible with the aid of telescopes on Earth due to the reflection of sunlight by the surface during daylight or by incident Earthshine during the night.

Nikola Tesla, the Serbian-born genius who introduced the world to alternating current, began experimenting with static electricity as early as 1899. If he had his way, we could charge our electronic devices remotely without plugging them into an electrical outlet. Tesla was certainly ahead of his time.

Interestingly, some of his experimental outcomes bear a striking resemblance to the electrical streamers being generated on the Moon (Fig. 11.3). They too feature long horizontal streamers with a burst of smaller ones, but they do not have organized patterns of flora, fauna, or monsters associated with them.

It is clear that the lunar entities are responsible for creating these massive and exaggerated representations. They must also understand Earth's aquatic creatures well enough to incorporate them into their displays.

Figure 11.3 Nicola Tesla seen happily zapping away in his laboratory in 1899 (Credit: "Hi-Story"/Alamy Stock Photo)

It seems curious how these lunar formations developed and endured over extended periods of time. The thin lunar exosphere cannot cause significant damage by wind, dust, or oxidation of metals exposed to it; only meteorite bombardment over time might be able to harm the surface. These formations are still intact today, suggesting that someone must have maintained them all these years.

Certainly, these formations must have been established long before the arrival of the Apollo missions. This could imply that these elaborate setups were designed to discourage unwanted visitors from Earth from visiting the Moon in ancient times using their Vimanas. The presence of a recognizable monster's face in some ancient Earth religions is a clear clue.

The lunar entities must have grown accustomed to the long periods of inactivity associated with the sporadic nature of lunar tourism from Earth. Who created these elaborate, eerie displays and why remains an unsolved lunar mystery.

* * * * * *

Chapter 12: What's in a Face?

A few years ago, friends of ours, identified only as the Jayaramans, were visiting us in Washington D.C. After giving them a grand tour of several monuments in the Capital, I distinctly remember chaperoning them on a visit to the *Freer and Sackler Galleries*. Mr. Jayaraman was flabbergasted by their beautiful South Indian collection of Chola Bronzes in the galleries. He took several pictures of one of his favorites from every conceivable angle. I would later learn that he was also a very accomplished painter, sculptor, and artisan in his own right.

I was completing Chapter 11 when my wife Jo and I decided to check ourselves into her favorite Ayurvedic Clinic in Coimbatore, India. My wife Jo passionately believes in the holistic approach taken by Ayurveda (Life Science as per the Vedas). You must check yourself into the clinic for a period of three to four weeks, eat their healthy, low-calorie vegetarian meals, drink a strict regimen of bitter concoctions called *Kashayams*, and enjoy their daily regimen of hour-long hot oil massages administered by a team of experienced therapists while you are lying, almost naked, on a seven-foot wooden massage table.

Massages during the first week are known as *Abhyanga* and are designed to prepare the body for the upcoming and more rigorous massages provided by a team of six therapists working simultaneously on you at sessions during the next two weeks. The second week consists of hot oil massages provided by a team of four therapists while another two slowly drip cold oil on the forehead from a dangling clay pot with a small hole at the bottom through which a wick made of coir rope drips oil in a process known as *Dhara*. The Dhara pot oscillates slowly over the forehead, dripping cool herbal oil and soothing one's nerves. The third week of the treatment focuses on your individual needs, with the hot oils being replaced by either a warm concoction of cow's milk and Ayurvedic herbs; or nine varieties of rice bundled into small coconut-sized balls wrapped in cheesecloth that are used to massage your entire body in a weeklong procedure known as *Navarakili*.

A regimen of internal gut cleansing is administered during the final week to rid the body of accumulated toxins deposited by years of allopathic medications and the consumption of processed foods. Many people benefit from the treatment as they return every year or two to rejuvenate themselves. Ayurveda is known to provide relief, particularly to patients with arthritis, back pain, neurological disorders such as Alzheimer's, Parkinson's disease, stroke, and even treatment of accident-related spinal cord injuries. It is rumored that the Russians may have incorporated Ayurvedic treatments to decontaminate and detoxify victims of the Chornobyl nuclear disaster.

During our stay in Coimbatore, our mornings usually began with oil massages and showers, followed by breakfast. I often catch up on world events and U.S. political primaries by watching TV news on CNN or BBC. The multitude of Bollywood and Tollywood movie channels, with their unconventional storylines and excessive violence, was a bit overwhelming. However, I found comfort in several religious channels that offered a variety of family programs. One of the religious channels was operated by the Tirupati Tirumala Devasthanam (TTDs), home to Lord Venkateswara, an eminent Hindu deity believed to be the most recent Avatar in the present Kaliyuga. The Tirumala temple, located in a seven-hill complex, attracts hundreds of thousands of devotees from all over the world daily. Pilgrims often wait in line for hours to catch a brief glimpse of the deity in His full splendor during the main darshan.

Chapter 12: What's in a Face?

Lord Venkateswara is always accompanied by his consorts, Goddess Padmavati, and Goddess Lakshmi, who is regarded as the Goddess of wealth. All three deities are elaborately decorated with fresh flowers and adorned with appropriate fine jewelry for each ceremony. The wedding of the deities is a very auspicious religious ceremony known as Sri Srinivasa-Padmavati Kalyanam, which is ritually celebrated daily by temple priests of the highest order. The deities themselves are placed on a swinging pedestal that is gently rocked back and forth by the priests while chanting prayers.

One morning, I was watching the Sri Srinivasa-Padmavati Kalyanam event on live TV. Suddenly, the camera operator focused on a monstrous face centered on the arch or stupa directly above Lord Venkateswara's idol. The center of the arch contains the face of a hideous beast, presumably to ward off any unforeseen evil or evil thoughts. I was instantly taken aback by the similarity of features between the face of this monster and the one I had noticed earlier in the lunar imagery (Fig. 11.2). The lunar monster seemed to have more stubble on the face and appeared less kept than the trimmer temple version. This striking similarity between the two was quite revealing and presented several possibilities for some of the events observed on the Moon.

Towards the end of our tenure at the Ayurvedic clinic, our family friend, Mr. Jayraman, invited us for lunch. His culinary skills were well known within his close circle of family and friends, and it was always considered an honor to be invited to share a meal. The lunch was excellent, and we all ate to our hearts' content.

It was a sweltering day, so we all adjourned into the formal air-conditioned living room to relax. The living room was an extension of his art studio with paintings in various stages of completion, easels, canvas frames, tubes of oil paint, brushes, and sketch pads scattered all over the place. Mr. Jayraman showed us some of the impressive paintings and sketches he had done over the years. He was an extremely talented artist, and his reproductions of paintings from the Mughal era and paintings and pencil sketches of Chola Bronzes were immaculately done.

I casually told him I had noticed something like the lunar monster (Fig. 11.2) on the TTD-TV's Channel the other day. "Oh!" Exclaimed Mr. Jayraman, "You must be referring to Kirtimukha, the Face of Glory. " He explained that this monstrous-looking face adorns the central segment of every arch with two pillars under which the main temple deity is placed, known as the Garbha Gruha or inner sanctum of the temple. Kirtimukhas can also be seen in the adorning temple gopurams (arches), entrances, and side walls.

The typical Kirtimukha features thick eyebrows, telescopic eyelids, bulging eyeballs, a prominent nose, and a wide mouth with a large tongue and protruding fang-like teeth (see Fig. 12.1). The overall shape may vary depending on the location or temple architecture.

Figure 12.1 Kirtimukha adorns the top central point of arches guarding most temple deities (Credit: "ephotocorp"/Alamy Stock Photo (subset))

The similarities between the Kirtimukha and the lunar monster are quite striking. This raises the question of how it became part of a strange lunar phenomenon. Traces of Hindu iconography on the Moon can also be observed in the form of "*U*" shaped markings and even a Sri Chakra engraved on a crater (reference: next chapter).

It is possible that ancient or alien gods visiting Earth may have used the Moon as a launch pad for various terrestrial missions described in religious texts. The descriptions of alien spacecraft in various religious scriptures worldwide cannot be dismissed as heresy, especially when there are clear indications of alien presence on the Moon in some form.

THE LEGEND OF KIRTIMUKHA

Brahma (The Creator), Vishnu (The Preserver), and Shiva (The Destroyer) are the three primary deities in Hinduism. According to ancient legend, Jalandhara, the son of the Ocean and king of the Daityas, develops feelings for Goddess Parvathi, who is Shiva's consort. To win her over, Jalandhara sends his headless messenger, Rahu, to Kailash to persuade Lord Shiva to give up Goddess Parvati. Jalandhara boasts to Rahu about his conquests and treasures as the ruler of the three worlds, convincing Lord Shiva that he is more deserving of Goddess Parvati.

Rahu arrives at Kailash escorted by Gana; a monster created by Lord Shiva. Outraged by the situation, Gana attacks Rahu. Rahu pleads with Lord Shiva to save him from Gana, and Gana releases Rahu, complaining that his prey has been taken away and asking whom he should devour now.

Lord Shiva commands Gana to start eating himself up to satisfy his hunger. After obeying orders to consume himself from his limbs, Gana is left with only his head. Lord Shiva exclaims that Gana is truly blessed for following His orders verbatim. Lord Shiva then bestows Gana with the title of Kirtimukha,

Chapter 12: What's in a Face?

His doorkeeper. He tells Kirtimukha that His devotees will always worship him. From then onwards, Kirtimukha was stationed at the entrance altar to all gods in every temple.

In the previous chapter, a creepy face (Fig. 11.2) appeared in one of the lunar images. Coincidentally, it strongly resembles Kirtimukha, blessed by Lord Shiva. It is quite probable that Lord Shiva may have visited the Moon an exceedingly long time ago.

In ancient times, Hinduism spread far and wide, stretching across the globe from Peru to Southeast Asia, including Cambodia, Thailand, Indonesia, and the Philippines. Kirtimukha occupies a very strategic position in temple architecture everywhere. Figure 12.2 shows a Kirtimukha (Yaksha) positioned to the left and right of the unknown deity in Banteay Srei temple in Angkor Wat, Cambodia. This monster also has characteristic telescopic eyeballs and a large mouth with fang-like teeth. The Banteay Srei temple is a Hindu temple dedicated to Lord Shiva and was built during the 10th century A.D.

In Bali, Indonesia, a Kirtimukha-like monster adorns a Boma sculpture at the Ubud Palace (Fig. 12.3). It is believed that nearly eighty-seven percent of Bali's population is Hindu. Many artistic handicrafts and batik paintings with themes from the Ramayana and Mahabharata characterize Indonesian art exports.

Figure 12.2 Kirtimukha (Yaksha) adorns the wall of Banteay Srei Temple in Angkor Wat, Cambodia
(Credit: "Sergeii Figumyii" - stock.adobe.com)

Figure 12.3 A Boma sculpture resembling Kirtimukha at the Ubud Palace in Bali, Indonesia (Credit: "Anna-Marie Palmer"/Alamy Stock Photo)

A stone idol of Lord Lakshmi Narayana, an avatar of Lord Vishnu, in Hampi, Karnataka, India shows the *Kirtimukha* at its apex and the seven-headed snake (*Adisesha*) shielding *Vishnu* right above His crown (Fig. 12.4). The idol perfectly features hand-carved circular telescopic eyeballs and wide mouth with large fang-like teeth of both the Kirtimukha and the deity in this avatar.

The statue was carved in 1528 A.D. during the reign of King Krishnadevaraya of the Vijayanagara Empire but was later vandalized. Themes revolving around number seven appear in Hinduism, Christianity, and Judaism, suggesting possible common linkages across religions (ref. to Chpt. 3); probably because we are in the 7th *Maha Kalpa* (Ref. Table 3.1).

Chapter 12: What's in a Face?

Figure 12.4 A stone idol of Lord *Lakshmi Narasimha*, an Avatar of *Vishnu* in Karnataka, India

Kirtimukhas can also be seen adorning many ancient temple gopurams (spires). Several are adorning the colorful Madurai Sundereswarar temple spire (Fig. 12.5) in Tamil Nadu, India.

Mystic Moon: A Lunar Odyssey

Figure 12.5 Several Kirtimukhas guard the Meenakshi Sundereswarar temple in Madurai, TN, India (Credit: 'Rafal Cichawa"/Alamy Stock Photo)

Kirtimukhas can also be seen guarding Vimanas. One such Kirtimukha can be seen adorning the golden *Vimana*-shaped temple gopuram of the *Ranganatha Swamy* Temple located in Tiruchirappalli, Tamil Nadu, India (Fig. 12.6). Its disproportionately enormous size relative to the idol of *Lord Vishnu* directly below signifies its importance as the protector against all evil. Hindu deities are believed to use Golden Vimanas often while traveling to Earth. One can always find these Vimanas carved in the temple architecture, or as stand-alone ornaments as mentioned earlier in Chapter 4.

Incorporating Kirtimukha-like caricatures in elaborate lunar light shows designed to deter unwanted visitors suggests a very ancient alien presence with probable roots in Hinduism long before the arrival of the Apollo astronauts. The elaborate light shows associated with such displays on the lunar surface would have taken considerable time and effort to set up. It is obvious that the lunar aliens had to deal with unwanted Earthly visitors long before the arrival of the Apollo astronauts. They set up elaborate light shows with demon-like displays to scare the daylights out of casual curiosity seekers.

Chapter 12: What's in a Face?

Figure 12.6 Kirtimukha adorns the golden Vimana arch of Lord *Ranganatha Swamy* temple in Srirangam, TN, India (Credit: "ephotocorp"/Alamy Stock Photo ID:2JBJK6C)

Several religions have images or idols of monstrous-looking creatures to protect the righteous and ward off or destroy all evil. Any appearance of such images on the Moon or elsewhere in our Solar system may indicate visitations by ancient travelers. Many scary creatures exist in other cultures and religions with interesting legends.

* * * * * *

Chapter 13: Sacred Religious Symbols

Earlier chapters presented the probability of our Gods traveling worldwide in their spacecraft. It is quite probable that they may have also traveled to our Moon, Mars, and other celestial bodies. Much like on Earth, they are likely to have left behind vestiges of their travels. As Mankind begins to explore our Moon, Mars, and other parts of our Solar system, there is a need for Astronauts, scientists, and others to familiarize themselves with some common religious symbols and their significance. Many appear on the walls of places of worship carved in stone, marble, or some other material.

Most of us are familiar with the neologisms of some of the major religions of the world, for example, Hinduism (ॐ), Zoroastrianism( ), Buddhism (☸), Judaism (✡), Christianity (†), and Islam (☪) to mention a few. There are also several symbols associated with each religion that are used in religious ceremonies and temple carvings.

One of the oldest symbols, the Swastika, holds a deep cultural significance for Hinduism and Buddhism. This symbol, whether left-facing (卍) or right-facing (卐), is a ubiquitous sight in Hindu temples and Buddhist monasteries. It has adorned religious temple artwork and festive decorations for millennia as a visual reminder of our shared human history and spiritual journey. Every temple and Buddhist monastery worldwide is adorned with hundreds of Swastikas, a testament to its enduring cultural importance.

The German Nazi party unfortunately adopted the Hindu/Buddhist Swastika, which became their infamous symbol after they rotated the original right-facing version of the swastika by 45 degrees. The Puranas, ancient Hindu texts, warned that the religious swastika should not be reversed or rotated, as it would create negative energy and lead to destruction. The version of the swastika used by the Nazis became associated with fear, death, and the war crimes committed against the Jewish people during the Holocaust. This tarnished the ancient religious symbol of Hindus and Buddhists, forever linking it to the despicable actions of the Nazis during World War II.

The Germans extensively researched Hindu Puranas in pursuit of scientific and technological clues from the superior Satya Yuga eras of the past. They gained insight into topics such as gravitation and anti-gravity, as well as powerful weapons like the Brahmastra (a mini atomic weapon) mentioned in epics such as the Ramayana and the Mahabharata. Additionally, they studied saint Bharadwaja's Vaimanika Shastra for their V-2 rocket, among other things.

The Puranas contain references to the existence of parallel universes, Brahma's Clock, galactic black holes (Vishnu Naabhi), wormholes, time travel, and weapons of Gods capable of destroying entire planetary bodies. Scientists such as Albert Einstein and Robert Oppenheimer found many valuable clues in their research of Hindu Puranas. The ancient medical practice of Ayurveda holds potential cures for many chronic ailments. The concepts of personal hygiene and remedies recommended in Ayurveda continue to help people combat dangerous viruses.

According to the Puranas, life can exist anywhere in the Universe, but only during the daylight Kalpa period of 4.32 billion years. After this period, the next Pralaya period of equal duration sets in (ref. Chpt.3).

Chapter 13: Sacred Religious Symbols

It is possible that other civilizations exist within our Universe or elsewhere with similar traits and parallel religions. In fact, the Puranas state that life exists in other galaxies and parallel Universes. One can then envision several parallel sets of religious divinities within the space-time continuum stretching across millions of galaxies and possibly numerous parallel universes.

Space travelers, space scientists, astronomers, and others interested in space exploration need to familiarize themselves with complex religious geometric shapes they may encounter during their missions within our Solar system and beyond. From a statistical perspective, given the 1.56 trillion years of our Universe's existence the odds of discovering other intelligent life forms on exoplanets are favorable. If such life forms exist, they may have left evidence of their civilizations, similar to humanity on Earth.

Previous chapters have delved into the intriguing concept of Gods or Alien Gods influencing Earth's history. They may have visited Earth to rejuvenate struggling civilizations, combat evil forces, or even trigger mini extinctions in response to human misconduct. Events like massive floods, droughts, famine, and disease epidemics could be interpreted as mini pralayas (extinctions) designed to test the resilience of mankind. This perspective adds a fascinating dimension to the discussion on the potential impact of extraterrestrial life on religious beliefs.

Numerous ancient civilizations have perished in mass extinctions or floods of Biblical proportions. Rising sea levels during the current warm interglacial period, which followed the last glacial period (100,000 to 25,000 years ago), were responsible for the gradual collapse of vulnerable land masses into the oceans, carrying the remnants of civilizations living ashore.

Rising sea levels also contributed to the disappearance of coastal cities, structures, temples, and other signs of ancient civilizations. The submergence of the legendary Atlantis, Dwarka, and the collapse of a continental land mass called Pumpuhar in southern India into the sea are examples of mass destruction associated with rising sea levels, floods, and tsunamis.

SRI CHAKRAS, MANDALAS, AND OTHER RELIGIOUS SYMBOLS

Several ancient geometric, religious symbols common to both Hinduism and Buddhism, known as Sri Chakras, Sri Yantras, and Mandalas, are complex Vedic depictions of the Universe in terms of the Hindu Trinity (Brahma, Vishnu, and Shiva) along with numerous other deities. Buddhist monks and Hindu priests are adept at creating these complex symbols in colorful art forms as part of religious ceremonies.

Sri Chakras and Mandalas are religious symbols signifying the flow of energy and order in the Universe. In its simplest geometric form, the geometry of Sri Chakras, also known as Sri Yantras, comprises a series of 9 isosceles triangles representing the nine primary forces of the Universe. Currently, we are aware of only four fundamental forces in the Universe: 1) the strong nuclear force binding nuclei and other fundamental particles but acting over molecular distances, 2) Maxwell's electromagnetic force, 3) the weak nuclear force, and 4) the gravitational force capable of acting over long distances. The other five forces of the Universe alluded to in the ancient Vedas remain elusive to modern humans.

The positioning of the triangles in the Sri Chakras (Fig. 13.1) holds symbolic significance. Four of the 9 isosceles triangles, attributed to Lord Shiva, stand upright, symbolizing his masculine energy. In contrast, the remaining 5 triangles, attributed to his consort Goddess Parvathi (Shakti), are placed with the apex pointing downwards, representing her feminine energy. According to Kulaichev (1984), it creates a total of forty-three mini-triangles at their points of intersection, with the innermost central triangle typically representing Mt. Meru. Occasionally, a dot-like feature may also be found (Fig. 13.2).

A Mandala is a sacred religious entity associated with Hindu and Buddhist worship. In a typical Mandala, the central Sri Chakra is surrounded by two concentric circular bands of lotus petals. The inner band consists of 8 large lotus petals, while the outer band includes 16 smaller ones (Fig. 13.2a). A series of concentric circles or walls (Fig. 13.1) surround the Sri Chakra. Every Sri Chakra rests on a square base with four entry points facing the cardinal directions (north, south, east, and west).

Figure 13.1 Intricate geometry of a Sri Chakra inside a Mandala surrounded by two concentric rings laced with 8 and 16 lotus petals each. All four gateways are aligned with the cardinal directions (N, S, E, and W) (Credit: "Paul Czyzak"/Alamy Stock Photo)

Typically, in Hindu and Buddhist ceremonies, a Mandala is drawn using colored sand by priests and monks specializing in its design. A Mandala's individual colors and patterns can vary widely, especially in the central part of the *Chakra*. Four different popular Mandala patterns are illustrated in Figure 13.2: (a) Tripura Sundari, (b) Bhuvaneswari, (c) Dhumavati, and (d) Devi Kamala. On numerous occasions Buddhist monks have been invited to demonstrate the drawing of Mandalas at the White House as well as in Asian Galleries at prominent museums across the United States.

Chapter 13: Sacred Religious Symbols

Figure 13.2 Four different Mandala patterns: (a) Tripura Sundari, (b) Bhuvaneswari, (c) Dhumavati, and (d) Devi Kamala
(Credit: "TRIKONA:"/Alamy Stock Photos IDs: T79K1P, T605DY, T605E2, T605E6)

Figure 13.3 A 3-dimensional Brass Mandala showing the legendary *Mount Meru* at the center of the Universe (Credit: Rao Achutuni)

A three-dimensional Mandala (Fig. 13.3) consists of a three-tiered square base over which three concentric circular disks rest. Nine concentric chakras of decreasing size and shape are placed over the circular concentric base. The uppermost chakra contains a solid geometrical (3-D-shaped) triangle representing the golden Mount Meru (Hinduism) or Mount Sumeru (Buddhism), the legendary center of the Universe.

SACRED RELIGIOUS SYMBOL OF ZOROASTRIANISM

Zoroastrianism is the world's oldest monotheistic religion, founded by the Iranian prophet Zarathushtra or Zoroaster (Greek) around 600 BCE. Some scholars believe that it could have been around Achaemenid King Darius I or even earlier during the reign of Cyrus the Great (Wikipedia Commons). Incidentally, this religion predates Buddhism, Judaism, Christianity, and Islam.

Chapter 13: Sacred Religious Symbols

According to Zarathushtra, Ahura Mazda created the universe and its cosmic order. He then introduced the twin spirits, *Spenta Mainyu*, symbolizing truth, light, and life, and *Angra Mainyu* (Ahriman), symbolizing deceit, darkness, and death. These two spirits represent the paths of good and evil one can pursue. The religious symbol of Zoroastrianism is known as the *Faravahar*, which means the guardian angel (Fig. 13.4). In modern times, it has taken on as a secular and cultural symbol for Iranians.

Figure 13.4 Faravahar, the sacred symbol of Zoroastrianism, adorns the Fire Temple (Ateshkadeh) in Yazd, Iran. (Credit: EmmePi Travel"/Alamy Stock Photo)

Scholars are considerably divided regarding the origins of the *Faravahar*. Some argue that the symbol was originally associated with the Achaemenid dynasties and subsequently embraced Zoroastrianism. Several descriptions of the symbolism associated with the *Faravahar* exist.

The central figure in the *Faravahar* is an elderly person signifying wisdom associated with age. One arm is facing forward, suggesting one must struggle to thrive. The second arm holds a ring known as the Ring of Promise, representing *loyalty and faithfulness,* the two tenets of Zarathushtra's philosophical teachings. The large upper feathers are arranged in three rows, each to the left and right, symbolic of "…*good reflection*, good words, and good deeds…" and associated with uplifting flight and advancement. Similarly, the tail section is arranged in three rows of smaller feathers symbolizing "*bad reflection, bad words, and bad deeds which cause misery and misfortune for human beings* '.

The large central ring around the subject's waist symbolizes mankind's immortal spirit. The ring has two arms on either side of the tail. The arm to the left and forward direction represents *Sepanta Minyu*, and that to the right represents *Angra Mainyu*[20]. In other words, one must embrace all that is good, move forward, and discard all that is bad and evil.

SACRED RELIGIOUS SYMBOLS OF JUDAISM

The Menorah and the Star of David are highly revered symbols in Judaism. According to the Jewish *Talmud*, G-d is said to have provided Moses with extremely specific guidelines on its design and construction. An authentic replica of the original seven-branched Holy *Golden Menorah*[21] It is believed to have been used by Moses and is on display at the Temple Institute in Jerusalem, Israel.

Figure 13.5 shows a typical 7-branch Menorah. The Menorah used during the Jewish 8-day holiday of Hanukkah is a 9-branched one. A candle is lit every eight days; the ninth branch is set aside for the candle used to light it. The ninth candle holder is typically offset slightly higher or lower than the eight.

Figure 13.5 A 7-Branch Menorah. (Credit: "Sadia" - stock.adobe.com)

Per the *Chabad*, an equilateral triangle links the three entwining knots connecting the entities: (1) the Holy One, (2) the Torah, and (3) *Israel*. Each of these three entities, in turn, consists of both an internal (*Primiyut*) and an external (*Chitzoniyut*) dimension. The *Jewish* soul is believed to attain the divine *Creator* through both the exoteric (the *Talmud*, Jewish Law, etc.) and *esoteric* (the *Kabbalah*) teachings as prescribed in the *Torah*[22].

---

[20] https://www.smp.org;Zoroastrians.net
[21] https://www.templeinstitute.org
[22] https://www.Chabad.org

Chapter 13: Sacred Religious Symbols

The Jewish *Star of David* (Magen David or Shield of David) consists of two inverted equilateral triangles (Fig. 13.6). In turn, these triangles generate six other smaller triangles at their points of intersection. The *Star of David* is also a symbol of the State of Israel.

Per the *Kabbalah*, G-d created the world from the following *seven emotional attributes: (1) Chesed* (kindness), (2) *Gevurah* (severity), (3) *Tiferet* (crown/harmony), (4) *Netzach* (perseverance), (5) *Hod* (splendor), (6) *Malchut* (royalty), and (7) the central *Yesod* (foundation). The relative position of each of these seven attributes in the *Star of David* is shown in Figure 13.4, respectively. The attribute *Yesod* (*foundation*) is the central and pivotal segment of the *Star of David* (Chabad.org)

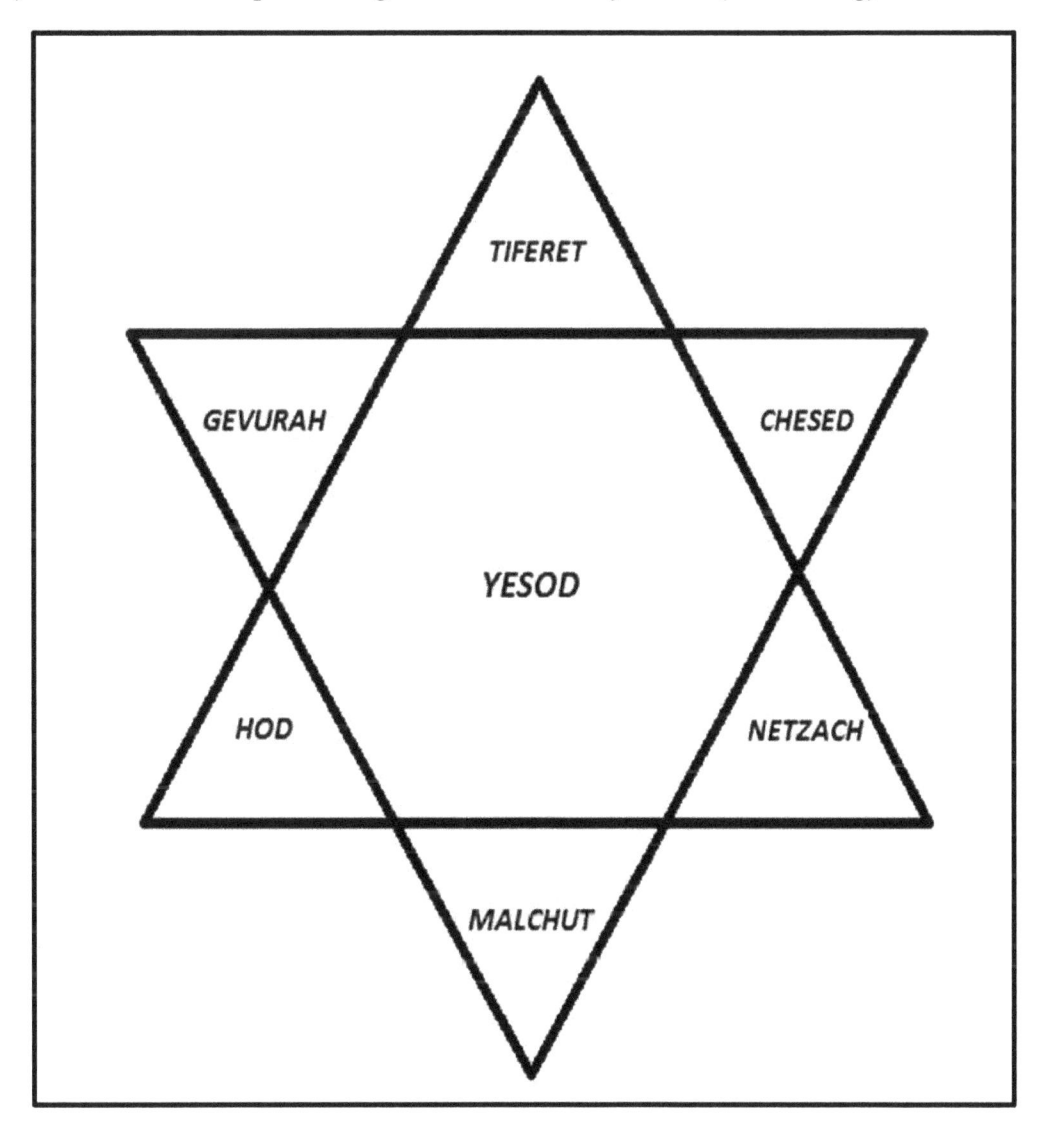

Figure 13.6 The double equilateral-triangle *Star of David* showing its seven attributes (Image Credit: Rao Achutuni)

Interestingly, variations of the Star of David also appear frequently in Mandala patterns of both Hinduism and Buddhism.

SACRED GEOMETRY IN NAZCA LINES

Some religious patterns, such as the chakras and mandalas presented above, can also be found in unexpected locations worldwide, far away from their known geographic origins.

The *Nazca Lines* of Southern Peru refer to geoglyphs drawn over various terrains scattered across the Nazca desert between *Nazca* and *Palpa*. These geoglyphs range from simple shapes of mammals, birds, spiders, giants, and ancient astronauts to complex geometric shapes, chakras, and mandalas (Aveni, 2015; von Däniken, 2011 & 2013; Forester, 2013; Hinman, 2015).

What is truly intriguing is the gigantic scale and precision with which they are transcribed on the dry desert plateau's surface, mountain tops, and hillsides. An interesting aspect of these geoglyphs is that they are best viewed remotely from the air. It is believed that the Nazca people created these graphics in the desert nearly two thousand years ago to be seen by the Gods from the sky above.

An artist's depiction of the Nazca Mandala geoglyph in Peru is shown in Figure 13.7.

Figure 13.7 Pattern of Nazca *Mandala* Geoglyph in Peru (Credit: "Zoonar GmbH"/Alamy Stock Photo)

LEGEND OF VIRACOCHA

Legend has it that the supreme Inca God *Viracocha* considered both the Creator and Destroyer, created these intricate geoglyphs, including the Mandala above. The presence of a complex and geometrically accurate Hindu-Buddhist Mandala in Nazca indicates that its creator must have had prior knowledge about ancient Hinduism. The *Bhagavatha Purana* describes how Lord Vishnu, during the early part of the *Treta Yuga*, came to Earth in the form of a short Brahmin as the *Vamana Avatar* (Lord *Vishnu's* 5th Avatar in a series of ten or *Dasaavataras)* to restore the status of *Indra* as the ruler of the heavens from the supreme Asura (giant or Nephilim) King *Mahabali*. He was the son of *Virochana*, the grandson of Prahalada as well as the great-grandson of the Asura King *Hiranyakashapu* whom Lord Vishnu had slain when He assumed the *Narasimha* Avatara (His 4th in a series of 10). King *Mahabali,* or *Bali,* was considered the supreme leader of *Svargaloka* (Heaven), *Bhuloka* (the Earth), and *Patala Loka* (the subterranean or underworld). In ancient times, South America, being to the south of the Indian subcontinent, was also referred to as Patala Loka.

In the story, the Brahmin Vamana visits the court of King Mahabali and is granted any gift of his choice. Vamana humbly requests just three steps of land. Despite warnings from his guru, King Mahabali feels obligated to honor his word to the Brahmin. Vamana then takes three steps, covering the earth and the heavens and finally placing his foot on King Mahabali's head. Pleased with the king's sincerity, Lord Vishnu allows him to rule Patala Loka (South America). Vamana promises to protect the king's palace and assures him that he will one day rule the Heavens. King Mahabali continued to rule successfully over the Americas and Antarctica.

The *Saksaywaman* temple in Cusco, Peru, is dedicated to the Inca God *Viracocha.* Some Hindu scholars believe that *Saksaywama*n[1] (meaning "one who travels on a hawk") refers to *Sakshat Waman,* the manifestation of *Vamana* or *Waman*, the 5th Avatar of Lord Vishnu. Lord *Vishnu's* mode of transportation is the *Garuda Vahana*, an avian chariot. Lord *Vishnu* travels to *Patala Loka* (South America) by the *Garuda Vahana* to assist King Mahabali in establishing his new empire.

The influence of Hinduism had spread all over the world as early as Lord Vishnu's 5th Avatar. Incidentally, King *Rama* of the Hindu epic *Ramayana* ruled Ayodhya also during the 24th *Treta Yuga*. He is known to have acquired the *Pushpaka Vimana* after killing King Ravana in a fierce battle and saving His beloved wife, *Sita*. This suggests that Hindu royalty from ancient times had access to *Vimana* spaceships and traveled the world with considerable dexterity. It is conceivable that *Virochana* (Viracocha) and King *Mahabali*, who also belonged to the *Treta Yuga*, may have had access to *Vimanas*. This may explain why Gods in the Inca and Mayan cultures descend to Earth as astronauts from the sky[23].

The Hindu ancestry of Viracocha and King Mahabali may explain the presence of complex Mandalas and Sri Chakras in the Nazca Lines of Peru. It is also conceivable that such traces of Hindu influences may be found in parts of North America and Antarctica that are considered part of ancient *Patala Loka*.

SACRED GEOMETRY ON THE MOON

---

[23] https://www.booksfact.com/religions/machu-picchu-saksaywaman-vamana-temples-cusco-peru.html

We have seen several instances across major world religions in which God communicates directly with humans or to His chosen disciples from the sky, usually from a spaceship or a Vimana. People down below tried their best to document these amazing and often bewildering moments to the best of their abilities. It is also highly likely that intelligent ancient civilizations existed long before our own. The Gods or Alien Gods may have provided or gifted some advanced space technology.

Nevertheless, alien Gods or our ancient ancestors may have acquired the ability to travel through space. This implies that they had the means to travel at extremely high velocities, both within our Solar system and farther away into deep space. If so, they may have left behind traces of their presence. These traces could be in the form of dwellings, structures, facilities, culture, religion, etc.

In this context, I accidentally stumbled upon an interestingly shaped crater known as *Franklin*. This crater has a pattern resembling a *Bhuvaneswari* Chakra engraved on it (ref. Fig. 13.2b). In *Vedic Tantrism*, this chakra is attributed to Goddess *Bhuvaneswari*, the protector of all *Universal* space. On the other hand, Goddess *Kali* is said to represent time, so between them, they represent space and time.

It is conceivable that alien Gods or superhuman races with access to advanced technology may have traveled freely between the Earth, the Moon, and their abodes in a distant constellation many light years away.

The ancient Gods or Alien Gods must have traveled freely across planet Earth and used this opportunity to establish their chosen rulers in faraway lands in mysterious ways thousands of years ago in the past.

* * * * * *

Chapter 14: Knocking on Mysterious Doors

Both conventional archeology and underwater archeology are fascinating disciplines. Ground-penetrating radar instruments have recently enabled archeologists to uncover hidden ancient riverbeds, roads, and trade routes. Deep Submergence Vehicles (DSVs) enable marine archaeologists to find sunken ships laden with gold and other treasures. They are also helping unravel submerged dwellings, ancient structures, cities, and coastal land masses that steadily rising sea levels have swallowed up following the *Holocene glacial retreat* that began around 11,700 years ago.

The time is now ripe for modern archaeology to logically extend its domain to include other planets and their moons. It is myopic to assume that we are the only civilization to ever inhabit Earth during its repetitive cycles of evolution, extinction, and life regeneration. Other planets and their moons could possibly harbor remnants of a bygone civilization from Earth or elsewhere. Planetary exploration presents humanity with numerous opportunities to investigate the mysteries of our Solar system.

A new generation of powerful space telescopes is also helping us explore our universe from light-years away. It is only a matter of time before a habitable exoplanet capable of sustaining human life will be discovered several light years away. Unfortunately, it will take us an exceptionally long time to develop the technology to get there.

A FAMILIAR SYMBOL SURFACES ON THE FARSIDE

Chapter 13 presents several religious symbols from around the world; several of these can be found in archeological sites and during excavations. For example, the complex Hindu or Buddhist mandala pattern embedded in the Nazca lines of Peru is particularly intriguing. These geometric patterns are challenging to draw and require considerable practice. It is a mystery who could have engraved them on the mountaintop.

Tsiolkovsky crater is a fascinating feature located in the southern hemisphere on the far side of the Moon. Its diameter is about 111 kilometers and boasts a relatively flat caldera that surrounds a characteristic central rocky mound, a unique geological formation that piques our curiosity (ref. Appendix 1-B).

Several spectacular pictures were captured from the Apollo 17 CM during its seventy five revolutions of the Moon. One that caught my eye was the sighting of a large bright "*U*" shaped symbol that appeared to the northwest of the central mound of *Tsiolkovsky* crater (Fig. 14.1) captured during the 74th orbital revolution of the CM. Generally, the image numbering sequence for Film Magazine "W" is the reverse of its exposure sequence, as with vintage 35mm camera film roll cartridges. Interestingly, the symbol bounced around the central mound of the crater as evident in subsequent scenes.

Mystic Moon: A Lunar Odyssey

(Image Credit: NASA/JSC/Project Apollo Archive/flickr)

Figure 14.1 A "*U*" shaped insignia appears northwest of central mound inside Tsiolkovsky crater

The following scene was captured a few seconds later during the 74th revolution of the CM (Fig. 14.2). Interestingly, the "*U*" shaped insignia now appears to the west; surprisingly, it has completely disappeared from its earlier location (Fig. 14.1) within a matter of seconds.

(Image Credit: NASA/JSC/Project Apollo Archive/flickr)

Figure 14.2 The "*U*" shaped insignia appeared to the "west" of the mound inside Tsiolkovsky crater

Chapter 14: Knocking on Mysterious Doors

When an orbiting spacecraft passes over a target, only the target's shape may be somewhat distorted by the oblique viewing angle; however, the target itself does not change coordinates unless it is bouncing around or being maneuvered remotely from above or below.

In a previous chapter, we discussed how lightning streamers and monstrous caricatures were possibly being projected from below ground. The reason to suspect projection is that these symbols appear transient in nature, moving from one place to another before eventually disappearing.

To determine the physical dimensions of this huge symbol or insignia, it had to appear near a crater of known dimensions. Fortunately, it appeared near the *Euler* crater (Fig. 14.3) with a known diameter of about twenty-eight kilometers (Wikipedia). Using this crater as a benchmark, the dimensions of the gigantic insignia measure up to about 17.5 kilometers in length and 3.5 kilometers in width. It is obviously quite huge and inconceivable by our standards.

One can imagine the level of technology required to project such a gigantic insignia onto the lunar surface dynamically. We have seen several examples in earlier chapters that attest to the advanced technological capabilities of the lunar entities in generating spectacular lighted patterns and bizarre displays involving 3-D patterns, lightning-shaped streamers, and monstrous caricatures, as well as "*U*" shaped arches and arrows in the lunar sky.

(Image Credit: NASA/JSC/Project Apollo Archive/flickr)

Figure 14.3 "*U*" shaped insignia north of Euler crater is about 17.5 km long & and 3.5 km wide

These "*U*" shaped insignias are not only found on the surface of the Moon but can also appear in the sky. This phenomenon is not caused by a charged atmosphere creating an auroral display like on Earth, as the Moon does not have a magnetic field. The origins of these displays are still unknown.

Interestingly, there seems to be some similarity between the "*U*" shaped insignia observed on numerous and the religious markings adorning the foreheads of some male Hindu deities. For example, the decorated idol of Lord Venkateswara or Balaji (the *Kaliyuga* incarnation of *Vishnu*: 3,102 BCE) (Fig. 14.4) shows a prominent "*U*" shaped *marking* on the forehead of the deity, as well as along the periphery of the ceremonial crown. Slimmer versions of this "*U*" shaped pattern also adorn the foreheads of other male deities.

Figure 14.4 Lord Venkateswara adorned with "*U*" shaped markings on forehead and crown

Legend has it that during the early part of the present *Kaliyuga*, Lord Venkateswara arrived on Earth in a three-tiered golden *Vimana* or spacecraft from *Vaikhunta*, Lord *Vishnu's* abode located deep within the *Ursa Major* constellation. A golden replica of this *Vimana* can be seen displayed near one of the entrances to the temple's inner sanctum.

As mentioned earlier, the Moon may have served as a springboard for launching divine missions to Earth by Gods or alien Gods belonging to several religions. They may have arrived on the Moon in large spacecraft capable of intergalactic travel and then switched to more versatile smaller *Vimanas* for terrestrial visits.

It seems that *Gods* depicted in major religions, such as Hinduism, Christianity, and others, appear to have used spacecraft to visit their followers on Earth (Ref. Chpt. 3 & 4).

Chapter 14: Knocking on Mysterious Doors

Interestingly, temple art from the Achaemenid Empire (550 BCE), founded by *Cyrus the Great* in ancient Iran, also has examples of the *"U"* shaped symbol. A decorative head-ornament of a warrior horse adorns a similar *"U"* shaped pattern (Fig.1 4.5). This symbol appears to be common in many cultures and religions.

Figure 14.5 U-shaped insignia pattern on a Horse Head in the ruins of Persepolis, Iran the capital of the Achaemenid Empire ruled by Cyrus the Great (Credit: "can yalcin"/Alamy Stock Photo)

ULTIMATE LUMINOSITY

It is difficult to ascertain whether an observed artifact on the Moon results from naturally occurring processes or something inexplicable and mystic.

When sunlight hits rain droplets, it creates a rainbow arc that can be seen from Earth. This happens because the light beam is split into different colors of the spectrum (Violet, Indigo, Blue, Green, Yellow, Orange, and Red) due to the sequential optical processes of refraction, reflection, and refraction. Each color is reflected at varying angles based on its wavelength, creating the beautiful rainbow we see. The order of colors in a rainbow, from the longest wavelength (top) to the shortest at the bottom, is *ROYGBIV*.

The Moon is known to have an exosphere consisting of extremely low concentrations of noble inert gases such as helium, neon, argon, xenon, radon, and krypton. In fluorescent lights, the inert gas neon begins to glow when an electric current is applied across two electrodes, but what about in the open lunar sky?

In Figure 14.6, you can see several blue and white inverted '*U*'- shaped bright and luminous arches rising high into the lunar sky across a region known as *Mare Australe* in the *Vallis Schrodinger* (an area formed by the triad of giant craters *Schrödinger*, *Humboldt,* and *Lyot*), on the lunar far side (ref. Appendix 2-B). It is worth noting that the familiar Blue spacecraft is hovering near east-northeast (rectangular inset).

The gaseous nature of these arches is evident from their translucent appearance. One can observe the lunar surface through the base of these arches, similar to observing a rainbow on Earth. How can the gaseous particulates in the sky retain their shape without eventually drifting or dispersing, such as due to the Solar wind?

In Figure 14.7, we notice the same series of blue-white arches again. However, this time, one can also observe the earlier 'Screw'-shaped spacecraft (Fig. 7.5A) towards the north-northwestern edge of the scene. This interesting feature is shown enlarged within the rectangular inset.

Chapter 14: Knocking on Mysterious Doors

(Image Credit: NASA/JSC/Project Apollo Archive/flickr)

Figure 14.6 A series of translucent inverted 'U' shaped blue and white gaseous lights observed over the *Mare Australe* region; notice the Blue spacecraft in the east-northeast corner

Mystic Moon: A Lunar Odyssey

(Image Credit: NASA/JSC/Project Apollo Archive/flickr)

Figure 14.7 Earlier 'screw' shaped spacecraft hovers over north-northwestern corner of image

The fact that both these spacecraft are hovering over the same area of the Moon suggests the probable presence of a spaceport nearby. Remember that these images are about sixty years old, and the situation could have very well changed by now.

The exact mechanism behind the formation of these lights remains a mystery. Unlike Earth, the Moon has no magnetosphere to generate optical phenomena like the Northern Lights. However, given the presence of lunar spacecraft, these features could be serving as their insignia, or some navigational lights directing spacecraft traffic towards a base or landing site In *Mare Australe* in the *Vallis Schrodinger* on the far side of the Moon.

Chapter 14: Knocking on Mysterious Doors

Imagine a situation in which airports on Earth were being identified by their unique symbols visible at flight level to assist pilots, or theme parks displaying their favorite comic characters in the sky to enthrall children while approaching their destination.

During the Apollo 11 mission, a pair of huge yellow-blue stacked *U*-shaped insignia were spotted over the lunar sky (Fig. 14.8). These arches appeared to reach an impressive height of about 750 miles (1,207 kilometers) above the lunar surface. The significance of changing the color of the arches from blue/white to blue/yellow lights or stacking them one above the other remains somewhat of a mystery.

Figure 14.8 A pair of Blue and yellow "*U*" shaped insignia tower ~750 km in the lunar sky

An example of this giant pair of yellow and blue "*U*" shaped insignia can be seen in the lunar sky (Fig.14.9) over the lunar craters *Kepler B* and *Milichius-A* located in a region towards the east of *Mare Procellarum* and west of *Copernicus* crater. They both appear to be gaseous in nature. One can try to

Mystic Moon: A Lunar Odyssey

explain such features in terms of atmospheric phenomena. Unfortunately, the lunar exosphere is extremely rare and, therefore, may not be responsible for such phenomena. One can also observe such *U*-shaped features on the lunar surface as well. A scientific explanation still remains elusive. However, the appearance of such gigantic artificially illuminated symbols in the lunar sky is quite an astonishing sight.

Figure 14.9 A pair of gaseous yellow, blue "*U*" shaped insignia adorns the sky over *Kepler B* crater

These mysterious, large, and transient U-shaped insignia kept appearing randomly on both land and in the lunar sky during the Apollo missions. They resemble a religious symbol, but this could be coincidental.

A series of inverted *U*-shaped insignia also appeared on land, and a couple of familiar lunar spacecraft were spotted hovering near them, suggesting the possible presence of a spaceport.

Chapter 14: Knocking on Mysterious Doors

In this Chapter, we encountered several situations that challenge conventional scientific wisdom. To confound the issue, many of these phenomena appear to be on the lunar. The documented display of gigantic insignia suggests the presence of an advanced civilization on the Moon. The colored U-shaped insignia made of gaseous material appears to maintain its form without dissipating quickly. These appear to be made by design and may not necessarily be the result of some optical illusion.

The *Puranas* state that the abodes of the Hindu divine Trinity Brahma (*Brahma loka*), Vishnu (*Vaikhunta loka*), and Shiva (Shiva loka) are all located within the *Ursa Major* (*The Great Bear* or *The Big Dipper*) constellation. In Sanskrit, this constellation is known as the *Saptarishi Mandala*. In Vedic cosmology, the seven brightest stars of this constellation are named after prominent *sapta* (seven) rishis in Hinduism.

The James Webb Space Telescope (JWST) has already begun to identify biosignatures in distant galaxies over one hundred light years away. It is only a matter of time before a planet beaming with life is discovered. Large space telescopes such as the JWST may soon allow us to observe God's neighborhood through the eyes of powerful telescopes, and we may soon be knocking on heaven's doors!

Imagine a reverse scenario in which a highly advanced civilization located about a hundred light-years away discovered our planet Earth long ago. They may have established a base on the Moon and frequently visited Earth to construct megalithic structures and accelerate mankind's evolution through genetic manipulation. Therefore, it is in their interest to help protect our civilization from harm. Over millions of years, no harm has been done, and we have nothing to fear. We must continue living in harmony and be going about our lives as usual.

* * * * * *

Chapter 15: Sustainable Lunar Exploration

One of the main objectives of lunar exploration is to search for life-sustaining elements such as water-ice and oxygen, as well as minerals and materials that will support rocket propulsion systems and meet the future needs of human settlements. Technologies to be developed and evaluated on the Moon will assist NASA in the future exploration of Mars and other planetary systems and their Moons. The proximity of the Moon to Earth is a big plus factor in further exploration. It so happens that the lunar South Polar region is prime real estate for exploration. This is why several countries are interested in exploring this region of the Aitken Basin, popularly known as the *South Pole-Atkin* (SPA) basin (Appendix 1-C).

The SPA basin is the largest impact crater in our solar system, measuring about 1,600 miles (2,500 km) in diameter and about 8.1 miles (~13 km) in depth (James et al., 2019). This huge impact crater is believed to have been formed about four billion years ago when a massive asteroid laden with metals crashed onto the Moon.

According to NASA's Jet Propulsion Lab (NASA/JPL 2015), the Moon contains three crucial elements: water, Helium-3 (^{3}He), and Rare Earth Metals (REMs). Apparently, ^{3}He is ideally suited for operating a fusion reactor when fused with deuterium to produce a nuclear reaction.

In addition to life-sustaining elements, one may also be interested in searching for other minerals such as gold, iron, titanium, magnesium, molybdenum, nickel, cobalt, lithium, etc. Rock samples brought back from earlier Apollo missions provided researchers with the mineral composition of the surface layer. Additional exploration of deeper layers will help develop a long-term lunar mining strategy.

MINING FOR ^{3}He

Earth-orbiting satellites and deep space exploration depend largely upon solar energy panels to generate adequate power for the entire spacecraft. The Moon has no clouds, but its long days and nights, each lasting about 14.75 Earth days, pose a real problem for generating solar power for long-duration missions.

The long duration of solar days may not be a problem in the equatorial regions, but solar intensity is a limiting factor over the polar regions. On the other hand, the long lunar nights will essentially shut down all solar energy production; typically, lunar landers and rovers must be put into sleep mode during the long nights to minimize energy consumption. Moreover, this is why everyone is rushing to find alternate energy sources to sustain long-term lunar missions.

NUCLEAR ENERGY: FISSION VS FUSION

Nuclear energy can be generated using two different processes known as *fission* or *fusion*. Conventional nuclear power plants are based on *fission* technology in which the bombardment of enriched Uranium 235 (U-235 or ^{235}U) or Uranium 238 (U-238 or ^{238}U) by neutrons splits it up into two or more smaller ones and unleashes vast amounts of energy (heat and radiation) along with some fission products. Neutrons are also released in the process forming a chain reaction.

In infusion technology, two or lighter atoms, such as Hydrogen (fuel), are combined (fused) into a Helium (He) atom. The energy released by the fission process is considerably higher and cleaner than that released by the chain reaction in a fission process. Unlike the chain reaction in a fission process, sustaining a fusion reaction for a long time is difficult due to the high temperatures and immense pressure required.

A promising future alternative being considered in lunar exploration is ^{3}He-derived power. This is the reason lunar missions from other countries, such as China and India, are also focusing their efforts on mining ^{3}He in the polar regions of the Moon. Fusion-based power plants can produce significantly higher and cleaner energy with no residual radioactivity.

However, ^{3}He is only available in low concentrations on the Moon; therefore, large quantities of regolith must be mined to sustain the demands of a future Moon base. Realistically, this can be accomplished only if heavy excavation equipment can be transported to the Moon for large-scale mining. Such equipment must incorporate technology that can function under anaerobic lunar conditions.

The SPA regions are believed to harbor higher concentrations of ^{3}He, especially in the *permanently shadowed regions* (PSRs) of craters. Due to the larger concentrations of craters there, the SPA regions are more rugged than the North Polar regions.

SEARCHING FOR WATER-ICE

Several deep lunar craters in the Moon's polar regions receive little to no direct sunlight and consequently register some of the coldest temperatures in our solar system.

The Moon's polar regions are of particular importance in lunar exploration as they are known to harbor ancient water ice in their *permanently shadowed regions* (PSRs)[24].

NASA's Moon Mineralogy Mapper (M^3) was launched aboard ISRO's Chandrayaan-1 and provided the first mineralogical map of the lunar surface (NASA/JPL-Caltech, 2008)[25]. In 2009, the M3 instrument confirmed the presence of solid ice in the Moon's polar regions.

Scientists (Li S, 2018) working with M^3 data were able to establish the definite presence of water-ice in the surface layers of the Moon in both polar regions. They could identify the presence of water in its different states (viz., liquid water, vapor, and solid ice). The SPA regions appear to have higher concentrations of surface ice located within the PSRs than the North polar regions

Unlike on Mars, where large subsurface water deposits appear lurking, the Moon may be more limited in this non-renewable resource, making its long-term exploration more challenging. Technology development to harness adequate quantities of this precious commodity on the Moon is considered an extremely high priority.

Several countries are focusing their lunar exploration efforts on the SPA basin in search of precious water. Technologies to harvest large quantities of water from the surface layers must be developed and evaluated before deployment.

---

[24] NASA Jet Propulsion Laboratory: https://www.jpl.nasa.gov/images/pia00002-north-pole-region-of-the-moon-as-seen-by-clementine

[25] NASA/JPL-Caltech: https://www.jpl.nasa.gov/missions/moon-mineralogy-mapper-m3

On the other hand, the supply of ^{3}He on the Moon is considered a renewable commodity. The challenge is to mine adequate supplies to meet the energy requirements for polar exploration.

Recently, NASA announced that its *Fission Surface Power Project*, currently under development with three industry partners, will build a reactor capable of delivering about forty kilowatts of power to meet requirements for its future exploration needs (Bausback, 2024). Once operational, this new technology can become a game changer in lunar and planetary exploration.

* * * * *

Chapter 16: A Review of NASA's Plans for Lunar Exploration

Following the phenomenally successful Apollo Program, NASA's crewed missions into low-Earth orbit continued through the Space Shuttle Era (1981-2011). Five Shuttle Transportation Systems (STSs) helped construct the International Space Station (ISS), shuttled astronauts and supplies to the ISS, deployed many new satellites, fixed, or retrieved problematic ones, and conducted state-of-the-art research (NASA-STS)[26].

The commercial sector continues to have numerous opportunities to assist in developing various aspects of the space program. A new partnership has also been established between the European Space Agency's 11-country consortium and its partner, Airbus Defence and Space.

NASA's mandate to revive crewed missions to the Moon and beyond was heralded by President Donald Trump in a Space Policy Directive issued on December 11, 2017 (NASA-ARTEMIS)[27]:

"Lead an innovative and sustainable program of exploration with commercial and international partners to enable human expansion across the solar system and to bring back to Earth new knowledge and opportunities. Beginning with missions beyond low-Earth orbit, the United States will lead the return of humans to the Moon for long-term exploration and utilization, followed by missions to Mars and other destinations."

NASA Administrator Tim Bridenstine reaffirmed his agency's commitment to return once again to lunar exploration and beyond, stating:

"President Donald Trump has asked NASA to accelerate our plans to return to the Moon and to land humans on the surface again by 2024. We will go with innovative new technologies and systems to explore more locations across the surface than was ever thought possible. This time when we go to the Moon, we will stay. And then we will use what we learn on the Moon to take the next giant leap – sending astronauts to Mars"

NASA responded to the challenge by establishing the ARTEMIS Program, which aims to return astronauts to the lunar surface by 2025-26. The plan includes the first woman astronaut to land on the Moon's South Pole.

The overarching goal is to develop technological capabilities in partnerships with the private sector and consortiums to meet the needs of lunar exploration. These capabilities can eventually be incorporated into future planetary explorations, especially Mars.

Focus areas include lunar geology, mineralogy, and harnessing water resources identified by earlier research in the polar regions. Experiments in radio astronomy are also planned for the far side in support of future exploration of Mars.

---

[26] NASA-STS: https://www.nasa.gov/mission_pages/shuttle/flyout/index.html
[27] NASA-ARTEMIS: https://www.nasa.gov/specials/artemis/

Space Launch System (SLS)

(The interested reader is advised to refer to Appendix-2 for a brief overview of the *Basics of Satellite Orbits* and Appendix-3 for Propulsion).

The Space Launch System (NASA-SLS)[28] is NASA's next-generation super-heavy launch vehicle for deep space human exploration? The new *Orion* spacecraft is designed to carry a crew of four astronauts and cargo for lunar exploration.

The SLS is designed to be a flexible and evolving series designated as Block 1, Block 1B, and Block 2 (NASA-SLS). Based on its scope, each block is further designated as either a Cargo or Crew mission. The typical SLS configuration for Block 1 *Crew* missions is shown in Figure 16.1.

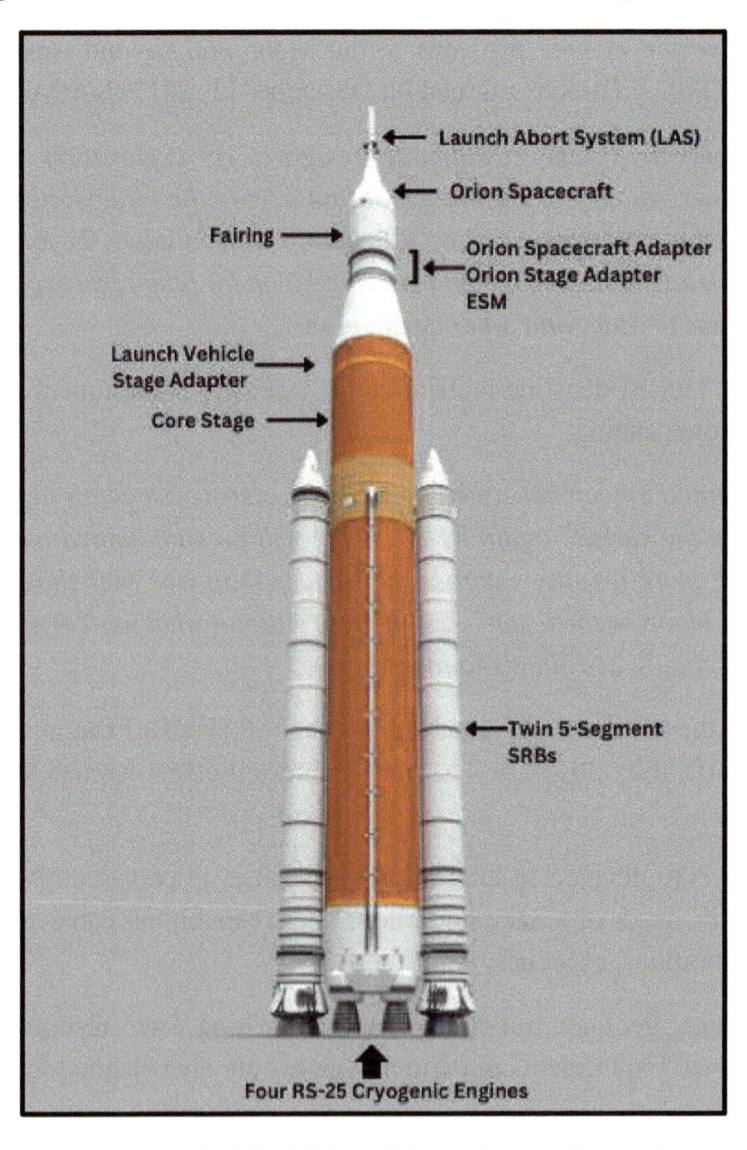

Figure 16.1 A schematic of the ARTEMIS I SLS launch Configuration setup shown in Crew Mode. (Credit: "Brandon Moser"/Alamy Stock Photo)

---

[28] NASA-SLS: https://www.nasa.gov/humans-in-space/space-launch-system/

The Orion Space Module (Fig. 16.1) consists of the *Launch Abort System (LAS)* at the top, with the *Crew Module* (CM) directly below it. The Cargo *Mode* (not shown) does not include the LAS. This configuration makes switching quickly from one mode to another easier based on mission requirements by incorporating a command module adapter (CMA), somewhat like a lens adapter ring in an SLR camera. The CM and the ESM are both mated together with the CMA (Also refer to Fig. 1.2).

A spacecraft adapter (SA) ring attaches the European Service Module (ESM) to the Core Stage. A set of three spacecraft adapter jettisonable fairings (SAJ) enclose the entire service module (SM) assembly (CMA+ESM+SA).

The large main *Core Stage* (cylindrical Orange object in Fig. 16.1) is attached to four cryogenic RS-25 engines powered by liquid oxygen (LOX) and liquid hydrogen (LOH) stored in separate tanks. The *Core Stage* delivers the entire spacecraft (ESM and Crew Module) into a low-Earth-orbit (LEO) before separating from it.

A pair of pencil-shaped Solid Rocket Boosters or SRBs (Fig. 16.1) provides additional thrust to meet payload requirements. Additional SRBs can be added later as needed for heavier payloads. These SRBs are self-propelled and can be recovered after separation (NASA-SRB)[29]. The Core Stage and the two SRBs can deliver about twenty-seven metric tons (59,525 pounds) of payload directly to Low Earth Orbits (LEOs).

The European Service Module

The earlier *Interim Cryogenic Propulsion System* (ICPS) used in ARTEMIS I has now been replaced by the *European Service Module* (ESM)[30] built by an 11-country consortium. The ESM provides the ARTEMIS II-IV Orion crew with spacecraft propulsion, electrical power supply, thermal control, water, oxygen, and nitrogen while in space.

The ESM includes 33 engines that provide the required thrust to maneuver the spacecraft: Orion's single *Main Engine* (~6,000 pounds thrust), 8 Auxiliary Engines (110-pound thrust), and 24 Reaction Control Engines (50 pounds thrust) (NASA-ESM)[31].

For power generation, the ESM is equipped with four solar array wings, each wing with a set of three solar panels (2mX2m). Altogether, 15,000 solar cells produce electricity (Fig. 16.2).

Once the core stage puts the lunar spacecraft into LEO and separates from it, the ESM is the sole propulsion system. The ESM fires short bursts of its engine to execute a Hohmann transfer orbit, which will bring it into a *Trans lunar-injection* trajectory towards lunar orbit (ref. Chpt. 1, Appendix-2).

Ultimately, the ESM is responsible for delivering the Orion capsule into lunar orbit and bringing the crew back safely to Earth once the lunar mission is completed and *Orion* docks with the ESM.

---

[29] NASA-SRB: https://www.nasa.gov/reference/space-launch-system-solid-rocket-booster/
[30] ESM: https://www1.grc.nasa.gov/space/esm/
[31] NASA-ESM: https://www1.grc.nasa.gov/space/esm/

Figure 16.2 An artist's rendition of the Orion Module attached to the new European Service Module. (Credit: "Claudio Caridi" Alamy Stock Photo)

The ARTEMIS II mission plans are to orbit the Moon and return to Earth. The lunar landing missions are reserved for ARTEMIS III & IV missions. Both these missions will be equipped with the ESM that will separate, land the crew on the Moon, and re-dock with the command module after the mission is completed.

Artemis III plans to spend about a week in the South Polar Region of the Moon. The Sun will appear on the horizon, casting long shadows in dim light conditions throughout the visit. The two astronauts designated to land will conduct several experiments and explore for water ice in the shadow regions of the craters. This is the mission in which NASA plans to land the first woman astronaut on the Moon.

The Lunar Gateway

A lunar-orbiting *Gateway* will serve as a base to support the future needs of the ARTEMIS missions (NASA)[32]. All crewed missions and supply lines to the Moon will first dock with this Gateway. Separate lunar modules will shuttle crew and cargo back and forth to the Moon from orbital heights. Overall, such a configuration will make lunar exploration safe, economical, and sustainable.

---

[32] NASA: https://www.nasa.gov/mission/gateway/   (NASA's Gateway Program)

Chapter 16: A Review of NASA's Plans for Lunar Exploration

Figure 16.3 The Gateway will serve as a space station for ARTEMIS missions to Moon and beyond. (Credit: "Geopix"/Alamy Stock Photo)

The ongoing partnership with U.S. aerospace companies, private sector contractors, and the ESA consortium aims to re-establish NASA as the world's premier leader in lunar and planetary exploration.

Developing propulsion systems capable of carrying heavier payloads is essential for colonizing the Moon. The rocky terrain of the lunar surface in the SPA basin presents several challenges for the safe and "upright" landing of crewed and cargo missions. These modules must be equipped with reliable propulsion systems capable of functioning in any position after landing.

This technology must be perfected to ensure successful crewed lunar missions. The other bells and whistles are nice after the essentials are perfected. Growing up in the 1970s, a popular adage ingrained in all budding scientists and engineers was the KISS (*keep it simple, stupid*) principle. It is always easier to guarantee the functioning of simpler systems than more sophisticated ones.

The proposed lunar orbiting Gateway (Fig. 16.3) will be a welcome addition. The crew can be shuttled to the Gateway and transferred to the lunar surface in smaller modules. The Gateway will enable the crew to receive immediate medical treatment and subsequently return to service. Technical problems on the lunar surface can also be quickly resolved from such a close orbit.

Sometimes the *act of getting there* is more important than the *art of getting there*. For example, when planning a long summer road trip, it is essential to have a workhorse that can take you to your destination without breaking down along the way. In an emergency, one can always request the services of a tow truck.

Presently, crewed space exploration does not offer a service call option. The crew must be able to fix any issues within the module or conduct spacewalks to rectify external issues. This situation could improve considerably in the near future, as vendors will be able to help if stationed on the orbiting Gateway.

Supply chains must be able to provide reliable components that will not fail. A common safety backup measure in crewed missions is planning with triple redundancy. Some critical components have triple backups to manage in case of failures. Failed components can be bypassed by switching to new ones. Ideally, it is preferable to have independent suppliers to avoid replication of failures. All such precautions can escalate costs and result in delays. Above all, quality workmanship is imperative for the success of any mission.

Setting aside catchy slogans, it is crucial to ensure long-term and consistent funding to maintain mission safety, upgrade infrastructure support, and establish a reliable supply chain. Modern-day lunar spacecraft are much larger and heavier than those in the earlier Apollo series, necessitating upgrades to aging facilities. It is unrealistic to expect private partners to contribute towards infrastructure development.

Space exploration is very specialized, and project vendors must retain specialized talent over the long term. Continuous baseline engineering research is necessary between major projects to assure long-term reliability and maintain global leadership.

Sustainable lunar exploration will generate numerous new technologies to meet its growing demands, creating high-paying jobs in the aerospace industry.

Educational institutions must step up by offering curricula tailored to the aerospace industry's needs. Higher education should be subsidized through scholarships funded by public funding and industry partnerships. This will help attract aspiring young men and women to pursue careers in space technology without being burdened by student loans.

* * * * * *

Chapter 17: The New Space Race to the Moon

In addition to the U.S. and Russia, Canada, and many European countries have been actively collaborating with NASA to develop space hardware and instrumentation in support of several ongoing programs. The U.S. and Russia have been working jointly to support their efforts in the modular development of the ISS.

The European Space Agency (ESA)[33] is a consortium of 22 EU states and several other cooperating members. Some of its meteorological satellites, known as *Meteosat*, and France's SPOT series of environmental satellites have been around for almost a quarter century. As stated in the previous chapter, the ARTEMIS program plans to include the European Service Module (ESM) in its ARTEMIS IV-VI mission to the Moon.

Canada has also been heavily involved with its own environmental satellites, such as Radarsat, which monitors sea ice and several others. Canada has also been highly active in NASA's Space Shuttle program by developing the shuttle's robotic arm for launching and retrieving satellites in orbit.

The Japan Aerospace Exploration Agency (JAXA) has also been a major space race player, developing advanced weather (GMS/Himawari), environmental monitoring, communications, GPS, and other applications. In 2014 JAXA launched a probe called *Hayabusa 2* to bring back samples from asteroid *Ryugu*, and in December 2020, they succeeded in bringing back small samples to Earth. They identified 23 types of amino acids in the samples; amino acids are key ingredients for life. JAXA collaborates with NASA and the European Space Agency (ESA) on numerous projects.

The modern industrial era has sparked a new space race towards the Moon, Mars, and even the Sun, with countries like China, India, Japan, South Korea, and the United Arab Emirates (UAE) joining the competition.

Additionally, several other countries, such as Saudi Arabia, Iraq, Morocco, Bahrain, Kuwait, and Pakistan, launched their own satellites through government or private vendors. Others include Algeria, Argentina, Australia, Brazil, Italy, Kazakhstan, Malaysia, Poland, and South Africa.

Recently, in June 2023, Indonesia had its communication satellite known as *SATRIA-1* launched into a geosynchronous orbit, parking it over equatorial Indonesia to provide free internet access to its people (Space.com)[34].

The future of space technology holds great potential as more countries recognize the importance of providing communication, the Internet, and other services to their people. Companies such as SpaceX, Blue Origin, and Boeing play a key role in making space technology accessible and affordable to many.

---

[33] ESA: tpts://www.esa.int/AboutUs/Corporate_news/Member_States_Cooperating_States
[34] Space.com: https://www.space.com/spacex-psn-satria-indonesian-satellite-launch

CHINA

Chinese Lunar Exploration Program

According to Wikipedia, the Chinese Lunar Exploration Program (CLEP) is a synonym for the *Change'* Project, named after the Chinese Moon Goddess. Change' refers to a series of lunar missions conducted by the China National Space Administration (CNSA). Since 2007, there have been a series of five missions to date:

- Change' 1 (2007)
- Change' 2 (2010)
- Change' 3 (2013) with Lander & Rover (*Yutu*)
- Change' 4 (2018/19) with Lander & Rover, *South Pole-Aitken Basin* on far side of Moon
- Change' 5 (2020) returned with 1.731 kilograms of lunar samples from the near side.
    - Discovers a sixth mineral by China named *Changesite-(Y)*, found to contain ^{3}He
- Future Change' 6-8 missions planned to all land on the *South-Pole Aitken (SPA) Basin*
- The Chang'e 6 spacecraft was launched successfully on May 3, 2024.
- As planned, it landed on the far side of the Moon and returned home safely with about two kilograms of soil samples ejected from the lunar mantle.
- Planned Crewed mission (2029-30) (Wikipedia)
- Queqiao-2 relay satellite was placed in lunar orbit on March 24, 2024 (Xinhua)[35]

Conducting lunar landings and experiments on the far side of the Moon requires the additional deployment of a 'relay satellite' called *Queqiao* in stationary orbit for all communications during the entire Change missions. This process adds another layer of difficulty to lunar exploration that the Change program has successfully accomplished.

In 2020, China's Change' 5 mission returned about 2 kilograms of lunar regolith samples from the lunar nearside. The China Space Administration (CNSA) and the China Atomic Energy Commission (CAEA) jointly announced that they had discovered a new mineral named *Changesite-(Y)*. This is China's sixth mineral to be discovered on the Moon as it joins the US and Russia in the quest to find new minerals on the Moon. Chinese researchers observed that Changesite-Y contains ^{3}He, the extraction of which can fuel the nuclear fusion process on the Moon.

---

[35] Xinhua, Huaxia (ed.): https://english.news.cn/20240325/edbf239ca39d48d2bdeabc975106e79e/c.html/

Chapter 17: The New Space Race to the Moon

According to the State Council of the PRC[36] Chinese experts analyzing lunar samples brought back by the Change' 5 mission "… discovered diverse glass materials with different physical origins -- liquid quenching, vapor deposition, and irradiation damage…".

They also found naturally formed glass fibers on the lunar surface, suggesting that lunar regolith could be used to process and produce glass-building materials.

INDIA

CHANDRAYAAN-3

On August 23, 2023, the Indian Space Research Organization (ISRO) successfully landed Chandrayaan-3 on the Moon, becoming the fourth country after the former Soviet Union, United States, and China. The *Chandrayaan-3* lunar lander known as *Vikram* successfully landed on the South Polar region of the Moon, a first for any country. A short while later, the lunar rover named *Pragyan* (Sanskrit for Supreme Intelligence) successfully rolled out of Vikram to begin its mission to probe the lunar surface. The mission was planned for a lunar day (14.75 Earth days).

During the Chandrayaan-3 mission, ISRO could restart the Vikram Lander and relocate it about 30-40 centimeters away by successfully firing its engines. They accomplished this incredible feat by conserving fuel through optimal orbital maneuvers during the mission.

The wide array of instruments onboard both the Lander Vikram and the Rover Pragyaan enabled ISRO to accomplish its mission goals encompassing soil thermal characteristics, presence of ice-water, lunar seismic activity, structure of lunar crust and mantle, and several others (DOS/ISRO)[37].

CHANDRAYAAN-4

The Chandrayaan-4 mission is scheduled to launch around 2028 or later. Its goals are to land on the Moon, collect lunar regolith, and safely return to Earth with collected soil samples.

THE UAE

The United Arab Emirates (UAE) astonished the world with its Emirates Mars Mission (EMM)[38] to orbit Mars and study its atmosphere's diurnal and seasonal characteristics. It carried a payload of three instruments to study the mechanisms involved in the upward transport of atmospheric gases like hydrogen and oxygen escaping from the planet. The UAE's Mars Mission *Hope* was launched on July 19, 2020, from Japan's Tanega Shima launch site and placed into Martian orbit on February 9, 2021.

JAPAN

Japan's JAXA is planning to launch a small-scale explorer lander called *the Smart Lander for Investigating Moon* (SLIM)[39] capable of performing pinpoint landings on the Moon's surface. Such miniaturization will enable the incorporation of lighter and more intelligent landing equipment for future

---

[36] PRC: https://english.www.gov.cn (January 11, 2024)
[37] DOS/ISRO: https://www.isro.gov.in/Chandrayaan3_Details.html
[38] EMM: https://www.emiratesmarsmission.ae/mission/about-emm
[39] SLIM: https://global.jaxa.jp/projects/sas/slim/

use in crewed lunar missions. In the past, the Apollo crew had to manually override the final landing maneuvers to select an optimal landing location.

Onboard SLIM is Japan's *X-Ray Imaging and Spectroscopy Mission (XRISM)*, a space telescope developed in collaboration with NASA and ESA. High-resolution spectral data from XRISM will enable scientists to study celestial X-ray objects in the Universe with massive imaging and high-resolution X-ray spectroscopy (NASA, 2024)[40].

On January 20, 2024, JAXA landed SLIM on the Moon, making Japan the fifth country to land on the lunar surface.

SOUTH KOREA

South Korea's first lunar mission is known as the *Korea Pathfinder Lunar Orbiter* (KPLO), also known as *Danuri*. It was launched by SpaceX Falcon 9 on August 5, 2022, from Cape Canaveral, USA, and placed into lunar polar orbit at 100 kilometers on December 16, 2022. Developed and operated by the Korea Aerospace Research Institute (KARI)[41] Danuri carries a payload of six instruments: five developed by KARI in collaboration with its university partners and NASA's Shadowcam, which will assist in mapping permanently shadowed areas located in the polar regions of the Moon containing water ice.

Danuri's program goals also include developing deep space communication and navigation technology, identifying potential landing sites for its planned lunar landing mission, testing a space internet, demonstrating the capabilities of its gamma-ray spectrometer for resource exploration of surface elements such as uranium, ^{3}He, silicon, and aluminum, and several other scientific experiments.

South Korea plans to make its first landing on the Moon utilizing indigenous launch technology developed by KARI.

ODYSSEUS

NASA's *Commercial Lunar Payload Services* (CLPS) industry partnership with *Intuitive Machines*, a Texas-based company, created history by returning to the Moon after 52 years. The Intuitive Machines lander named Odysseus[42] was launched by SpaceX on February 15th and landed successfully on the Moon's SPA basin a week later. It was carrying several instruments to the Moon. Intuitive Machines became the first private company to join the distinguished list of countries that have landed on the Moon.

PAKISTAN

Pakistan's Inaugural lunar cubesat, named iCube-Qammar, was launched successfully by China's Change'6 mission on May 3, 2024. The lunar module was designed by Islamabad's Institute of Space Technology (IST) in collaboration with China's Shangai University (SJTU), and Pakistan's space agency SUPARCO (*The Dawn*).

---

[40] NASA (2024): https://heasarc.gsfc.nasa.gov/docs/xrism/
[41] KARI: https://www.kari.re.kr/eng/sub03_07_01.do/
[42] Odysseus: https://www.intuitivemachines.com/

The iCube-Q Orbiter, weighing seven kilograms, carries two optical cameras to image the lunar surface over a period of three to six months, transmitting images to Earth.

According to *The Dawn*, the Change'6 opportunity was offered to Pakistan by CSNA after their proposal was accepted by the Asia Pacific Space Cooperation Organization (APSCO).

SOME CAVEATS AND CHALLENGES

The new lunar space race is on for access to life-sustaining resources such as water-ice, oxygen, and ^{3}He for fusion power generation. Many future missions are planned within the SPA basin of the Moon, which encompasses both the near and far sides. Missions on the far side must also rely on the presence of relay satellites for communication purposes.

Unlike on Mars, where day-night transitions are somewhat similar to Earth's, the long lunar nights add a considerable energy burden on missions. New sustainable energy production sources must be developed to overcome limitations posed by the polar regions. ^{3}He-based fusion energy seems plausible, but this resource requires considerable mining of lunar regolith. The catch-22 is that ^{3}He mining operations also require energy to operate equipment under lunar conditions. Traditional combustion engines will not work on the Moon, and solar options may be limited to its equatorial regions. NASA is also developing portable nuclear fission reactors.

Lunar regolith produces oxygen, and ^{3}He may not be a limiting factor, but water-ice distribution is confined primarily to the permanently shadowed regions (PSR) within the polar regions. Several countries will compete fiercely for this limited non-renewable resource vital for human survival on the Moon. The long-term exploration of the Moon will put a significant demand on harnessing this precious resource. New international agreements must be established and honored to continue harmonious lunar exploration.

More research and development must be supported in the energy sector to meet these new challenges in lunar exploration. Artificial intelligence (AI) shows considerable promise in quickly resolving issues and optimizing solutions when provided with the full spectrum of possibilities. Several countries will use AI to develop promising solutions to complex problems in space exploration.

More importantly, all lunar missions must perfect the art of landing right-side-up on the Moon. Earlier, the Apollo Program perfected this art because of its simple yet *sure-fire* engine technology. Another important requirement is to conserve fuel for performing unforeseen maneuvers during landing. In crewed missions, the final selection of the landing site can be performed manually by taking control. Nowadays, well-trained AI algorithms may be able to accomplish perfect and safe lunar landings when trained with detailed images of the terrain in combination with sure-fire engine technology.

* * * * * *

Chapter 18: Epilogue

NASA's phenomenally successful U.S. Apollo Program of the sixties and seventies deserves many accolades for the picture-perfect lunar landings, surface explorations, and capture of myriad artifacts and anomalies before safely returning home. They established a new benchmark in lunar exploration that remains challenging for all. The astronauts demonstrated unwavering courage, a keen vision, and a passion for documenting everything they encountered.

The success of the Apollo Program was not just the result of NASA's efforts but also a testament to the collaboration between engineers, scientists, technicians, contractors, academia, and others. Their collective achievement of landing Man on the Moon and meeting President Kennedy's challenge is truly monumental.

The Apollo Program also produced a wealth of satellite imagery, photographs, videos, and scientific papers. Many of the Hasselblad images are now available in *Flickr's* Project Apollo Archive. These fascinating images provide a deeper insight into the mysteries of our Moon.

Upon examination of the Project Apollo Flickr archives, a fascinating array of artifacts and anomalies from the lunar missions came to light. These archives reveal the presence of several types of large spacecraft, UFOs, or UAPs observed around the Moon, each with its unique shape, size, and propulsion system. The presence of drones among these lunar spacecraft only deepens the mystery, as their functions and ownership remain unknown. The lunar entities have adapted to the Moon's harsh environment by utilizing light drones capable of taking off and landing without any infrastructure support.

A large, dilapidated glass tower behind a glass wall suggests that the Moon may have been colonized thousands, if not millions, of years ago. The use of readily available glass aggregate in lunar regolith for use in structures must have been known to these early lunar visitors. We are now probably observing new and different groups or entities that followed them.

The Hasselblad imagery reveals the recurring presence of significant, transient '*U*' shaped markings or insignias over several parts of the lunar surface. These symbols also appear randomly in the sky, sometimes towering to heights reaching 700-800 kilometers in the lunar sky. Their exact significance, origins, or mechanisms remain unknown.

The indications of early lunar settlements piqued my interest in ancient spacecraft, especially any references to them in major world religions. In Chapter 5, I discussed examples of Hindu temples incorporating Vimanas, used by the primary deity, into their architecture.

Additionally, biblical texts allude to unknown entities interfering with God's creation, indicating that God intervened to rectify this situation by re-engineering or purifying evolution by reintroducing His preferred genetic stock.

Many religions also refer to humanity's ongoing struggle with giants that tormented societies in numerous ways. Rama's first order of business on Earth was to confront thousands of giants that were menacing societies. Several other significant religions also mention the existence of giants or Nephilim.

Numerous anecdotal accounts suggest that Gods or Alien Gods visited our planet in spacecraft thousands, if not millions, of years ago to establish their presence on Earth. This could be one of the reasons why ancient religious icons such as *Mandalas*, *Sri Chakras*, and *Yantras* keep showing up in different parts of the world. Interestingly, one of the lunar craters (*Franklin*) located towards the northeast of the *near side* appears to have a faintly distinguishable *Bhuvaneswari chakra* etched on its surface. This pattern seems to have weathered considerably over time, attesting to its antiquity.

The ancient Puranas yielded several important clues: (1) Mahayuga cycles of 4.32M years each, (2) the Four Yugas within each Maha Yuga, (3) the specific yugas during which giants (Nephilim) inhabit the Earth, (4) formulation of the Life Cycle of the Universe (Viz., *Brahma's Clock*), and (5) that Lord Shiva is credited with mantric (voice activated) Vimanas mentioned in the epics Ramayana and Mahabharata.

We have seen how the Mahayuga cycles provide a simple mathematical formulation to navigate into our past. For example, the Ramayana occurred during the tail end of the 24th Treta Yuga, about 18.156M years ago. At the same time, the Mahabharata took place during the tail end of the 28th Dvapara Yuga, about 5,126 years ago. Interestingly, the dinosaurs became extinct about sixty-six million years ago during the Satya Yuga, associated with the 16th Mahayuga cycle.

The Yuga cycles also suggest that evolution is cyclical and that, paradoxically, human attributes appear to diminish in successive yugas within each Mahayuga. Individuals from the Satya Yuga are significantly more intelligent than those in the Kali Yuga by divine genetic design. Therefore, it is highly probable that some intelligent civilization from an earlier Yuga may have developed the technological means to explore the Moon and other parts of our solar system.

We have seen how Vedic Cosmology arrived at the age of our Universe in trillions of years, starting from a simple Mahayuga cycle, all without supercomputers. We are now said to be halfway through the 7th cycle of our Universe; that is, the world has already experienced not one but six *Big Bangs*! This may explain the auspiciousness of the number 7 in several world religions. There are also seven days in a week!

The Gods or Alien Gods have already assigned names of the next seven Manus responsible for completing the remaining Manvantaras associated with the current *Sveta Varaha Kalpa* (Tables 3.2-3.3). After that period, the world is scheduled for a planned deluge for the next Manvantara. Fortunately, we may not have to worry about this impending cataclysm.

Early Christian texts allude to large subterranean wells that seem to upwell massive volumes of water deep within the Earth during significant flooding events. Recent research has shown that the Earth contains a vast interior ocean around four hundred miles below the surface, surrounded by layers of ringwoodite. The mechanism behind the upwelling of this underground water is currently unknown. These deep wells could have a modulating influence on rising sea levels. Future research must comprehend the Earth's hydrological cycle over the millennia.

It is proposed that the Gods or Alien Gods may have used the Moon as a base to launch their various religious campaigns on Earth for thousands, if not millions, of years. It is important to note that all religions appeared sequentially over time without any overlap. Each religion has stories about how the Gods communicated with them from above.

They may have arrived on the Moon in large spacecraft and then transferred to smaller spacecraft, shuttling freely between the Moon and the Earth. We may find their technological prowess incomprehensible compared to our relatively modest accomplishments. It is even probable that some of the UAPs observed by the public around the Earth may, in fact, be located on the Moon.

The Moon, our nearest neighbor, and our only natural satellite is quite literally a stone's throw from Earth compared to other celestial bodies in our Solar system. The examples cited in this book indicate the highly probable presence of unknown advanced civilizations on the Moon. The current situation on the lunar surface may have changed somewhat since the Apollo era; more *in situ* validation may be required to substantiate these claims.

The concept of spacecraft, *UFOs,* or UAPs is nothing new to Earth; it may have already witnessed these alien *thingummies* far longer than any of our ancient religious texts can narrate. However, the frequency of UAP sightings on Earth is rising as more people now have the technological means to quickly document such incidents with their cell phone cameras and post them instantly on social media platforms.

A few of the spacecraft presented in this book may have occasionally appeared on some social media sites. Gone are the days when you may have your SLR camera safely tucked away in the mess of the glove compartment in your car to avail yourself of when the occasion suddenly arises.

The modern-day *Space Race* has already begun, with several new entrants from across the world exploring the Moon, Mars, and even the Sun. The race is on for access to limited life-sustaining resources on the Moon, Mars, other planets, and their moons.

Sustainable space exploration will require significant investments in new technologies involving propulsion, energy production, mining, and harnessing water and oxygen to meet new challenges. Sustained funding is also essential to maintain the lunar and planetary exploration momentum.

With its proposed lunar Gateway, the ARTEMIS mission will revolutionize lunar exploration and provide the framework for planetary exploration. Partnerships with the European consortium and the U.S. Industry will usher in a new era in lunar exploration. Technological innovations will facilitate the establishment of lunar colonies, enable long-term planetary exploration, and create significant employment opportunities for scientists, engineers, and highly skilled workers.

Mystic Moon is an *Odyssey*, a long journey from ancient visitors to contemporary lunar explorers. The future of space exploration is limitless and will surely provide opportunities for future generations of humanity. The development of innovative new technologies in space exploration will also require the continued nurturing of our educational systems and challenge younger generations to avail themselves of the available opportunities.

* * * * * *

References

Achutuni, R., and Menzel, A. (1999). Space Systems Considerations in the Design of Advanced Geostationary Operational Environmental Satellites. *Advances in Space Research*, *23*(8), 1377–1384.

Ahrens, C. (unknown): Lunar Length of Day. NASA Goddard Spaceflight Center, Greenbelt, MD, pp.1-4 (Caitlin_Lunar Length of Day_paper.pdf).

Aveni, A. F. (2015). Between the Lines: The Mystery of the Giant Ground Drawings of Ancient Nazca, Peru. Peru. Univ. of Texas Press.

Barra, M. (2012). Ancient Aliens on the Moon. Adventures Unlimited Press, pp. 256.

Basu, B. (1916). Matsya Puranam, Chapters 1-128. Vol. XVII-Part 1. The Sacred Books of the Hindus. ISBN Volume 17, pt. 1: 0-404-57841-1. Reprinted (1974) by AMS Press Inc. N.Y. 10003

Bausback, E (2024). NASA's Fission Surface Power Project Energizes Lunar Exploration. In *Glenn Communications*. January 31, 2024.

Biggs, R., (2009). F-1 Saturn V First Stage Engine (Rocketdyne). Chpt. One. In Fisher, S.C., and Rahman, S.A., (Eds.) **Remembering the Giants: Apollo Rocket Propulsion Development**. PP. 15-26. NASA Monograph In Aerospace History No. 45. John C. Stennis Space Center

Bird K & Sherwin, B. (2006). American Prometheus: The Triumph and Tragedy of J. Robert Oppenheimer. Borzoi Books. Published by Alfred A. Knopf.

Boyce, C. (2009). AJ-10-137 Apollo Service Module Engine (Aerojet). Chpt. Five. In Fisher, S.C., and Rahman, S.A., (Eds.) **Remembering the Giants: Apollo Rocket Propulsion Development**. PP. 51–58. NASA Monograph In Aerospace History No. 45. John C. Stennis Space Center.

Budge, E.A.W. (1920). The Babylonian Story of the Deluge and the Epic of Gilgamish: With an Account of the Royal Libraries of Nineveh. British Museum, Printed by the Order of the Trustees, pp:1-61.

Childress, D. H. (2004). VIMANA Aircraft of Ancient India & Atlantis. Adventures Unlimited Press.

Coffman, P. (2009). J-2 Saturn v 2nd and 3rd Stage Engine (Rocketdyne). Chpt. Two. In Fisher, S.C., and Rahman, S.A., (Eds.) **Remembering the Giants: Apollo Rocket Propulsion Development**. PP. 27–38. NASA Monograph In Aerospace History No. 45. John C. Stennis Space Center.

Däniken, E. v. (2011). Arrival of the gods: Revealing the alien landing sites of Nazca. Tantor Media.

Däniken, E. v. (2013). Evidence of the Gods: A visual tour of Alien Influence in the ancient world, ISBN-13: 978-1-60163-247-0, The Career Press Inc., New Page Books.

Filipovic, M. D., Horner, J., Crawford, E. J., & Tothill, N. (2013). Mass Extinction and the Structure of the Milky Way. Serb. Astron, J. No, 1, 1–6.

Forester, B. (2013). Nazca: Decoding the Riddle of the Lines. CreateSpace Publishing, 142–9781492327585.

Harmon, T. (2009). SE-7 and SE-8 Engines (Rocketdyne). Chpt. Four. In Fisher, S.C., and Rahman, S.A., (Eds.) **Remembering the Giants: Apollo Rocket Propulsion Development**. PP. 51-58. NASA Monograph In Aerospace History No. 45. John C. Stennis Space Center.

Hinman, B. (2015). The Mystery of the Nazca lines. Core Library. ISBN 10:1680780255/ISBN 13:9781680780253.

Jeffrey, C. (2014). Structure and evolution of the lunar Procellarum region as revealed by GRAIL gravity data. **Nature**, 514, pp. 68–71.

Josyer, G. R. (1973). Maharshi Bharadwaja's Vymaanika-Shaastra or Science of Aeronautics: Part of His Unknown Work "Yantra Sarvasva" or "All About Machines. Mysore, India: " Coronation Press.

Kindy, D. (2023). The Man Who Fell to Earth, Air and Space Quarterly, Summer 2023. The Smithsonian.

Kulaichev, A. P. (1984). Sri Yantra and its Mathematical Properties. Ind. Jour. of Hist. of Sci, 19(3), 279–292.

Leonard, G.H. (1977). Somebody else is on the moon. Pocketbooks, PP. 266.

Medvedev, M. V., & Melott, A. L. (2007). Do Extragalactic Cosmic Rays Induce Cycles in Fossil Diversity? The Astrophysical Journal, 664, 879–889.

Mukunda, H. S., Deshpande, S. M., Nagendra, H. R., Prabhu, A., & Govindaraju, S. P. (2021). A Critical Study of the Work of "Vymanika Shastra. 1–23.

Neufeld, M. (2008). Von Braun: Dreamer of space, engineer of war. Random House.

Penrose, R. (2006). Before the Big Bang: An Outrageous New Perspective and its Implications for Particle Physics. In Proceedings of EPAC 2006 (pp. 2759–2762).

Penrose, R. (2012). Cycles of Time: An Extraordinary New View of the Universe. Vintage Books.

Pisacane, V.L., and Moore, R.C. (1994). **Fundamentals of Space Systems**, JHU/APL Series In Science and Engineering, Oxford University Press, ISBN 0-19-507497

Rampino, M. R., Caldeira, K., & Zhu, Y. (2020). A 27. 5-My underlying periodicity detected in extinction episodes of non-marine tetrapods. Historical Biology.

Rice, D. (2020). Mass extinctions of Earth's land animals follow a cycle study finds. In USA Today.

Richard, D. T., Glenar, D. A., Stubbs, T. J., Davis, S. S., & Colaprete, A. (2011). Light Scattering by complex particles in the Moon's exosphere: Toward a taxonomy of models for the realistic simulation of the scattering of lunar dust. Planetary and Space Science, 59, 1804–1818.

Roy, M. (1984). The Concept of Yantra in the Samarangana-Sutradhara of Bhoja. Ind. Jour. of Hist. of Sci, 19(2), 118–124.

Schmandt, B., Jacobsen, S.D., Zhenxian Liu, D., K.G. (2014). Dehydration melting at the top of the lower mantle. **Science**, 13 Jun 2014, Vol. 344. No. 6189, pp. 1265-1268.

Sutton, G.P., & Biblarz O. (2016). *Rocket Propulsion Elements*, ISBN-10: 1118752658, (9th Ed.), Wiley.

Swami Prakasanand Saraswati, H. D. (2007). The True History and the Religion of India: A Concise Encyclopedia of Authentic Hinduism. Macmillan India, Ltd. PP.1-807, ISBN13: 978-0230-63065-9.

Valmiki and Griffith, R.T.H. The Ramayan of Valmiki, Translated by R.T.H. Griffith. Kindle Books.

Veda Vyasa, Swami Paramananda (2020): Mahabharata: The Complete Collection with bonus of the Upanishads (18 Volumes), Ageless Reads (Editor), translated by Kisari Mohan Ganguli, Kindle Edition.

Veda Vyasa: Puranas – All 18 Maha Puranas (English): Vishnu, Naradiya, Padma, Garuda, Varaha, Linga, Shiva, Skanda, Markandeya, Bhavishya, Vaman, Brahma. Kindle Edition., pp. 1,679.

Wilson, H.H. (1840). The Vishnu Purana, Kindle Edition published by Evinity Publishing Inc, 2009

Worthy, T. H., Hand, S. J., Archer, M., Scofield, R. P., & Pietri, D. (2019). Supplementary material from "Evidence for a giant parrot from the Early Miocene of New Zealand." Royal Society Collection.

XENON Collaboration* (2019). Observation of two-neutrino double electron capture in 124Xe with XENON1T. Nature, 568(7753), 532-535. https://doi.org/10.1038/s41586-019-1124-4

Some Relevant WEB Publications:

Penrose, R. (2018, August 21). New evidence for cyclic universe claimed by Roger Penrose and colleagues –. Physics World. https://physicsworld.com/a/new-evidence-for-cyclic-universe-claimed-by-roger-penrose-and-colleagues/

Wikipedia contributors. (2023, December 26). **Ararat anomaly**. Wikipedia, The Free Encyclopedia.https://en.wikipedia.org/w/index.php?title=Ararat_anomaly&oldid=1191877387

Wikipedia contributors. (2024, January 16). *Kardashev scale*. Wikipedia, The Free Encyclopedia. https://en.wikipedia.org/w/index.php?title=Kardashev_scale&oldid=1196180428

Wikipedia contributors. (2022, December 21). **List of craters on the moon**. Wikipedia, The Free Encyclopedia. https://en.wikipedia.org/w/index.php?title=List_of_craters_on_the_Moon&oldid=1128616333

CERN: (January 23, 2024): http://home.cern/:

Mersmann, K (May 29, 2019): Three Ways to Travel at (Nearly) the Speed of Light. https://www.nasa.gov/solar-system/three-ways-to-travel-at-nearly-the-speed-of-light/

Blue Origin (2023, December 19): https://www.blueorigin.com/

History and timeline of the ISS. (n.d.). Issnationallab.org. Retrieved January 23, 2024, from https://www.issnationallab.org/about/iss-timeline/

Apollo Photographic Support Data. (n.d.). Asu.edu. Retrieved January 23, 2024, from http://Apollo.sese.asu.edu/ABOUT_SCANS/index.html

Tool for interactive plotting, sonification, and 3D orbit display (TIPSOD) (GSC-14732-1). (n.d.). Nasa.gov. Retrieved January 23, 2024, from https://software.nasa.gov/software/GSC-14732-1

Ladd, D., Wright, E., Ladd, D., Petro, N., & Ladd, D. (2017, October 6). NASA scientific visualization studio. SVS. (Lunar Day). https://svs.gsfc.nasa.gov/12739

Apollo Browse Gallery: ASU Apollo Image Archive (Retrieved March 28, 2024): https://wms.lroc.asu.edu/apollo/browse/

NASA. (2009a, July 8). Apollo 8: Mission details. https://www.nasa.gov/mission_pages/apollo/missions/apollo8.html

Loff, S. A. (2015, April 17). Apollo 11 mission overview. NASA. https://www.nasa.gov/mission_pages/apollo/missions/apollo11.html

NASA. (2009a, July 8). Apollo 12: The pinpoint mission. NASA. https://www.nasa.gov/mission_pages/apollo/missions/apollo12.html

NASA. (2009a, July 8). Apollo 13: Mission details. NASA. https://www.nasa.gov/mission_pages/apollo/missions/apollo13.html

NASA. (2009a, July 8). Apollo 14: Mission details. NASA. https://www.nasa.gov/mission_pages/apollo/missions/apollo14.html

NASA. (2009, July 8). Apollo 15: Mission details. NASA. https://www.nasa.gov/mission_pages/apollo/missions/apollo15.html

ARTEMIS SLS: NASA. (2019, November 1). Rocket to the moon: What is the exploration upperstage? NASA. https://www.nasa.gov/exploration/systems/sls/multimedia/rocket-to-the-moon-what-is-the-exploration-upper-stage.html

Mohon, L. (2014, October 30). Getting to know you, Rocket Edition: **Interim cryogenic propulsion stage.** https://www.nasa.gov/sls/interim_cryogenic_propulsion_stage_141030.html

The Moon - NASA science. (2023, March 27). Nasa.gov. http://www.nasa.gov/moon:

Moon Facts (Interactive). Nasa.gov. Retrieved January 23, 2024, from https://science.nasa.gov/moon/facts/:

Scott, D. R. (n.d.). **The Apollo program**. NASA. Retrieved January 23, 2024, from http://www.nasa.gov/mission_pages/apollo/missions/index.html

Apollo Landing Sites: Usra.edu. Retrieved January 23, 2024, from http://www.lpi.usra.edu/publications/slidesets/apollolanding/:

Apollo Missions. Usra.edu. Retrieved January 23, 2024, from

Appendices

http://www.lpi.usra.edu/lunar/missions/apollo/

Apollo 70mm Slide Catalog: Usra.edu. Retrieved January 23, 2024, from

http://www.lpi.usra.edu/resources/apollo/catalog/70mm/

Lunar Orbiter Photo Gallery: Usra.edu. Retrieved January 23, 2024, from
http://www.lpi.usra.edu/resources/lunarorbiter/

Lunar Orbiter-4 Gallery: Usra.edu. Retrieved January 23, 2024, from

http://www.lpi.usra.edu/resources/lunarorbiter/mission/?4

Lunar Orbiter-5 Gallery: Usra.edu. Retrieved January 23, 2024, from
http://www.lpi.usra.edu/resources/lunarorbiter/mission/?5

Steigerwald, W. (2015, August 17). NASA's LADEE spacecraft finds neon in lunar atmosphere. NASA. http://www.nasa.gov/content/goddard/ladee-lunar-neon

The Apollo Lunar Roving Vehicle. Nasa.gov. Retrieved January 23, 2024, from http://nssdc.gsfc.nasa.gov/planetary/lunar/apollo_lrv.html

Apollo17: Mission details. http://www.nasa.gov/mission_pages/apollo/missions/apollo17.html

Weather on the Moon: NASA Science. Retrieved January 23, 2024, from https://moon.nasa.gov/inside-and-out/dynamic-moon/weather-on-the-moon/

The lunar gold rush: How moon mining could work. NASA Jet Propulsion Laboratory (JPL). Retrieved January 23, 2024, from https://www.jpl.nasa.gov/infographics/the-lunar-gold-rush-how-moon-mining-could-work

Mystic Moon: A Lunar Odyssey

Appendix-1A:
Lunar Near Side

(Annotations Credit: Rao Achutuni) (Credit: "Claudio Caridi" - stock.adobe.com)

Appendices

Appendix-1B:
Lunar Far Side

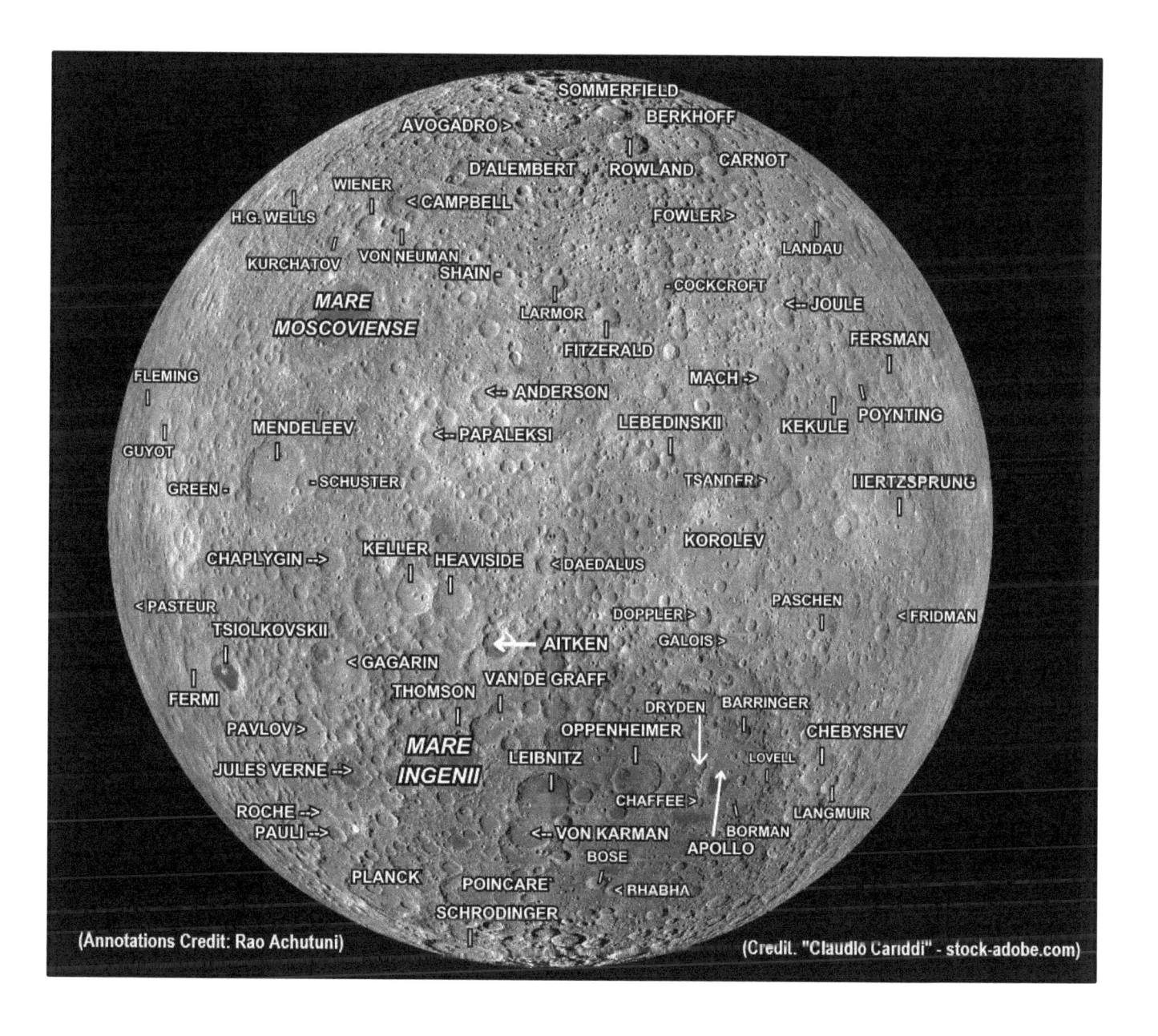

Mystic Moon: A Lunar Odyssey

Appendix-1C:
Lunar South-Pole Aitken (SPA) Basin

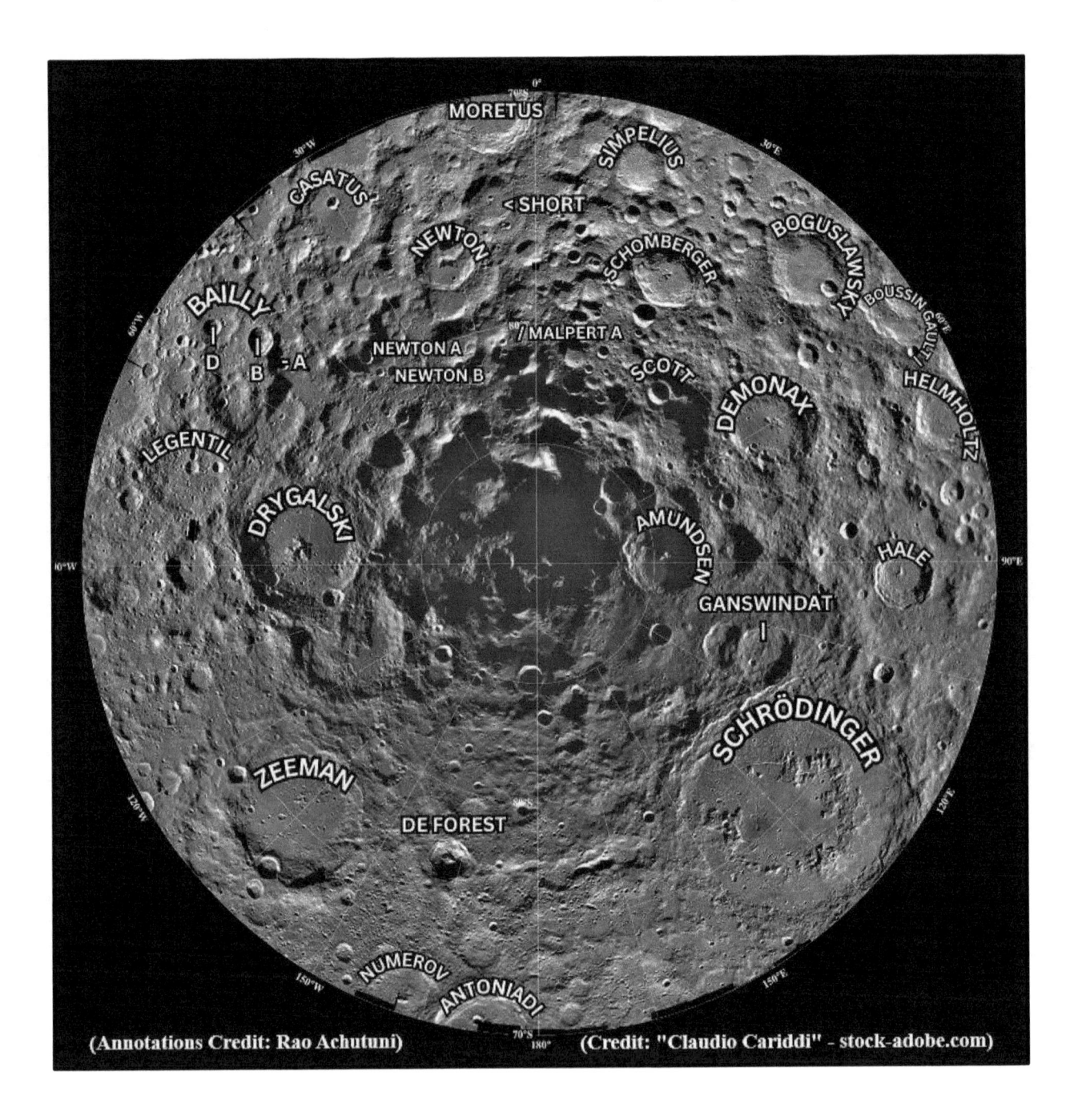

(Annotations Credit: Rao Achutuni) (Credit: "Claudio Cariddi" - stock-adobe.com)

Appendix-2:
Basics of Satellite Orbits

Kepler's Laws of Motion:

1. All planets move in elliptical orbits, with the Sun at one of the foci

2. A planet sweeps across equal areas in equal intervals of time

3. The square of the orbital period (T) of a planet is proportional to the cube of the semimajor axis

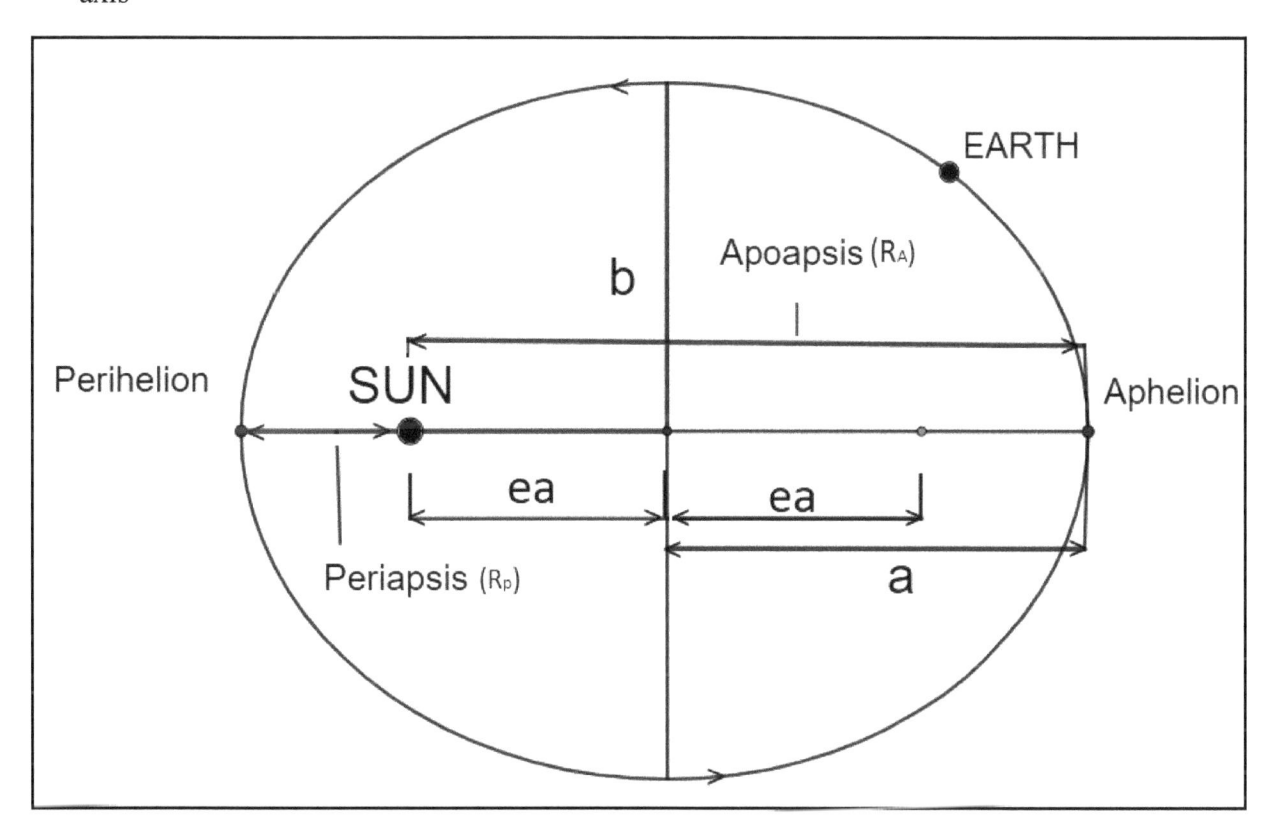

Fig. A2.1 Orbital parameters of Earth's elliptical motion around the Sun. Perihelion is the closest approach of Earth to Sun and Aphelion is the farthest; Periapsis and Apoapsis refer to their corresponding distances. The parameter a = semimajor axis; b = minor axis; e = eccentricity; and T = orbital period (Earth year).

Kepler's First Law: Planets revolve around the Sun in elliptical orbits.

The orbital plane is known as the *Ecliptic*. The Earth revolves around the Sun in an elliptical orbit (Fig. A2.1). It also revolves around its own axis over a period of 24 hours. The axis of the Earth is tilted at an angle of 23.5° to the ecliptic.

The direction of motion of Earth around the Sun is counterclockwise and rotation around its own axis is from west to east. That is the Sun appears to rise from the east and sets to the west.

The closest point of approach of the Earth to the Sun is known as the *Perihelion* while the farthest point in the orbit is known as the *Aphelion*.

In the case of satellite orbits, these two points are known as the *Perigee* and *Apogee*, respectively.

The corresponding distances (in kilometers or miles) from the Sun are referred to as *Periapsis (Rp)* and *Apoapsis (R_A)* and given by:

$R_P = a(1-e)$ and

$R_A = a(1+e)$

where *a* is the semi-major axis and *e* refers to the eccentricity of the ellipse. In the case of a circular orbit, e = 0.

Kepler's Second Law: A planet traverses' equal areas (segments ΔA) in equal intervals of time (Δt) as it orbits the Sun (Fig. A2.2).

In simple terms the ratio:

$\Delta A/\Delta t = H/2m$ = constant, where H is the angular momentum of planet and m= mass of planet.

Kepler's Third Law: The square of the orbital period of a planet (T) is proportional to the cube of the semi-major axis (a): In the case of the Earth,

$T^2 \propto a^3$ or $T = 2\Pi\sqrt{(a^3/\gamma)}$

where $\gamma = Gm_E$

G = the gravitational constant (6.670×10^{-11} N m^{2}kg^{-3}) and

m_E = mass of Earth (5.977×10^{24} kg).

$V = 1037.5646 \times \cos\theta$

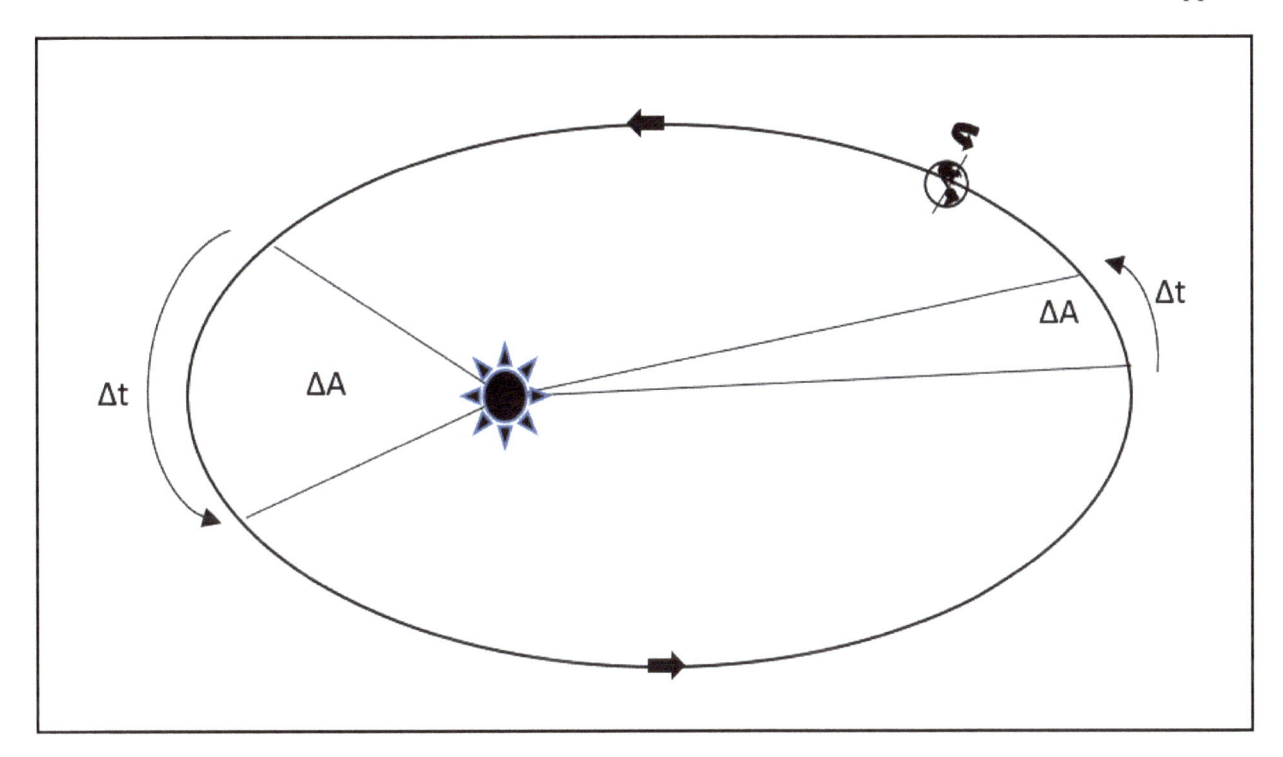

Figure A2.2 Kepler's Second Law: Equal areas (ΔA) are traversed in equal intervals of time (Δt) by Earth and other planets orbiting the Sun. Objects speed up as they approach closer to Sun (Perihelion) in orbit.

Prograde and Retrograde Orbits

In *Prograde Orbits* the direction of rotation of the object is in the same direction as its primary (Fig. A2.3a). All planets, except for Venus and Uranus, rotate in the same direction as the Sun. The Sun rotates in an anticlockwise direction with a slight tilt of 7.25° from the perpendicular to the plane of the ecliptic.

In a *Retrograde Orbit* (Fig. A2.3b) the direction of rotation of the object is in the opposite direction to that of the primary (P).

Both Venus and Uranus have retrograded orbits since they rotate in a direction opposite to that of the Sun. Triton, the largest of Neptune's 13 moons, is the only 'large' moon in the Solar system to have a retrograde orbit.

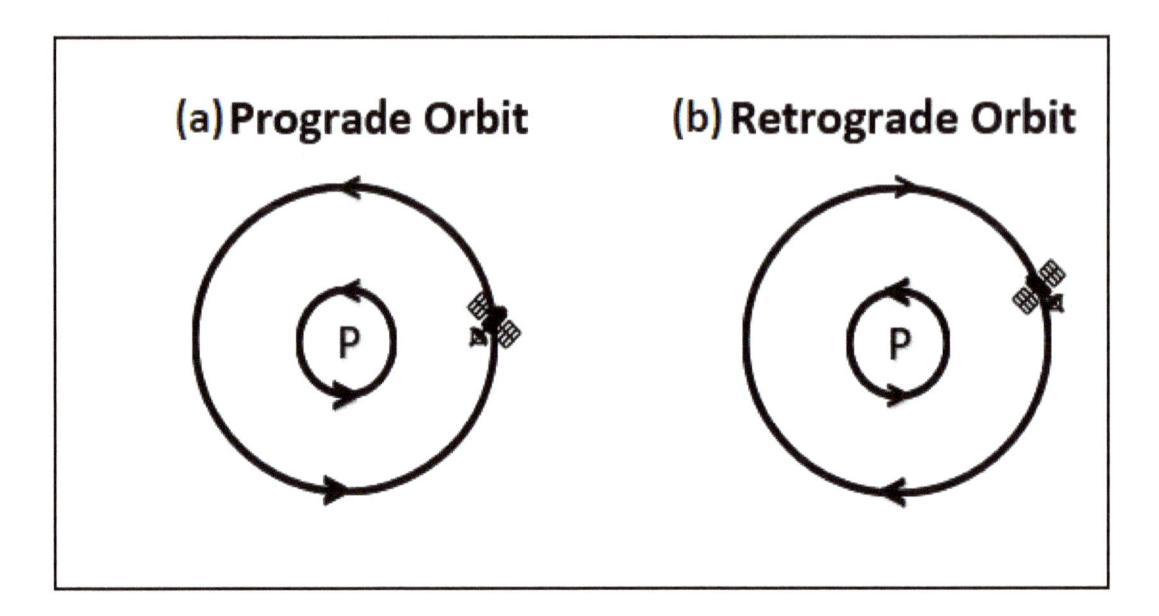

Fig. A2.3a-b. In a Prograde Orbit the Primary Object and Satellite Both Revolve in Same Direction (Clockwise or Anticlockwise), Rotational Direction is Opposite to One Another in Retrograde Orbits

Most satellites orbiting the Earth are known as *artificial* or manufactured satellites. The Moon is the Earth's only natural satellite. On the other hand, Comets and asteroids are not considered to be Earth's satellites since they are mostly passing by. Comets such as *Halley's comet* orbit the Sun and pass by Earth once every 75 years. There may be many others with extremely long orbital periods that we may not be aware of yet.

TYPE OF ORBITS

Basically, there are three types of Earth orbits: (1) Low-Earth Orbits (altitude range of 180 – 2,000 km); (2) Medium Earth Orbits (2,000 – 35,780 km); and (3) High Earth Orbits ($\geq$ 35,780 km) (NASA, 2009)

Low-Earth Orbits (LEOs)

Low-Earth Orbits (LEOs) are used largely in situations where frequent temporal coverage with high spatial resolution is desired, such as in environmental monitoring, agricultural monitoring, military applications, space telescopes, astronomical applications, and others.

Crewed missions such as the earlier Space Shuttle Missions and the International Space Station (ISS) belong to this domain. All the Apollo missions were initially inserted into equatorial LEOs before being injected into a Trans-Lunar trajectory (Fig. A2.4).

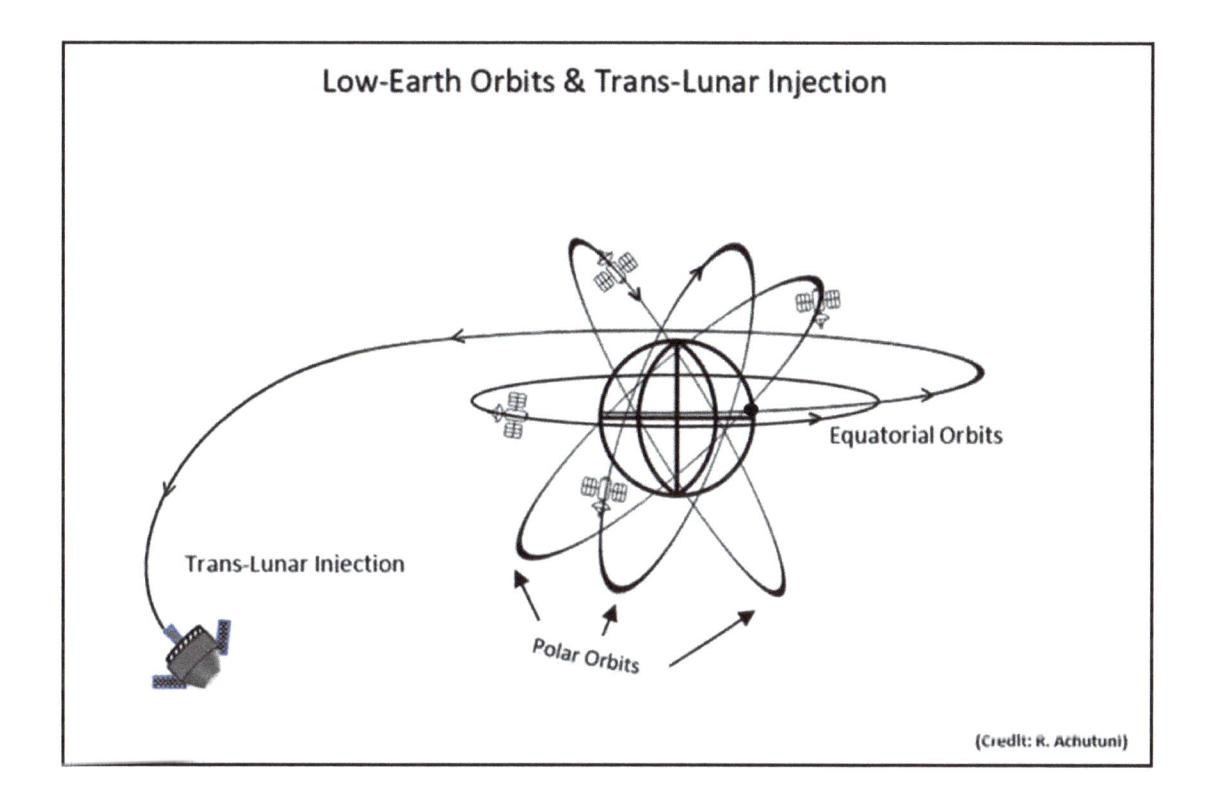

Fig. A2.4 Schematic of Low-Earth Polar orbiting satellites and initial Equatorial Orbits of crewed lunar missions which are transferred from the parked orbit to another coplanar orbit via a Hohmann transfer prior to the Trans-Lunar Injection.

Hohmann Transfer or Hohmann Transfer Orbit

Initially, the spacecraft is launched into a low-Earth equatorial orbit to take advantage of the Earth's Coriolis force which happens to be a maximum at the equator. This is the reason many rocket launches are from locations close to the equator. A much larger thrust is needed to launch from locations at higher latitudes. For this reason, all the Soviet *Soyuz* rockets had to deliver heavier thrusts than their American (Kennedy Space Center) or French (Kourou, French Guiana) counterparts when launched from the Baikonur Cosmodrome in Kazakhstan (45. 97°N latitude). The landings of all Russian as well as former Soviet Union's crewed missions is always on land and not on water.

The spacecraft must be moved from its initial or *parking* orbit to its *final* orbit through an intermediary two-stage transfer process known as a *Homann Transfer* or *Hohmann Orbit*. There are several types of transfer orbits available with varying degrees of time and energy requirements. The selection of the appropriate transfer orbit is dictated by the mission requirements, energy constraints and available onboard fuel, and time constraints. A faster direct *radial transfer* approach may be preferable when time is of the essence, such as in an emergency.

The Homann Transfer is a slow but energy-efficient way to move a spacecraft from a smaller circular orbit to another of a larger radius in the same orbital plane and is termed an *outward transfer*. The reverse process of transferring a spacecraft from a larger outward orbit into a smaller inner one is termed an *inward transfer*.

The Homann Transfer or orbit for an outward transfer is illustrated in Figure A2.5. Consider two circles with a common center C. The inner circle represents the spacecraft's *Parking Orbit* while the outer circle with a larger diameter represents the desired *Final Orbit*.

The transfer ellipse is tangential to both the inner and outer circles at the Periapsis (A) and Apoapsis (B) points as shown. The distance CA is the radius of the inner circle, whereas CB is the radius of the larger outer circle, and the distance AB represents the major axis of the transfer ellipse. The transfer is accomplished in two stages by firing thrusters to achieve incremental changes in velocity of ΔV_1 at the Periapsis and ΔV_2 at the Apoapsis. The total change in velocity to affect the transfer is given by the sum of ΔV_1 and ΔV_2. Sometimes the spacecraft may have to be slowed down during the transfer by firing a thruster in the opposite direction.

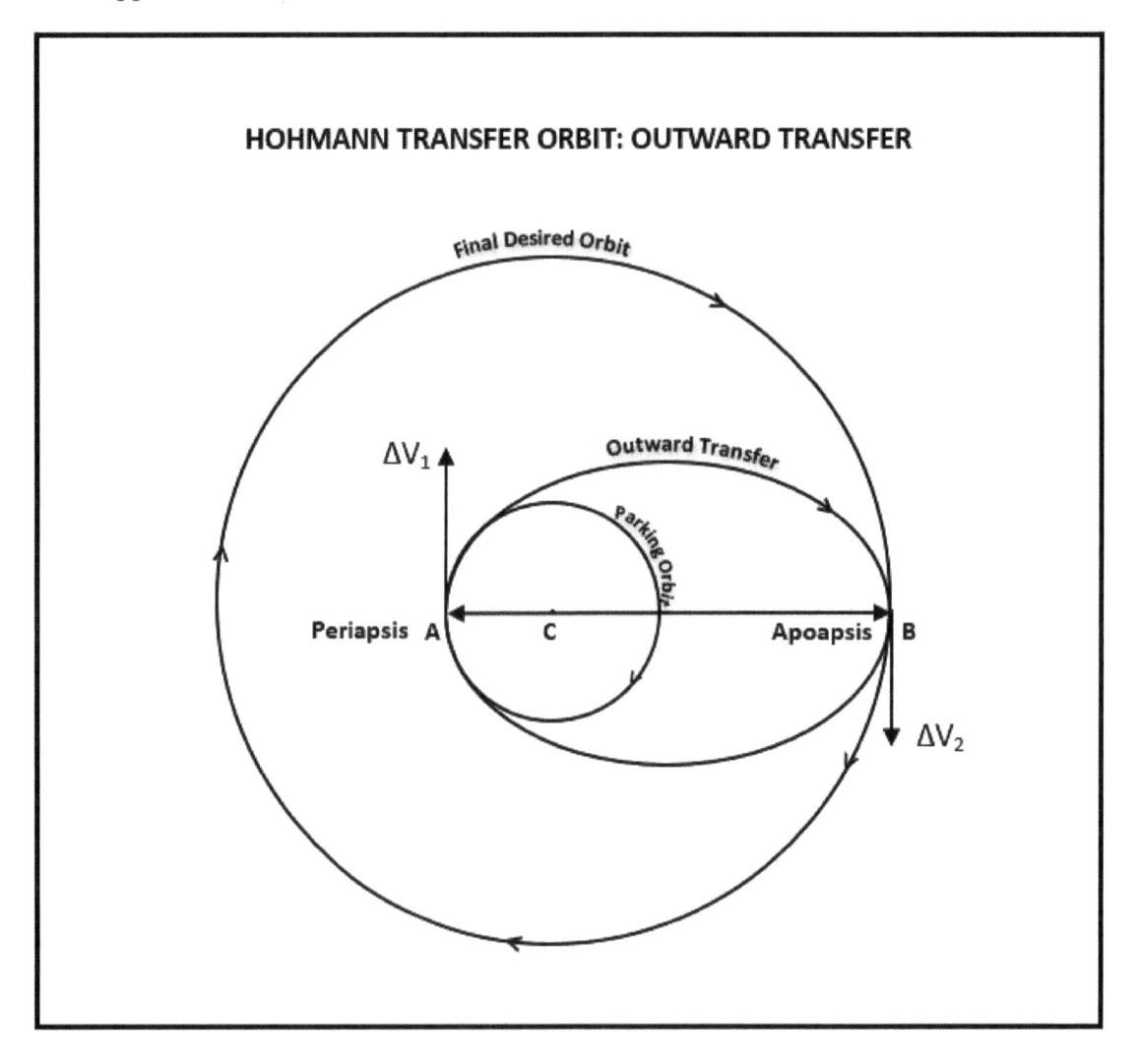

Fig. A2.5 Hohmann Transfer Orbit: Outward Transfer

International Space Station

Appendices

The first segment of the International Space Station (ISS) was originally launched on November 20, 1998, from the Baikonur Cosmodrome in Kazakhstan. The ISS has a perigee altitude of 408 kilometers (253.5 mi) and an apogee altitude of 410 kilometers (254.8 mi). It has an orbital inclination of 51.64° and an orbital period of 92.68 minutes. The rest of the ISS was launched in another thirty missions spanning a period of over 10 years involving collaboration from 5 space agencies and 15 countries. Its components weigh about 460 tons and are spread over an area of a football field (ISS, 2006). Of course, the ISS is a continuously evolving scientific endeavor in terms of scientific scope, instrumentation as well as multi-disciplinary astronauts from several participating countries.

The global orbital tracks of the ISS are shown in Figure A2.6. The northern orbital extent does not cover Alaska, but the southern extent covers the tip of the South American continent.

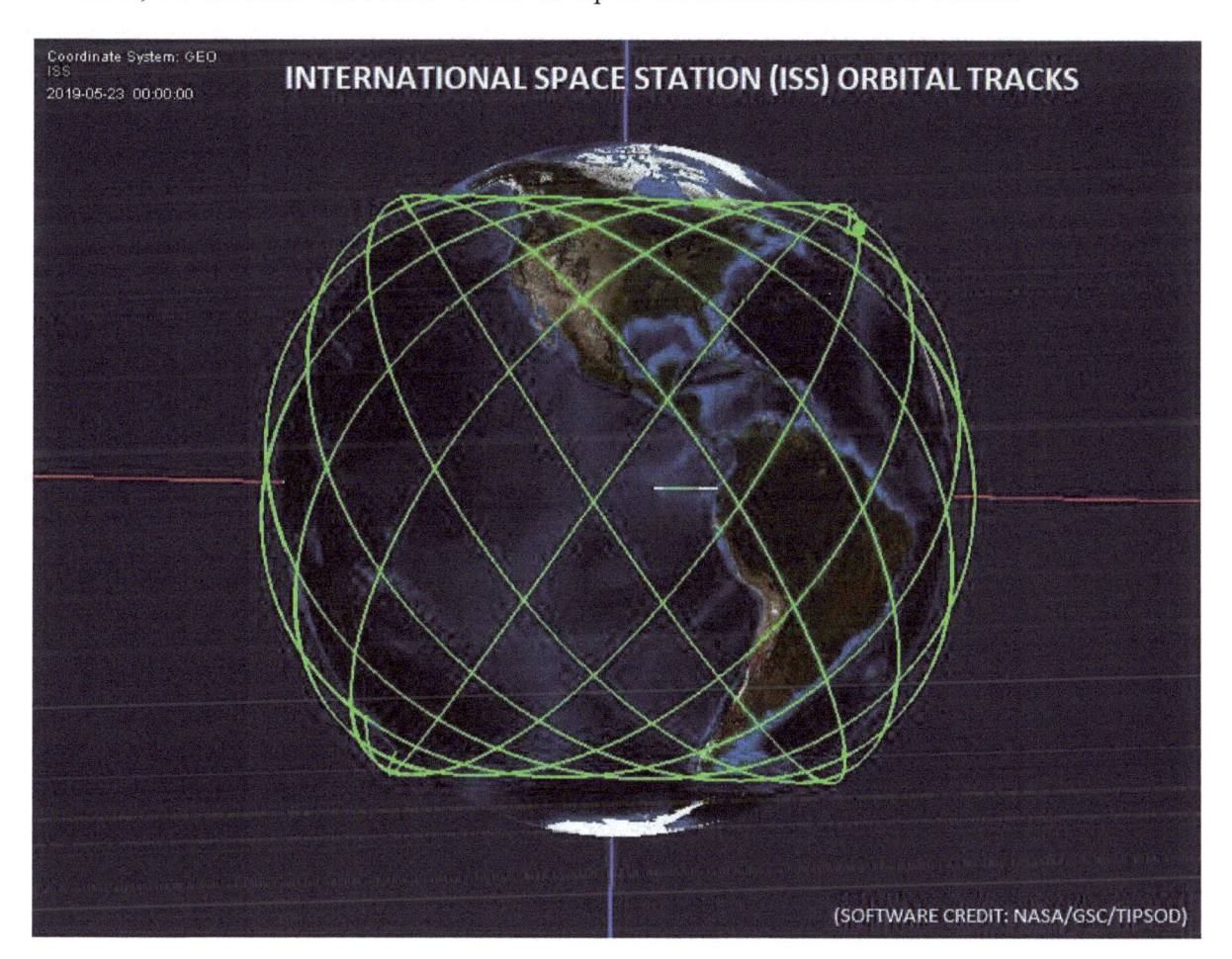

Fig. A2.6 Global orbital Tracks of the International Space Station (ISS) generated using an inclination angle of 51.64°.

Polar Orbiting Environmental Satellites (POES) orbit the Earth at various inclination angles depending upon the application, desired coverage, and return frequency. A high inclination of about 98° provides frequent coverage along narrow swaths. The satellite return period can be adjusted by varying its inclination. Typically, the POES have an orbital period of about one hundred minutes. The orbital paths generated by NOAA's polar-orbiting NOAA-19 satellite are shown in a North Polar view in Figure A2.7. Notice the circular gap in coverage when viewed from above the North Pole. A similar gap in coverage occurs over the South Pole.

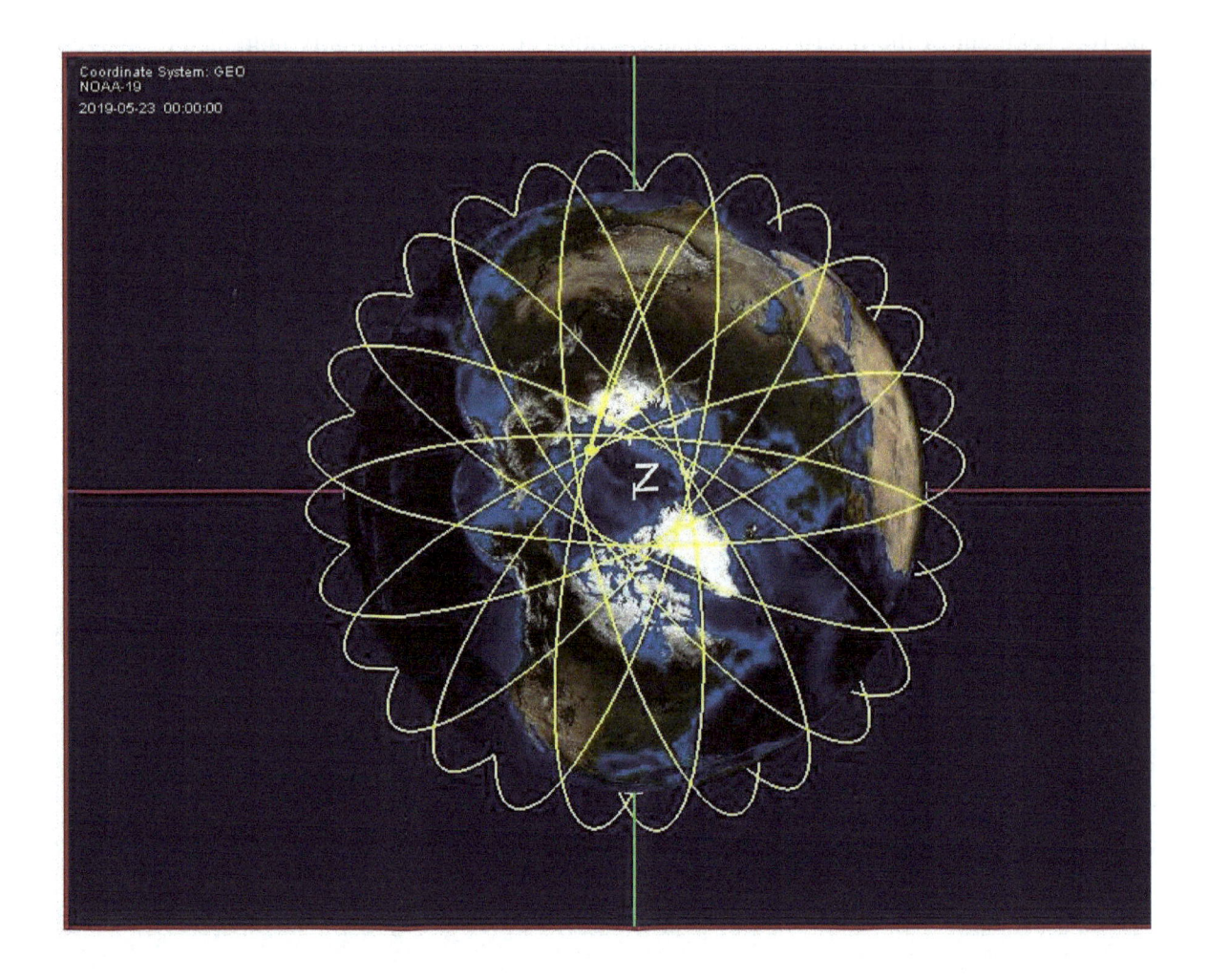

Fig. A2.7 Orbital tracks of NOAA's polar-orbiting NOAA-19 satellite, notice a gap in coverage in the polar region as viewed from over the North Pole. A similar gap in coverage occurs over the South Pole

Low-Earth orbits require periodic trajectory corrections by burning thrusters to stay on course. Therefore, the life of the spacecraft is dependent upon the amount of onboard fuel, assuming everything else is operational.

Medium-Earth-Orbits (MEOs)

The orbital domain in space ranges from Low-Earth orbits, and the Geosynchronous orbits (altitude of 2,000 to 35,786 km) are designated for Medium-Earth Orbits (MEOs). This domain is primarily used for navigation by Global Positioning Systems (GPS) at about 20,200 kilometers; Galileo (23,222 km) for global navigation; the Russian Global Navigation Satellite System (GLONASS-K) (19,100 km); and Telstar 12 communications satellite constellations and several others (ESOA, Wikipedia).

Communications satellites serving customers at extremely high latitudes are generally placed in highly eccentric elliptical orbits known as *Molniya orbits*. Satellites in such orbits have high dwell rates (time

Appendices

spent) while passing over high latitudes serviced all along the orbital Apogee (Fig. A2.8). A pair of such satellites, each with an orbital period of 12 hours, can provide continuous coverage over high latitudes.

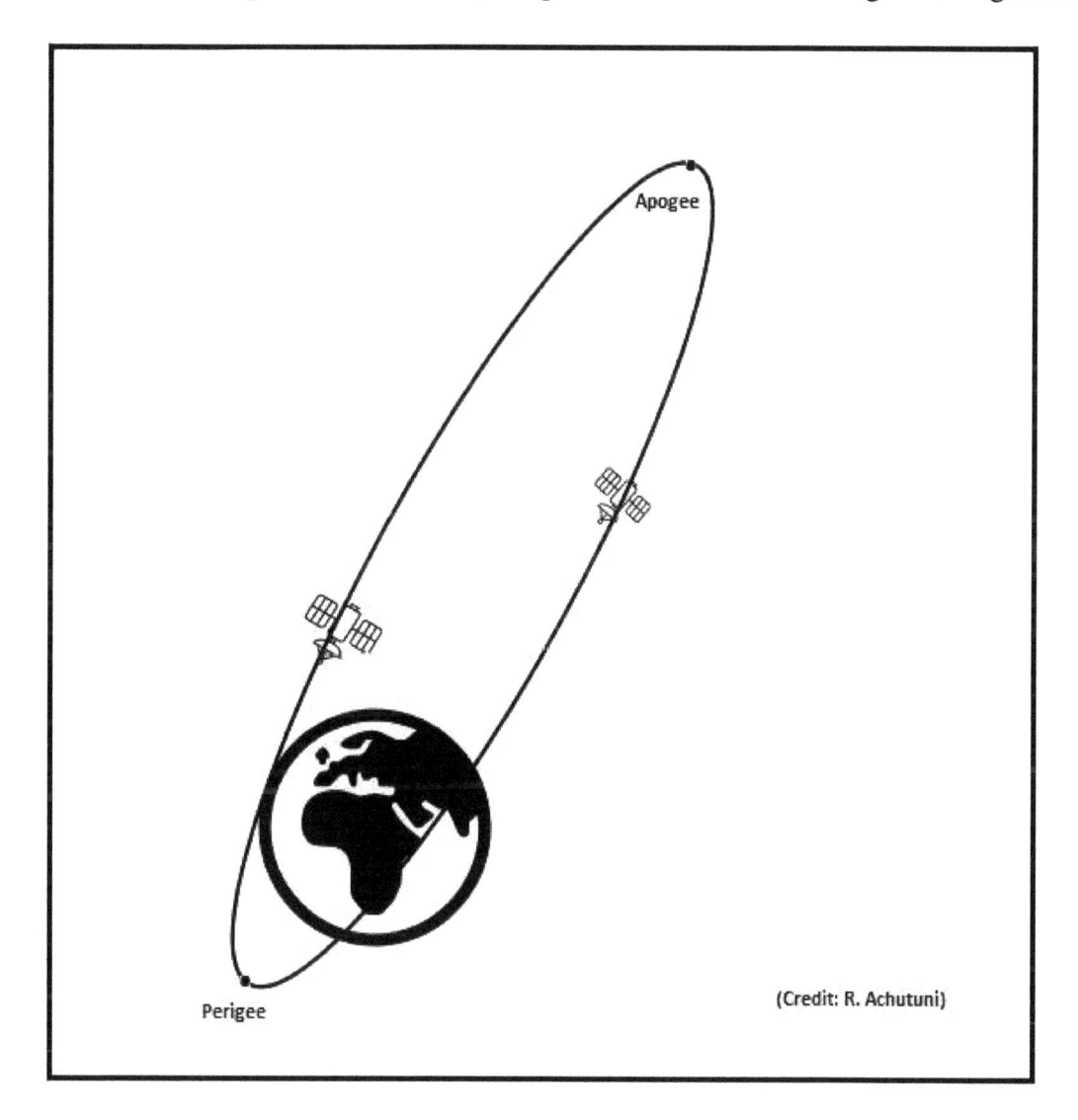

Fig. A2.8 A pair of satellites in a highly eccentric Molniya Orbit provides 24-hour coverage over high latitudes due to high dwell rates towards orbital ascent and descent from Apogee.

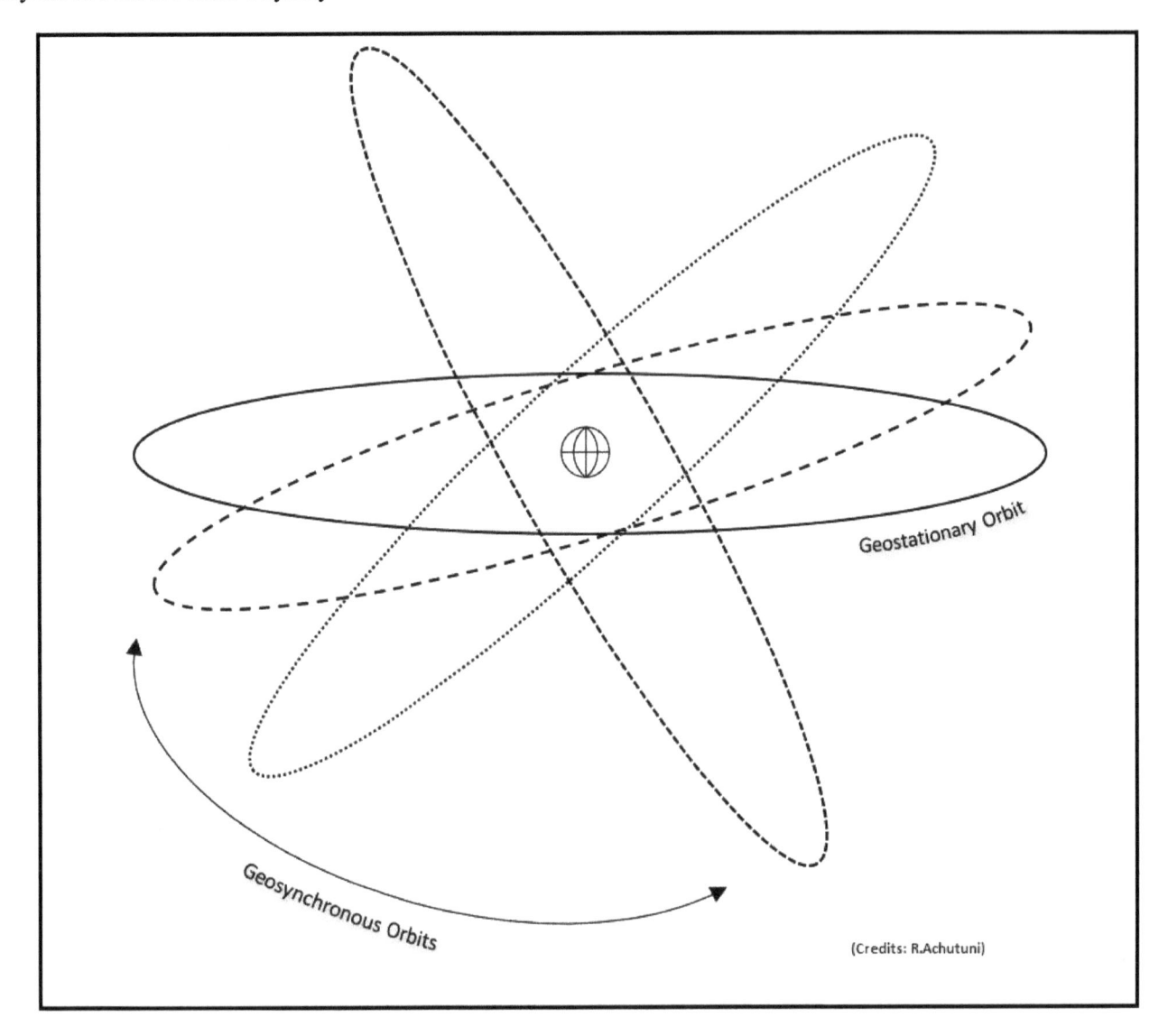

Fig. A2.9 Geostationary and Geosynchronous orbits have an orbital period of a sidereal day (~24hrs). Geostationary orbits lie in the equatorial plane while Geosynchronous orbits are inclined to the equatorial plane.

Geosynchronous and Geostationary Orbits (GEOs)

Satellites in *Geosynchronous* and *Geostationary* orbits, broadly classified as GEOs, have a circular orbit with an orbital period identical to that of the Earth around its own axis (~24-hrs) and so they appear stationary to an observer on the ground. Geostationary orbits are located along the equatorial plane at altitudes of about 22,500 miles (36,210 km) and at the desired longitude that provides optimal coverage of the full-disc field of view. On the other hand, the orbital plane of Geosynchronous satellites may be tilted at an angle with respect to the equatorial plane (Fig. A2.9)

Geosynchronous orbits are used when continuous coverage of the Earth's surface or atmosphere is desired, such as when weather satellites are placed. These orbits are ideal when continuous full-disc coverage is desired. For example, the U. S. National Oceanic and Atmospheric Administration (NOAA) operates two satellites called GOES-15 (West) (parked at longitude 128°W0 and GOES-16 (East) (parked

Appendices

at 75.2°W) to provide image coverage over the Eastern and Western U. S., Canada, Mexico, and countries in Central and South America 24/7 (Fig. A2.10).

Similarly, commercial communication satellites that depend upon continuous coverage rely upon geosynchronous satellites. A constellation of such satellites can achieve global coverage.

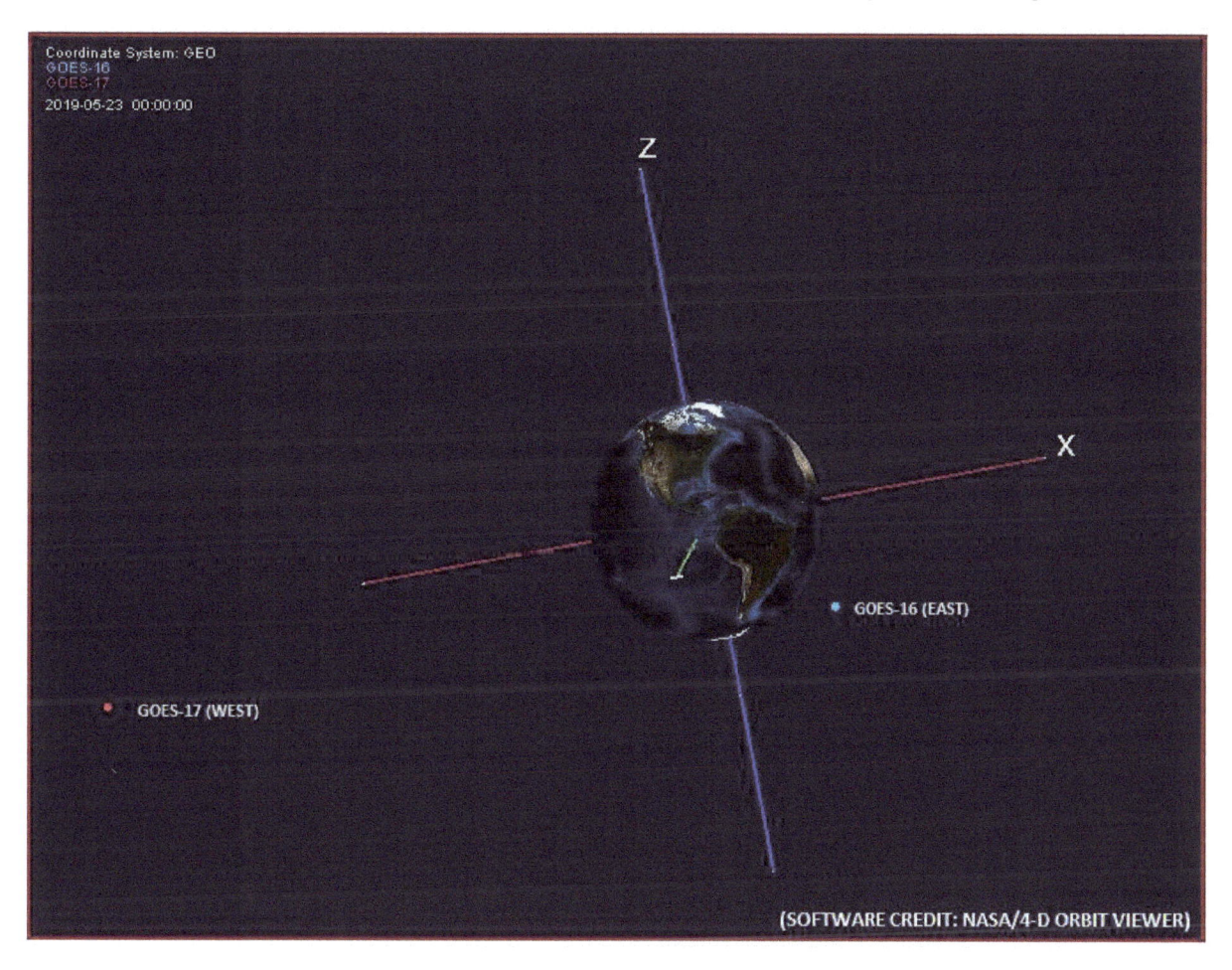

Fig. A2.10 Schematic showing orbital positions of the NOAA GOES-16 (EAST) and GOES-17 (WEST) geostationary weather satellites orbiting at an altitude of about 25,000 mi (~40235 km) over the equator in the XYZ plane.

The miniaturization of satellites has made it possible to deliver multiple small satellites or *smallsats* into orbit from a single launch. NASA's Space Shuttle Program successfully launched numerous smallsats into low-Earth orbit. Many of NASA's as well as the European Consortium's space telescopes and observatories, such as Spitzer, Chandra X-Ray, Kepler, Herschel, Planck, Astrosat, Hitomi, and several others, were launched as smallsats in a very economical manner. Future crewed missions will also capitalize on this opportunity to deliver *smallsats* to defray some of the program costs based on mission priorities.

The Moon

Our Moon, the Earth's only natural satellite, has a prograde orbit that is nearly circular (e=0.05) around the Earth (Fig. A2.11) and completes one revolution relative to the stars in about 27.32 days, this period

Mystic Moon: A Lunar Odyssey

is known as a *sidereal month*; while the same revolution measured relative to the Sun, has a period of 29.53 days and this is known as a *synodic month* (Wikipedia).

The difference of 2.2 days between the synodic month and the sidereal month of the Moon arises because the Earth moves during the 27.3 days the Moon takes to rotate around its axis. Consequently, the Moon takes an additional 2.2 days to compensate for this difference and align itself precisely at the same position relative to the Sun.

The Moon and Earth both rotate around their axes in an anticlockwise direction. It takes the Moon about 27.32 days to rotate around its axis. Consequently, observers on Earth will see the same near side of the Moon that appears stationary; this is known as *synchronous rotation*.

The Moon has a nearly circular orbit around the Earth (e=0.05). The difference in orbital distance from Apogee to Perigee is about 69,171 kilometers. The Moon appears about fourteen percent larger and thirty percent brighter when closer to Perigee, this is known as a *Supermoon*; similarly, the Moon at transit closer to Apogee is termed a *Micromoon*.

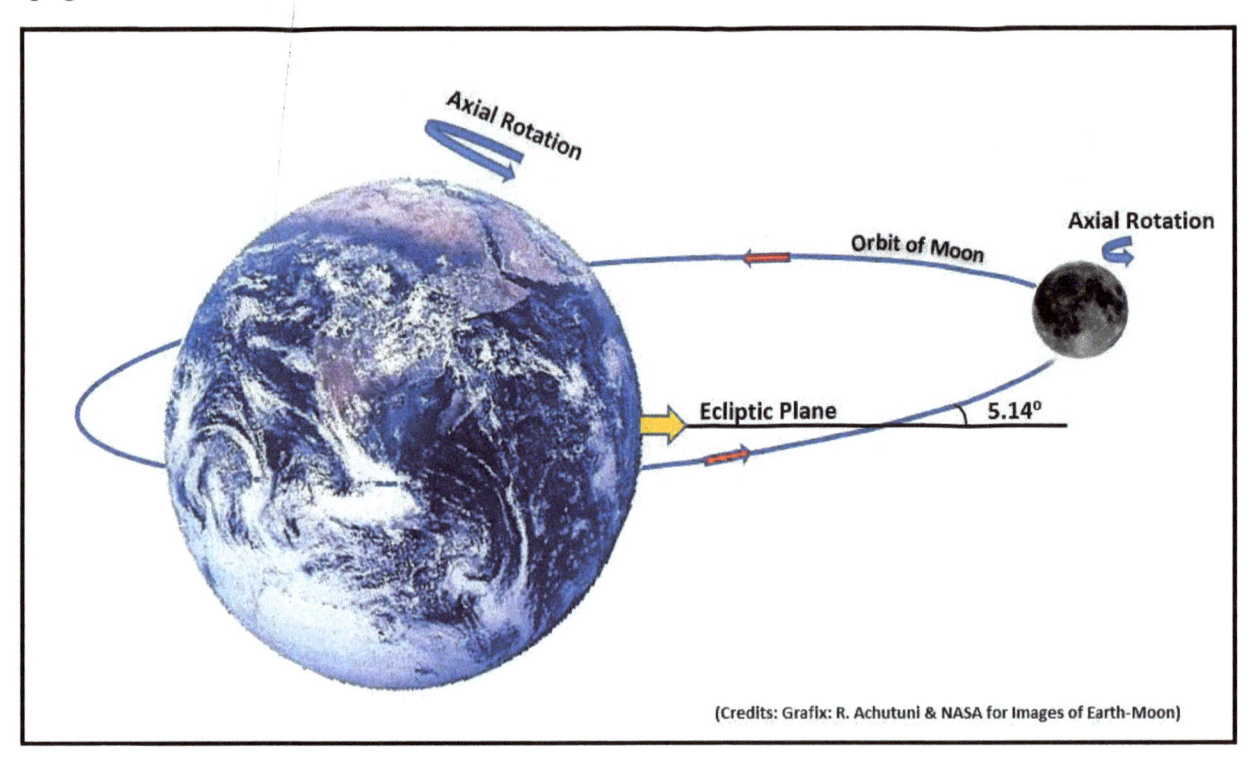

Fig. A2.11 Schematic showing the Moon's orbit around the Earth (not to scale). The orbital plane of the Moon is inclined at 5.14° to the Ecliptic plane. The Moon and Earth rotate counterclockwise on their axes while traversing their respective orbital paths.

Appendix-3: Propulsion

To successfully place a spacecraft into Earth orbit, considerable force is required to overcome the gravitational pull and atmospheric resistance encountered during ascent. The amount of force required is also a function of the spacecraft's total mass at launch. It is important to realize that the spacecraft mass decreases rapidly with time as the propellant is used up during ascent.

The direction of the Earth's rotation around itself is from west to east. The Earth's angular momentum is maximum at the equator and diminishes with increasing latitude. Consequently, it is desirable to have rocket launch pads as close to the Equator as possible to take maximum advantage of the Earth's angular momentum.

Typically, most rocket launches are in the eastern direction. However, geostationary satellite launches such as NOAA's GOES series of weather satellites are sometimes launched toward the west from Vandenberg Air Force Base in California.

Another important aspect to consider in selecting a launch site is its proximity to large open bodies of water towards the east. This is important because any debris falling off during launch will land in open water rather than over land in heavily populated residential areas. Access to open waters is also essential for developing and testing rocket engines.

With the development of super heavy rockets capable of carrying large payloads into orbit, it is imperative to reinforce the aging launch pads to withstand the stress during launch. Also, the newer launch systems are significantly taller than their Apollo Era counterparts, resulting in delays due to accessibility issues. The spacecraft launch infrastructure may have to keep up with the rapidly evolving propulsion technology and the massive scale of the spacecraft. The burden of developmental costs will typically fall upon governments as private sector partners may be unwilling to invest in infrastructure development.

THRUST

Rocket propulsion equations are inherently complex and mathematical in nature. I will try to explain the fundamentals in as simple terms as possible. The interested reader is encouraged to refer to NASA-Glenn Research Center[43], Sutton and Biblarz (2016), or Pisacane and Moore (1994) for a comprehensive treatise.

NEWTON'S LAWS OF MOTION

Newton's Laws of Motion describe the forces acting upon an object and its motion.

First Law (Law of Inertia): An object at rest will remain at rest or continue moving in a straight line at a constant speed unless acted upon by a force.

Second Law: The force on an object is equal to its mass multiplied by its acceleration

---

[43] NASA Glenn Research Center: https://www1.grc.nasa.gov/beginners-guide-to-aeronautics/thrust-force/

Force = m * a Where m is the mass of a body, and a is its acceleration.

Third Law: For every action, there is an equal and opposite reaction

The spacecraft's total mass is a function of time as it decreases rapidly with height with fuel consumption during launch. Therefore, the varying mass is represented by $\dot{m}=dm/dt$.

In a rocket engine, the fuel and oxidizer are combined and expelled through the narrow throat of the nozzle. This creates a Bernoulli effect and expels the combusted material through a bell-shaped exit area to produce the desired thrust. The design of the nozzle throat restricts the reverse or backup flow of gases to prevent an explosion.

The amount of thrust (force) produced by a rocket engine is a linear function of the mass flow rate ($\dot{m}$) through the engine, the exit velocity V_e, the Δp - the pressure difference at the bell-shaped nozzle exit (p_e), and the ambient atmospheric pressure p_o, and the exit area A_e:

$F = f(\dot{m}, V_e, \Delta p, A_e)$

Def: Thrust (measured in Newtons (N)) is the amount of force needed to accelerate a kilogram of mass at the rate of 1 meter per second per second.

The units of thrust are in pounds (British/American units) or Newtons (MKS-metric units)

The combined thrust generated by the Apollo Saturn V launch vehicles by stage is as follows: Stage-I: 7,610,000 lbs.; Stage-II: 1,150,000 lbs.; Stage-III: 230,000 lbs. Maximum thrust is required during liftoff and diminishes considerably by the time of orbital insertion.

By comparison, the 4 RS-25 Engines of Artemis II crew missions can generate a combined thrust of about 8.8 million lbs.

On the other hand, SpaceX's new Raptor engines can deliver thrust exceeding 16 million lbs.

SPECIFIC IMPULSE (Isp)

The Specific Impulse (I_{sp}) measures a rocket engine's efficiency in producing thrust from its propellant mass. In other words, the higher the I_{SP}, the more efficient the engine.

PROPELLANT TYPES

Rocket propellants can be broadly classified as Solid, Liquid, or Hybrid.

Solid Propellants: In solid propellants, both the propellant (fuel) and oxidizer are combined, molded into a cylindrical form, and ignited to provide thrust. They resemble old-fashioned nylon eraser material.

Solid rockets can be stored in ambient conditions and are easy to ignite. However, once ignited, the launch cannot be aborted. For this reason, crew missions do not initiate the liftoff process with solid propellants.

One of the disadvantages is that it does not store well over long durations as internal cracks can develop; these cracks can quickly transmit the ignited flame upward resulting in a massive explosion.

Liquid Propellants: In 1914, Robert H. Goddard demonstrated and patented the feasibility of using liquid propellants in rockets.

These are broadly classified as either *monopropellants* or *bipropellants*.

Monopropellants: Both the fuel and oxidizer are combined, and the mixture is combusted. Examples: Hydrogen and oxygen; Hydrazine (N_2H_2); Monomethyl hydrazine (MMH), Unsymmetrical dimethyl hydrazine (UDMH).

Bipropellants: Both fuel and oxidizer are stored in separate tanks until combustion.

Liquid propellants: Either *storable* at room temperature or *cryogenic* propellants stored at extremely cold temperatures.

The entire Apollo lunar mission relied upon the flawless performance of a single gimballable SPS engine capable of delivering a thrust of 20,000 pounds. Its surefire reliability is attributed to using Aerozine 50 (as fuel) and dinitrogen tetroxide (N_2O_4) as oxidizer.

Liquid propellants are ideal for crewed missions since the launch can be aborted if necessary. Hypergolic propellants can combust spontaneously upon contact without the need for igniters; typically, they are used to initiate the launch process.

Hybrid Propellants combine polymer-based solid fuels with liquid oxidizers (Liquid Oxygen (LOX), Hydrogen Peroxide (H_2O_2), N_2O_4, etc.). Both propellants are individually inert and can only combust when the solid fuel is converted into a gaseous state and mixed with the oxidizer in the combustion chamber.

Appendix-4:
Accessing the Apollo Image Archive on Flickr

(URL: https://www.Flickr.com/photos/projectapolloarchive/albums/)

The Apollo Hasselblad Imagery in Public Domain is available on *Flickr*. The interested reader can access the individual scenes, display, zoom, print, or download as described based on the Mission and Magazine Number.

Apollo Mission# and Magazine#:

Apollo 7: Magazine: 3/M, 4/N, 7/S, 11/P

Apollo 8: Magazine: 12/D, 13/E, 14/B, 15/F, 16/A, 17/C

Apollo 9: Magazine: 19/A, 20/E, 21/B, 22/C, 23/D, 24/F

Apollo 10: Magazine: 27/N, 28/O, 29/P, 34/M, 35/U,

Apollo 11: Magazine: 36/N, 37/R, 38/O, 39/Q, 40/S (v1/levels-adj), 40/S (v2), 41/P, 42/U, 44/V

Apollo 12: Magazine: 46/Y, 47/V, 48/X, 49/Z, 50/Q, 51/R, 54/T, 55/EE

Apollo 13: Magazine: 58/N, 59/R, 60/L, 61/II, 62/JJ

Apollo 14: Magazine: 64/LL, 65/KK, 66/II, 67/JJ, 68/MM, 72/L, 74/N, 75/R

Apollo 15: Magazine: 81QQ, 82/SS, 84/MM, 85/LL (v1 / mixed dpi), 85/LL (v2), 86/NN, 87/KK, 88/TT, 89/WW, 90/PP, 91/M, 92/OO, 93/P, 95/RR, 96/Q, 97/O, 99/N

Apollo 16: Magazine: 105/M, 106/K, 107/C, 108/I, 109/G, 110/H, 111/J, 112/L, 113/A, 114/B, 115/D, 116/E, 117/F, 118/NN, 119/RR, 120/V, 121/PP, 122/QQ

Apollo 17: Magazine: 133/J, 134/B, 135/G, 136/H, 137/C, 138/I, 139/K, 140/E, 141/L, 142/M, 143/N, 144/R, 145/D, 146/F, 147/A, 148/NN, 149/KK, 150/LL, 151/OO, 152/PP, 153/MM, 157/VV, 159/XX, 160/YY, 162/SS, 163/TT

The 'Main Menu' screen in *Flickr* (Fig. A-4.1) stores all images by the corresponding 'Mission Name' and all of the 'Magazines' by number. Click on the desired magazine number in order to access the images. You may have to move the mouse cursor over the image thumbprint in order to see the image number.

Appendices

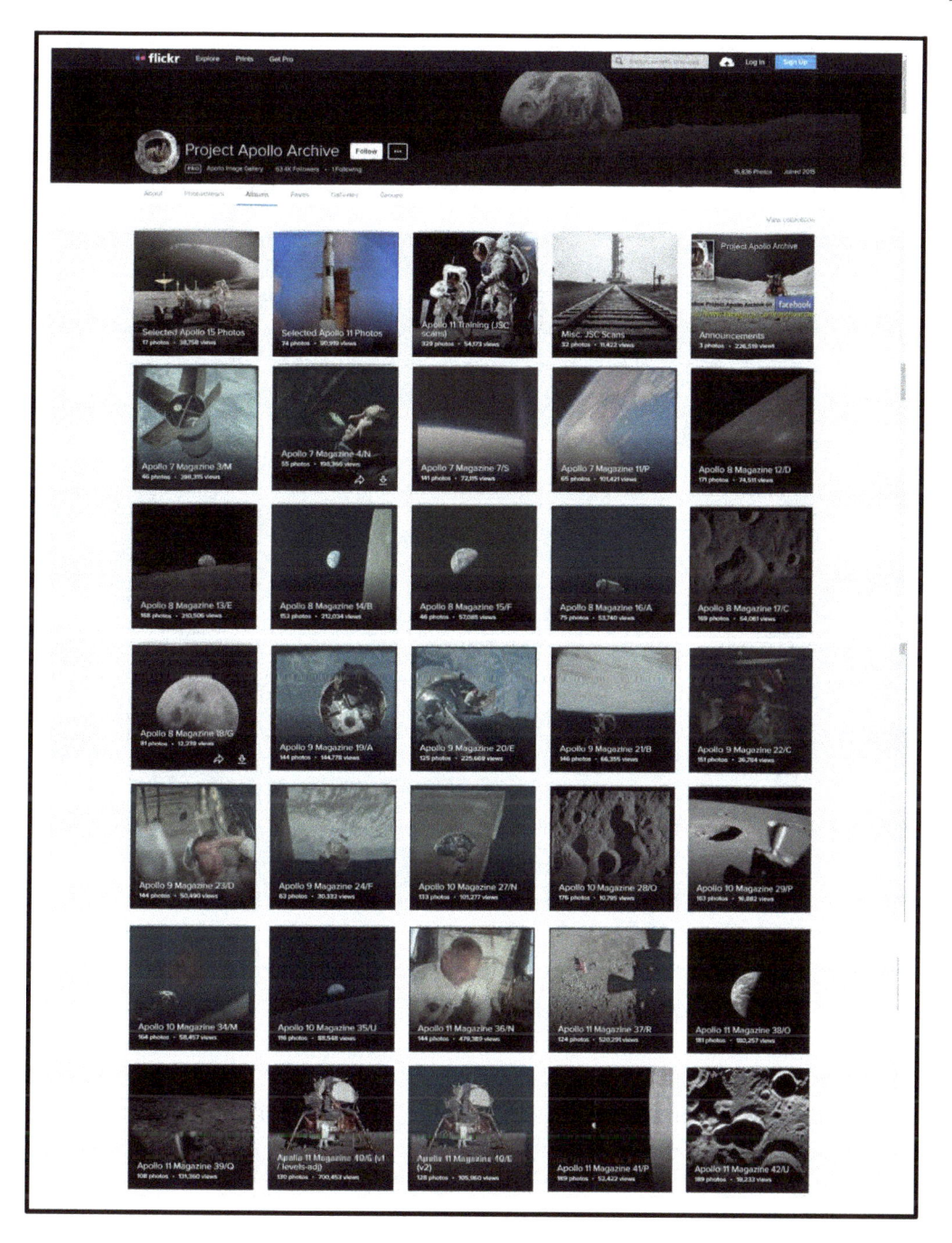

Fig. A4.1 Project Apollo Archive Menu Screen

The Main Menu screen in Flickr lists Apollo 7 - Apollo 17 Images by Frame#s. Scroll down to the desired Mission and Frame# and click the mouse to select an image. Additional pictures may be on second page.

AN EXAMPLE:

Let us display an image of the Tsiolkovsky Crater (AS15-87-11727) located on the far side of the Moon on *Flickr* (Fig. A-4.2).

> https://www.Flickr.com/photos/projectapolloarchive/albums/

Mystic Moon: A Lunar Odyssey

- Locate Apollo 15 Magazine 87 in the Album set and click to open it. Next, we need to locate Image Number 11727 from the images displayed on the Menu screen.

- Moving the cursor over the image will display its five-digit number; scroll down till you find the Image AS15-87-11727 and click on it. The following screen will then appear:

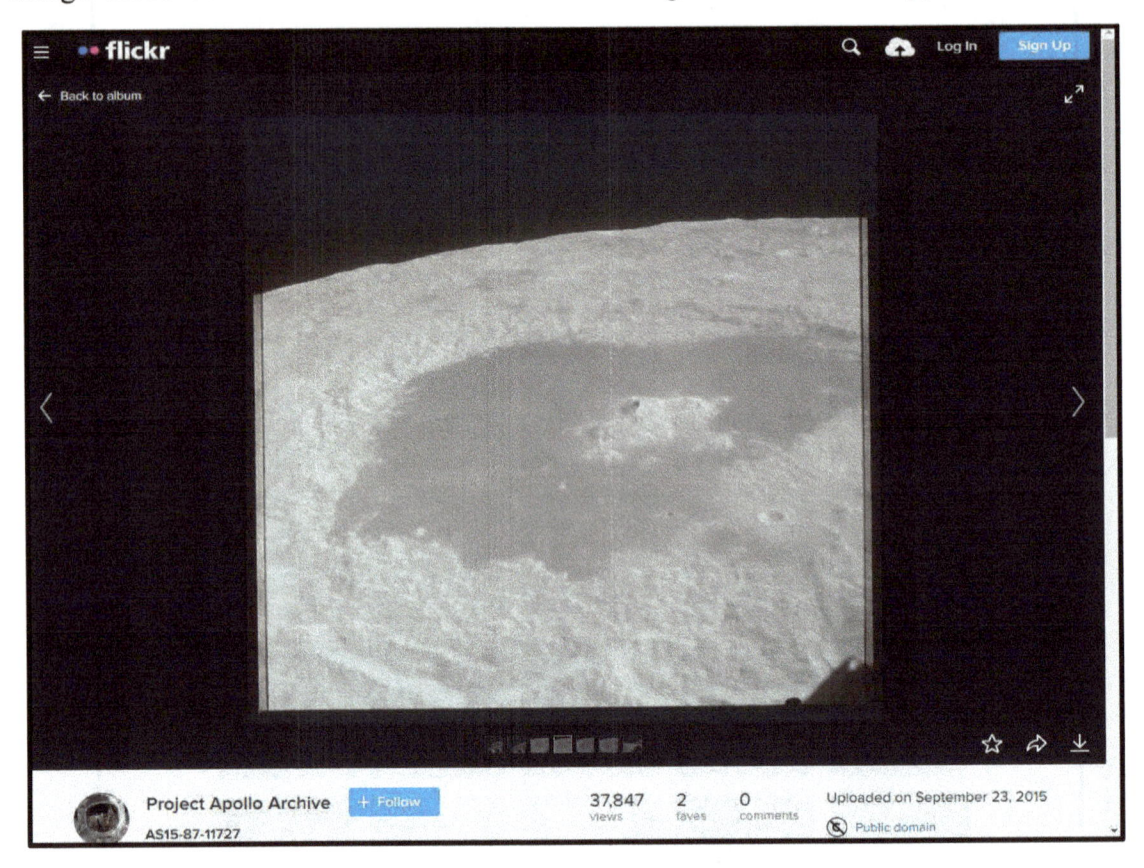

Fig. A-4.2 Uploaded Image of Tsiolkovsky Crater

- Click on Image to magnify it. It can be zoomed by clicking the "magnifying lens" icon once or twice as desired. Clicking on image for a third time (-) will restore it to its original size.

- To display the image in full-screen mode, click on the icon. Pressing the [ESC] key will revert the image to its original size.

- To print or save a copy of the image, press the 'Down Arrow' icon; it lets you download the image

- To see other images in the magazine, click the 'Left Arrow' (<) or the 'Right Arrow' (>) key on the screen to shift to the previous or next image as desired. Sometimes the desired image may be on the second page of the Menu screen. You may scroll down to flip to second-page content.

- To return to 'Album' screen, click "□ Back to Album" and move slider button to the top.

- Next, click on the "□" key in the top left corner and select "Albums" to return to the Album list.

- Repeat the above procedure to display other images of interest.

Milton Keynes UK
Ingram Content Group UK Ltd.
UKHW052027141124
451150UK00005B/25

9 798991 597906